PIXIE DUST

Merry Christmas 2023
Love,
Mindy

To Diane

Jenna E. Faas

PIXIE DUST

❖ A JELF ACADEMY NOVEL ❖

JENNA E. FAAS

SPARKS AND CINDERS PUBLISHING
PITTSBURGH

First published by Sparks and Cinders Publishing 2021

Pixie Dust. Copyright © 2021 by Sparks and Cinders Publishing

First U.S. Edition

Cover art and formatting by Damonza

Editing by Alexandria Groves

ISBN 978-1-956207-00-2 (paperback)
ISBN 978-1-956207-01-9 (ebook)

Pixie Dust

To my parents, for always supporting me in my endeavors and giving me the confidence to pursue my writing dreams. Without your love and encouragement, this book wouldn't be possible. I love you both so much.

xoxo
Infinity and Beyond

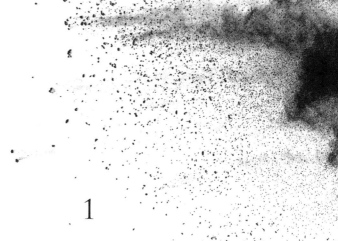

1
THE ONLY LIFE I HAD
EVER KNOWN

IRT AND GRIME clung to the rafters in the attic of the manor house. Spider webs glistened from the small amount of light coming from the dirt specked circular window near the ceiling. Shadows, in odd, contorted shapes, bounced off the walls. The wooden floorboards creaked from the light scampering of mice somewhere in the corner.

I was curled up in the middle of the floor on top of a dirty mattress. Tears fell slowly down my face, like a gentle rain, while my heart clenched in pain. I pushed a strand of my long blonde hair away from my sticky cheek and brushed my palm along the damp line. Down below I heard movement, and I knew I would soon have to get up. Though I felt exhausted, I hadn't been able to sleep. It seemed like a very long time since I had gotten a good night's rest.

The last memory I had of a real bed with soft, comfortable pillows, was when I was five years old. Since then, all the luxuries I'd known had been snatched away. The pain of losing my father ripped through my chest and I stifled a sob. Though eleven years have passed, my heart has not healed.

Slowly, I sat up, careful to avoid the sharp springs that had torn their way through the fabric. Concentrating, I stared across the room to the sheet-covered vanity. The sheet blew to the side, and a small box levitated off the furniture and floated toward me. When it was close enough, I grabbed it and placed it in my lap. Inside were brushes and combs that had belonged to my mother. This box was one of a few things I had to remember her by, besides my appearance in the mirror. She had passed away when I was only a year old. My father had always remarked that everything about me reminded him of my mother, including my "special ability". The traits I inherited from my mother would be the reason I would spend the rest of my life in captivity.

I was only five years old when I lost my father unexpectedly. I had never seen him sick in bed before. My father was always so strong, and I never imagined that anything would happen to him. He was always up before the servants and had never taken a sick day in his life. He embraced running the manor house with an exuberance, not allowing anyone else to take care of it.

My father wasn't a controlling man, but he was willing to take full responsibility for what was his. No one worked as hard as he did, whether it be overseeing the production of crops or making sure everything ran according to plan. He had so much to take care of, including me. People who remembered him said that he had worked himself to death, which was difficult for me to believe.

On the day he died, I remember I had been in a little white dress, and my nanny had just bathed me. My hair held a matching bow and it had been done up in beautiful curls. My hair had always been beautiful back then and was taken care of, unlike now. I was ushered into my father's bedroom where my stepmother, Marie, and her two children stood.

Emily, who was a few years older than me, had a ribbon similar to mine in her dark brown, almost black, hair. She stood close to her mother, the two almost like identical twins. On Emily's left stood Preston, two years old and barely able to concentrate on anything very long, a trait which carried into his later years. His grubby little hands were busy ruining his new clothes. His nimble fingers pulled at the red bow tie under his neck. Preston's bright red hair was combed neatly, but it was obvious that it would soon be messy.

I came up next to them and gazed at my father in his bed. I didn't know what was going on as I stared at his handsome face. His once blonde hair had begun graying in areas, and his face looked whiter than the pillow. He was wearing the blue robe that my mother had made for him, the robe that matched his eyes perfectly.

As I stood by my father's bed, I knew something was wrong, but being so young, I couldn't even fathom what the reason might be.

"Papa!" My small voice penetrated the silence in the room.

I wanted to climb up beside him on the silk sheets, but Marie stopped me. My father's eyes fluttered open, and he looked at me.

"Jane," came his barely audible response. His voice sounded scratchy, and his skin looked so swollen.

"Papa, I love you!" I cried as I felt my face grow hot.

"I love you too," my father said. He groaned and clutched at his stomach. His face contorted with pain. His eyes found Marie's gray ones. "Take care of Jane. Make sure she has the best," he told her, his voice barely above a whisper. With a shudder, my father closed his eyes and never moved again.

"Papa, Papa," I yelled. I broke away from Marie and rushed to my father. I shook his arm repeatedly and screamed in panic. It was at that moment I realized why my father had called my mother and me special. All at once, every door in the house closed with a resounding bang. Somehow, I realized it had happened because I had wanted it to and that I could move things without touching them.

Before I knew what was happening, I was being dragged by the arm out of my father's room. I looked into the enraged gray eyes of Marie as she dragged me toward the stairs that led to the attic.

"You are a disgusting little creature!" she shouted as she pulled on my arm. "I knew there was something odd about you the moment I met you."

"What did I do?" I cried out, though I knew it had been my fault the doors had closed mysteriously. I had felt it in my heart, and I had thought it into being. Marie gripped my arm even tighter.

"You know damn well what you did! I just knew something was strange about you. When I first married your father and you were a baby, I noticed things. The toys in your room moved without anyone touching them!" she shrieked.

I fought to stop moving as my mind processed what Marie had said. Was it true that she had seen me move things before? I couldn't recall doing anything like that.

"Come on!" Marie said as she tugged harder.

At that moment, I imagined that my arm would be too hot to hold on to. Sure enough, Marie yelped and let go. I turned to sprint away, but she was too quick and caught hold of my hair. I sensed that my hair was a part of me that I could not control. She pulled me up the steps in the direction of the attic. When we reached the top, she threw me onto the attic floor.

"You will stay up here from now on, and I will assign you chores to complete. If I see any trace of your abnormality, there will be hell to pay!" she shouted. Then she slammed the door, and I heard the big brass skeleton key turn in the keyhole. From that moment on, I never defied Marie again.

A loud knock on the attic door pulled me out of my memories.

"Jane, I need you to get down here and help me make breakfast. Why are you still up here?" came the loud voice of the cook, Ellen.

"Hurry it up! You know that Marie doesn't like to wait! I've brought up some water. Make yourself look presentable."

I heard the familiar noise of a bucket being dropped outside the door, and then I heard Ellen stalking back down the stairs. When I was sure Ellen was gone, I made the door open softly, and the bucket floated into the room, stopping at the foot of the mattress. This was the only place I could use my special talent. I had been forewarned that if any of the staff caught wind of my powers, I would be kicked out of the house forever and left to die in the street.

I leaned over the bucket of crystal-clear water and looked at my reflection. My tears had left streaks down my face, and my violet eyes stared back at me.

I placed my hands in the cool water, splashing it on my face. My body shivered. Ellen hadn't bothered to warm the water. When I felt as refreshed as I could be, I levitated the bucket away and ran the brush through my hair one more time. Then I got up from my small dirty mattress and replaced my mother's intricately carved box to its hiding place. With a deep sigh, I crossed the room to the door. When I was halfway down the attic steps, I heard the attic door close just as I imagined it would.

I briskly walked into the kitchen and found Ellen chopping vegetables. Her chubby fingers closed around the knife as she quickly julienned the carrots. Some of her mouse-brown curls had slipped from her blue bonnet and fell across her forehead. Ellen had on a matching blue dress and a white apron that covered her round midsection. Ever since my father passed away, She had been my overseer, and when Marie wasn't assigning me chores, Ellen was.

"Come over here, girl! Don't just stand there. Heat this water so I can boil these carrots!" she yelled at me over her shoulder.

Quickly, I grabbed the pot of water and moved beside her to put the pot on the stove. Ellen continued chopping vegetables and as she finished, she dropped them into the water. I gazed out the kitchen window above the sink. The sun was streaming in through the glass, creating a bright pattern on the gray countertops. I could tell that it was going to be a beautiful day. Maybe if I got all my work done, I could go swimming in the lake that was in the woods on the manor's property.

Glancing down at the pot on the stove, I took the wooden spoon and began stirring the stew. After a few minutes, my mind began to wander, distracted by the scenery out the window. I hoped that I would complete all my chores and that Marie would not think to assign me extra ones. I hardly noticed when Ellen moved beside me to continue prepping the day's menu.

As I monotonously stirred the pot, I didn't realize that my subconscious mind was affecting the stew. I heard the lapping sounds of the liquid hitting the sides, not realizing that the ingredients were rising from the pot. Ellen's voice brought me back from my daydreams.

"Girl, watch what you're doing! You are splashing the stew everywhere! Quit your daydreaming because it will get you nowhere around here! Come back to reality and accept it!" Ellen yelled.

"I'm sorry. I'll clean it up right away," I said as I went to get a towel.

"You better clean it up," Ellen said with a shake of her head.

I hurried to clean off the stove and then replaced the towel in its proper place. I couldn't believe how foolish I had been. I was letting my magic run away with me. What if I hadn't controlled something else? What if the pot would have levitated right off the stove? Despite the harshness of Ellen's advice, it would benefit me to listen to it. If Ellen ever saw something abnormal, I wouldn't doubt that she would report it to Marie. I did not doubt Marie would follow through with her threat and expel me from the house. I had to be more careful next time.

At Ellen's instruction, I began cooking the eggs for breakfast. When all the food was prepared, Ellen demanded that I carry the meal up to Marie, Emily, and Preston. The family commonly took breakfast in bed, and it was my duty to serve it to them. The hot, fluffy rolls, scrambled eggs, and browned sausages had to be presented on our best china plates. Marie couldn't stand to use anything unless it was of quality. The fanciest china sets were not only used for guests.

The plates were deep and tiny light blue flowers decorated the outer edge. I had never eaten off plates like these. My food was served in a wooden bowl and typically it was whatever was leftover. I didn't mind that much because Ellen was a good cook, and she sometimes saved a little something for me.

Even though Ellen was brisk, I believed she cared about me a bit. She wasn't much of a mother figure but compared to others around the house, she was the closest to me. Ellen had worked for my father's household when my mother was still alive. She had known my father's grief at the loss of his wife, so I hoped she was somewhat sympathetic toward my situation since she had known both of my parents.

My father had been lonely, and heartbroken when my mother died. It was his concern for my upbringing that convinced him to remarry. A year after my mother died, he met and married Marie, a widower in town.

Marie's husband was rumored to have been murdered by a band of outlaws on one of his many trips out west. She didn't seem to care about the death of her husband. Not long after his death, she married my father even though the official mourning period had not ended. This had caused much gossip within the town, but Marie didn't seem concerned.

Marie was beautiful, but she was nothing like my mother. I believed my father compared them too much, and I knew Marie grew aggravated and jealous when he commented on how much I looked and acted like the love of his life. Though my father had married Marie so that I would have a mother figure in my life, she hardly ever paid much attention to me, nor I her in the beginning. How could he have known that my upbringing with Marie as a mother figure would not be what he envisioned?

Even with a new wife, my father would still make time for me. When he could find moments in the evening to spare, we would sit in his office. It was a large room with a big oak desk in the middle. Red curtains hung on the windows behind the desk. The brass sconces on the walls would light up most of the room when night fell. The room was very masculine, and it was one of my father's favorites. He would sit in there for hours going over figures for the manor's expenses and the payments he would receive from clients. Everyone knew that he did not like to be disturbed when he was in his office, but he would always make exceptions for me. It was our special place outside of my nursery and playroom. I would sit in his lap, and he would tell me about my mother and how special she still was to him.

"You are like her in almost every way, Jane," he would tell me. "You have her eyes, her smile, and her soft complexion."

I would look up into his deep blue eyes and nod. He always talked about her as if she were a mystical creature, not possibly human. He made her sound perfect and to me she always was. My father was convinced that I would grow up to be just like her. How disappointed would he be if he knew I had grown up to be Marie's slave?

As I reached the top of the stairs, the first door I arrived at was Marie's. Just like every morning, I knocked three times on the big brown wooden door and waited for Marie to tell me to enter. It was taking a long time for Marie to summon me, so I knocked again. I had to quickly step back as the bronze doorknob turned and Marie burst through the doorway.

"What do you want?" she shouted. Her hair was undone, and it hung wildly around her shoulders. I could see faint streaks of gray near her ears. Marie had on a white robe that hung open to reveal her gray night dress, which matched her steel-colored eyes.

"Breakfast, ma'am," I whispered.

She looked me over from head to toe. "Well, bring it in then. Don't stand in the hallway looking like a half-wit!" Marie turned back into her room, and I knew she expected me to follow. I watched as she collapsed onto the silken sheets covering her bed.

"Bring the tray over here," Marie commanded. Slowly, I brought the tray to her bedside and handed it to her. "Good, now get over to the window and open the curtains. I would like to see what I'm eating."

I drew back the curtains like I did every morning. Blinding light flooded the room and illuminated the dark corners. The room was painted emerald green and the accent carpet matched the walls. Marie's nightdress stuck out among the green pillows. She looked small in the huge bed, but I knew from experience that she was a very powerful woman. Her iron eyes seemed to follow me as I opened the curtains to their full extent.

"That will be all for now, Jane. Make sure Emily and Preston get their breakfast. I'll call you when I am ready to be dressed," Marie told me.

I picked up the trays and moved on to the next room: Emily's room. At the door, I knocked three times just like I had done at her mother's.

"Come in!" I heard through the door. Quickly, I pushed the door open and moved to the bedside. Emily had the covers pushed up beneath her arms so I could see the red, puffy sleeves of her nightdress. Unlike her mother, she almost blended into the bed except for her dark hair and pale skin.

"Put my tray on my nightstand and open my curtains," Emily commanded.

While I drew back the curtains, Emily glared at her breakfast tray. Then she climbed out of her bed and went to the closet.

"Help me get dressed," Emily said as she held out a blue dress with ribbons around the bodice. I stifled a sigh as I took the dress from her and unbuttoned the back of it. I helped Emily out of her nightdress and straightened her undergarments before I held the dress open for her to step into. She pressed down hard on my shoulders to maintain her balance as she lifted one foot and then the other into the dress. I pulled the decorated sleeves up on her shoulders, and when I finished fastening the buttons, Emily turned to look at me.

"Jane, I want to wear my hair up today, so pick one of my pretty ribbons and begin fixing it," she said as she moved towards the chair of her vanity.

"Miss, I have to get your brother his breakfast before it gets cold," I stammered.

"He can wait. I'm sure he is still sleeping." She sat in the chair and looked at me expectantly.

I stood there debating what I should do. Should I fix Emily's hair or take Preston his breakfast tray? Before I could decide on the best option, Emily spoke.

"Hello Jane, what are you waiting for?"

I moved toward her with her brush in my hand and began brushing out the knots. As soon as I finished, I went over to the dresser and picked out one of her satin blue ribbons. I was in the middle of tying up Emily's hair when a scream echoed down the hall in the direction of Preston's room.

"Where is my breakfast? I'm hungry! Breakfast! Breakfast!" he shouted.

Before I could even comprehend what was happening, Marie had flown into Emily's room. Her face looked cloudy, and her gray eyes pierced through me.

"What are you doing?" she asked.

"I'm fixing... um... Emily's hair," I mumbled.

"Why doesn't Preston have his breakfast yet?" she asked, her voice rising.

"I told Jane to take Preston his breakfast before she began on my hair, but she insisted that he could wait," Emily spoke up before I could.

"I... I..." I stammered.

Marie rounded on me. "Jane, give Preston his breakfast immediately. Then I want you to come to my room. Hopefully, your brain will not become sidetracked in the short distance it takes to travel down the hall."

Quickly, I grabbed Preston's breakfast tray and hurried to his room. Preston was jumping on his blue bedspread, still screaming the word "Breakfast!"

"Preston, come down from your bed," I said as I slowly set the tray down.

At thirteen years old with flaming red hair and bright green eyes, he was past the age of jumping on his bed. Preston acted much younger than his age and had an appetite for causing trouble. I didn't want to imagine what today would bring. Though eleven years later, Preston still acted as if he were two.

I moved to the window to draw his blue curtains as he climbed down from his bed and crawled toward his breakfast tray like an uncivilized beast. While he ate, I took a deep breath and headed back to Marie's room. I braced myself for an ear beating.

"Come here now," Marie yelled as soon as she saw me in the doorway.

Slowly, I walked toward her not knowing what to expect.

"Help me into my dress," she said pointing to a red dress, with lace around the collar and the bottom, lying on her vanity chair.

At once I helped her put on the dress and stalked behind her to work on her hair as she instructed.

"Jane, do you remember what the rules are?" she asked in a

chillingly calm way. "What were you instructed to do every morning since the death of your father?"

"I am to wake up with Ellen and help her cook breakfast. After that, I'm supposed to… suppose to…" I mumbled while trying to hold in my tears.

"Supposed to… suppose to…" Marie said mimicking me. "Suppose to what, Jane because you apparently forgot this morning!"

"I'm supposed to bring up and serve breakfast," I choked out.

"Well, what happened today?" Marie's voice went from sounding calm to yelling.

I stopped my French braiding. It was pointless to tell her that it was Emily's idea.

"I just thought…"

"You just thought? What you didn't think about was a hungry boy starving in his bed. Did I say stop braiding?"

"I'm sorry ma'am. It won't happen again," I said as I continued weaving her strands of hair.

"You're right it won't happen again and to help you remember, you will not be permitted to spend time outside when you are finished with your chores. After you are done with your regular cleaning of the house, you will go back to the kitchen and help Ellen," Marie demanded.

My heart sank into the pit of my stomach. It was foolish of me to hope for some time to myself. I should have anticipated disappointment because I had wanted to go to the lake so badly. I finished with Marie's braid and stepped back from the chair.

"Now, I want you to get back down to the kitchen and do everything Ellen tells you, but when you are done, you will go upstairs and not come down until dinner," Marie commanded.

"Yes, ma'am," I said sadly as I gave her a small bow and left the room. Slowly, I walked back down to the kitchen full of sadness and anger, but I had to control my emotions. If I got too angry or sad, things could happen. It was fine to lose control in the attic, but down here, where someone would see could be horrific.

Once I was back in the kitchen, I set to work scrubbing the floors, washing off the countertops, and assisting Ellen with whatever she asked. When I had finished, I began my routine in the rest of the house. I had bedspreads to change and wood to stack in the fireplaces. I dusted and polished the furniture to perfection and shook out the rugs over the balconies.

By the time I was finished, I was exhausted and sweaty. I regretted the episode with Emily and Preston and made my way into the hot, dusty attic. With each step up the stairs, I felt the sweat trickling between my shoulder blades. When I got into the attic, I collapsed on my mattress. Once the door closed behind me, I knew it was safe to let my emotions go. The sheets over the old furniture ruffled as if a wind was blowing and the old furniture creaked.

I cried on my mattress missing my father more than ever. If he were alive, I would have a room downstairs, I would never have known what the attic looked like let alone have to live in it, and above all else, I wouldn't be treated this way. Was it foolish to think Marie would be nice to me if he were still alive? I also cried for the mother I couldn't remember. What had she been like? If she had not passed away, would my life still have turned into a disaster? Did I resemble her with more than just my looks? Death had robbed me of so much, beginning with my mother.

Ellen called me down from the attic when she needed me to help serve dinner. I proceeded with my pre-dinner routine: carrying hot plates of delicious entrées into the dining room, which I placed neatly in front of Marie and her children. Marie sat at the head of the long, mahogany dining table. On her right was Emily, who sat pencil straight in her seat just like her mother. Their steely gray eyes scrutinized the room. With one glance, one would know Marie and Emily were related, but Preston was entirely different.

Preston was the complete opposite of his mother and sister. While Marie and Emily's skin appeared porcelain white because of their dark hair, Preston's cheeks were rosy with a spattering of freckles. His green eyes were bright and always had a mischievous glint to them. Preston's red hair had become wild and curly over the years, while Emily's hair was as straight as her posture. Preston had obviously inherited his looks from his father. I often wondered what kind of man he had been.

The family only occupied a small spot at the long mahogany dining table. The table was made to seat large parties, and beneath it was a beautiful oriental rug that I knew Marie had paid a pretty penny for. The top half of the walls were painted white and at about the middle, dark wood paneling extended to the floor. The floor was hardwood which matched the paneling. Even though the dining room was too big for the small family, Marie had insisted that they should be served dinner there every night. She had to be surrounded by her fine things at all hours of the day and would accept nothing less.

When I was finished serving them, I went back into the kitchen to eat my dinner, which Ellen had spooned into a small wooden bowl. I was in the middle of eating my soup when I heard a loud crash coming from the dining room.

"You better get in there and see what he has broken this time," Ellen said, referring to Preston. Both of us knew that Preston was prone to breaking things. I grabbed the broom from the corner along with a washcloth and made my way into the dining room.

"Hurry up and get that soup off my rug!" Marie yelled.

It was on the tip of my tongue to tell her to control her son, but I knew it would only cause more trouble. Sure enough, it was Preston's bowl that was on the floor, shattered to bits. Gently, I picked up the larger pieces of glass and threw them in a dustpan. I did my best to sweep the small shards of glass off the rug, and then I got down on my hands and knees with the washcloth and began scrubbing. Everyone at the table continued to eat as if nothing had happened. I reminded myself to keep my anger in check as I finished with the rug and headed back into the kitchen.

Anger consumed me and I didn't feel like eating anymore, so I cleaned up my bowl. Now I was required to wait for the family to finish their meal. I waited at the kitchen table for what seemed like hours, and when I finally heard them leaving the dining room, I began cleaning up. It took a few hours to scrub and put away the dishes, wipe down the dining room table, mop the kitchen floors, and make sure everything was returned to its place. My muscles ached with exhaustion as I left the kitchen and began my ascent up to the attic.

Once in my safe haven, I collapsed onto the broken mattress and fell into a restless sleep, where I tried to dream of better days.

2

MR. WICKER

THE DAYS OF summer fell upon the house with stifling heat and dry windless air. The attic was even hotter than before, making it difficult to stay up there for long periods of time. I made sure I completed all my chores correctly so Marie couldn't find a reason to punish me.

One day at the beginning of the summer, Marie commanded all the servants to labor until the house was immaculate. The staff's normal hours were extended, and I was given double chores which included cleaning all the windows on the first and second floors. Soon, everyone was wondering what had brought on this dramatic cleaning of the manor.

Ellen was the first to find out when Marie demanded preparations for a feast later on in the week. Apparently, we were receiving company. Marie wanted everything perfect, so she supervised the work effort. Nothing passed Marie's sharp eyes and she targeted me more than anyone else. I had to be very careful not to upset her.

On the day of our guest's arrival, Marie was all a flutter and she rushed into Emily's room, threw open her closet, and rifled through Emily's dresses. She made sure to stress the fact that Emily had to look her best today. I assumed a suitor was coming to court Emily since she was of age. Sure enough, I was right.

He pulled up in a black carriage drawn by four black horses. I watched from the front window as a boy, about six-foot-tall with auburn hair, jumped down from the carriage and opened the door. An older man, who appeared to be in his fifties, stepped out of the carriage. He had gray hair and a mustache. In his hand, he held a ruby-encrusted cane, and he sported a top hat. He turned to the boy, and I saw his mouth snap open as he yelled. Swiftly, the boy ducked into the carriage and emerged with a small bag in his hand. I was interrupted from my watching by Marie.

"Jane, get back into the kitchen. I'll call you to serve tea when I am ready," Marie yelled. "and do straighten your skirt before you come out."

Hastily, I moved out of the bright hall and into the kitchen. I smoothed out my skirt like Marie had asked and waited for her to summon me for tea. Soon after I settled in the kitchen, I heard a commotion in the dining room. I knew Marie had retrieved Emily from her room, but I didn't know if Preston would be joining them.

Marie's call for tea snapped me to attention. Grabbing the rose-colored tea tray, stacked high with biscuits and small sandwiches, I went into the dining room. The elderly gentleman was sitting on Marie's right. He had taken off his top hat, but he still held onto his cane. The boy who had come with him stood in the corner. I proceeded to pour out the tea after I had inquired whether the man wanted milk, lemon, or sugar.

"As I was saying, Mr. Wicker, Emily is a delightful young lady," Marie said, ignoring me and addressing her guest.

"Yes, I see," Mr. Wicker said as his gaze shifted over to Emily. I couldn't be certain, but I thought I had seen Emily flinch.

"I'm sure when we are done with tea, Emily will be glad to escort you around the grounds. However, please excuse the stables because we are short a stable boy," Marie explained.

"I might be able to help with that," Mr. Wicker said as he leaned back in his chair. "Recently, I've been looking for a new position for my stable boy, and I would be happy to pass him off to you."

"I don't think I'm in the financial position to pay a stable boy's salary," Marie said.

"Don't worry ma'am. This boy won't need paying. He will be happy just to have room and board, I can assure you. It was lucky that he came with me today," Mr. Wicker said, pointing to the corner. "Come here, Robert."

The boy in the corner slowly made his way over to the table. His face had slightly reddened, and his deep brown eyes gazed at Marie. My eyes were drawn to the collar of his blue button-up shirt. Around his neck was a tarnished silver chain with a charm of some sort hidden beneath his shirt.

"Robert is seventeen years old and a good worker. I'm sure he will do whatever you ask of him, especially if his life depends on it," Mr. Wicker said.

"If he is such a good worker, why do you wish to be rid of him?" Marie asked, her eyes full of suspicion.

"How about after Emily shows me the property, you and I will further discuss this proposition," Mr. Wicker said as he got up from the table and extended his arm to Emily. She hesitated in getting up, but finally stood and linked her arm through his.

Robert moved back into the corner, and I came forward to clean up the half-eaten biscuits and tea. I watched him out of the corner of my eye. He stood very still, and I wondered if he was in a similar predicament as me, working for food and a place to sleep.

I walked back into the kitchen with the plates and decided to stay there until I was summoned again. It wasn't until after dark that I was called to help with dinner. Ellen handed me bowls of mashed potatoes and corn to carry out onto the table. Surprisingly, Ellen even helped by carrying out the steaming turkey on a platter.

She put the platter in the middle of the table and beamed at the family before backing the kitchen.

Marie was once more at the head of the table, and Mr. Wicker was on her right. This time Preston was on Marie's left and Emily was seated next to Mr. Wicker. Her thin mouth formed a pout, and her arms were crossed. It was apparent that she wasn't very fond of Mr. Wicker. Robert was still standing in the corner, and I wondered if he had ever left that spot.

"Jane, take Robert into the kitchen and let him eat in the servant quarters. He needs to know how things work around here. After he is finished, I want you to take him out to the barn. Help him set up the loft since that is where he will be staying from now on," Marie said. It seemed Marie and Mr. Wicker had come to a conclusion about where Robert would live.

Robert silently followed me into the kitchen. I showed him where to find the wooden bowls, and I pulled down two.

"I'm always instructed to eat my meals in the kitchen," I explained. Robert looked at me but didn't say anything. He took one of the wooden bowls and helped himself to the remaining food. After filling my bowl, I sat down beside him at the small table. Robert didn't say anything while we ate, so I ate in silence.

About halfway through dinner, we heard a commotion in the dining room. I jumped up and ran for the broom thinking that Preston had broken something again. I entered to find Emily standing. Mr. Wicker's eyes were wide, and he had food all over his face and in his mustache. He stopped chewing on his turkey leg to look up at Emily. I noticed that his plate was piled high with everything on the table.

"I can't take this anymore!" Emily screamed. Her face was red, and she reminded me of an angry Marie. "You cannot possibly expect me to marry this man! He is repulsive!"

"Don't you talk to our guest that way! Apologize, this instant!" Marie shrieked.

"I refuse to apologize to that fat, pompous pig!" Emily cried. She moved away from the table and headed for the door.

"Emily, get back here! You will marry Mr. Wicker! You must!"

Marie dashed out of the room after Emily. I could hear their screams fading into the distance. Mr. Wicker looked disturbed but continued eating his dinner. His face was very red. I stood frozen, dumbfounded by the scene that had just unfolded.

"What are you starring at, girl? Get back in the kitchen where you belong. Maybe I should take you back to my kitchen and explain your place as a servant," he said with a nasty glare and a glint in his eyes.

Rapidly, I turned to head back into the kitchen. On my way in, I ran right into Robert. It was with enough force to knock us both off our feet. I tumbled on top of him, and we hit the kitchen floor with a crash.

"I'm so sorry!" I muttered, feeling extremely embarrassed as I got to my feet.

He glared at me as he stood, his right hand rubbing his lower back.

"I didn't mean for that to happen. I'm very sorry. Are you okay?" I mumbled as I smoothed my skirt. Robert didn't reply.

I walked past him to continue cleaning up the bowls from dinner, too embarrassed to look at him. I knew my cheeks were flaming red, and I turned to the sink and started scrubbing the dishes. I set the dishes in the rack beside me, intending to dry them when I was done washing them. To my surprise, Robert stepped up beside me, grabbed a rag, and began drying the dishes.

"You don't have to help me," I said as I watched him from the corner of my eye. He just shrugged his shoulders.

I was beginning to wonder if Robert was mute and that was the reason Mr. Wicker wanted to pass him off. I continued to subtly watch him as he stacked the dishes next to the sink. Once everything was clean and dry, Robert stepped back into the corner of the kitchen, and I could feel his eyes on me. I stopped putting the cutlery away when I heard more commotion coming from the dining room. Marie's voice penetrated through the wooden door.

"I'm so sorry for my daughter's rudeness. I've tried to get her to come out of her room, but she has locked the door. Please take my apology for her."

"That was one of the most offensive things I've ever heard in my life," I heard Mr. Wicker say, and by the sound of his voice, I could tell he was still eating. "I cannot accept that apology from you."

I risked peeking through the door and heard the scrape of the chair as Mr. Wicker stood. He grabbed a pink cloth napkin from the table and wiped his mouth, but not all the food had come off. Mashed potatoes still clung to his mustache. He whipped around and grabbed the ruby-encrusted cane that was leaning up against the wall.

"I'll take my boy and we will be on our way."

"No, we had a deal about the boy!" Marie shouted.

"That was before the better piece of the deal fell through," Mr. Wicker said.

"What part of the deal are you referring to? I only agreed to give you one-eighth of my wheat production." Marie replied.

"I've changed my mind since that little outburst," Mr. Wicker said.

"My daughter had nothing to do with this deal. Now, get out of my house," Marie yelled. I watched a very harassed Mr. Wicker lean on his cane as he limped toward the door.

Slowly, I slipped out of the kitchen and watched Marie barge after Mr. Wicker toward the front door. Instead of remaining in the dining room, I followed suit and watched as she slammed the door behind him.

Marie and I watched from the window as Mr. Wicker got into his carriage, shot a dirty look toward the house, and told the coachman to crack the whip. The black horses cantered away, and the carriage rocked dangerously down the drive. Marie turned on me so sharply that I wasn't expecting it.

"What are you standing here for?" her sharp voice rang through the empty hall.

"I wanted to know what else you wanted me to do," I replied in a whisper.

"Go finish with the dishes. I don't know why I should have to tell you that," Marie said.

"But ma'am the dishes are already done," I pointed out.

"Then you can take Robert out to the stables and show him the quarters he will be occupying."

I left the front hall and headed back into the kitchen where I found Robert in the position I had left him. He turned to face me when he heard me enter. "If you follow me, I'll show you to the stables where you will be sleeping," I said.

He gave me a nod to show that he understood, but his lips remained closed. We went out the back door in the kitchen and crossed the lawn to the big red barn that was only a shadow in the dark night. I went along slowly, not wanting to trip on an upturned stone or twig. Also, the ground was steeply sloped, and I didn't want to embarrass myself any further by falling.

When I reached the barn, I fiddled with the rusty latch until it opened. I could hear Robert breathing behind me. I pushed the doors open and felt for the lantern that was hanging against the wall. My hand grazed a sharp nail, but I continued to grope forward. Finally, my hand contacted the lantern, and I pulled it down from the wall. Bending down into the dampened hay, I lit the lantern, and a blazing light filled the stable. I could hear the snorting of the horses as they restlessly moved in their stalls. Now in the light, I looked down at my hand. There was a small cut that didn't seem very deep, but blood beaded across my hand. I tried to hide it as I turned toward Robert.

"Follow me. You will be sleeping in the loft above the horses," I said as I headed for the far side of the barn where a ladder went into the ceiling above. "I'll climb up and you can hand me the lantern."

Giving him the lantern, I began climbing up, careful not to put pressure on my injured hand. Once in the loft, Robert handed the light up, and I hung it from a nail that was sticking out of the rafters. In the illuminated space, I saw bare brown wooden walls, and the floor was littered with hay. I set to work trying to find the least damp hay while Robert climbed up the ladder.

"I've found the driest hay for you to sleep on for tonight," I said.

He crossed the room and settled on the fresh hay while I slowly sat down across from him. Glancing around, I searched for something to cover my hand. Suddenly, I sensed him watching me, and I tried to hide the wound, but it was too late. Robert assessed the injury and then ripped off some fabric from his shirt. Tentatively, he wrapped it around my hand.

"Thank you," I said, wondering even more so if he was mute. I decided the best thing to do was ask. "Do you know how to speak?" I asked.

"Yes," came his hoarse reply. "I choose not to. Mr. Wicker didn't like it when I talked," Robert said quickly, and then he fell silent again. He looked guilty.

Instantly I felt the need to ask him questions. Perhaps with Mr. Wicker gone he would talk to me. I hoped so because I hardly had anyone to converse with, especially someone around my age.

"What was your life like with Mr. Wicker? Why would he want to excuse you from your services? Do you have any family? Have you always lived with him?"

I know I didn't give him time between questions to answer, and my questions were a bit nosy, but I was so eager for conversation.

Robert gave me an odd look. I couldn't tell if he was mad or not.

"Maybe I don't want to share that kind of information with you," he said suddenly.

I was taken aback by his response. Didn't he also need to talk to someone after Mr. Wicker had kept him silent? Robert gave me a cold look and turned away from me. Judging from his reaction toward me, I knew he had tired of my company. I decided it was time for me to leave.

Slowly, I got up from the hay and moved to the ladder. I gave him an angry look as I turned around to lower myself down from the loft. A small part of me expected him to call down and ask me to come back, but no call came. I stalked out of the barn.

Through the dark night, I felt my way up to the house, careful not to trip on the uneven land. A small light was shining in the kitchen, and I moved toward the soft glow. The kitchen was empty, and slowly I turned the brass doorknob, hearing a click as the heavy door opened. Marie and her children seemed to have retired to bed, and I knew there would be hell to pay if I woke them. Like a thief, I stole into the house and made my way to the stairs. Practically holding my breath, I took each step at a time, grateful that I was able to remain silent. I was a few steps from the top when I started to breathe easier.

Then, it happened on the last step. The step creaked under my weight and echoed in the silent, old house. I froze and strained my ears to see if anyone had heard. My heart began to drum in my chest. I noticed candlelight moving under the door to my left, Marie's door! Slowly, the knob on the door turned and I closed my eyes wishing I could disappear. When I opened them, I saw Marie standing in the doorway holding a slim candle in her hands. If it weren't for the candle, I would have thought her eyes were creating the fire.

"What are you doing?" Marie asked in a harsh whisper.

"I was just heading up to my room," I replied.

"I don't need you sneaking around my house like a common criminal," Marie said.

"I was showing Robert out to the barn, like you asked," I stammered.

"Well, get up to bed. I hope never to find you out this late," Marie said as she slammed her door in my face.

Shuttering, I continued toward the attic. Today had been so confusing. I had thought Emily would be forced into marrying Mr. Wicker, and I would finally get someone to talk to if Robert came to stay. When would I learn I should never be hopeful?

If only my father could be here. He would have been able to make things better, I thought as I closed my eyes. Though I felt tired, I wasn't foolish enough to believe that my mind would descend into the darkness of sleep.

3

AN UNEXPECTED SURPRISE

THE SUMMER DAYS moved by swiftly, and I kept to my routine in the house. I had little to no contact with Robert. I spent my free time in the woods around the house, and on rainy days, I would retreat to the attic. My life progressed the same as it always had, except for the fact that more men came to have dinner with Marie and her family in hopes of courting Emily. Emily, however, was not to be won that easily, and she managed to find something distasteful about every man that walked through the door. Marie seemed to be on pins and needles every day, and she yelled at me frequently. Her irritability was the reason I enjoyed disappearing into the woods. Each day I found myself going deeper and staying later than I should. I didn't know how long the manor's property extended, but I didn't care. The woods became my sanctuary, a place where no one could bother me.

I often thought about my mother during my woodsy walks. There was so much I would never know about her. I wished that someone would be able to tell me what she had been like. Though some of the servants had worked at the manor when my mother was the lady of the house, none of them talked about her. I believed they were afraid that Marie would find out and punish them. When Marie married my father, she insisted on hiring some of her previous servants. However, my father could not afford to hire more staff members, and he dismissed some of his employees. Ever since then, the remaining long-term staff feared that they would lose their jobs if they displeased Marie.

As soon as my chores were completed for the day, I made my way down to the forest. My breath slowed as I stepped into the cool, shadowed green. The trees were so beautiful, and the sun shone through the leaves creating shafts of light on the forest floor. I stepped over the mossy fallen logs making sure I didn't step on the sharp stones. My mind wandered as I continued to walk further into the forest, where the trees became thicker, and sunlight broke through less often.

I walked for what I suspected was a half hour before I stopped. This was the farthest I had ever been. I lowered myself onto a log and gazed around admiring the beauty of nature. A cool breeze ruffled the leaves above, and it felt so good against my skin. I closed my eyes and leaned back on the log noticing that the forest was uncommonly quiet. My eyes snapped open, and I looked around wildly. Usually, the forest was full of life and the constant chirping of birds could be heard, but today the woods were still. Was it because I was so deep in?

In the bush directly behind me, I heard a rustling and immediately jumped up from the log. Had someone followed me? What kinds of animals lived this deep in the woods? Slowly, I backed away from the noise. Since I hadn't paid attention to where I was stepping, I tripped over a broken branch, and I fell onto my back. As I struggled to get up, a man stepped out from behind the bush. He wore a bright purple vest and black pants. The man had a short gray beard and oval glasses that sat on the brim of his nose. He appeared to be shorter than average, but I couldn't tell from the ground. I began to scream for help, but I didn't know if anyone would hear me this far into the woods.

"Hush Miss Fitzgerald, your stepmother can't hear you from here which is probably for the best," the man said.

"How do you know my name?" I asked in a terrified voice.

"Calm down, Miss Fitzgerald. I've been watching you for a while now, and I'm positive you are who I'm looking for," he replied.

How could I calm down when he had just admitted that he had been following me for some time now?

"Why would you be looking for me?" I asked while I tried to keep my voice from shaking. If worse came to worse, I could use my powers to escape from this man with the hope that Marie would never find out.

"I'm quite sure that you have the same ability as your mother," the man replied.

"What do you mean by ability?" I asked.

"I think you know what I mean." He smiled at me, and I was sure he meant it to be encouraging.

"So, you knew my mother?" I asked, not wanting to reveal my powers to this stranger.

"Of course, I knew her! She was one of my best students at my school and you look just like her," the old man said.

"What are you talking about?" My father had never told me anything about this man.

"Your mother attended the Jelf Academy of Magic for five years," the man said. "She had the same capabilities you do."

"Are you saying that my mother was, and I am a witch?" I blurted.

At this point, the strangely dressed man laughed at me. "Heavens no! Witches and Warlocks do not exist! They are just fictional characters that humans make up out of fear of anything magical. You, my dear, are a pixie. Your mother was one of the best pixies I have ever had the pleasure to teach."

"Aren't pixies supposed to be small and impish? I don't think I fit the description," I said.

"That is another misconception that humans make about the magical world. Pixies control things with their minds. We can create charms using the rocks and minerals around us. If you agree to attend the Jelf Academy, you can learn to control your powers and be able to do so much more with them," the man said.

"I'm not so sure Marie will approve," I replied. I was sure she would immediately say no to any place that would help enhance my powers.

"She must approve! I personally think you were meant to go to the Jelf Academy of Magic and be trained like your mother," the man burst out. "All pixies must complete their education. How else are you going to learn to create charms and control your powers?"

"I'm sorry, but I don't even know who you are," I said as I pulled myself up from the ground. I had just realized that I had been talking to this man the entire time from the forest floor. I was so baffled by his presence that I couldn't even think clearly. Could there really be an entire school of people like me?

"Oh, how silly of me," the man chuckled. "My name is Dr. Tweedle, and I'm the headmaster of the Jelf Academy." He reached into his pocket and pulled out a folded piece of cream-colored paper. "This is your letter of introduction to the school. I apologize since it seems I forgot to tell you more than my name."

I opened the paper and stared at the neat, scrawled print.

Dear Miss Jane Fitzgerald,

I am pleased to inform you that you may possess the magical ability that is required to attend the Jelf Academy of Magic, and you have recently reached the appropriate age to begin your magical education. Enclosed is a list of required items for your education. I would be delighted if you were to accept the proposal to come and study at the Jelf Academy of Magic. School begins at the end of August and students are allowed to return home on weekends. I anticipate your acceptance.

Sincerely,

Dr. Oliver Tweedle

Headmaster.

My eyes scanned down the letter to the list of items I would need if I were to attend.

SCHOOL SUPPLIES

- *School uniform*
- *Set of twelve astrological gemstones*
- *Set of star charts*
- *One pixie dust case*
- *Set of stone mixing dishes*

BOOKS

- *The Power of Gemstones* by Ruby Pebble
- *Divination for Beginners* by Moon Shadowveil, Master Seer
- *Pixies of the Modern Age* by Walter Brown
- *Understanding the Zodiac* by Leonardo Flitz
- *Predicting the Weather and Other Catastrophes* by Merle Greenhouse
- *The Movement of Stars and What They Mean* by Orion Nebula
- *Mixing Stone Powders Vol. 1* by Randolph Talc

Dr. Tweedle was watching me intently over his oval spectacles.

"Well, even if I were allowed to attend Jelf Academy, where would I get the money to buy all these things?" I asked as I looked up from the very long list.

"Not to worry," Dr. Tweedle said as he pushed up his glasses so that they sat higher up on his nose. "We have a wonderful program for students who do not have the money to pay for their supplies. You don't have to worry about paying any sort of tuition to attend the school. The Jelf Academy is considered a public school, in which all of the pixies of the eastern United States can attend."

My eyes went back to the letter:

You have the option of bringing a small pet, which you may keep in your dormitory. Also, you may bring a formal dress/suit if you qualify for the school dance.

"This can't be real." the words came out of my mouth when I had only meant to think them.

"This is very real. Now the only thing I have left to do is convince your stepmother. I've already managed to convince the pixie government for now," Dr. Tweedle sighed.

"What do you mean by the pixie government?" I asked confused. Also, what did he mean when he said for now?

"Within our hidden community, there is a pixie government that deals with pixie affairs. The pixie government of the United States is skeptical about allowing you to attend because your father was human. They have this irrational fear that you would expose the pixie world to humans, and they also don't believe that you will be talented enough since you are not a pure-blooded pixie. I've convinced them to offer you admission as long as I keep them updated on your progress."

"Why would you want to convince them? You don't even know me," I stammered.

"I knew your mother, and I am sure that you have her ability," Dr. Tweedle responded.

31

"Marie will never let me go. She would never let me attend a school that focused on magic especially since she is repulsed by me. Marie has threatened to throw me out of the house because of my magic. She even denies that I'm her stepdaughter," I cried.

"Then we shall not let her know that your attendance is for magical purposes." With that, Dr. Tweedle snapped his fingers and blue dust surrounded his body in a glittery cloud. When the dust settled, Dr. Tweedle emerged dressed in a black suit and his glasses looked cleaner. I gaped with shock because I had never seen another person perform magic.

"Wow, will I learn to do magic like that?" I asked in amazement.

"Yes, you will learn the powers of charm making and how to focus your mind. Pixie magic requires a great deal of mental stability that will help you control your powers. Let me explain my impromptu plan. You will head back to the house, and I will come by later. Do not give any indication that we have met. Let me have that letter back so I can properly present it to your stepmother. Without a doubt, she will accept this invitation for you to attend."

Dr. Tweedle plucked the letter from my hands and instantly the letter resealed itself as if it were never opened. As Dr. Tweedle confidently turned on his heel and made his way farther into the woods, I headed in the opposite direction toward the house. My stomach clenched and my head spun. Dr. Tweedle did not know Marie, so how could he be so sure she would agree?

When I got closer to the house, I heard Marie calling my name. Had Dr. Tweedle arrived already?

"Jane, where have you been?" Marie demanded.

"Just in the woods, ma'am," I replied.

"Get in the kitchen and put on some tea. Emily has a dreadful headache, and she has requested some tea with lemon," Marie said.

Hastily, I went into the kitchen and put on a kettle of water. While the water boiled, I sat nervously waiting for Dr. Tweedle to appear. I began fidgeting, and my nerves jolted when the tea kettle whistled. Trying to stay calm, I grabbed some tea leaves and added them to the porcelain pink cup. Even though my hands shook, I managed to pour out the hot water. Then, I took two slices of lemon and squeezed them into the tea along with a lump of sugar. Was Dr. Tweedle telling me the truth about a magic school or was this an elaborate hoax? Could I even allow myself to hope? Hope had never worked in the past.

I was on my way up to Emily's room when I heard a knock on the door. Spinning around on the staircase, I watched Marie head across the foyer and fling the door open. I felt a flutter of excitement at the sight of Dr. Tweedle on the front steps. I prayed this all wasn't a joke for Marie's amusement.

Before Marie could notice me on the staircase, I headed up to Emily's room to deliver the tea. Marie couldn't yell at me for not doing what she had asked. Emily was lying in her bed with the covers up to her neck and her eyes closed when I entered the room. Her red curtains were drawn tightly to keep the light out. She must have sensed someone was in the room with her because she started to moan dramatically.

"My head, my head!"

As I moved closer to the bed, Emily's eyes opened. "There you are! I've been waiting for ages for that tea. My poor headache won't go away with cold tea."

"Don't worry, the tea is hot," I sighed as I walked to her bedside.

"Well, since you're here, there is an awful dirty spot on my fireplace mantel, and it's hurting my eyes," Emily sighed.

I set her tea down on her bedside table. "What spot?" I asked. "I don't see one."

"Believe me, it's there! It's been glaring at me all day," Emily replied.

Slowly, I moved to the mantel and grabbed a cloth that was hanging on the rack near the fireplace.

"To the left. No, more to the right." Emily was shouting at me as I wiped all over the mantel. I could hear the suppressed laugh in her voice, and I knew that Emily wasn't sick at all. She was probably acting to get a break from the line of suitors Marie had waiting.

"Jane, Jane!" I heard Marie calling from downstairs. I smiled to myself as I dropped the rag at the foot of the fireplace.

"Where do you think you're going?" Emily asked.

"Your mother calls," I replied as I exited her bedroom and made my way downstairs. Marie was in my father's old office, and I almost cringed when I saw her seated at that old oak desk. Dr. Tweedle sat in the chair in front of the desk with his back to me, facing Marie. The curtains were thrown open, and I blinked to get used to the light because Emily's room had been a sea of shadows.

"Yes, ma'am," I asked attentively, and I tried not to look at Dr. Tweedle.

"This man, Dr. Twaddle…"

"Tweedle," Dr. Tweedle cut in.

"Dr. Tweedle," Marie smiled sweetly, but I knew she was furious about being corrected. "Has informed me that you have the qualifications to attend his school, but what the qualifications are I do not know," she sneered.

Dr. Tweedle twitched in his chair, and I could tell he was embarrassed for me.

"Well, Jane, why do you think I should let you go? I still haven't found out what they teach there," she inclined her head toward Dr. Tweedle.

I remained silent not knowing what to say. Do I beg and plead? Was I supposed to come up with a lie for what the school taught? Suddenly Dr. Tweedle gasped. "My, my, look at that extraordinary bird just out the window there."

Marie and I both looked out the window, but out of the corner of my eye, I saw Dr. Tweedle pull a bag out of his jacket. Marie's back was still to Dr. Tweedle.

"What bird? What are you talking about?" she asked in an aggravated voice.

"Oh, it's just out the window there," Dr. Tweedle replied.

Marie continued to look, but I was not interested in the bird anymore. I was more interested in what Dr. Tweedle was doing. He took a pinch of green powder from the pouch and sprinkled it into Marie's cup of tea. Green smoke rose from the glass and then magically vanished when Marie turned around. She gently picked up her cup and took a sip. If Marie could taste anything different, she didn't show it.

"Maybe you should take a look at Miss Fitzgerald's acceptance letter," Dr. Tweedle suggested as he pulled out the cream-colored letter. I held my breath as he handed it over to her.

"Mm… the Jelf Academy," Marie mumbled. "So, your school teaches etiquette." I breathed a sigh of relief. Whatever Dr. Tweedle had slipped into Marie's tea must have changed what she saw on my acceptance letter.

"Her mother attended, and I believe her father would have wanted her to attend as well. She has a small amount of money saved in an account which she will be able to use toward supplies. We can help her finically with the rest," Dr. Tweedle said.

"It wouldn't hurt for the girl to learn some manners, but I definitely won't pay any money towards it. How long will she attend this school?" Marie asked.

"She will attend the school for five years and she is allowed home for the holidays and weekends," Dr. Tweedle replied.

"Well, that is not going to do. I need Jane to help with cleaning the house every day," Marie said.

"Please, ma'am," I said. "I will work extra hard on the weekends to make up for the week."

Marie sat staring at my acceptance letter, and Dr. Tweedle sat patiently. It seemed like an eternity before Marie said anything.

"If I let you go, Jane, you must promise me that you will work harder than ever. You will not have any time off except for supper." Her cold gray eyes looked me over.

"Yes, ma'am, I understand," I said as looked down at the desk.

"You may go only on those conditions. It certainly wouldn't be a waste for you to acquire proper etiquette. Maybe then you won't be a complete embarrassment in the future," Marie said. "but, if I find your housework lacking, I will never let you return If your education doesn't benefit me, I won't tolerate it."

"Good, that seems settled," said Dr. Tweedle as he got to his feet. "I'll be back on August twenty-sixth to take Miss Fitzgerald to get her school supplies, and then I will make sure she gets to the school."

"Surely you don't take all the students to get their school supplies," Marie said with that suspicious look on her face.

"Miss Fitzgerald's case is different, seeing that she is an orphan who does need our financial help. I didn't think you would mind so much if I took her out of your hands. If you would rather take her yourself, then by all means…" Dr. Tweedle stated.

"No, no that's fine. I supposed I'll have to see you again on the twenty-sixth of August," Marie said snootily as she stood and gestured Dr. Tweedle toward the door.

My heart felt lighter as I made my way up to the attic. Soon, I would escape this prison, even if it were just for a little while.

On the twenty-sixth of August, Dr. Tweedle kept his word and arrived in a horse-drawn carriage. He was dressed in a finely pressed suit, and his beard looked neater. I stood silently at the top of the stairs as I watched Marie open the big wooden door and saw him standing in the doorway. The light bounced off his oval glasses and he looked up at me and smiled.

"Are you ready to go, Miss Fitzgerald?" Dr. Tweedle asked completely ignoring Marie, which I knew she couldn't stand.

"Oh, Jane, I didn't know you were there," she said as she spun around to face me.

"Come along, Miss Fitzgerald, and remember to bring your acceptance letter," Dr. Tweedle said with a wink.

"It's in my room. I'll just be a minute," I said and dashed up to the attic. I grabbed the letter and looked around the musty old room. It would be a week before I would have to sleep here again. I turned my back on the dismal space and hurried down the stairs to Dr. Tweedle in the hall, not feeling any sadness about leaving.

"Are you ready?" Dr. Tweedle asked. The tension in the hallway felt like it could be sliced with a knife. I had never seen Marie so uncomfortable in her own home. "Don't you have a suitcase or something special that you would like to take with you?"

I shook my head as I watched Marie out of the corner of my eye.

"You don't have anything at all, dear?" he asked.

"No, I don't, but I'm ready to go now," I replied as I watched Marie's dangerous stare,

"Alright then, Miss Fitzgerald, let's be off," Dr. Tweedle said. He started to head to the door. I was on my way out after him when Marie grabbed my arm and pulled me very close to her face.

"Remember what you promised me." Her gray stony eyes scanned my face and made me shutter. It was only for a moment, and then she shoved me toward the door.

Shaken up, I followed Dr. Tweedle to his carriage and he helped me in. I looked back at the house as the carriage pulled away, and I saw Marie disappear behind the curtain. I began to breathe easier as the carriage rounded the bend down the drive by the barn. I was so afraid Marie would change her mind at the last moment. A flash of movement caught my attention. Watching me from the shadow of the barn was Robert. We made eye contact for a split second before I lost sight of him as the carriage pulled me into my new life.

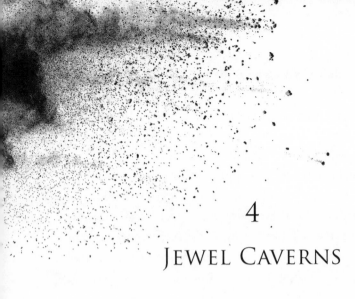

4

JEWEL CAVERNS

THE CARRIAGE LEFT the manor's grounds, taking me into a world I had never seen before. Suddenly, Dr. Tweedle stopped the horses and pulled off to the side of the road. "Why are we stopping?" I asked.

"You'll see in a moment, my dear," he replied as he reached into the back of the carriage. I waited as he pulled out a small pouch. "This will get us where we want to go faster than this little carriage. Now, hold tight to my arm and the side of the carriage. It is imperative that you do not let go."

I did as I was told, grabbing his arm probably a bit too tightly. From the pouch, Dr. Tweedle extracted a vial containing a mixture of purplish powder. The powder was a variety of shades and was as fine as sand in an hourglass. He uncorked the vial and held the powder aloft.

"Now Miss Fitzgerald, are you holding on tight?" Dr. Tweedle asked as if he couldn't feel my death grip.

I nodded my head, and Dr. Tweedle tipped his hand. The powder poured out into the air and everything around me went black. It felt like I had entered a cloud of dust. I began to cough.

My head suddenly felt dizzy, and my feet felt like they had lifted off the carriage floor. When the cloud cleared, the surroundings were different. I couldn't see the manor house anymore, and tall mountains surrounded the carriage. Dr. Tweedle took hold of the reins and began steering the horses up the mountains.

"What just happened?" I asked, bewildered by the change of scenery.

"We just teleported," Dr. Tweedle explained. "With the right combination of a few minerals and mental concentration, you can go anywhere you imagine."

"Will I learn to do that at the Jelf Academy?" I asked as I sat in amazement.

"Not in your first year. You will begin learning about teleportation in your fourth year and will continue your study of it into your fifth year," Dr. Tweedle explained. "If the pixie government approves your continued education, of course."

The carriage was now climbing rockier terrain. Where were we going? Dr. Tweedle finally steered the carriage into the shade of the mountains. He climbed down and began examining the rock formation. He stroked his beard, and I wondered what he was looking for. Finally, his hand came in contact with a rock that looked like a lever. To my surprise, Dr. Tweedle pulled on the rock, and instantly the side of the mountain split opened. I watched as a wall of rock slid away to reveal a cave in the mountainside.

"Our society is expertly hidden from humans. They wouldn't be able to find this place due to our extensive charms," Dr. Tweedle said as he hopped back onto the wagon. He snapped the reins, and the horses entered the cave, which I realized was lit by what looked like little people with wings. Each one gave off a different colored glow.

"If I'm a pixie, then what are those?" I asked as I pointed to the light source.

"Those are sprites. They can be very helpful. There are many different kinds of sprites. Some reside in caves, some underwater, and some in the forest. Sprites get along with pixies very well, but they are not one of our main light sources. We don't need them to produce light, but they are friendly, and we love the company," Dr. Tweedle explained.

The sprites circled us as we went deeper into the cave. Darkness enclosed us from behind as the wall of rock slid back into place, hiding the cave entrance again. I realized how much I didn't know about the world my mother had belonged to. I wanted to know everything about it because this was the missing piece of a mother I had never known.

"I hope you don't mind me asking, but where are we going?" I asked.

"This is Jewel Caverns, the best place to get school supplies and everyday charm supplies,' Dr. Tweedle replied.

As we went deeper into the cave, I noticed that the ceiling was getting wider, and the walls seemed less narrow. Suddenly and so unexpectedly, the carriage reached a wide space where the cavern became deep. A road spiraled down to the bottom, and when I looked above me, I could see a domed ceiling. The domed ceiling appeared to be made of glass and sunshine shone brightly down into the cavern. As we traveled down the spiraling road, I saw that shops had been cut into the rock wall. I couldn't believe that an entire town had been hidden inside the mountain. There were so many people walking along the edge of the street. When Dr. Tweedle spoke, it was hard to draw my attention away from all the new sights around me.

"We have to make a quick stop at the very bottom, so I can get the money you have saved and the financial aid the school offers," Dr. Tweedle said as the horses trotted down the long road.

As soon as he had finished speaking, my eyes darted back to all the activity around me. I couldn't get enough, and I wished I had more eyes. If I did belong at the Jelf Academy, this could be my new world. This place was more exciting than anything I had ever known. More sprites seemed to have appeared and they were flying around the cavern; small little lights that bounced and flashed off the walls.

People moved from shop to shop as the carriage made its way down the street. Some waved to Dr. Tweedle and tipped their hats, while others called out a friendly greeting. Most of the people were dressed in brightly colored clothing. The servants at the manor house all wore drab colors and only Marie and Emily had a wardrobe of variety. Even so, Marie and Emily's clothing lacked in comparison to the people we passed.

When we finally reached the bottom, Dr. Tweedle told me to stay in the carriage as he went into the last building on the street. It had big silver double doors and a huge sign over the entrance. I couldn't make out what the sign said, but I was afraid if I moved all of this would disappear, and I would wake up from this dream.

I waited for a few minutes, and then Dr. Tweedle reappeared with a small blue drawstring bag in his hand. He crossed the street and climbed back up beside me.

"Here is the money you can use to buy your school supplies," he said as he tossed the bag in my lap. "Now we can head back up to those shops."

The carriage was steered back up the street, and the first shop we stopped at was *Mr. Murray's Wardrobe*. The small, printed sign in the window stated that the store now had school uniforms and formal attire.

"We better get your school uniforms first," Dr. Tweedle said as he helped me from the carriage.

We walked across the street to the shop, and Dr. Tweedle held the door open for me. Inside, racks of clothing stretched to the back counter. The walls of the shop were bright yellow and rocky, while the floor looked smooth. A man in a colorful vest, much like the one Dr. Tweedle was wearing when I had met him, stood behind the counter. Though his hair was also gray, I could tell he was younger than Dr. Tweedle.

"Good afternoon, Oliver. Here to see our new fashionable dress clothes?" the man asked.

"Not today, Timothy. I'm here to help Miss Fitzgerald with her school supplies. It's going to be her first time attending the Jelf Academy. Her mother was Rachel McCalski," Dr. Tweedle almost whispered his last sentence, but I had heard it.

"Oh," the man at the counter said in wonderment which I didn't understand.

"We don't have much money to spend, so could you please show us the used or clearance school uniforms?" Dr. Tweedle asked.

"Of course, right this way," said Timothy Murray as he moved from behind the glass counter. "These school uniforms are on sale and those on that rack are used. All the used uniforms have been thoroughly laundered and pressed."

"Thank you. I'm sure this selection will fulfill our needs," Dr. Tweedle said.

All the school uniforms on the rack were of the same design though they were all different colors. The boys' uniforms consisted of a button-up shirt, colored vest, and slacks, while the girls' uniforms included a blouse and long skirt. I began looking through the rack of clothes.

"Dr. Tweedle, none of these clothes have sizes on them," I remarked. "Shouldn't my measurements be taken for the uniforms? If so, they won't be ready for school tomorrow." I was feeling uneasy. How could I go to school without uniforms?

"These are pixie clothes. They shrink or expand to the size of the wearer. Pixie fabric is very special. We don't need to take measurements for alterations. All clothes that we put on will become the perfect size," Dr. Tweedle explained. "Here is a uniform with a purple skirt that will match your eyes."

I held the clothing up to my body and looked down at it. It

was the prettiest skirt I had ever seen. I had been wearing rags most of my life, so I was very excited to try it on. Dr. Tweedle alerted Mr. Murray and he showed me to a dressing room. The uniform fit perfectly and the fabric felt cool and soft against my skin. I looked in the mirror at my reflection and was surprised to see how well my eyes shinned. The blouse was white with short sleeves, and Dr. Tweedle was correct in the fact that the skirt matched my eyes.

"That looks beautiful on you," Dr. Tweedle remarked. "I think this is the perfect choice for you. Now let's see about shoes. All uniform shoes are black, and they work the same as the fabric in your uniform."

From the rack of shoes, I picked a pair of black ones with a small heel. They also fit perfectly and looked wonderful with the skirt.

"I think we have found one of your school uniforms. Go ahead and change and we will pick out a few more," Dr. Tweedle said.

Dr. Tweedle and I continued to quickly browse through the racks of uniforms on sale. He helped me select a few more varieties so that I could have clean uniforms that would last the week. The majority of the uniforms were shades of purple and some blues that Dr. Tweedle believed would go well with my eyes. The blouses had short and long sleeves for different times of the year. It was hard to believe that these new clothes were all for me.

"Would the girl be interested in a formal dress for one of the dances?" Mr. Murray asked.

"You know, Timothy, we are only here for the essentials. She can only afford what she needs," Dr. Tweedle replied.

"She is beautiful enough to be asked," Mr. Murray stated, and I blushed from his compliment and mumbled a thank you.

"In that case, I'm sure we will be back. Come along, Miss Fitzgerald."

I followed Dr. Tweedle from the shop, holding the wrapped package. He helped me back into the carriage, and we moved onto the next shop which was called *Jewels and Powders*. The shop was crowded when we entered. Some of the customers waved to Dr. Tweedle as he steered me to a rack titled Astrological Gemstones.

"You need a bagful of each of these twelve stones," Dr. Tweedle explained.

I grabbed twelve bags and waited for the crowd to clear around the display.

"Here, let me hold those bags while you fill them to the brim," Dr. Tweedle said. I handed him all twelve bags. Then I picked up the small shovel and began with the gems on the farthest left, which were dark red.

"This is a garnet... ," Dr. Tweedle explained as I scooped them into the bag. "... and that purple one is an amethyst."

When I was finished with all the gemstones that Dr. Tweedle told me represented each month of the year, I followed him around the shop. In the very last aisle were odd-looking cases and stone mixing dishes.

"Let me explain to you about these pixie dust cases. They hold all the different rock and mineral types you will need for class and anything needed to make any charm. These cases have secret compartments that only the owner can find and will shrink with only the owner's touch. That way you can store it in your pocket," Dr. Tweedle said.

"Wouldn't the case be very heavy since it stores all the gems you will need to make charms?" I asked.

"These cases are pixie made, and the material is infused with different charms. The charms make the case and everything in it as light as a feather with the ability to shrink and expand."

There were many different pixie dust cases on the shelves. I chose a gold one with an intricate design consisting of flowers and leaves that wove around every side of the box. The design was beautiful and since it had drawn my eye, I knew I had to have it for my pixie dust case. I was really surprised by how light the box actually was when I lifted it from the shelf.

"Do you see the indention on the front of the box that looks like a regular keyhole?" Dr. Tweedle asked. I nodded in response. "You will press your right pointer finger onto that keyhole. The box will only respond to your touch. Do not do that until we have paid for all of this though," Dr. Tweedle instructed.

I followed Dr. Tweedle to the counter, after I had picked out a set of stone mixing dishes, and placed the twelve bags of gemstones, my pixie dust case, and my mixing dishes in front of the shop owner.

"That will be thirty kryptos and sixty coodles," the woman at the counter said. I stared at Dr. Tweedle looking confused at what the woman had meant. I hadn't overheard the exchange when Dr. Tweedle had purchased my school uniforms since I had been in the changing room. Dr. Tweedle took some bills and coins from the blue drawstring bag and handed them across the counter. Dr. Tweedle then grabbed my purchases and we headed back to the carriage.

"What are kryptos and coodles?" I asked.

"It is pixie money. Are you hungry? I'll take you to lunch, and then I can explain the money," Dr. Tweedle offered.

I agreed, feeling famished, and Dr. Tweedle drove the carriage to one of the restaurants. He ordered for the both of us, and as we sat waiting for lunch, he explained the pixie currency.

"Coodles are like coins in human money. There are different types of coodles just like there are different types of human coins. Five splicks make one beezle, four beezles make one magnus, and five magnuses make one krypto."

Dr. Tweedle reached into his jacket pocket and pulled out three coins. He laid them out on the table and looked at me again.

"This is a splick," he said as he picked up the smallest of the three. The coin was silver, and it had a picture of a man with small, slightly pointed ears. "This is a picture of Waldrick the Great. He was one of the greatest leaders in the pixie world even though he is fairly young in terms of history. This coin was actually reminted to have his face on it. Waldrick made sure that the pixie society remained well hidden from humans."

"Why do pixies try to hide from humans? My mother married my father, and he was a human," I said.

"Your mother disappeared from the pixie world to be with your father, but just imagine if all humans found out about magic. Everyone would want to have it, though humans wouldn't understand that they do not have the ability to control it. Also, we do not want to be found by the W.A.S.P." Dr. Tweedle said looking down at his plate. It seemed that he had become instantly sad.

"What is the wasp?"

"I shouldn't be the one to tell you, but I would hate for you to hear it while at school. The W.A.S.P. is a secret human society that stands for World Association for the Slaying of Pixies. The humans who join this club believe magical creatures exist. Typically, humans won't openly announce that they are members because to admit it would be crazy. I'm sure they would be afraid of being carted off to an asylum. That's why it is so secretive. The main goal of the W.A.S.P. is to find pixies and destroy them," Dr. Tweedle said with a deep breath.

"Now, I'm going to tell you something that is very hard for me to say. Your mother was one of the best pixies I have ever known. Rachel was the best in her year. She topped every class she was in. During her last few years at the Jelf Academy, Rachel acquired an internship. She worked with Waldrick the Great, which made her slightly famous for being his youngest employee. Rachel worked while she attended her last year at Jelf Academy. After she graduated, the other teachers and I expected her to achieve great things, but when she met your father, she gave it all up. Some say that meeting your father was her downfall, the pathway to her demise.

"I remember a conversation where she seemed curious about humans and what would happen if a pixie fell in love with one. I tried to explain to her that marrying outside of the magical world was unwise and dangerous, not to mention against pixie law. I didn't understand at the time what possessed her to ask me such questions. When she disappeared, I had no idea that she had left the pixie world to marry a human. Until her death, I didn't know what had become of your mother," Dr. Tweedle paused to take a drink.

"I feared the worst when she disappeared after graduating from the academy. When pixies discovered where she had been, most thought it was ironic of her to run off with a human when her whole career had been based upon hiding the magical world from them," Dr. Tweedle shifted uncomfortably in his chair and was silent for a moment. Then he cleared his throat and continued speaking.

"You must not think this is your father's fault, but without knowing it, he hired a loose-lipped man. The man must have caught her using magic and spread rumors of what he had seen at the local tavern. I can only assume that a member of the W.A.S.P. overheard what the man was saying. The W.A.S.P. discovered the location of your father's farm. They took your mother and… and…" Dr. Tweedle stopped talking and his eyes welled up with tears. He grabbed a napkin and wiped them.

My throat felt like it was going to close up because I knew what he was going to say.

"The W.A.S.P. killed your mother and later returned her body to the property. She had been missing for a few days before she was found. Your father was distraught when I explained to him what had happened and why. He vowed that he would hide you from the magical world. I told him that would probably be impossible because even at the age of one, you showed signs of magical ability by making your playthings move around the room. Stopping your magic would be like stopping a river from flowing. That is when your father put a down payment on your education.," Dr. Tweedle said.

"Since I knew of the magic you possessed as a child, that was how I convinced the government to allow you to attend. You are a special case, Miss Fitzgerald. Since the pixie law states that pixies cannot marry or have relations with humans, you are the only person that has both pixie and human heritage. It is because of organizations like the W.A.S.P. that the government officials were leery of letting you attend. If you were to expose any details about the pixie world, the W.A.S.P. might find us. Our government officials also believe you won't be able to keep up with the lessons due to your human blood. I hope you will prove them wrong. Don't focus too much on what the government thinks. I'm sure you will do fine."

We sat silently for a moment after Dr. Tweedle's story. My mother had the same magical ability as me, and she had been killed for it. This society called the W.A.S.P. was the reason my mother was no longer alive. I swallowed back tears. I didn't want to cry in front of Dr. Tweedle, but it was hard not to when I had just discovered that my mother had been murdered. I had always assumed she had been sick. I reached for my napkin and raised it to my eyes.

Despite Dr. Tweedle's reassurances, I was nervous that I wouldn't be allowed to stay at the Jelf Academy. I didn't know anything about magic or the pixie world. How would I be able to keep up with the other students? Dr. Tweedle's arrival at the manor had been the best thing to ever happen to me. I had to make sure I did well enough to continue my education. Now that I knew about the magical world, I couldn't give it up.

"I'm so very sorry to upset you, Miss Fitzgerald. Your mother's story isn't a secret in our world, and I didn't want you to hear about it from someone else," Dr. Tweedle apologized.

"No, thank you for telling me. I'm glad that I won't have to hear about my mother from another student. I never knew how she passed. I think about her every day and have always wondered about her, so thank you again. Also, you may call me Jane instead of Miss Fitzgerald. I'm not used to being addressed so formally," I replied.

"From now on, I'll call you Jane if that is what you wish. Shall we return to our lesson about pixie money? This is a beezle," he said as he pointed to the middle-sized coin on the table. The coin was gold, and it had a picture of a funny-looking man with a shamrock in his hat. "We chose to put the face of a leprechaun on the beezle because the beezle is made of gold, and leprechauns were the first creatures to find gold."

Again, I was surprised to hear about other magical beings.

The last coin on the table was the largest and was a bright copper color. I assumed that this coin was the magnus. The picture on the magnus was of a horse with a horn sticking out of its head. Of all the coins, the magnus was the brightest and shinier than all the rest.

"As you can tell, this is the magnus," Dr. Tweedle said. "We have placed a picture of a unicorn on the magnus because it is the most powerful creature in our world. They are very rare and very pure. It is said that if they touch their horn to a pixie, they can heal any ailment. Unicorns cannot be hunted because they only reveal themselves to pixies that they deem worthy. I did have the pleasure of seeing a unicorn once in my lifetime."

I looked back at the coins and tried to remember what Dr. Tweedle said. Five splicks make one beezle, four beezles make one magnus, and five magnuses make one krypto, I repeated in my head. Dr. Tweedle put the coins back into his pocket, and next, he pulled out some bills.

"Kryptos are bills and they come in amounts of one, three, nine, fifteen, thirty, and sixty."

He laid all the bills out on the table in front of me. These wouldn't be hard to deal with because they had the numbers printed in the corner. I nodded my head in understanding, and Dr. Tweedle slipped the bills back into his pocket. As we finished our lunch, Dr. Tweedle looked at my list to see what else I needed for school.

"All you need is your books and your star charts. We can get all those at *Paper and Ink*," Dr. Tweedle said.

We left the restaurant, got back into the carriage, and made our way up the street to *Paper and Ink*. The shop was a small bright bookstore, with shelves that reached the ceiling. There were sections for simple charm work, magical creatures, medical and herbal remedies, and even books on how to get back at an enemy. I was amazed at the selections of books and was very eager to find the ones on my list. Dr. Tweedle walked around the shop picking out the books I needed. He even surprised me with a bag to carry my books and a pen whose ink was the same color as my eyes. I thanked him profoundly as we left the shop.

"Now that all your shopping is done, I'm going to have to leave you and return to the school to make sure everything is ready for the first day. I have already arranged for you to stay at the *Leaf and Lily Inn* for the night. In the morning, a carriage will arrive to take you to the Jelf Academy. You don't need to worry. Mrs. Dimple, the owner of the inn, is very kind and she will help you with whatever you need," Dr. Tweedle explained.

The *Leaf and Lily* was a tiny, humble place cut neatly into the mountainside. Warm candles glowed in all the windows which made the inn look cozy and inviting from the outside. The door to the inn had a large glass window in the center that was etched with the name and two lilies decorated both sides of the writing. Dr. Tweedle helped me carry my school supplies inside and from the minute I entered the small inn, I felt more at home than I ever did at the manor house. A woman with kind, light blue eyes stood behind the counter. She looked motherly and I immediately knew I would like her, but from my experience with Marie, I knew looks could be deceiving.

"Oh, my Lord! My heart almost stopped a-beating! I thought

Rachel McCalski had entered my inn again," the woman said with emotion.

"Irene, this is Jane Fitzgerald, the new student I was telling you about," Dr. Tweedle said.

"Hello, my dear. I'm pleased to finally meet you. I'm Irene Dimple," she said as she came out from behind the counter. Mrs. Dimple approached me and shook my hand. Then she grabbed one of my bags. "I have already set up a room for you. Come along."

I followed her up the granite stone steps that led to the second floor. Mrs. Dimple was slightly overweight, and she had bleach blonde hair that was cut around her shoulders. Her appearance seemed to match her joyful personality. The longer I followed her along, the more I liked her and the happier I felt. The room that she had set up for me was as homey as the rest of the inn. A candle glowed by the bedside, and the bed was covered with a soft-looking quilt. I was excited at the thought of a real bed, and the first thing I did after I put my school supplies down, was lay on it.

"You must be tired after your travels. Let me go into the kitchen and fix you some of my famous soup. That should take the ache out of your bones. Poor dear, losing your mother so young," Mrs. Dimple sighed as she left the room.

"Jane, it is time for me to go now," Dr. Tweedle said as he stood in the doorway. "I will see you tomorrow at the Jelf Academy. Sleep well."

"Thank you, Dr. Tweedle," I called as he left my room.

Pleased with my accommodations, I crawled under the covers and waited for Mrs. Dimple to return with the soup. The bed was the best I had ever laid on and the pillows were soft and comfortable. My body relaxed, and I felt better than I ever had in my life. Mrs. Dimple bustled into the room a few minutes later carrying a steaming bowl.

"Here, my dear. This should make you feel better and refresh you for tomorrow. I don't have many customers this evening so if there is anything else that you need or want, please feel free to ask me for it." Mrs. Dimple hesitated a moment. She seemed unsure of saying what was on her mind. Finally, she cleared her throat. "I hope you won't mind me asking, but do you remember your mother at all?"

"No, I don't remember her, but sometimes I have dreams where I hear a soft voice speaking to me. My father always told me I looked like her. He died when I was five," I added.

Mrs. Dimple's bright eyes shadowed over, and her rosy cheeks paled. "Who are you living with now, my dear?"

"My father remarried, so now I live with my stepmother and her two children," I explained. I didn't want to tell Mrs. Dimple how they treated me because I feared she would be upset. I did not want to be pitied or worried about.

"I knew you mother," Mrs. Dimple said. "I was two years ahead of her in school, but we became very close. She was a very intelligent pixie and all the teachers loved her. She was a very brilliant girl, even helped me, though I was ahead of her. She always absorbed all the information we were taught. What subjects are you best at, my dear?"

"I don't know ma'am. I just found out I was a pixie. I don't know anything about this world," I explained.

"I'm sorry. That was so silly of me to ask. I was always best at Zodiac Signs. Your mother was good at every subject: Charms, Transfiguration, Teleportation, Magical Creatures, Predicting the Future. Now that I think about it, the only class that your mother was satisfactory at was History. Maybe because it wasn't as hands-on as the other classes," Mrs. Dimple said.

"I don't have any books on creatures, teleporting, or transfiguration," I said, scared that something on my list had been left out.

"Don't worry. In the second year, you'll learn about creatures. Transfiguration is not until year three and Teleportation is in year four, I think. I can't recall. It's been nineteen years since I attended the Jelf Academy."

I breathed a sigh of relief. I would learn about those things if the government let me stay, I thought. "Mrs. Dimple…" I started but was quickly interrupted.

"Please call me Irene. Mrs. Dimple makes me feel so old."

"Irene," I said, the word sounding foreign to my mouth. It felt so strange to address an older woman by her first name. "Do you live here alone?"

"Yes, I live here alone with only guests like you for company," she replied.

"If you don't mind me asking, where is Mr. Dimple?" I asked.

"My husband was a kind and giving man, but he was also a fool. The drink was his downfall, though he wasn't a mean drunk. Two years after we were married, he went out for a drink one night and never came home. I suspected that he had too much and let secrets of this world slip to the wrong people. A few days after his disappearance, pixie authorities came to my house with the news that they had found him. The authorities suspected that it was the W.A.S.P. who was responsible. I assume you know what the W.A.S.P. is?" Irene said. I nodded my head. "You and I are sitting in the same boat, child. We've lost the ones that we love to that evil society. After his death, I have never loved again."

"Irene, I'm so sorry," I said as I looked down at the blue quilt.

"Well, dear, it's getting quite late, and you have a big day tomorrow. It would be best if I let you sleep and not trouble you with my thoughts," Irene said as she patted the bed. Slowly, she got up and as she did, she accidentally hit the candle on the bedside stand. I might have screamed as the candle fell to the floor, but Irene just sighed and picked it up.

Not a single thing had been burned, but my heart was still beating very fast. Irene must have seen the expression on my face because she lightly chuckled.

"This kind of fire doesn't burn, my dear," she said as she put her hand in it. "This is goblin fire which shines brightly but doesn't scorch. Goblin fire is one of our main light sources."

I smiled at her and began breathing easier. Snuggling under the sheets, I watched Irene move toward the door with the candle in hand.

"Sleep well, dearie. I'll wake you bright and early with breakfast," she said nodding once before leaving the room.

Deep under the covers, in the most comfortable bed I had ever laid on, I looked up at the shining stars out the window and far up into the sky through the domed ceiling of the cavern. What would tomorrow bring? Hopefully, my life would be better in this world than it had been in my old one.

5

THE JELF ACADEMY

A SOFT WHISPER AND a small nudge woke me from my sleep. Never before had I been woken like this. "Wake up, dearie. You don't want to be late for your first day of school," Irene whispered in my ear. I rose from the bed feeling very refreshed for the first time in years. I assumed it was because of the wonderful bed and the fact that Marie was far away. Irene was sitting on the edge of the bed, and her round cheery face smiled down at me. "You should get dressed and come downstairs for breakfast."

I climbed out of bed and moved over to the bags with my school supplies. Irene left the room while I dressed, saying she had to get back to the kitchen. I pulled one of my wonderful uniforms from the bag. I slipped on the purple skirt and buttoned up the blouse. Once again, I was surprised by how well the clothes fit. I couldn't help but spin around in front of the mirror. As soon as I finished getting ready, I left the room.

Sunlight streamed into the kitchen making it bright, and the opened windows allowed a light breeze to move through. The green countertops were incredibly clean, and the cabinets were a lovely shade of brown. Mrs. Dimple stood at the brown stove. The smell of something delicious caught my nose.

"Sit down there at the table, my dear," Irene said sensing my presence. "I'll serve you in the kitchen today since I don't have any other customers. Usually, I serve all the guests in the dining area when the inn is full. I'll just have to pay attention in case anyone walks in. Some people just like to come to the inn's restaurant to have a meal."

I sat at the table inhaling the delightful aroma. I was caught off guard when Irene made the rolls levitate and land lightly on the table. I needed to remind myself that I was not the only one in this world who could perform magic.

I lifted one of the rolls from the dish and took a bite. It was one of the best things I had ever tasted in my life. Compared to Irene's cooking, Ellen's looked like sludge. Happily, I ate the rest of my breakfast, feeling more at home in a stranger's house than I had ever felt anywhere else. Irene talked about what I might expect on the first day of school. She said it probably would be an introduction day for the new students which would be fairly easy. Her words made me feel less anxious about attending. After breakfast, Irene told me to collect my belongings since my carriage would be here soon. With a heavy heart, I headed back up to my room to collect my bags.

"Jane dear, your carriage just pulled up outside. Do you have everything?" I heard Irene call from downstairs.

"Yes, I have it all," I said as I descended the steps.

"Oh my, you look even more like your mother today. I believe she also had a purple uniform to match her eyes. Oh, I'm going to miss your company. Promise to come back and visit when you can," Irene replied.

"I promise," I said, full of hope that I would see her again. To my pleasant surprise, Irene pulled me into a warm embrace.

"Now, now don't let me get all teary-eyed. You don't need to be late for your first day," Irene said pulling away. "Farewell dear, I hope you have a good school year."

I moved to the door, gave her one last look, and then stepped into the bright sunshine. I was surprised by how much the light came through the dome despite the town being inside a mountain. Waiting for me was a black carriage pulled by two winged horses. I had to pinch myself to make my eyes weren't playing tricks on me. The horses were both white with large wings protruding from their shoulders. I noticed that the carriage did not have a coachman. How would I get to Jelf Academy without one?

After I had my belongings situated in the carriage, I waited for the coachman to appear, but no one did. Suddenly, the horses pawed at the ground and started to gallop away. Did they know where to go without a coachman to direct them? What if I did not arrive at Jelf Academy because the horses had taken me elsewhere? The horses entered the darkness of the cave that had led into Jewel Caverns. I watched out the window as sprites flew beside the carriage, lighting the way. The mouth of the cave opened, and we burst into light.

Suddenly, with fright and excitement, I realized that the carriage was no longer traveling on the ground, but in the sky. I looked out the window and saw rolling hills and pastures beneath me. The ride was surprisingly smooth. After a while, the fields turned into forests and the horses began to fly lower. At a clearing in the trees, the horses finally landed. I noticed other carriages were landing all around me. Where was the school? Did we need to pull a special lever to get to it just like in Jewel Caverns? Would this be a test to prove I was a pixie?

The people getting out of the carriages were dressed in the same uniforms as me but in all different colors. The scene before me looked so strange and foreign. I wondered what a group of humans would think if they stumbled upon this. Having no idea about where to go or what to do, I clasped my bag and waited by the carriage. I caught bits of conversation from the students around me. Hearing words like coodle, krypto, and beezle made me glad that Dr. Tweedle had spent the time to tell me about pixie money or I would have felt even more lost than I already did.

No one seemed to notice me as students ran toward their friends. I felt awkward just standing in the forest clearing, and I wished somebody would direct me to the school. My hopes rose when I noticed a pretty girl with dark blonde hair walking my way. The girl had on a white blouse with a pink skirt and matching silk scarf tied loosely around her neck. She walked with confidence across the grassy field, stopping a few feet in front of me.

"Hello, I'm Betty Ann Barber." She said her name in a way that made it sound important as if I should recognize it. However, I was not familiar since Dr. Tweedle hadn't mentioned anyone by the name of Barber yesterday.

"Hi, I'm Jane Fitzgerald," I said stretching out my hand. Betty Ann looked at my outstretched hand, but she didn't raise hers. Her sneer indicated she had no intention of reciprocating.

"Your mother was Rachel McCalski, right? Everyone proclaims what a great pixie she was, but I don't understand. If she was so brilliant, she wouldn't have run off with a human," Betty Ann said.

Shocked by the candor of her opinion, I gave her a nasty stare. Who was she to judge my mother? Before I could respond, Betty Ann was speaking again.

"My father told me all about you. He works for the pixie government and had mentioned that a half-human would be in my year. The first of... your kind to attend the Jelf Academy. It's my first day as well. My father told me everything I need to know about the Jelf Academy. I bet you've heard of him, Arnold Barber, he donates a large sum of money to the school every year. With his generous donations, you would think they would have at least named the library after him," Betty Ann said.

"No, I haven't heard of him," I replied in an irritated tone.

"I should have known you would be a simpleton. You probably love humans just like your mother. I would never marry a human and anyway, that would be breaking the law. I guess I'll see you in school unless you do get expelled on the first day," Betty Ann said as she turned on her heel, walking back into the crowd.

I was dumbfounded by our encounter. I didn't like her. My hope that she would explain where the school was, or potentially become a friend, vanished. Did Betty Ann think she was something special because of her father? Also, if he worked for the government, he could be one of the people judging my progress at the academy. Instantly, I was even more determined to prove them wrong.

As I recovered from the encounter, I noticed everyone else was still milling around. What were we waiting here for? I looked to the sky as more carriages approached. Suddenly, I jumped when I felt a hand touch my back. At first, I thought Betty Ann had returned, but the person who tapped me was a girl with black hair and tanned skin. With her was a boy who had the same physical features.

"Hi, you look lost," the girl said with a kind voice.

"Yes, I guess I am. This is my first year at the Jelf Academy," I told the girl.

"This is our first year too. Luckily, our older brother is starting his third year, so we don't have to worry. He promised to explain everything. I'm Josefina Martinez and this is my twin brother, Miguel," the girl said pointing to the boy beside her.

"It's nice to meet you both. I'm Jane Fitzgerald," I said as I shook both their hands.

"We should go find Juan, so he can tell us where to go next," the boy named Miguel said.

"Come with us! I'm sure Juan won't mind," Josefina insisted.

I smiled as I followed the twins across the field full of people. As I walked behind them, I noticed they had matching uniforms. Josefina was wearing a white blouse with a red skirt, while Miguel had on a red vest with black pants. The color suited their darker complexion. Easing our way through the crowd, the twins stopped in front of a boy in a yellow vest. He had to be their older brother.

"Juan, this is Jane Fitzgerald. She is new to the school this year. Do you mind if she joined us?" Josefina asked.

"No, I wouldn't mind. Hello, Miss Fitzgerald, my name is Juan Martinez," he said, sticking out his hand for me to shake.

"Hi," I replied as I shook his.

"Since Josefina and Miguel are attending their first year, you'll probably be in the same classes," he said.

"I don't understand what we are doing in this forest clearing. Where is the school?" I asked.

Juan chuckled. "Don't worry, you'll see the school soon enough. We just have to wait for the signal. It should not be long now. Most of the students seemed to have arrived."

I stood with Juan, Josefina, and Miguel, looking for the signal Juan said would come. While we waited, I listened to the three siblings talk about school supplies and classes. I didn't know what to say, so I silently listened. Suddenly, Juan looked up from the conversation.

"Finally, it's here!" he cried as he looked over my shoulder. I spun around to see a cloud descending from the sky. The people in the center of the clearing moved out of the way as the cloud landed lightly on the ground. Miguel and Josefina looked at the scene with the same amount of awe I felt.

"What's the cloud for?" Josefina asked.

"We board it," Juan said. "The cloud will take us up to the school, which is in the sky. We just have to get in line," Juan pointed with his right hand up to the clouds that hung above us.

"Why couldn't the winged horses have flown us up there?" I asked. "Wouldn't it have been easier?"

"The school is surrounded by protection charms around it. The winged horses can't penetrate the charms," Juan explained.

Slowly, we moved into the line waiting to board. Each time

the cloud filled with students, it would rise into the sky and come back down empty. I saw Betty Ann farther ahead in the line talking with other girls who appeared to be in the same social group. The girls' blouses appeared to have lace sewn into the cuffs of the sleeves while light caught and reflected off the jewelry around their wrists. Betty Ann's hair bounced across her back as she boarded the cloud and the next moment she was out of sight.

I was a little bit nervous about climbing onto the cloud. What if I fell off? I didn't want to hurt or embarrass myself on the first day. As the line continued to grow smaller, I felt my stomach clench.

When it was time for me to board, I bit my lower lip and took a step up. The cloud was light and fluffy. I bounced as I moved to make room for the Martinez's. Under my feet, I felt a small sign of movement as the last of the students climbed on board. When I looked down, I was surprised to see that my shoes had sunk into the fluffy whiteness.

"This is really exciting," Josefina said as the cloud began to rise into the sky.

"I'm very nervous. What will we do on our first day?" I asked Juan.

"First, Dr. Tweedle will usher all the first years into the dining hall where you will receive your class schedule. The first day is supposed to be a day where you familiarize yourself with the school. Older students will be there to help new students navigate the building and grounds. The first day is usually a free day to meet your teachers and discover where all the classrooms are located," Juan explained. "The classes are shortened today, so you may only be assigned some light reading for tonight."

I sighed in relief. At least older students would help me get around, and I wasn't expected to perform magic on the first day.

Slowly, the cloud rose into a big cluster of clouds. When we were level with the others, the sight before me almost took my breath away. Sitting on the top of the clouds was a magnificent building, with bricks as white as the clouds and a blue gabled roof. It looked like a fantasy castle that only existed in my dreams. Even though we were in the clouds, I noticed that green gardens surrounded the school.

The group of students stepped off the cloud, and I followed them forward in awe. My feet bounced as I went over the clouds, and my body felt light as air. I didn't know if the altitude had done something or if it was just my excitement.

We reached the path where the clouds ended, and the grass and gravel began. I couldn't tell I was in the sky whatsoever. Across the grounds to my right, was the largest willow tree I had ever seen. Around its base, I could make out what appeared to be desks and chairs. Looking to my left, I could see a barn-like structure in the distance, and a fenced-in meadow that also had desks and chairs. I wondered if those areas were used as classrooms.

The closer we got to the building, the cooler I felt as its great shadow draped over me. The words, Jelf Academy of Magic, were written across the white doors in a blue cursive script. A murmur of anxiousness swept through the crowd. The white double doors swung open on their own, and we stepped into the entrance hall. Dr. Tweedle was standing at the top of the marble staircase, patiently waiting for us.

"All first-year students, please move through the door on your right, and enter the dining hall where you will receive a class schedule. Everyone else, feel free to go upstairs to the fourth floor to be assigned a dormitory. Then unpack your belongings," Dr. Tweedle said.

We murmured goodbye to Juan, and then I went through the door with Josefina and Miguel. We entered the largest dining hall I had ever seen. Dozens of round and rectangular tables made of dark oak wood were scattered around the length of the room. Each round table seemed to have eight to ten chairs, while the rectangular ones looked as if they could seat double that. Along the left wall were several long buffet tables. Four large chandeliers hung from the ceiling with huge dangling crystals. Everything in the dining hall seemed to sparkle and shine. I sat down at one of the tables with the twins as Dr. Tweedle walked towards a lectern at the front of the room.

"Welcome all first-year students to the Jelf Academy of Magic. In a moment, your schedules will be passed out by a member of the staff. Before we get to that, let me explain some very important school rules. First, performing magic in-between classes is prohibited. Anyone who intentionally uses magic to harm another student will be expelled. Secondly, boys are not allowed in the girls' dormitories and vice versa. Any student found breaking this rule will receive detention, and in extreme cases, expulsion. The rest of the rules can be found on the dormitory bulletin boards.

"Now, for those of you who don't know, the Jelf Academy of Magic was founded in 1701 by Edward Jelf. It was one of the first pixie schools in America, and only male students were allowed to attend. This changed about twenty-nine years later when Edward's granddaughter, Emeline, begged to be able to continue her magical education outside of the home. So, in 1730, Edward Jelf opened the doors of this academy to all students, so every pixie could gain an education."

Dr. Tweedle stopped speaking for a moment and motioned to a woman with white curly hair. She walked toward him with a stack of envelopes in her hand. "This is Mrs. Rowley, your Gemstones 101 teacher. She has everyone's schedules which will be passed out momentarily. Once you obtain your schedule, you will go to every class to familiarize yourself with the building. Older students will be in the hallways in-between classes and are under strict orders to point you in the right direction. This way no one can have an excuse for being late to class tomorrow. I highly encourage you to report any student who hinders your way to class," Dr. Tweedle stated.

"Once in the class, the teacher will give you a brief speech on the subject and what he or she has planned for the year. Now, without further ado, I will let Mrs. Rowley pass out the schedules," Dr. Tweedle said as he stepped back from the lectern, allowing Mrs. Rowley to take his place.

Mrs. Rowley was still holding a stack of envelopes in her hand. I expected her to call each student up one by one, and I hoped I didn't trip when it was my turn. Mrs. Rowley interrupted my thoughts with her sharp, attention-grabbing voice.

"These envelopes contain your schedules. As soon as I pass them out, I do not want students to get up and begin running to their first classes," she stressed the word *not* with a sharp movement of her tongue. "No matter how excited you are to get started with this school year, I expect you to leave this hall in an orderly fashion."

She raised her hands, and to my surprise, the envelopes rose and stayed suspended in the air level to her face. With a pushing motion, all the envelopes flew at the students. One of the envelopes fluttered near me, landing on my lap. I was shocked to see I had received the correct envelope with my name on the cover. Slowly, I ripped it open.

Gemstones 101-8:00 a.m.-8:55 a.m.

Predicting the Future-9:00 a.m.-9:55 a.m.

History of Pixies-10:00 a.m.-10:55 a.m.

Lunch-11:00 a.m.-12:30 p.m.

Charms-12:35 p.m.-1:30 p.m.

Earth Catastrophes-1:35 p.m.-2:30 p.m.

Zodiac Signs-2:35 p.m.-3:30 p.m.

"What does your schedule look like?" Josefina asked. She was already comparing her schedule with Miguel's. "Miguel and I have every class together."

I offered them my schedule, hoping they would be in at least one of my classes. They were the only people who had been kind to me. I held my breath as I waited for the verdict.

"Jane, you're lucky," Miguel said. "You have Gemstones 101 first."

"Why? When do you have it?" I asked my heart failing a little.

"You're lucky because two of the best people are in there with you," Josefina said. I gave them both blank stares not fully understanding what they meant.

"Us, of course!" Miguel said laughing as he handed me back my schedule. "We're in every other class too!"

I smiled at both of them, relieved that they were not only in one, but all of my classes. I noticed Dr. Tweedle had begun dismissing tables by sections. When he got to our section, Miguel, Josefina, and I got up and walked toward the entrance hall. We now had to find our way to our first class, Gemstones 101.

"Look, there is Mrs. Rowley. We could ask her," Josefina suggested. We fought our way through the crowd of students toward Mrs. Rowley. "Excuse me, Mrs. Rowley!" Josefina called.

Mrs. Rowley stopped at the foot of the staircase and pivoted to face us. "Yes?" she asked.

"Mrs. Rowley, could you please tell us where your classroom is? We have Gemstones 101 first," Josefina replied.

"It is on the second floor, in the east wing. You can reach it by going up the grand staircase," Mrs. Rowley said, pointing to the enormous flight of stairs in front of us. "I have to make a quick detour before class starts or I would take you there myself."

Mrs. Rowley hastily walked in the opposite direction, as we made our way to the staircase. Thankfully, her classroom wasn't hard to find because on the door, in twelve different colors, were the words Gemstones 101 written in humungous letters. Upon entering the classroom, we noticed that Mrs. Rowley's desk was encrusted with all twelve gemstones. Each one had the name of a month with a description in print too small to read at a glance.

The three of us chose seats in the middle of the class and waited for the arrival of Mrs. Rowley and the other students. It didn't take long for other first-years to come into the room, and a short while later Mrs. Rowley entered, taking a seat at her desk. I heard the sound of tinkling bells from somewhere overhead, and the class quieted.

"That, students, was the bell to signal the start of class," Mrs. Rowley explained. "When that bell rings, I expect you to be in your seat and ready to start."

As she spoke, I examined the room. I noticed two candles on her desk which I assumed to be goblin fire because they reminded me of the candle at the inn. The walls were covered in brightly colored pictures that depicted a different gemstone. The blackboard behind her desk also didn't strike me as ordinary because it seemed to shimmer. Mrs. Rowley's classroom felt bright and airy, and I began to relax.

"Welcome to Gemstones 101. This course is an introductory course, which means you will only be taking it this year. Over the course of the year, I will teach you everything there is to know about the twelve astrological gemstones. You will learn their powers, how to make charms with them, and what their protective abilities are," Mrs. Rowley explained while she stood behind her desk. "Now, since we only have a few minutes, we'll just write the names of the stones on the board. I'll go into more detail tomorrow."

Mrs. Rowley moved closer to the blackboard. I noticed that there wasn't chalk, and I wondered what she was going to write with. In the blink of an eye, the word Garnet appeared in sparkling maroon letters. Everyone gasped.

"This is simple magic that you will learn how to do this year. The only thing you need to do is use your mind. Now, I'll call on someone and we'll see if they can master writing on the board using their minds," Mrs. Rowley said.

Instantly, my palms became sweaty. I didn't want her to call on me. I probably would fail and then Dr. Tweedle would tell me that I had to leave the Jelf Academy.

"Miss Martinez, why don't you think of a gemstone and imagine writing the name in the gemstone's color on the board."

Josefina stood up from her seat and stared at the blackboard. Her face scrunched up in concentration. It took a few seconds, but finally the word emerald appeared in dark green letters.

"Very good, Miss Martinez. That was great!" Mrs. Rowley complimented. "Now, let's see... How about Miss Fitzgerald?"

Suddenly, my mind went completely blank for a moment. What if I couldn't make anything appear on the board? The first gem I could think of was an amethyst, which I recalled was the exact color of my eyes. I concentrated on the word and the color. To my surprise, the word popped up on the blackboard almost as soon as I thought of it.

"Well done, Miss Fitzgerald. Not many students in their first year can accomplish that as quickly as you just did. It would please me if you could stay after class for a few minutes," Mrs. Rowley said in awe.

I nodded my head slowly as I sat back into my seat, stunned by how well I had done. Mrs. Rowley called on someone else to put a gem name on the board. The class got most of the gem names displayed by the time I heard the tinkling sound that signaled the end of the class. The other students got up from their seats, and I lagged behind to speak to Mrs. Rowley.

"Do you want us to wait for you outside the door?" Josefina asked.

"No, you go on ahead. I don't want you to be late," I replied.

I walked to the front of the classroom and stood before Mrs. Rowley's desk.

"Miss Fitzgerald, I must say that was one of the best displays of magic I have ever seen on the first day of class in many years."

"Thank you, ma'am."

"Who are your parents?"

"My father was a human, and my mother was a pixie. Her name was Rachel McCalski. They both passed away when I was young," I sadly replied.

"No wonder you have so much talent! You have my sympathy. I am saddened to hear about your parents. Who has taught you?" Mrs. Rowley asked.

"No one," I said nonchalantly.

"I should let you get to your next class, so you are not late. We can talk more about this later. I knew your mother very well. I can't believe I didn't see the similarities."

I said goodbye to her and left the classroom. Where was the Predicting the Future classroom located? Students rushed in every direction in the hallway, and I was unsure of who to ask. After what seemed like a few minutes, I began to panic. I didn't want to be late. I was so distracted trying to find the class, I almost ran into somebody.

"I'm sorry," I said. "I was not paying attention to where I was going."

I looked up into the bluest eyes I had ever seen. They looked like two floating pools of ice water, and his long eyelashes lightly brushed his cheeks when he blinked. The boy standing in front of me was incredibly handsome. His blonde hair was short and cut neatly around his ears. His full lips opened in a smile as he looked down on me.

"I'm guessing you need help," he said.

"Yes, I do," I replied truthfully, hoping he would help me.

"Where are you going?"

"Predicting the Future," I replied.

"I know where that room is. Come on, follow me. You were heading in the wrong direction," the boy replied. "My name is Thomas Whitmore by the way."

He extended his hand to me as we walked down the hall. "I'm Jane Fitzgerald," I said smiling.

"It's nice to meet you, Miss Fitzgerald. I'm in my third year at the Jelf Academy," Thomas said. "How do you like it so far?"

"Everything is wonderful here," I replied. He quirked his brow and slightly chuckled.

We continued to walk down the hall, passing the Gemstones 101 classroom, until he pointed to a door at the end of the hall. I felt rather foolish since I had turned the wrong way when I had left the Gemstone 101 classroom. I stopped at the door and turned to look at Thomas. "Thank you for helping me," I said.

"It was no problem," he assured me.

As I stood looking at his handsome face, a girl's arm slipped through his. Betty Ann Barber came to his side. "There you are, Tom. I've been looking everywhere for you," Betty Ann said. Then her eyes fell on me. "Oh, hello, Jane. I see you've met Thomas. We've been courting for a while. Our fathers work in the same department." She sounded like she was bragging.

"I was just showing Miss Fitzgerald to her class," Thomas replied.

"Seriously, Tom, I don't know why you insist on helping riff-raff. This is the one who is part human," she sneered at me. "Well, I need to get to class and so do you. I'll see you later." Betty Ann said as she leaned toward him and kissed him on the cheek. Her eyes continued to watch me. Then she walked into the Predicting the Future classroom.

"Goodbye, Jane. I'll see you around," Thomas said as he winked at me and walked off.

Thomas seemed so nice, I thought as I watched him go down the hall. It was a shame that he was taken by someone who didn't seem deserving. I walked into the classroom only to be confronted by Betty Ann.

"I don't know what you think you're doing," she said.

I gave her a blank stare. What was she talking about?

"Everybody knows that Thomas and I are together and will probably get married. Don't expect to just waltz into this world and do what you please. Do not talk to him again or else... or else," she faltered.

"Or else you might finish your sentence?" I said smartly as I walked past her toward Josefina and Miguel. My legs were shaking as I stood beside the twins. I had never talked that way to someone in my life. Oddly enough, it felt good.

I followed the twins down a set of stairs, glancing around at the room. The room was circular like a theater, but instead of chairs, there were pillows lined up on each level. Down the stairs, in the front of the classroom, was a shiny blackboard with a table in front of it. On the table sat a crystal ball.

"Why did Betty Ann come up to you before class?" Josefina asked as we slowly sunk down onto a few pillows next to each other.

"Oh, I was talking to Thomas," I replied.

"Her intended beau?" Josefina looked shocked.

"Yes..."

"Betty Ann is insanely jealous. She doesn't like it when any girl talks to him. All of the Barbers think they are entitled to everything. Her father is a very powerful man. I wouldn't mess with her," Josefina warned.

"She can't have complete control over him, but alright, I won't talk to him," I mumbled.

"Josefina is right. The Barber family is one of the most powerful families. Generation after generation of Barbers has been involved in big businesses or government. I'm sure they feel superior because of it," Miguel explained. "Just a few years ago our father found a hidden gem mine which made our family quite a bit of money. Our family is still looked down on by old-money families like the Barbers. They still see us as the lower-class."

Our conversation was interrupted when a woman entered the room from behind a beaded curtain at the bottom of the stairs.

She walked out as if she had just entered a stage, wearing an orange bandana over her dark hair. Long earrings dangled from her earlobes, but smaller studs adorned each ear. Around her waist was an orange shawl which was bedecked in gold charms. She reminded me of a gypsy, and sure enough, she moved to the front of the room and sat behind the crystal ball.

"Welcome class. Please have a seat," she said. "My name is Ms. Crescent and I'm the Predicting the Future teacher. This year, we'll begin with the tarot cards for minor fortunes and then progress into bigger insights of the future when your minds are ready."

Looking over my shoulder, I noticed Betty Ann talking to a group of friends. She wasn't even paying attention to what Ms. Crescent was saying.

"Can anyone tell me what types of methods we use to tell the future?" Ms. Crescent asked.

A girl at the back of the classroom raised her hand. She had frizzy, blonde hair and wore square glasses. Her uniform looked shabby, and I noticed nobody was sitting by her.

"Yes, my dear. What is your name?" Ms. Crescent asked.

"My name is Taylor Miller. Some of the methods used to predict the future are tarot cards, palm reading, meditation, connection to the spirit world, and, of course, the crystal ball."

"Very good! It looks like someone has read the textbook," Ms. Crescent replied.

"I've actually read the whole book ma'am," Taylor said.

A loud snort came from the group of Betty Ann's friends and distinctly Betty Ann said, "Of course she read the whole book, what has she better to do?" The group broke out into new fits of laughter.

"That is enough. I wish I had more dedicated students," Ms. Crescent said. "The bell should be ringing soon due to these shortened periods. Tomorrow, we will begin discussing the art of the tarot."

It only took a moment for a slow murmur of whispers to

move through the classroom. Apparently, we were allowed to talk because Ms. Crescent didn't raise any objections. She sat with her eyes closed and it seemed she was completely oblivious to the noise.

"What class do we have next?" I asked the twins.

"History of Pixies," they replied simultaneously.

I almost laughed at how accurately they had said it, not missing a beat with the other.

When the bell finally rang, and we got up from our seats, moving into the hallway as Ms. Crescent continued to sit still with her eyes closed. "Where is the History of Pixies room?" I asked.

"I think it's on the first floor," Josefina replied as I followed her down the stairs. She boldly walked up to another student in the hall to confirm where the room was. It occurred to me that Josefina was very outgoing while Miguel was more reserved. Quickly she came back to us. "Yes, it's on the first floor in the west wing."

Just like our previous two classes, we made it on time and sat down next to each other. An older gentleman sat behind the desk, his perfectly round spectacles sitting on the bridge of his nose. The classroom walls were crowded with maps and what I assumed were historical figures. The man waited patiently at his desk while everyone filed in. I saw Betty Ann slip in right before the bell, and she sat in the back of the classroom. I sighed at the thought of seeing her in another class.

When it was apparent that everyone was present, the teacher stood up from his desk. Behind him, letters began to appear on the blackboard that spelled out Mr. Collyworth.

"Good morning, class. As you can see, my name is Mr. Collyworth. I will be your History teacher for the next five years. If you decide to pursue a career in history studies, you can attend some of my summer classes after your third year. Looking around the class, I recognize some of you from either having had your parents or older siblings in class."

His light gray eyes scanned the room and stopped on me. "Ah,

Jane Fitzgerald, I was wondering if I would see you." I blushed though I probably should have expected it. "Your mother was a very talented and wonderful pixie."

I heard someone in the back of the room let out a deep sigh, and I knew instantly that it had been Betty Ann.

"Yes, I remember your mother, but though she was uncannily good at everything else, she only managed satisfactory in my class." At this, I heard a snicker from Betty Ann. "Let's hope you do better," Mr. Collyworth finished.

I ducked my head, in embarrassment. Josefina gave me a questioning look. I remembered that Josefina and Miguel did not seem to recognize my last name like so many others had. She remained silent, but I had a feeling she would ask me about it later.

Mr. Collyworth had moved on from examining the students and was now explaining our course schedule. "This year, we will discuss American pixies and their achievements from the 1700s until now. This will include different ideas and wars. In the years to come, we will discuss other countries, but the curriculum focuses on America. By the looks of it, we only have a few minutes left, so feel free to talk among yourselves. Tomorrow, we will start our lesson about pixies in the 1700s." Mr. Collyworth moved back behind his desk.

"I didn't realize how many people were pixies," I said leaning across the aisle to talk to Josefina in hopes that she wouldn't bring up my mom, at least not here.

"Yes, pixies live all over the world. Our grandparents are pixies, and they were born in Mexico," Josefina explained. My plan to change the subject worked because Josefina started talking about her Mexican heritage.

When the bell rang, we were instructed to go back to the dining hall for our lunch period. Once every student appeared to be in the dining hall, Dr. Tweedle returned to the lectern.

"Before everyone eats lunch today, I would like to assign the first-year dormitories. You are allowed to choose a roommate, but for those of you who do not know anyone or would rather not choose, we can assign you one."

Josefina touched my arm, and I looked her way. "Do you want to be my roommate?" she asked.

"I was just about to ask you," I said smiling.

"Now those of you who already have a roommate in mind, please get in line and Mrs. Rowley will assign you a room. We ask that you keep the rooms clean at all times. Every weekend, we perform a check to make sure you keep to the rules. After we have assigned you a room, we encourage you to put your belongings in the room and then come back here for lunch. Your trunks and bags can be found in the entrance hall," Dr. Tweedle concluded.

Josefina and I rose from the table and walked toward Mrs. Rowley. A line had formed already so we waited patiently. I took the moment to observe my surroundings, still in awe at the world around me. It was still sinking in that there were others like me, and they lived in secret: a huge "underground" society. A chill also ran through me as I thought about my mother walking these same halls and sitting at these same tables.

When we reached Mrs. Rowley, we gave her our names and received a dorm number. Then she briefly instructed us on how to get there.

"When you leave the dining hall, climb the grand staircase to the fourth floor, and head toward the east wing. Your dormitory should be down that hallway."

"I wonder what the rooms will be like," I stated as we ascended the stairs to the fourth floor.

"I don't know, but Juan told me that they were really nice. He said they made him feel like he was at home," Josefina replied.

At the top of the stairs on the fourth floor, Josefina and I started looking for room 114. It wasn't long before we found it, but when we did, we were surprised to find that the door did not have a doorknob.

"How do we get in?" I asked puzzled as I stared at the door. I couldn't see an obvious form of entry.

Josefina stepped forward to examine the door more closely. She felt all over the wood and she pushed against the doorframe, but nothing happened. I stood watching her while I pondered how to get in. Maybe this was some kind of test.

I closed my eyes and imagined the door opening. Maybe if I thought about it hard enough, the door would open just like the day my father died. Normally, I found things like this easy, but when I opened my eyes, the door had not budged. I was disappointed. Whatever held the door shut must be strong magic. Josefina's eyes moved to what looked like a small panel on the right side of the door. Josefina stuck her hand in the middle of the panel, and after a few seconds, she pulled away with a yelp.

"Ouch! It pinched me," she exclaimed.

Suddenly, a voice spoke in a smooth monotone. It seemed like it was coming from the door.

"Josefina Martinez, brown eyes, black hair, of Mexican descent, a first-year student to the Jelf Academy, and granted access to this room for the school year. Ready for next occupant."

"Wow, how did it know all that?" Josefina asked as she stepped back from the door to let me get closer.

I placed my palm on the panel and anticipated the pinch. Quicker than I expected, I felt a sharp pain in the palm of my hand and pulled away.

"Jane Fitzgerald, violet eyes, blonde hair, of English and Polish descent, a first-year student of the Jelf Academy, and granted access to this room for the school year," the monotone voice said. "This room has been programmed to read the palms of the occupants only. This allows belongings to remain secure. Have a good school year," the voice continued.

The door slid open to reveal our dorm. A white puffy carpet lay on the floor and the walls were a light purple. Lamps that looked like flowers sat on the tables between the two matching beds. Both beds had purple comforters with huge purple pillows. I crossed the room and sat on the second most comfortable bed I'd ever sat on in my life. Josefina sat across from me on the other bed.

"Juan wasn't lying," Josefina remarked. "It is almost as good as home."

"Better than home," I mumbled under my breath.

Josefina must have heard because she leaned toward me with concerned eyes. "What is your home like?"

Could I trust Josefina enough to tell her about my life? I debated on whether or not I should lie. I didn't trust anyone, but something inside me wanted to tell Josefina. I wanted to have an actual relationship with someone. Maybe if I shared my personal difficulties, I would feel better.

"I live with my stepmother, Marie, and her two children, Emily and Preston. Both my parents died when I was very young. When my mother passed away, my father remarried. Marie never liked me because I looked like my mother, and I wasn't what she considered normal. When my father passed, Marie sent me to live in the attic. Every day I have chores to complete, and I've never left the manor's property until now."

Josefina looked horror-struck. "You live in the attic?"

"The attic is my bedroom. Marie makes me stay in the attic because she wants me to stay hidden from the outside world. She doesn't want me to exist, except for when I do things that displease her," I replied.

"How did she ever allow you to come here? Did your magic scare her?" Josefina asked in awe.

"No, Marie was never frightened by my magic. Just as long as I keep it hidden, I can continue to live in the house. Marie doesn't even know this school is for magic. She thinks this school will teach me etiquette. Dr. Tweedle kept that aspect hidden from her," I replied.

"Who is your mother? Why did Mr. Collyworth speak so highly of her in class today?" Josefina asked.

"My mother's name was Rachel McCalski."

"Rachel McCalski! THE Rachel McCalski? She worked with Waldrick the Great. You know about Waldrick the Great, don't you? He is the whole reason that we are more effectively hidden from the W.A.S.P. Your mother was one of the best pixies in this century! Wow… Rachel McCalski's daughter," Josefina exclaimed.

I blushed at her enthusiasm. "I'm sorry, I've never really heard of my mother's accomplishments until Dr. Tweedle spoke of them yesterday. I never knew my mother. She died when I was one," I told her.

"Oh, Jane I'm so sorry," Josefina said as she got up from her bed, crossed the room, and gave me a quick hug. Once again, I was surprised by the show of affection by a stranger. Never in my sixteen years did Marie ever comfort me when I was hurting. Not only was the magical world something to get used to, but also the kind-heartedness of some people.

"Don't be sad!" Josefina said as she jumped up. "Today is a great day because it's our first at the Jelf Academy and Rachel McCalski's daughter is my roommate!"

I laughed at her bubbly personality. I couldn't help it. "Don't make any assumptions. I don't think I'll ever be as good as my mother, nor do I have her talent. The pixie government didn't even want to let me in, but Dr. Tweedle convinced them somehow. If I don't do well enough here, I'll probably be expelled."

"You don't know that yet. It's only the first day," Josefina pointed out.

"Tell me about your home?" I asked to change the subject.

"We live in a nice home, but that wasn't always the case. Like Miguel mentioned earlier, our father stumbled upon a gem mine. He has a few different companies where he sells the gemstones. Our dad is also very creative, so he makes his own jewelry designs.

It was very lucky for our family that he made this discovery," Josefina explained.

"That's great, Josefina. Do you have any other siblings besides Miguel and Juan?" I wondered.

"No. My mom is very caring, but sometimes she worries about us too much. She used to be a governess but was able to quit when my father started his business. Ever since we moved to our new house, she was able to teach us instead of focusing on others. My mom is amazing. Maybe you'll get to meet her one day."

"I would love that. Josefina, don't you have anyone at the Jelf Academy that you know? Friends from home?" I asked wondering why she had chosen to be my roommate.

"The friends that I have at home are neighbors, but they are all a year younger than me and won't be starting at the Jelf Academy until next year. Their names are Marley Thornton, Candi Vaughn, and Bellony Sandhu. When we moved into the new house, none of the neighbors' children would talk to Miguel and me, but finally, those three girls started being nice," Josefina said as she glanced around the room.

Suddenly, she appeared startled. "I didn't realize how long we've been up here. We better get to lunch."

We had been so consumed with getting to know each other that we didn't realize we were late.

6
NOT SO CHARMING

WE WALKED OUT of our room and back down to the dining hall where we grabbed trays and helped ourselves to the buffet. Josefina found Miguel at a table waiting for us to arrive.

"How is your first day so far?" Juan asked as he sat down at our table next to Miguel.

"It's alright. So far, we had Gemstones 101, Predicting the Future, and History of Pixies," Josefina said between mouthfuls.

"Ms. Crescent is melodramatic, so don't take everything she says seriously. She's one of the best pixies at predicting the future, but things never get as bad as she says. Mr. Collyworth can get a little boring, but I swear all history teachers are. Mrs. Rowley is one of the best teachers here. She'll teach you a lot and is very understanding," Juan said.

"We have Charms next," Miguel said after he had dug his schedule out of his bag.

"That's with Mr. Withermyer. He is one of the youngest teachers on staff. I think he is in his early thirties. He's okay. Sometimes he can have a temper and is unfair, though I've never had a problem with him," Juan replied.

Once we finished our lunch, the twins and I headed off to Charms. The classroom was in the west wing on the second floor, so we turned left at the top of the grand staircase. The room was the last in the hallway, and I was the first to enter. Seated at the big brown desk in the corner was a dark-haired man with piercing green eyes. He looked up from his work the moment I walked in. The look in his eyes confused me. First, they were wide with shock and then this dreamy look made his inhumanly bright eyes glaze over.

"Rachel," he mouthed but no sound left his lips. I blushed because, once again, I was being confused for my mother. He rose from his chair, eyes focused solely on me. I noticed the deep circles under his eyes as if he had not slept well in weeks, but there was something darkly handsome about him that I couldn't put my finger on.

"Jane, where do you want to sit?" Josefina asked coming in behind me.

The glazed look in the man's green eyes instantly disappeared and was replaced by a look of anger which confused me more. Quickly, I dropped my gaze and looked toward the twins. They had moved toward the middle of the classroom, and I took a seat beside Josefina. Mr. Withermyer, for I assumed that's who he was, continued to watch me.

More students started to file into the classroom, and my heart dropped when Betty Ann waltzed in with a few of her followers. Mr. Withermyer seemed to recognize Betty Ann, and I assumed he knew her father. As soon as the class got settled, Mr. Withermyer went to his lectern.

"Good afternoon class. My name is Mr. Withermyer, and I am your Charms teacher. I will teach you different ways of combining stone powders to make charms for everyday uses, special powers, and some that are lethal." He sneered as he said lethal, his eyes roaming around the classroom. His angry eyes settled on me. "This class will be one of the most difficult you will have this year. This will not be an easy course like Zodiac Signs or Predicting the Future. Charms class will weed out the better students from those who just can't make the standard." Once again, his eyes shifted around the room. It was almost like he already knew which of us would succeed or fail, just by our appearance. I swallowed the lump in my throat. What if I couldn't meet the standard?

"Tomorrow, we will start something moderate and from your performance on it, I will have an idea of how well you can complete a task. I would have you start today, but we don't have the time. You may sit quietly until the bell rings. Do not talk." With another dark look, he sat at his desk.

I cast Josefina a glance of terror which she returned. What did he have prepared for tomorrow? I sat in the uncomfortable silence, which felt as if it was bearing down from all sides. The tension in the room was unbearable. Looking around, everyone seemed to be worried about tomorrow. No one dared utter a sigh about their anxieties.

Relief washed over me when I heard the tinkling little bells. It seemed like everyone was fighting to get out into the hallway, but nobody dared to run. I followed the tight group of students out into the hall, which seemed bright and airy compared to the Charms room. Breathing in deeply, I pulled my schedule out of my bag to see what was next.

"Looks like Earth Catastrophes is our next class," I told Josefina and Miguel.

"I think that's outside," Miguel said.

We headed toward the main entrance and out the double doors. Looking left and right, we decided on the classroom underneath the large willow tree. Again, it amazed me that the school was in the clouds. Glancing up, I saw higher clouds, which meant the school was probably still affected by the weather.

As we walked over to the willow, it appeared that we were the first to arrive, but then, I noticed a frizzy blonde head sitting in the front row. Taylor Miller, who had been in Predicting the Future, sat perched in her seat reading *Predicting the Weather and Other Catastrophes*. She must have heard us approach because she looked up, uncertain about whether she should say something. Now that I had a chance to closely observe her, I noted how small she was. Her uniform had several small holes in it and her glasses were slightly bent.

"Hello there," Josefina said. "I'm Josefina Martinez, this is my twin brother Miguel, and this is Jane Fitzgerald."

"You have a twin," Taylor said as she looked almost sadly at her book.

"Yes," Josefina said slowly.

"Twins are powerful," Taylor commented.

I was confused by this exchange and looked at both girls with a questioning expression.

"Twins are the most powerful unexplained part of the magical world. We can read each other's minds when we choose to, and if we combine our charms and thoughts, they will be more powerful. Nothing but death can break the bond we have," Josefina explained.

My gaze shifted toward Taylor. I could have sworn I saw her wipe a tear from her eye, but perhaps she was just brushing away an eyelash. We took our seats near Taylor and waited for the class to start. After a while, I was beginning to wonder if we were in the right place because a teacher hadn't arrived. Josefina and I glanced around, and after a few more students took their seats, I became more confident we were in the right place. How could we all be wrong?

Running across the lawn toward us was a much-frazzled-looking man. He was balding in the middle but had two tufts of blonde hair that stuck out on both sides of his head. It was sort of comical the way he sprinted at us with some books under his arm.

"So sorry, so sorry. I lost track of time. At least you found the classroom."

The man jogged over to the tree and placed the books in a large knothole. Then he came to stand in the front of the class as a few students shifted in their seats.

"Hello, my name is Mr. Laruse. Welcome to Earth Catastrophes. Before I begin, I would like to compliment you all on arriving here in an orderly fashion despite the fact that I was running late. I have a free period before this, and I didn't keep track of time. Anyway, let's get started.

"Earth Catastrophes is a course based on predicting the weather and other events like earthquakes and brush fires, just by reading your surroundings. By paying attention to the atmosphere, the earth, and the reaction of different species, you will gain an insight into weather conditions for the future. I will teach you how to use all five senses to get in tune with the earth.

"I hope you all have your copies of *Predicting the Weather and Other Catastrophes*. I'm sure you've noticed how large the textbook is. We will be using it for the next three years. Does anyone have any questions about the course?" Mr. Laruse asked.

Taylor's hand shot in the air. "Could you predict the weather for tomorrow, Mr. Laruse?" she asked.

Mr. Laruse closed his eyes and breathed deeply. The class watched as he concentrated. After a few minutes, he opened his eyes. "Well class, I would bring some raincoats tomorrow because it is going to pour," he replied.

The bell rang, and the class picked up their books to head to the last period of the day.

"I wonder if Mr. Laruse will be right tomorrow," Josefina said. "The Zodiac Signs class is next. I think that's on the third floor."

The Jelf Academy towered over us as we entered. The grandness of it all continued to shock me. The climb to the third floor was exhausting. Josefina was walking in silence and though I had only just met her, I sensed this wasn't normal for her.

"You are quiet all of a sudden," I pointed out. "Is there a reason?"

"I was just thinking of something," she mumbled.

"About?" I probed as we continued our lengthy climb.

"Taylor's reaction when I said I was a twin was very odd," Josefina commented.

"It seems like she loves to read, so she probably read about twins," I said. "She seemed sad though."

"I wouldn't worry about it. Taylor might know someone who has a twin or maybe as Jane suggested, she read about it. Twins are studied all the time because they are magically rare," Miguel pointed out.

"You're probably right," Josefina said instantly brightening out of her brooding mood.

We ceased the conversation as we entered the Zodiac Signs classroom. The desks were arranged in a circle, which was different from any other classroom. On the walls hung star charts, zodiac symbols, and drawings of the zodiac figures. The ceiling looked black, but I could make out a few specks of light. We sat close together and waited for the class to begin. More students filed into the classroom along with Taylor. She chose a seat close to us and propped open a book. It looked like the book *Understanding the Zodiac* was our assigned book for this class.

A woman walked into the classroom a few seconds after the bell rang, closing the door behind her. "Hello, class. My name is Mrs. Harris." She had flaming red hair that was pinned back with a few clips. Her light blue eyes scanned the class as she moved to the center of the circle. "I will be your Zodiac teacher. In this class, we will use two different books. *Understanding the Zodiac* will be our main book. Sometimes we will look at lessons in *The Movement of Stars and What They Mean*. You might also use that book in Predicting the Future. So, can anyone tell me what topics we will study?"

Naturally, Taylor's hand was in the air, so Mrs. Harris called on her. "We will learn what the Zodiac constellations mean when they are in the sky and how people under different zodiac signs react with one another."

"Correct! I see you are already deep into reading *Understanding the Zodiac*. I know it is only the first day, but I'm going to assign a bit of homework."

Some people groaned as we watched Mrs. Harris circling to stare at each of us in turn.

"I would like you to read the preface to *Understanding the Zodiac*. It's only a few paragraphs long, so it won't be very time-consuming. This will prepare you for our discussion tomorrow," Mrs. Harris said.

Taylor had a smile on her face, and I assumed it was because she already read the preface and therefore had no homework. I turned toward Josefina and Miguel. "Guess we have something to do tonight," Josefina said.

The bell rang to end our short day, and Josefina and I left Miguel to head back to our room until dinner. When we arrived, I laid my hand on the pad and anticipated the pinch, but none came. The door slid open.

"Did it pinch you again?" Josefina asked.

"No, it must have the first time, so it would recognize our handprints," I replied.

I dumped my schoolbooks on my bed as soon as I entered. Josefina did the same, and then we stopped to stare at each other.

"What do you think of our teachers?" Josefina asked.

"Mrs. Rowley seems nice. I think I like her the best so far," I replied.

"Ms. Crescent seems nice too, but I think Juan is correct; she seems dramatic. I'm sure her class will always give us something to talk about. Her jewelry and her orange bandana made her look like a gypsy," Josefina laughed.

"Yeah, she did seem a little melodramatic. I bet History of Pixies is going to be boring," I complained thinking of what Mr. Collyworth had said about my mother. He was probably the reason her grades were only satisfactory.

"Do you want to know what was really strange?" Josefina asked. "The way Mr. Withermyer was staring at you."

I closed my eyes, remembering Mr. Withermyer's deep stare. His green eyes had looked right through me and sent shivers down my spine. Why had he looked at me first with a dazed expression that had suddenly turned angry? There had to be something behind that. I shook my head to rid myself of the chilly memory.

"Yes, I thought it was strange too, but I'm not going to think too much about it. Dr. Tweedle told me I looked like my mother and a lot of people here seem to know who she was."

"If Mr. Withermyer wouldn't look so brooding and mean, I would actually think he was handsome," Josefina giggled.

"Josefina! He is our Charms teacher!" I laughed. "Speaking of that class, we are going to have to make a charm in there tomorrow," I reminded her.

"That's right! What do you think he will make us do? Do you think it will be difficult or dangerous?" She grabbed her copy of *Mixing Stone Powders Vol. 1* and flipped through the pages.

"We should look at every charm," I suggested.

Josefina put down the book. "Even if we study all night, it probably won't help! We never tried to make any of these charms!"

"Don't worry about it. Everything will be fine," I comforted, even though I was worried myself. "What did you think of Mr. Laruse?"

My idea to change the subject worked perfectly.

"He seemed scatterbrained. Can you honestly believe he forgot he had a class?" Josefina said.

"Maybe he was busy, and time just slipped away from him," I replied.

"This year is going to be good" Josefina stated. "I can just feel it."

"I hope so. I know nothing about the pixie world. What if I can't do magic like everyone else? I didn't grow up in this world. I might not even make it through the year."

"I'm sure you will do fine. You did make that word appear on Mrs. Rowley's chalkboard. She said it was the fastest display of magic she had ever seen," Josefina said. "Don't think about all the rules. That's what I'm here for. I'm glad that I met you this morning in the field."

"I am glad that I met you too. I don't know how I would have gotten through the day," I smiled at her.

"We better get started on the Zodiac homework before we go down to dinner," Josefina said.

I sifted through my stack of books and found *Understanding the Zodiac*. Flipping open to the preface, we sprawled out on our beds and began to read:

The Zodiac is a very ancient magical talent developed in ancient Greece. The ancient pixies realized that by examining the stars, one could find shapes and meaning in them. Different events have been commonly known to occur when different zodiac signs are in the sky.

Zodiac signs influence the people born under them. Understanding these signs can help you predict a person's characteristics. Though these predictions might not be a hundred percent accurate, they still give one general insight into others around them. The Zodiac sign one is born under also deals with how compatible they are with others. Throughout this textbook, you will learn how the zodiac signs move in the sky,

how they affect people's characteristics, and how the zodiac
signs affect people's compatibility toward each other.

When I finished the rest of the text, I put the book down and waited for Josefina to finish. Reading the preface did not take long at all. As my stomach growled, I wondered what time dinner would be served. Looking around the room I couldn't find anything that resembled a clock.

Josefina looked up from *Understanding the Zodiac.*

"What are you looking around for?" she asked.

"I was looking for a clock. How are we supposed to know the time?" I replied.

Josefina got up from the bed and strolled over to an object that looked like a miniature solar system. The planets around the sun looked like they were hardly moving at all.

"Right now, it's almost four-thirty," Josefina said after examining the instrument.

"How do you know that?' I asked amazed.

"This is our form of a clock," Josefina replied. "It is more accurate than the mechanical clocks humans use. The planets rotate in the same time measurement as the real planets do. They also orbit the sun in the same number of days. To find the correct time, you have to read the shadow on the earth for your time zone. These three levers help you get a more accurate reading: one for hours, one for minutes, and one for seconds. You just have to get used to reading the shadow. After that, it's easy,"

I examined the earth and the levers to see what she was talking about. I hoped in time I would be able to read the clock effortlessly. It was amazing that my mind didn't explode from all this new information. For the next half hour, Josefina and I sat talking about our families, our classes, and our worries about the Jelf Academy. Josefina told me what it was like to have two brothers, one of which was sometimes in her head.

"How do you read each other's thoughts?"

"Miguel and I don't read each other's minds all the time. I can easily block him from entering my mind, just like he can block me. Even if I do let him in, he won't be able to read all my memories and thoughts unless I let him. I have to think of whatever I want him to hear if we decide to communicate that way."

"So right now, you could tell him I said hello?" I asked, still wondering how their magic worked.

"Well, only if he lets me in. It's like knocking on a door. Once I knock, Miguel has to decide if he lets me in or not. I could try."

Josefina paused and deeply concentrated. After a moment, she smiled. "He says hello."

"So, it doesn't matter how far apart you are? You can still hear him?" I asked.

"I could stand on the North Pole and Miguel could stand on the South Pole, and I would still hear him clear as day," Josefina smiled.

"That's amazing. I wish I had someone to share my thoughts with," I said.

"You say that now because you don't have someone in your head. Sometimes it can be annoying, but it's nice to have the option of an unspoken conversation," Josefina said.

We sat in silence for a while. Josefina got up from her bed and walked back over to the desk to peer at the solar system. "It is almost five o'clock. Maybe we should head down to dinner," she suggested.

I stacked my books in an orderly fashion, took one last look at the slowly spinning solar system, and followed Josefina out of our room. The door closed silently behind us.

In the dining hall, we met up with Miguel and Juan again. After we chose what we wanted to eat, we picked a table. As we ate, Juan talked about his day.

"I have a new class this year. In the third year, every student gets to study Transfiguration. I can't wait to change my appearance and the appearance of objects!" he told us.

I hoped I would be able to prove I belonged here and continue my education. Even though I was scared about my classes, I felt my life was complete. Finally, after all these years, I knew where my mother had come from and that others like me existed. Tension left my body, and I relaxed on that thought. Now that I knew about my mother, I would try to live up to her legacy in my new world: The Jelf Academy of Magic.

7

GEMSTONES, PREDICTIONS, AND THE SEE ALL CHARM

REAKFAST BEGAN EARLY the next morning at six-thirty. Last night, Josefina had set the funny-looking clock to wake us up a six o'clock, so we would have enough time to dress. After our wonderful breakfast in the great hall, Josefina, Miguel, and I headed off to Gemstones 101.

"Good morning, class," Mrs. Rowley said as she got up from her desk. "Today, we are going to start learning about our first astrological gemstone. Please open *The Power of Gemstones* to page five. As you can see, we will begin with the garnet. Take out your notebook and jot down this information."

The word garnet flashed on the shimmering board.

"The gemstone garnet is associated with January," Mrs. Rowley's words appeared. "The garnet is used in the quick complete charm. Can anybody tell me what that charm does?"

Josefina raised her hand. "The quick complete charm allows one to complete chores or tasks quickly without getting tired. My mother uses it a lot."

"Yes, this charm is very useful, and it saves time and energy. However, we do not encourage the use of this charm at this school or the use of it on children younger than your age group. Pixie families should allow their children to experience the trials of hard work and sacrifice as it builds stronger characters in the future. Young pixies will better respect the effects of the quick complete charm," Mrs. Rowley said. "Now, as a quick note before I forget, by wearing these gemstones one can enhance their ability only a little. Who can tell me what happens when you wear a garnet?"

Again, Josefina's hand shot up. "A garnet will allow you to move faster, but not as quickly as the charm. The garnet just enhances one's speed a little," she said.

"Very good, Miss Martinez," Mrs. Rowley said. "Tonight, I would like you to read pages five through ten about the garnet and its properties. I'll let you get started now. You may read until the bell."

The class started reading, and when the bell rang, the twins and I moved on to Predicting the Future. When we entered, we noticed a soft mist floating around the room, and at the center of it all was Ms. Crescent. On top of each desk was a packet of cards. I moved through the misty room and sat in the same place I had yesterday.

"Come in and quickly have a seat," Ms. Crescent said in an eerie mystical voice. "Today we will start on the art of the tarot. Choose a partner and then we will get started. Once you have a partner, pull out your copy of *Methods of Seeing the Future* and open to the tarot section."

Josefina and I partnered up while Miguel moved toward someone else. I opened my book and found the chapter on the Tarot.

"You will take turns reading each other's fortunes with the tarot cards. The best way to understand the tarot is to practice it. While reading, try to memorize the meaning of each card and what each means in the past, present, future, and reversed. In a few weeks, I will call you one at a time into my office, where you will be tested on your ability to read the tarots. Do your best to study and memorize them," Ms. Crescent said.

For the rest of the lesson, Ms. Crescent let us read each other's tarot cards. Our homework that night was to practice reading them for ourselves.

When the bell rang, I gathered the cards and placed them back into their box. I slammed my book closed, stuffing it back into my bag. Then, we left for History of Pixies. Mr. Collyworth was standing stiffly by his desk. He raised his eyes when we entered.

"Good morning, Miss Fitzgerald, Miss Martinez, and Mr. Martinez. Please have a seat. Good morning, Miss Barber," he said as he acknowledged Betty Ann who slipped in behind us. "We have a lot to discuss today. Pull out your notebooks, and we will get started."

There was a shuffling of paper and a moving of seats as everyone took out their pencils and paper.

"Today, we will start our study of American Pixies." Just like in Mrs. Rowley's class, his words appeared on the board. "As you might know, Christopher Columbus landed in the West Indies, thus discovering the American continents. We'll skip ahead a few hundred years to the late 1700s. The American Revolution began in 1775, but what you may not know is that pixies were involved in our own separate war. Not only did we fight for our independence from Britain, but there were also conflicts with the W.A.S.P.

"Before we delve even further into the 1700s, let me just explain that pixies have existed since the beginning of time. There once was a time when pixies didn't need to hide their magic. It wasn't until humans became hateful and greedy that the W.A.S.P. was formed."

Mr. Collyworth was interrupted by a loud cough in the back of the room.

"Mr. Collyworth, if pixies have magic and the W.A.S.P. are only humans, what do we have to fear?" Betty Ann asked sarcastically.

"Well, Miss Barber, the W.A.S.P. is speculated to have a way to incapacitate pixies. Somehow, they can painfully extract our magic. I do not know if the magic is useful or not after it is sucked from our bodies, and I hope no one has the misfortune of ever finding out. Now, let's get back to the lesson at hand.

"In 1775, it was very difficult for pixies to join the Revolution in fear our magic would be revealed. Even British pixies did not like the American resistance," Mr. Collyworth continued in his monotone.

For the next hour, Mr. Collyworth continued speaking about the 1770s and the role pixies played in the American Revolution. My stomach began to rumble. I realized it was almost lunchtime.

With the tinkling of bells, everyone looked up sleepily from their notes and mechanically made their way to lunch. The noise and flutter of students greeted us as we entered the great hall. Just like the day before, we chose to sit with Juan and his older friends. I noticed Thomas Whitmore, with his neat blonde hair and bright blue eyes being led across the hall with Betty Ann on his arm. Grimacing in disgust, I bit into my sandwich. Josefina appeared to be distracted. I could tell she was nervous from the way she was eating so quickly. When I asked what was wrong, she looked at me with panicked eyes.

"You know what's next, don't you? Charms! Mr. Withermyer said he would give us something moderate, but we don't know what that means. I'm going to fail!" she squeaked.

"Let's get our Charms book out and try to study some more."

For the next half hour, Josefina and I sat in our room pouring over our book looking for any charm that seemed to be the right difficulty. We became so absorbed in studying; we barely heard the bell ring. Quickly packing up our books, we raced down to the second floor of the west wing. We found the room half full of students with all the blinds closed. Mr. Withermyer sat darkly behind his desk, waiting for the bell. Though we were not late, Mr. Withermyer rose from his desk.

"Take a seat, ladies," he said in a rough voice, and his eyes pierced right through me. "As we wait for the rest of the students, please take out *Mixing Powders Vol. 1*."

"Today you will attempt to create the charm I display on the blackboard. You cannot copy off anyone else and believe me, I will know if you did. This will be your first test. You will get forty-five minutes to complete the task. In the last ten minutes, we will test your charms. When the forty-five minutes pass, I will tell you to stop working, which means all materials down and hands behind your backs. Do you understand?" The class slowly nodded. "Good. Now, open your books and get started." Mr. Withermyer said.

On the shimmering board, the words *See All Charm* were displayed. I opened my book and shifted through the pages until I found the charm instructions.

The See All Charm helps one see anyone or anything that is not in their immediate view. Advanced-Year One.

Of course, Mr. Withermyer would choose an advanced charm. My palms began to sweat, and I tried to calm down enough to read the directions.

Extract one cup of tiger-eye stone and place it in a stone mixing dish. Crush the stones into a very fine dust.

I pulled my stone mixing dishes and my pixie dust case from my bag and set them both in front of me. Opening my pixie dust case with my pointer finger, I looked through the different stones until I found the one labeled tiger-eye. It was a brown and amber color. I scooped up a cup full adding it to my mortar and then picking up the pestle. It took a moment to work up a rhythm, but soon it became easier to crush the stones. When I had the tiger-eye crushed into fine brown dust, I stopped to read the next set of directions.

Measure a half cup of azurite, and in a separate mixing dish, also crush into a fine dust.

I found the azurite, a blue crystal, and added it to another dish. Then, I proceeded to crush it as well. My arm was becoming sore from the grinding of the mortar and pestle, but I kept at it. I wasn't sure how much time I had left. When I had ground the azurite, I paused only a moment to look up from my book. Other students were also struggling with their mixing dishes. With a deep breath, I continued.

Add the azurite to the tiger-eye and fold the dust together gently. DO NOT STIR VIGOROUSLY! Fold until thoroughly mixed together.

Slowly, I did as I was instructed. My classmates appeared to be approaching the same stage. To my left, I noticed Josefina was sweating, but I continued to concentrate on the task in front of me.

Measure out another cup of tiger-eye and crush it into dust. Before adding it to the mixture, slightly heat the mineral. DO NOT MELT IT.

I looked around the class. How were we supposed to accomplish that? I didn't see any heat sources. I began to crush the second cup of tiger eye, pondering on how to accomplish this step. How did Mr. Withermyer expect us to do this? Was this supposed to be a trick to prove we couldn't accomplish a difficult charm?

I don't know what inspired the memory, but as I was grinding down the tiger-eye, I remembered the day my father died. When Marie had tried to drag me to the attic, I imagined my arm being so hot she couldn't hold onto me. Amazingly it had worked then. If I could heat up my body, I could use my hands to heat the tiger-eye. Concentrating really hard, I focused all my energy on the mixing bowl. I imagined heat, and after a few minutes, I placed my finger in the dust. Excitement coursed through my body when I felt warmth beneath my fingers. Glancing around at the class, it appeared other students were puzzling over what I had just figured out. A boy in the back of the class had his hand raised.

"Sir, how do we…"

Mr. Withermyer quickly cut him off with his sharp voice. "I will not answer any questions."

I returned to my work, but I felt like someone was watching me. As expected, I looked over my shoulder to see Betty Ann's eyes trained on me. Had she figured out what I was doing? Her brown eyes flashed with realization. I focused all my attention on my dish which finally reached the proper temperature.

After the tiger-eye dust is heated, fold it in with the rest of the mixture. DO NOT STIR VIGOROUSLY.

I spooned the hot mineral into the dish with the other ingredients and began folding it in. Gently, I scrapped particles from the sides, thoroughly combining them. I noticed that some parts had crystallized when I added the heated mineral. I wondered if it was supposed to do that.

When thoroughly mixed, let the charm sit for two minutes before use.

I set the bowl down and calmly reread the steps, making sure I hadn't missed anything. I didn't need to fail this first assignment seeing that Mr. Withermyer had already judged me. Would I be instantly expelled if I failed?

"Time's up. Put down all your materials and place your hands behind your back. If I see anyone continuing to work, you'll automatically fail," Mr. Withermyer said as his eyes passed over the room. When he seemed satisfied, he continued. "Form a line and bring your newly made charms up to my desk for testing."

Betty Ann rushed forward with her charm and became third in line. I wondered why she had rushed, as I got in line behind Josefina. Mr. Withermyer pulled out a bowl of water and set it on his desk for everyone to see.

"The See All Charm will allow you to see what anyone in the world is doing at that moment. All you have to do is think of someone or someplace, take a pinch of your charm, and sprinkle it in the water. If your concentration is strong and your charm is accurately configured, you should be able to see whom you're searching for. When it is your turn, think of someone who is not in this room.

Then add your charm. If you have concocted the charm correctly, this should be easy. Let's begin."

The first student stepped up to the bowl and added their charm. The water seemed to lighten a bit, but no image appeared.

"Not heated enough," Mr. Withermyer declared.

The next student had the same results as the first. Then, Betty Ann was next. She smiled as she quickly stepped up to the bowl and added her charm. A blurry image of a salt-and-pepper-haired man appeared. He looked like he was sitting at a desk. I couldn't make out his other features because the picture was not clear enough.

"Your one cup of tiger-eye could have been heated longer. Good job on your first try. When this charm is created correctly, what you see in the water should be as clear as glass. Next."

The line continued to move forward as each student got a different verdict: some didn't crush the stones enough, some didn't add enough heat, and some tried adding heat after all the ingredients were mixed. Before I knew it, it was my turn to present my charm. To the best of my knowledge, I had followed each step, but I couldn't help being nervous under the scrutinizing green eyes of Mr. Withermyer.

"Miss Fitzgerald, what do you have to show us?"

As I thought of Marie, I took a pinch of the charm and dropped it over the water. Almost instantly the clear water turned into an even clearer picture. I could see Marie bustling around the manor house, instructing other servants on what they were supposed to be doing. Although I couldn't hear what she was saying, just by watching her actions, I felt like I was right there in front of her. The image I had conjured had been sharper and clearer than Betty Ann's.

"Satisfactory, Miss Fitzgerald," was all Mr. Withermyer said to me. I stared at him waiting for more, waiting for the compliments he had piled on Betty Ann. They never came. What had I done to deserve his angry glare? Why did I feel his eyes pierce right through me every time he looked at me? Confused and puzzled,

I picked up my remaining charm and moved so the next student could step forward.

Josefina gave me a questioning look, which confirmed that she was just as puzzled. I was so lost in thought that I almost didn't hear the bell. Josefina had to grab my arm and drag me to Earth Catastrophes.

"That was strange. Your charm was immensely better than Betty Ann's, yet she got all the praise. I had no idea how to heat mine. Between Miguel and me, we couldn't figure it out. Through that entire class we communicated, and we both couldn't come up with an answer. You're a great pixie, Jane. You completed that assignment with ease while the rest of us floundered. I bet you're more like your mother than you think."

I blushed from her compliments and shrugged my shoulders. "Beginner's luck," I replied.

When we got to the front doors, we were shocked by the heavy downpour outside. Rain pelted the ground as we made a wild dash for the outdoor classroom. Taylor was already under the giant boughs of the huge tree. Once again, she was sat hunched over one book or another. It was surprisingly dry underneath the tree. Josefina, Miguel, and I took the same seats as yesterday.

"Good afternoon, Taylor," Josefina said.

"Oh, hello," came Taylor's soft reply as she looked up from her book for a second to acknowledge us.

Mr. Laruse sprinted across the grounds through the rain. He shook the rain off his jacket and put the books he was carrying in the knothole.

"Good afternoon, students who are early! It brings a smile to my face to see you here before me. What dedicated students!" he exclaimed.

Mr. Laruse's blonde hair was platted against his head. He combed his hands through it, trying to dry it, but that made it worse.

"It's raining," Taylor said, stating the obvious.

"Yes, it is," Mr. Laruse said, not noticing how strange her statement was.

"You predicted it yesterday," she replied.

"So, I did. I haven't been wrong in thirty years. Here comes the rest of the class."

Trudging through the slick rain, the students crossed the lawn.

"Good afternoon," Mr. Laruse said as the class crowded under the tree, shaking off excess raindrops. "When you have dried off a bit, open your copy of *Predicting the Weather and Other Catastrophes* to page one. We will begin learning how to predict the daily weather forecast. The first lessons will be easy since we will only be predicting one day at a time."

I pulled out my book, glad that my bag was waterproof. Page one in the book had a short paragraph in the middle and the page border was made up of all different types of weather symbols. The paragraph summarized that we should be able to predict any type of weather or catastrophe after taking this course for a few years. Mr. Laruse then instructed the class to read the first half of chapter one, which explained how to sense moisture in the atmosphere, hence, how to feel when it was going to rain. By the sound of the bell, Mr. Laruse still hadn't explained how to predict the daily forecast, but he did ask us to write a prediction just for fun.

"I'm going to write down a tornado," Miguel said laughing and shaking his head. "Mr. Laruse didn't even touch on the process of predicting the weather."

"It is probably best if we focus on Zodiac Signs now. At least I read the pages assigned," Josefina said casting a look at Miguel.

"You can help me if I don't know," Miguel said.

"Maybe I'll close my mind from you, and you'll have to figure it out yourself," Josefina replied, but from the way she smiled, I knew she wouldn't follow through with her threat.

The bright colorful posters and the circle of desks greeted us as we entered the classroom. Today, Mrs. Harris had her bright red hair pulled up in a messy bun on the top of her head. She stood in the middle of the circle of desks, watching as the class filed into their seats.

"Hopefully, you read the preface last night. Who can tell me where the powers of the zodiac were first discovered?" she asked.

I raised my hand and Mrs. Harris pointed at me. "The powers of the zodiac were first discovered in ancient Greece."

"Very good. The ancient Greeks examined the stars and found meanings and shapes in them. They found out that people born under these signs had different characteristics according to the sign. It was not in the reading, but does anyone know the name of a zodiac sign?"

Taylor had her hand in the air, but Mrs. Harris did not call on her. "Is Miss Miller the only one who knows?" Mrs. Harris inquired. No one spoke or raised their hands. "Okay, take out a notebook, and we will start with that. The zodiac signs are broken down into months, but not how we define the months. One cannot say everyone born in January is a Capricorn. These cycles normally start and end in the middle of a month. Today, we will just start with the names of the signs and what object, or animal represents them. Let's start with Capricorn. The sign Capricorn is in the form of a sea-goat," Mrs. Harris said, pointing to the picture on the wall.

"People born under Capricorn have birthdays that fall between December twenty-second and January twentieth."

The scratching of pens filled the room as everyone was busily writing.

"The next sign is Aquarius, which is represented by the water bearer. People whose birthdays fall between January twenty-first and February nineteenth have the sign Aquarius. After that is Pisces, the two-jumping fish, and those dates are from February twentieth to March twentieth."

As Mrs. Harris spoke, she moved along the posters on the

wall, pointing to each as she talked about them. It was so much to remember, but I planned to study as hard as I could. When the class ended, Mrs. Harris told us that we would explore the zodiac signs and their meanings in depth. Josefina and I retired to our room to work on our assignments before dinner.

I picked up the Zodiac signs book and began paging through it. "According to this, my sign is Pisces because my birthday is February twenty-fourth," I commented.

"Miguel and I are born under Gemini," Josefina said. "We were born on June fifteenth."

"Twins born under the twins," I replied as I resumed my homework.

The night progressed quickly, and before I knew it, Josefina and I had finished our supper in the great hall. We made our way sleepily back to our room, our stomachs and minds bursting. I couldn't believe that the second day at the Jelf Academy was almost over. For the remainder of the night, Josefina tried to teach me how to read the pixie clock. It took some time for me to understand, but I hoped I would be able to read it as well as Josefina. That night, I fell asleep anxious for the next day, but being here felt right.

8

THOMAS'S PROPOSAL

THE WEEKS FLEW by at a steady pace and in a flash, autumn had arrived. The days were getting colder. I had fallen into the routine of returning to the manor house every weekend and leaving for the Jelf Academy Sunday evenings. Marie worked me to the bone during the weekends, and I barely had time to rest, but it was worth it.

I was learning so much, enhancing my magic ability. In Gemstones 101, I learned how to create the quick complete charm. We were strictly advised never to use it for assignments, but Mrs. Rowley never said it couldn't be used otherwise. So, whenever I was alone in the manor, I would use the charm to finish my work faster. However, I was very careful when I risked the charm because I didn't want to jeopardize my newfound freedom. Most days I couldn't use the charm because Marie or the other servants were watching. Even with the charm, I felt tired all the time under Marie's strenuous workload. All the things I used to accomplish in a week had to be crammed into two days.

When I would return to the school Sunday nights, Josefina

and I would stay up late talking about how horrible Marie and her children were.

"It isn't fair," Josefina stated one evening. "Why do you have to live with them? Isn't there anywhere else?"

"No, I have nowhere else to go," I replied. "My father didn't have siblings. I don't remember any relatives coming to visit."

I didn't know if my mother had any living relatives. It wasn't something I ever thought about since I doubted it would change my situation. Once I had gotten into the pattern of working on the weekends, it wasn't so bad. I kept myself motivated with thoughts of returning to Jelf Academy.

In mid-October, the students couldn't stop talking about the Harvest Festival, which was the autumn dance. Third through fifth years were allowed to attend, but first and second-year students had to be invited. The dance was scheduled to be held on a weekend, so I didn't care that I couldn't attend. Marie would never allow it. Still, it was fun to watch the older students prepare.

"I wish someone would ask me," Josefina exclaimed. "If only Juan would agree to take me. Instead, he is escorting one of his friends."

"Don't worry. You'll have plenty of chances to go once we're older," I replied. "In a few years, you will have your turn."

Since the dance was in two weeks, that was all anyone could think about. Josefina talked about it excessively, and she demanded that Juan share all the details at lunch the Monday after. My attention was solely focused on my classes, so after dinner, I told Josefina that I was going to the library to do research for the essay Mr. Collyworth had assigned.

"I would go with you, but I still don't understand the concepts Mr. Withermyer had us outline today," she replied. "Do you mind if I stay here?"

"It's alright," I said, wishing she would come. "I'll take notes on what I research in case you want to use the information in your paper," I offered.

She looked guilty as she glanced up from her Charms book. "Maybe I'll come down a little later."

I nodded and then set off for the library. It was on the first floor in the east wing, next to the dining hall. The first-floor corridor was almost empty as I headed for the east wing. It amazed me how eerily silent the school was once classes had ended. Most of the students retired to their rooms after dinner.

When I entered the library, the silence was deafening. The librarian, Miss Pierce looked at me over the tops of her reading glasses, taking note of my presence before returning to her book. She had light brown hair and brown eyes that were magnified by her glasses. If I had to take a guess, I would say she was in her late thirties. Miss Pierce was very serious about what books could be signed out of the library and had a strict policy on talking. Students were allowed to study with each other, but voices had to remain a whisper. Miss Pierce had total authority to ban students from the library for any reason she deemed worthy. Completing essays would become nearly impossible if you were banned from the library.

Slowly, I walked between the big brown bookcases, looking for books on the American Revolution. It amazed me how tall the shelves were; they almost touched the high ceiling with a ladder in every aisle. The library was enormous, and it seemed to stretch on forever. It would be lovely to have the time to look through every shelf.

After I found what I had been looking for, I settled down at one of the wooden tables in the back and began taking notes. I was so absorbed in my work that I didn't even notice when someone sat down across from me.

"Hello there," he whispered.

I looked up into the startling blue eyes of Thomas Whitmore. I hadn't seen or talked to him since the first day of school, so his presence shocked me. He looked like he was waiting for me to say something, but I couldn't find the words. I noticed again how his wonderfully long eyelashes brushed his cheeks. When he smiled, I felt my heartbeat quicken.

"How have you been?" he asked.

I closed my notebook and looked at him again. "I'm fine. How are you?" I whispered.

"Actually, I've been thinking about you," he said, leaning across the table.

A blush began to creep from my face, down to my neck. I couldn't look at him. "That can't be true. What about Betty Ann?"

Thomas just shrugged his shoulders and shook his head. "What about her?"

"Isn't Betty Ann your intended?" I asked.

"Every time I'm with Betty Ann, I feel like it's just another business arrangement my father set up."

Thomas looked deeply into my eyes, making me feel self-conscience. He was so handsome, but there was something off about him I couldn't place. Maybe it was his mysterious air.

"You have such beautiful eyes. I've never seen eyes such a vivid violet."

I shifted in my seat, blushing again. I had never been shown this much attention before. It felt good, but it made me slightly uncomfortable. Why did he feel the need to talk to me now?

"Thank you," I replied, looking down at the table.

Thomas reached across the table and lifted my chin with his finger, forcing me to look at him.

"I'm glad I found you alone. There is something I've been wanting to ask you. The Harvest Festival is in two weeks, and I was wondering if you would do me the honor of allowing me to escort you? Betty Ann has accepted an invitation from one of my friends." He looked sad as he said this.

"I don't know, Thomas. My stepmother probably won't let me. Plus, I don't think Betty Ann would be too pleased, even if she did accept your friend," I replied.

"Who cares what Betty Ann thinks? Go with me!" he said grabbing at my hand. "We will have such a great time. I'm sure if you talked to Dr. Tweedle he could talk to your stepmother."

Thomas's pleading blue eye met mine, making me feel weak. Dr. Tweedle had confused Marie before with his charm. Maybe he could do it again. Besides, Thomas was so devastatingly handsome. It felt like a dream that he was asking. Thomas seemed like such a nice person, and he looked sincerely hurt when he had told me about Betty Ann. Not only did I feel sorry for him, but I also sincerely wanted to go. I would feel like a princess on his arm.

"Ok," I said nodding. "I would love to go with you. I'll ask Dr. Tweedle what can be done about my stepmother. However, I can't guarantee he'll be able to change her mind," I said, being honest.

He smiled at me as he got up from the table. "Let me know if you get the approval to go. Maybe we can meet again in here sometime next week." He winked as he began backing up. I noticed Miss Pierce walking toward us out of the corner of my eye.

"This is a library. I suggest you two keep quiet or get out!" she harshly whispered to us.

"Sorry, ma'am," I said as I glanced at the table. I hadn't realized that we were talking so loudly.

"Remember," Thomas leaned in to whisper as Miss Pierce walked away. "Meet me here next week with your answer," he winked again as he smoothly turned and walked away from me.

My heart was racing, my palms felt sweaty, and I knew my face was flushed. I tried opening up my notebook again, but I couldn't concentrate. In the end, I slammed the book closed, put it back on the shelf, and left the library.

I wanted to run all the way to my room to tell Josefina everything, but I held in my excitement. Running was frowned upon, and I didn't want to get in trouble. Hugging my notebook to my body, I ascended the steps to the fourth floor and walked down the corridor to my room. Placing my palm on the panel, I waited patiently for the door to slide open. When it did, I found Josefina on her bed still pouring over her Charms book. I came rushing into the room, full of the pent-up energy I had to contain in the hall.

"You'll never guess what just happened to me!" I said, flying onto my bed.

"What?" she said as she sat up and closed her book. "You're back early."

"I was in the library taking notes when I was interrupted."

"By whom?" Josefina asked impatiently.

"As hard as it is to believe, Thomas Whitmore sat at my table."

"Thomas? You don't mean Betty Ann's suitor? Jane, I warned you about that."

"It's not what you think. Betty Ann's being escorted to the Harvest Festival with one of Thomas's friends. He said their courtship's over. He invited me to the Harvest Festival!" I said, hugging my pillow.

"Did you say yes?" Josefina asked with excitement.

"I did, but I doubt Marie will let me stay the weekend. I'll have to talk to Dr. Tweedle. He might know what to do."

"Wow, I'm so excited that you got asked! You have to talk to Dr. Tweedle because then I can live vicariously through you!" She leapt from her bed and came over to hug me.

"I can't believe Thomas asked me. He is so handsome with his beautiful blue eyes," I replied.

"Jane, I just want you to be careful," she said pulling away from me. "If Betty Ann's going to be there, you have to be cautious. Even if Thomas isn't courting her anymore, she won't be thrilled to see you there, on his arm."

"I promise, but what could happen?" I asked.

"I don't know, but the Barber family is very devious. She could have anything up her sleeve," Josefina warned.

"I'll ask Dr. Tweedle first thing in the morning," I said as I nestled under my covers. The Harvest Festival was one of the biggest events at the Jelf Academy. My heart felt like it was going to fly out of my chest when I thought about Thomas. The dance could be the most special night of my life, but first I had to make sure I could be there.

≈

I found myself outside of Dr. Tweedle's office the next morning. He persuaded Marie about Jelf Academy; maybe he could convince her to let me have one weekend at the school. I raised my fist to knock on the door when suddenly it opened. Dr. Tweedle stood in the doorway with a familiar glint in his eye.

"Come in, Miss Fitzgerald," he said as he backed away from the door, revealing the inside of his office. I entered the room confused by the fact he knew I was there.

Dr. Tweedle's office was a soft baby blue that made me feel instantly comfortable. He directed me to a pillow-covered sofa, and I sat down.

"How did you know I was at the door?" I asked. Dr. Tweedle sat down at his desk and folded his hands on top of it.

"The ability to open your mind and sense the people and things around you is another talent you can acquire here, Miss Fitzgerald. To what can I contribute your delightful presence?"

"Dr. Tweedle, the Harvest Festival is in two weeks, and I was wondering if you could talk to Marie."

"You know first years can't attend the dances," he said, leaning forward.

"I know, but I have been asked by a third-year. I would really like to go. I know Marie will say no, but with your authorization, she might," I said looking at him intently.

Dr. Tweedle smiled at me as he took his oval glasses off and cleaned them on his handkerchief. He pulled out a fancy, heavy-looking paper and began writing in his elegant scrawl with a feather pen. I waited patiently while he finished the letter. Then he handed it over to me.

"It's the best I can do."

To the Guardian of Miss Jane Fitzgerald,

In a week's time, on the twenty-fifth of October, our students will have an opportunity to meet with respected individuals of society so that they can exercise and be judged on the manners and etiquette they have learned so far. Since this event takes place on the weekend, students will need to stay at the school. It is highly recommended for the students to attend since it is a once-in-a-lifetime experience.

Thank you for your consideration.

Dr. Oliver Tweedle

Headmaster of the Jelf Academy.

After I read the letter, Dr. Tweedle motioned for me to give the letter back. When I did, he sprinkled what looked like opal powder on the letter and inserted it into an envelope that he sealed with his mind.

"Give this to Marie. I have inserted a deciding charm, and hopefully, it will be the decision you are looking for. I normally don't do this for students, but your situation is very different. You have no one from our world at home. Also, I see so much of your mother in you. I see her determination for success and the want to experience everything.

"Next Sunday evening, when I come to pick you up, if Marie has said yes, then we will go to Jewel Caverns to get you proper dress attire," Dr. Tweedle said.

"Thank you so much, Dr. Tweedle! I don't know how I can ever repay you. You've done so much for me already!" I said as I stood up from the sofa. He extended his hand with the letter. I took it, storing it safely in my bag.

"Don't worry about repaying me, dear. I'm not one hundred

percent certain that the letter will work, but it's the least I can do. Now hurry off to your first class. I wouldn't want you to be late."

I thanked him again and hurried off to Gemstones 101.

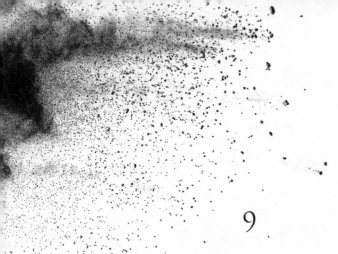

9

THE BEGINNING OF
A FRIENDSHIP

BEFORE I KNEW it, the week flew by, and I found myself standing weak-kneed in my father's office with Marie seated behind the desk. She looked severe with her black hair pulled tightly into a bun. The red curtains were closed, casting most of the room in darkness except for what was illuminated by the small candle on the desk. If Marie was intimidating in the daylight, she was even more so in the dim lighting.

"You said you needed to speak with me about something important. I doubt the significance but speak before I change my mind and decide not to listen," Marie demanded coldly.

"I have a letter for you from the headmaster of my school," I said. My hand shook as I passed her the letter.

"Yes, that school. Have you been learning your manners?" she asked as she tore open the envelope.

"Yes, ma'am, I have." I curtsied, hoping that effect was enough.

"So, you received an invitation to attend a party that will allow you to exercise your newly learned manners. I wonder what kind of respectable people you will be meeting. I guess it couldn't hurt for you to attend. The way you acted when all of Emily's suitors arrived at this house was unacceptable. You were constantly staring and looking through cracks in the doors as if you've never seen a man before. It was such disgusting behavior. I'm sure those men were bothered by your actions.

"Do you realize if I let you attend, you'll be missing a weekend of work? I have been more than kind in this situation, Jane. I will let you attend this event since you have been socially handicapped all of your life. It is only out of pity for you that I'll allow it," Marie said.

Though her insults stung me deeply, she still gave me permission. "Thank you, ma'am. Thank you," I said bowing to her.

"Don't grovel at my feet! We already have enough work to get done. Robert needs help in the stables," Marie smiled wickedly. "Get a move on!"

Quickly, I left the dark office and went towards the front door. It was obvious that Marie would assign me one of the dirtiest jobs since I asked to remain at the academy next weekend. For a quick moment, I rested my head against the door frame. I closed my eyes, and Thomas's face flashed in my mind. We were going to have a wonderful time, and I was sure he would be happy when I gave him the news.

Opening the door, I stepped into the bold sunshine, ready to complete the chore set in front of me. As I stumbled over the small hills and bumps to the barn, I thought of Robert. I had not spoken to him since his arrival, and I wasn't planning on breaking the silence now. His reluctance to talk to me or tell me about himself had hurt. We both could've had someone to talk to, but if he hadn't pushed me away. I hoped he enjoyed the silence now because I wasn't going to break it.

When I reached the barn, I swung open the doors with more force than I intended, causing them to bang against the front of the barn. I believe Robert was shocked to see me for he had stopped working, shovel in hand, and stared at me with his mouth opened. His auburn hair looked bright in the places the light hit it, and his dark brown eyes gazed at me for a long moment. I shrugged off his stare and moved off to the corner of the barn where the shovels were kept. When it became apparent to him that I was here to help him work, he continued shoveling.

Starting in another stall, I began shoveling manure into the aisle. Marie wanted the manure collected into bags to be delivered to the other side of the manor where it would be used as fertilizer. For the next half hour, I worked in the stall, and when I had cleared it out, I laid new hay and moved on to the next one. Perspiration was soaking my back, and I was sure I was smeared with dirt… or worse. The smell clogged my nostrils, making me want to choke. My arms were becoming sore, and it took every bit of determination to walk into the next stall.

I was surprised when Robert came into the stall and spoke. "I heard that you attend a school for etiquette during the week and come back here on the weekends," he said.

"Oh, you feel like talking now?" I asked sarcastically. "Maybe I don't feel like sharing that information with you," I returned the comment he had used so many months ago. Robert's expression looked like I had struck him across the face. For a slight moment, I felt guilty, but I turned away from him and continued with my work.

For another hour we worked in silence. My back ached, my palms blistered, and my lungs filled with disgusting odors. The Harvest Festival was the only thought that ran through my mind.

Suddenly, Robert spoke again. "You know, your reply wasn't very polite or mannerly."

"It took you that long to come up with that," I huffed as I shoveled another load into the aisle.

"I'm sorry for how I acted when I first arrived here. I've

been meaning to tell you that, but I haven't seen you. I was very withdrawn. Mr. Wicker didn't like it when I talked, and it was prohibited. You can accept my apology or choose not to," Robert said, turning back to his work.

I didn't waste my time replying. I needed to save my energy for the physical work. Once we had emptied all the stalls, it was time to bag everything.

"I'll get the bags. They are on the other side of the barn," Robert commented.

I nodded feeling guiltier for lashing out at him. It was just so strange to hear him talk. While he was gone, I surveyed the barn wondering how to do the work faster. I always carried a tube of garnet dust in my pocket for the quick complete charm. How could I get Robert away long enough to use it?

Robert came back into the barn with his arms loaded down with burlap bags.

"Are you sure those bags are enough for all this?" I asked thinking quickly.

"Yes, I think these might do," he replied.

"It's better to be safe than sorry. Maybe you should go across to the fields and collect more bags while I get started on this."

Robert looked at me skeptically, but then shrugged his shoulders and nodded. As soon as he disappeared out the barn doors, I had a pinch of garnet dust between my fingers. As I cast the charm, s familiar red cloud formed around my body. When it cleared, my body pulsed with pent-up energy. I launched into action, shoveling the manure, filling bag after bag. My muscles tightened under the strain of the work, but it felt good. For twenty minutes, I worked at filling the bags. The effects of the charm were beginning to wear off when the barn door creaked open, and Robert entered. Thankfully, I had estimated enough pixie dust. He looked shocked to see a third of the bags filled and stacked against the side of the barn. The bags he carried fell from his hands.

"How?" was all he managed to say.

"I've been working since you've been gone," I replied.

"I couldn't have done this so quickly!" he stuttered. "How did you manage this?"

"I'm a woman," I said.

I thought I saw Robert smile as he leaned down to pick up the bags he had dropped.

"Give me your shovel," Robert said walking up to me. I gave him a questioning look. "You did a lot. I can take care of the rest. Unless you want to hold the bags open, I wouldn't mind if you went up to the loft to rest."

He took the shovel from my hands, and I looked at the ladder contemplating the loft. The quick complete charm hadn't made me tired, and I was afraid the moment I rested, Marie would check on our progress. Picking up a bag with my dirty, blistered fingers, I held it opened for him. Robert scooped the remaining manure, not saying another word or commenting on why I was helping him.

My hands were the sorest they had ever been. Marie had never assigned me outdoor work before. All the scrubbing I ever did in the manor did not add up to the way my body ached now. When the last bag had been loaded and sealed, I collapsed on a bale of hay. Robert hauled the last bag over to the others and then came to sit on the hay next to me. I held my hands up to my face, inspecting them in the opaque barn. Robert looked over at me to see what I was doing. He motioned to see my hands just as he did the first day when I had cut myself.

"These blisters look bad," he said, holding my small hand in his rough calloused one. "I have a small bucket of cool water in the loft that I use for washing. You should go up there and use it while I haul the fertilizer onto the wagon. My next chore is repairing one of the saddles. You can stay if you want to. I might need help, but I have to figure out how to pull the saddle up into the loft," he commented, talking more to himself now.

As he went to load the wagon with the fertilizer bags, I climbed up to the loft. Without any trouble, I found the bucket and dipped my hands into the water. It felt cool against my skin, and I was grateful that he had offered it to me. Robert was being so nice, and I felt guilty. What could I do for him? We were both so tired, and he still had to fix the broken saddle. Perhaps I would be able to levitate it into the loft for him.

Climbing down from the loft, I looked through all the stalls for the broken saddle. Once I found it, I used my remaining energy to concentrate on the task at hand. I imagined that the saddle would lift from the dirt and make its way into the loft. Little by little the saddle rose from the floor of the barn and floated up. I finally let go of my concentration, and the saddle dropped down onto the soft hay of the floor above. I climbed the ladder again and returned my hands to the bucket. Soon after, Robert reentered the barn, and I called down to him.

"Robert, I've already brought the broken saddle up to the loft."

I looked down into his amazed face as he changed directions and grabbed onto the ladder.

"You amaze me," he said as he climbed. "How did you ever manage to carry that heavy saddle up here after all the hard work you did today?"

"I can accomplish anything I put my mind to," I said, smiling at the private meaning of my statement.

Robert sat down across from me and began to repair the broken stirrup. I watched his hands gently go over the tough leather, and his dark eyes were deeply concentrated.

"Does this mean we're on talking terms?" he asked, not looking up from his work.

"I accept your apology, and I must return one of my own. I'm sorry I was so short with you," I replied.

He nodded and uttered, "I understand."

We sat in a comfortable silence as I continued to soak my hands, and he worked on the saddle. I could tell he had changed from the first day I met him. Before, he had looked like a scared, caged animal. Now he looked more relaxed. How bad had Mr. Wicker been for Robert to look comfortable here? Drying my hands on my dirty dress, I stood up in the loft and moved toward the ladder. I couldn't stay up here all day. Marie would get suspicious.

"Perhaps I shall see you in two weeks? Next weekend I have a school function that Marie has allowed me to attend," I said with my foot on the first step of the ladder.

"Thank you for forgiving me. I'm sorry we got off on the wrong foot," Robert replied.

I left the stables, my muscles complaining the entire way to the house. I entered the foyer and headed to the stairs when I was suddenly startled by Emily's voice.

"Where have you been? I need help getting ready for a party." I turned to see her emerging from the shadows. Her eyes raked over my body, and she scrunched up her nose. "Why do you smell like that?"

"Sorry miss. Your mother assigned me to the stables."

"That's disgusting!" Emily shrieked. "Go wash up before you touch my pretty things. Then, hurry to my room. I don't want to be late."

Emily turned around to ascend the steps, and I made a face at her back. I regretted it immediately.

"I wouldn't make such an awful face. The Devil might freeze it that way," Marie said, slinking into the room. It was on the tip of my tongue to ask her if she was going to freeze my face, but I held back. Too much was at stake. "Remember Jane, I might rethink my decision if your behavior doesn't improve."

I bowed to her and then went to wash up. With a heavy heart, I climbed the stairs and headed toward Emily's bedroom. She was seated on her bed in her undergarments with an impatient look on her face.

"What took you so long? Are you that incompetent that you don't even know how to wash up?" she grumbled.

I said nothing as I moved to her side and began brushing her midnight black tresses. She sighed, looking down at her beautiful long nails.

"What to wear?" she asked herself. "It's a very important party," she said to make me jealous, but I kept on brushing, remaining speechless. That seemed to aggravate her. "There will be many important, rich young men at this party. I must make a good impression, but I assume you know nothing of attracting a suitor. Well, I imagine when mother passes away, you can live with me and my rich husband. We might find work for you, or your other option would be to stay here with Preston when he inherits the house."

I clenched my teeth at her comment. My face heated as I thought of Preston inheriting my father's house. I swallowed my anger, which I was better at now with my training. After so many brush strokes, Emily shrugged me off and moved to her closet. Dress after dress flew over her shoulder as she looked for something special to wear.

"I guess I'll wear this red one. It brings out my dark hair," she said throwing a lace-covered red dress in my direction.

I held the dress opened for her to step into, and after I had buttoned up the back, she looked in the mirror. "I am so beautiful. I really cannot believe I'm not married yet, but my mother has such gruesome choices." Her menacing laugh filled the room. "Mr. Wicker was a bore, and he was two times my age. All we got from that rotten man was that awful boy."

As she mindlessly talked, I picked up all the dresses she had thrown out of the closet. After so many years of listening to Emily's rants, I knew how to tune her out and nod my head at the right moment. When it was time for her to go, I sighed in relief. Helping her down the steps in her long red dress was a hassle, and she shoved me aside when she got to the bottom.

"Hurry up. Open the door! My carriage is waiting!" she complained as I rushed to the door.

She stepped through with her nose up in the air. The coachman helped her board the carriage that whisked her away into the dark night. Very tired from the day's hard work, I climbed up to the attic and crashed on my mattress. Dreams of frilly dresses, dances, and handsome young men floated under my eyelids. If only Emily knew that I would soon attend a dance of my own.

10

THE HARVEST FESTIVAL

S UNDAY EVENING CAME quickly. I was too excited to wait at
the front door, so I walked down to the front gates to meet
Dr. Tweedle. It wasn't long before his carriage appeared.

"Good evening, Jane," he said taking off his top hat and tipping
it to me. "I'm surprised to see you out here. Am I taking you to
the school or Jewel Caverns?" he asked hopefully.

"Marie said that I was allowed to go!" I smiled at him as I
accepted his outstretched hand.

With the use of a teleporting charm, we were suddenly outside of the Jewel Caverns. Once we entered the cave, Dr. Tweedle
looked over at me.

"We will go to Timothy Murray's shop. He always has the best
deals." I nodded my head, just grateful to be here. Mr. Murray was
behind the counter greeting us as we entered.

"Miss Fitzgerald, to what do I owe this pleasure?" Mr. Murray
asked making me blush.

"Jane was invited to the Harvest Festival, Timothy," Dr. Tweedle answered for me. "We are here to pick out a dress."

"What did I tell you, Oliver? I knew she would be asked. Let me show you the new arrivals," he said leading us to the back of the shop. "I have a nice selection of dresses that just came in."

Different types of dresses were thrown my way, overwhelming me instantly; so many wonderful, lacey, frilly dresses all for me to try on. I disappeared into the changing room multiple times trying every single dress until I came across a light blue one. It had short frills over the shoulders and glitter cascading to the bottom. The dress was a ball gown, and I felt like a princess for the first time in my life. I didn't see a slave girl when I looked in the mirror. The tale of Cinderella my father used to read to me came to mind, and I smiled because for once in my life I was going to a fancy ball.

"That dress is beautiful on you, Jane," Mr. Murray said as I stepped out of the changing room.

"I do love it," I replied as I spun around to look at my reflection in the mirror.

"So, is this the one? What do you say, Oliver?"

"Alright, what do I owe you?" Dr. Tweedle asked smiling as he inclined his head toward Mr. Murray.

"I'll tell you what," Mr. Murray said pulling Dr. Tweedle off to the side, so I wouldn't be able to hear.

I was curious about their conversation, but I went back into the changing room to put on my clothes. When I had reemerged, Dr. Tweedle had collected the dress, and he smiled at me.

"I've already paid. Come along so I can get you back to the school."

I stared at him in awe. "But Dr. Tweedle, how much did this cut into my funds?" I asked with concern.

"No need to worry about that, Jane. It is all taken care of," Dr. Tweedle motioned his hand to quiet me.

I followed him out of Mr. Murray's, shocked by his response.

∽

The trip up into the clouds was perfect as I held the dress close to my body. Nothing could ruin my happiness at this moment. When I got up to my room, Josefina wanted to see my dress, so I modeled it for her. The glitter shone under the lighting, and I turned in a circle, showing her every inch of the blue fabric.

"The dress is so beautiful," Josefina said as she lightly touched the belled-out bottom. "You're so lucky."

"I wish you were going as well. This won't be as fun without someone to share it with," I replied.

"Now, don't go feeling guilty. You're going with Thomas Whitmore, one of the most handsome boys in this school. I know you'll tell me all about it, all the way down to the last detail," Josefina said as she got under the covers of her bed.

I slipped out of my dress and hung it securely in the closet. As I climbed into bed, I couldn't help but imagine what the dance would be like, and I fell asleep with a smile.

The week seemed to crawl as I anticipated the dance. Every day after dinner I snuck off to the library where I promised to meet Thomas. I was beginning to worry that he had changed his mind. On Wednesday, he finally appeared.

"Thomas, I thought you had reconsidered," I softly whispered when he stood beside the table. He grabbed my hand and led me between two bookshelves in the back, away from the eyes of Miss Pierce.

"Why would I change my mind on someone as beautiful as you?" he asked. I felt myself blush pleasantly all over. "Will I be escorting you to the Harvest Festival?"

"Yes," I replied.

"Good," he said looking into my eyes. "I'm glad you can go."

Thomas reached up to brush a strand of my blonde hair back into place. He was leaning very close to me. I felt my heart rate quicken as I stared up into his deep, blue eyes. Was he going to kiss me, right here between the two musty bookshelves? I had never been kissed before. The thought of it made me nervous, but I wanted him to. His long lashes played on his cheeks as he blinked. The spicy scent of his cologne delighted my nose. I wanted to be impulsive and just throw myself into his arms, but I hesitated not sure of myself. He probably knew everything about kissing and romancing, and I didn't want to make a fool of myself. Suddenly, he paused and backed away from me. I tried not to look disappointed as his eyes traveled over my face.

"What is your room number, so I can properly take you to the dance?" he asked.

My mind went blank. It was hard to think about anything at that moment with him only a few feet away. "My room number is 114," I told him, finally remembering.

"The dance starts at seven, so I'll come by then," he said smiling at me. "Until Saturday."

He backed away from me even further. "Until Saturday," I mimicked breathlessly. "Goodnight, Thomas."

He winked at me in his classical way as he left the library. Feeling weak-kneed, I sank to the floor and propped my back against the bookshelves. Why hadn't he kissed me? Did I do something wrong? Should I have made the first move? No, that would've been completely unladylike. Maybe Emily was right, I thought sadly. Maybe I knew nothing about men.

I returned to the room to find Josefina sitting on her bed waiting.

"Was Thomas there?" she asked anxiously. Every day she posed the same question.

"Yes, he was. I told him I could go," I said smiling as I recalled his face.

"You'll have a great time, but remember you have to mentally document everything!"

I shook my head and smiled at her as I pulled my pajamas out of the closet.

"I promise I will let you know every single detail down to the color of the decorations. I won't be able to wait until Sunday evening to tell you everything. Hopefully, Betty Ann won't be hateful."

"Oh, she will be, so just be careful," Josefina warned.

"Don't worry, I will," I promised.

﹏

Saturday came and soon I found myself alone in my room trying to get ready. I missed Josefina's incessant chatter and wished she had stayed. I combed my long, straight blonde hair until it shone. Smiling at my reflection in the mirror, I rose from the vanity table and straightened the long skirt of my dress. Everything seemed so perfect, but I couldn't help feeling sad that my best friend wasn't here. I had said my goodbyes to Josefina yesterday. She had hugged me and told me to have a good time.

"Don't trip in that long dress," she had joked. I now swallowed the lump in my throat as I gazed at my reflection.

The loud knock sounded on the door making me jump. With a deep breath, I answered the door. Thomas stood there in a very dapper in a white suit. His blonde hair fell across his forehead, making him look even more dashing. It was hard to look away from his sparkling eyes. He was devastatingly handsome, and I couldn't help but smile. I still couldn't believe he was my escort.

"You look so beautiful," Thomas said with a playful grin as he slipped a ring of white flowers onto my wrist.

"Thank you. They're lovely," I said examining the flowers.

"Just like you," he complimented me again. "Are you ready to go, my lady?"

He extended his arm to me, and I slipped mine through his. I lifted my head, feeling prouder than I ever had.

On Thomas's arm, I followed him down the steps from the

fourth floor to the main hall. The dance was taking place in the main hall and the dining hall, so we would make our grand entrance on the staircase. Around the balustrades were fall leaves in bright reds, oranges, and yellows. Below me, the dance was already underway.

"Are you ready?" Thomas asked as he glanced at me. I nodded my head vigorously, and he winked at me. We descended the steps, and I felt like royalty. I was expecting someone to announce our arrival just like the balls in storybooks. My heart fluttered as I noticed some of the students glance up at us, and I prayed that I wouldn't fall. I was so nervous with all the attention; I wished I had cast a calming charm before I had left my room.

Thomas led me through the gigantic crowd toward the buffet tables. The decorations were so beautiful, and everything looked so crisp like a fresh autumn day. The light fixtures were decorated with the same leaves that had adorned the balustrades. Bales of hay with pumpkins decorated the edges of the dance floor. Excitement seemed to pulse and vibrate through the floor. Thomas poured a cup of punch from the flowing fountain and handed it to me. I took a sip and it pleasantly burned in my throat.

"This is different from any punch I've ever had before," I commented.

Thomas pulled me close and whispered in my ear. "That's because alcohol was added to it. Shh, don't tell anyone. We don't want the teachers to know. They don't allow drinking at school functions. I can trust you to keep a secret, can't I?"

I found myself nodding my head even as I put my glass down, promising myself not to have anymore.

"Come on, let's dance. I will be the first on your dance card," Thomas said, grabbing my wrist and penciling his name on my card. Then he began dancing me back into the crowd, right after he downed a glass of punch. He spun me around in the middle of the floor and pulled me into his arms. As we whirled around, I realized Thomas was a great dancer. He had rhythm and never lost the beat. Our first waltz was wonderful.

After the first dance, we took a break, and Thomas went back over to the punch bowl. He offered me another glass, but I refused it. Thomas just shrugged and downed both glasses. Other young men tried to approach me to fill in the dances on my card, but they strangely turned away when Thomas spoke to them. Even though Thomas had escorted me to the Harvest Festival, it seemed improper for him to not let anyone else dance with me. Perhaps he just wanted me all to himself and planned on dancing every dance with me.

"Hello Tom, I see you couldn't resist bringing riff-raff to this dance," Betty Ann cackled as she came up to the refreshment table with a handsome dark-haired boy. "You really need to stop feeling sorry for unfortunates."

Thomas didn't reply and sipped his punch instead. Betty Ann pushed her way past me toward the punch. She took a sip and didn't seem surprised by the taste. Betty Ann then faced me. "Are you having fun, Jane?"

I gave her a cold look. "Yes, until you showed up," I replied.

"Now Jane, don't be so nasty," Betty Ann said in a voice that was shockingly similar to Marie's. "Don't worry. You'll regret that comment. Come on, Adam, let's dance," Betty Ann said tugging on Adam's tie.

"Let's go, Jane," Thomas said, using one hand to lead me to the dance floor while his other hand clung to the glass of punch.

Once we were on the dance floor, Thomas whirled me to the beat again. Despite Betty Ann's comments and threats, I began to enjoy myself. After one of the faster dances, the band played a slow waltz. Thomas pulled me closer. I stared into his eyes, feeling so content and happy for the first time in my life. This night was magical, and I didn't care what Betty Ann had to say. As we spun around, Thomas got a silly grin on his face, causing me to wonder what he was thinking. All of a sudden, his hands slipped down my back, stopping in an improper place. Instantly, I grabbed at his hands and moved them back up into position.

"What are you doing, Thomas?" I asked. He just stared at me with a big dumb smile on his face.

"What do you mean?" he asked dumbly, his smile still plastered on his face.

"What's wrong with you? Please stop!" I said as I pulled away from him.

"Nothing is wrong. I'm just trying to have fun, darling," he said leaning close to me again. The pungent smell of alcohol hit me in the face, and I coughed.

"Are you drunk?" I asked with comprehension.

"Don't be so uptight, darling. It was just a couple of drinks," Thomas replied.

I took a step away from him, but he grabbed my wrist and forcefully pulled me into the dance again.

"Come on. Let's have a good time." Thomas finally lost the silly grin and almost looked like himself again. He smiled at me and whispered in my ear. "I'm sorry you're upset."

Although Thomas didn't try to touch me again, he did begin to lose some of his balance and sway a little. By the end of the song, I was practically holding him up.

"Maybe we should sit down," I suggested.

Thomas stepped back from me and slightly nodded. He was looking over my shoulder, and that dumb grin appeared again. "Why don't we go sit down?" I suggested again.

Thomas continued to stare. I stepped toward him, but before I could reach him, a thick red liquid came crashing down on my head. The next sound I heard was a crash and the punch bowl exploded at my feet. Thousands of eyes glanced in my direction. I turned around to see Betty Ann standing by the refreshment table laughing. Instantly I knew it was she who had levitated the punch bowl and dumped it on me. I turned away from her to look at Thomas hoping he would be my defender. Instead, my heart lurched when I saw him laughing as well. He was finding just as much enjoyment as Betty Ann.

"I told you that you'd regret being so nasty to me," Betty Ann said as she came to a stop in front of me. "Nobody wanted you here anyway."

I looked at Thomas expecting him to say it wasn't true. I wanted him to say that he invited me because he liked me, but he just continued to laugh.

"Thomas, what is going on?" I whispered, but I was sure I already knew the answer.

"Did you honestly think I asked you to this dance because I liked you?" he slurred stepping closer to Betty Ann. "If you thought that, you're more naïve than I thought. What would possibly make you think that I'd want to court you? You're a poor half-breed?" Thomas stared at me with an awful grin on his face.

I felt tears well up in my eyes as I stood in front of everyone at the dance utterly humiliated. My wet hair continued to drip. "You told me that you couldn't tolerate Betty Ann anymore," I whispered.

Betty Ann laughed. "Jane, what don't you understand?" she asked in a voice as if she were talking to a child. "Thomas had no intention of courting you. In fact, he went along with my little plan quite nicely. You're such a fool. Why would Thomas leave someone like me for someone like you?"

"You're a real laugh, Jane, and such a stuck-up prude. I would've never asked you in the first place if Betty Ann hadn't insisted upon it," Thomas added as he slipped his arm around Betty Ann and kissed her.

"Why?" I sobbed. "Why would you do this to me? What have I ever done to you?"

Betty Ann pulled away from Thomas. "You existed," she replied hatefully.

I felt a hand touch my arm. I turned quickly anticipating another assault, but Juan stood staring at me.

"Jane, I'll take you back up to your room."

I nodded my head as I gazed down at his black suit. His friend clutched his arm, looking at me with sympathy.

"I'll help you," she said to me as she reached for my hand.

Thomas stepped toward me. "Juan Martinez comes to the rescue." Thomas clapped slowly. "His social standing is one notch above yours."

"Leave us alone, Thomas. Don't you think you've done enough damage for one night?" Juan asked, stepping in front of me while his friend held my arm.

"How typical of you to care for the poor and downtrodden. I should've expected this, but helping a half-human? It seems you Martinez's have lowered your standards," Thomas spat.

"Do well to remember, Thomas, that the Martinez's are no longer poor. Money isn't everything anyway."

"How could I forget that stupid gem mine your father stumbled across? The money made you rich, but you'll never fit in our social class no matter how much money you have," Thomas sneered.

"I don't want to be one of you. If this is how you treat good people, I don't want to be involved. Jane is better than either of you. Now excuse me, the decent and civilized people will be leaving now," Juan said

Thomas lurched forward, and I thought he was going to jump on Juan, but he didn't. "Just remember who I'm connected to. I wouldn't upset me if you know what I mean," he threatened, pointing a finger at Juan.

Ignoring Thomas, Juan turned away from Thomas and led me out of the dining hall, helping me up the grand staircase. I hadn't realized that I had been sobbing until Juan reached over and wiped some tears off my cheeks. "Don't worry, Jane. It's okay now," he said in a soothing voice.

When we reached my room, Juan's friend helped me inside. "I'm going to help her get cleaned up," she said to Juan as my room door began to slide closed. Then she sat me down on the vanity stool and knelt before me. "Hello Jane, my name is Helena Rodriguez, but you can just call me Lena," she said as she unstrapped my shoes and pulled them off.

"I'll help you with whatever you need, and I'm here if you need to talk," Lena said sweetly.

I looked into her dark brown eyes and nodded. "Thank you very much," I replied.

I stood as Lena unbuttoned my blue dress, which was now ruined by the red punch. My skin and hair were sticky, and I could not control my sobbing. I stepped out of my dress and Lena held it up unsure of what to do with it.

"Go get a bath, Jane," Lena said as she pointed to my bathroom. "I'll take this dress to my room and try a cleaning charm my mother taught me. I hope that the stain will come out. When I come back, I'll knock three times on your door, so you'll know it's me," she said. "You looked so beautiful tonight. I'm so sorry for what they did." She stroked my cheek with the affection of an older sister before she left.

Slowly, I walked into the bathroom defeated and weak. I didn't feel like myself. The hurt cut into my body like a knife, far worse than anything Marie had ever done. The warm water washed over my body, and I scrubbed at my skin and hair. My tears melted and formed into the water until I couldn't tell the difference. I succumbed to the internal pain that had me doubled over.

How could Thomas do this to me? Their words rang in my head: "You're such a fool Jane... why would Thomas want to court you... you're a stuck-up prude." I cried even harder, leaning my head against the side of the tub. "Why would you do this to me? What did I ever do to you?" I had asked, and Betty Ann had answered "You existed."

The pain stabbed at me, cutting to my very core. It would be so much better for everyone if I did not exist, I thought, remembering how Marie hated my very existence as well. I finished my bath and toweled myself dry. The soft and familiar fabric of my pajamas comforted me a bit, and I wrapped my wet hair in a towel. Slowly, I walked to my bed and sat down. My eyes felt dry and sore, but I could feel more tears coming on.

I wasn't sitting long when I heard the sound of Lena's knocking. Lena brought in my dress which still looked to be in the same state as when she had left.

"I'm sorry, Jane. I tried everything, but the stain won't come out. I'm not sure if they added a permanent charm to the punch," Lena said as she reached for me. I allowed her to hug me, and then I retreated to my bed. Lena hung my blue dress in the closet and then came to sit next to me.

"I know you don't know me very well and trust is probably hard right now, but you can trust me," Lena said looking me in the eyes.

I noticed that she had changed out of her orange party dress and her dark brown hair was now pulled off to the side.

"What they did was wrong and evil. My heart aches for you," Lena said as she reached for a tissue and wiped at my tears.

"Thank you so much for taking care of me. I don't know what would've happened if you and Juan hadn't come to my rescue. I can't believe I was so stupid," I said bursting into tears again.

Lena reached out and pulled me into her arms. "You're not stupid," she said, patting my back as I cried on her shoulder. She reminded me so much of Irene Dimple that I began to feel comfortable. "It's not your fault. None of this is your fault."

"Betty Ann hasn't been nice from the moment I met her. I should've known he was going to be exactly the same," I sobbed.

"You couldn't have known, Jane. Let's get your hair out of that towel," Lena suggested.

I took off the towel and hung it in the bathroom. Lena offered to brush my hair.

"Thank you."

"No one has ever done this for you before?" Lena asked as she ran the brush through my wet hair.

"No, my mother died when I was an infant. My father remarried. Marie is nothing like a mother to me. She hates my very existence. I'm just a thorn in her side. Tonight, just confirmed that I really am nothing," I said as my shoulders heaved.

"That's not true, Jane. Don't ever tell yourself that. You are important," Lena said stroking my hair. "Marie and all the others who have treated you badly are at a loss, Jane. I can tell that you are a great person."

"Thank you again, Lena. I'm really glad that you helped me tonight. I don't know how I would have gotten through it. If you don't mind me saying, you almost feel like the big sister I never had. Thank you for making me feel better."

"You're welcome, Jane. I figured you needed someone since Josefina isn't here," Lena replied.

I nodded in agreement. Lena rose from my bed and put the brush back on the vanity table. Then she returned to my side. "The Barbers think they can do whatever they want to people and get away with it," I said.

"That's because their entire family is involved in big business and the government. They are pretty powerful and hard to defy. Don't worry about Betty Ann, she isn't worth your tears. Forget about what she says because it's not important. Anyway, it's getting late, and I don't want to miss curfew," Lena said as she got up from my bed. I followed her to the door and before she could exit, I hugged her.

"Thanks again, Lena," I said holding back tears.

Lena patted my arm and then she was gone. I turned back into my empty room and took a deep breath. My body felt numb, and the pain still lingered as I suspected it would for a while. Emptiness was all I could feel now. Empty of tears, empty from all the joy I had imagined, and empty from all I had lost, beginning with my mother's death.

11

THE AFTER EFFECTS
OF A BETRAYAL

Sunday was the hardest day for me, and I stayed in my room waiting for Josefina to return. I laid on my bed, not wanting to move and feeling unable to anyway. I skipped breakfast and lunch, not wanting to leave the room and risk seeing Thomas or Betty Ann. Despite what Lena had said to me last night, I still couldn't help feeling insignificant.

At eight o'clock, Josefina finally arrived, her bubbly personality completely filling the room. "How was the dance? You have to tell me everything!" she exclaimed, closing the door behind her. However, the moment she looked at my face her smile fell. As soon as I looked into her kind brown eyes, I burst into tears.

Josefina threw her belongings on the floor and raced over to me. "What's wrong? What happened?" she frantically asked me. It only took her a few moments to deduce the cause of my pain. "Betty Ann," she whispered

"At the beginning, it was everything I dreamed of. I felt so beautiful. Then before I knew it, everything was ruined," I said.

"What did she do?" Josefina asked with malice in her voice. "Start from the beginning and leave nothing out."

I began with Thomas arriving at my room like a perfect gentleman; how the first half of my night had been absolutely wonderful. "The punch had alcohol added to it by the fifth years as a tradition, so I only had a sip, but Thomas had more than a few glasses," I explained. "He started acting funny when Betty Ann first approached me."

I then told Josefina how Thomas had been a great dancer at first, and then everything had gone sour, just like the punch. "Betty Ann levitated the punch bowl and dumped it on me. The worst part was when Thomas laughed along with her. He didn't defend me and admitted he had only invited me because it was Betty Ann planned to embarrass me," I said sadly.

"I can't believe he did that to you! I wish I would've been there to help," Josefina replied. It was the first time I had ever seen her that disturbed and distressed. "What did you do after that?"

"If it wasn't for Juan, I don't know what I would've done. He saved me and helped me back to the room," I replied.

"I'm glad Juan was there," Josefina said as she patted my arm. "How did he handle it?" She looked at me intently, probably wondering if Juan had gotten into a physical fight.

"He didn't punch Thomas or anything like that," I said to quiet her fears. "Juan just stepped in and led me away." Memories of the sticky punch dripping off of me made me shiver.

Josefina rose from the bed and walked over to the closet. She sifted through the clothes until she found my ruined blue dress. Josefina held it out and inspected the damage.

"Can't anything be done about it?" she asked glancing at the red splotches.

"No, Lena already tried to get it clean. She said a permanent charm must have been added to the punch," I replied.

"You met Lena?" Josefina asked as surprise lit up her face.

"Yes," I said cautiously. "She was very nice to me."

"Isn't Lena great? She's such a good person. I can't believe Juan isn't trying to court her. Miguel and I keep trying to talk him into it."

"They aren't courting?" I asked confused. "They sure looked like they belonged together."

"No, but I know for a fact that she is crazy about him. It would be wonderful if Lena would become my sister-in-law. I think Juan needs to wake up and realize they're made for each other," Josefina said.

"I'm grateful for Juan and Lena," I said.

Josefina moved closer to me and gave me another comforting hug. "I'm so sorry. The time when you needed me, I wasn't there. I wish I could've been. I would've given anything to be there for you."

"It's okay," I said, gazing over her shoulder. Even as I said the words, I felt my chest tighten. I knew more tears were coming so I moved from Josefina's embrace and turned in my bed to face the wall. "I'm glad you're back. I'm sorry Josefina, but I'm really tired. I think I'm going to try to get some sleep now."

Josefina didn't get up from my bed, but as I laid there facing the wall, I felt her patting my shoulder as I drifted off to sleep.

By Monday morning, my mood hadn't improved. Even though I wished I didn't have to get up, I hauled myself out of bed and got dressed for breakfast. Miguel gave me a sympathetic look when he saw me. Josefina must have told him about everything using their telepathy. Lena smiled and waved as I sat down, and I weakly smiled back. I just wanted to put my head down and disappear. Mostly everyone in the dining hall had seen what had happened on Saturday, and I didn't feel like being gawked at.

"It'll be okay," Josefina said, laying a hand on my shoulder as she sat down next to me.

I continued to look down and slowly eat my food when a loud noise caught my attention. Looking up, I watched as Betty Ann walked into the dining hall with Thomas, a few of her friends, and Adam. They were laughing loudly at something. I tried to slide down in my seat but hiding under the table wouldn't have stopped me from hearing what they were saying.

"I can't believe you dumped that punch on her."

"Yes, she had no idea what was about to happen. The teachers don't even know what went on. The other diversion worked nicely. No teacher was present when you taught her a little lesson," someone cackled.

"I bet she couldn't get the stain out of it. Her dress has to be completely ruined! It's probably the only nice outfit she owns," Betty Ann laughed evilly.

I couldn't take anymore. I picked up my tray and dropped it off where the dirty dishes were supposed to go, before heading out of the dining hall. Loud bouts of laughter followed me as I headed back to my room to collect my morning textbooks. I dreaded the thought of being in class with Betty Ann.

I was the first student to enter Gemstones 101. Mrs. Rowley gave me a quizzical look because normally I'd arrive with the twins.

"Good morning, Jane," Mrs. Rowley said. "Is everything okay?"

I bit back tears and nodded my head. I didn't want anybody to see me cry, and I didn't want to be pitied.

"Are you sure?" Mrs. Rowley asked with concern. "I want my students to be able to come and talk to me about their problems."

"No, Mrs. Rowley, I'm fine," I told her.

Sooner than I expected, Josefina and Miguel arrived. Once Mrs. Rowley saw that my friends had taken seats next to me, she continued into the lesson and didn't ask again. My morning progressed rather easily despite the fact that Betty Ann was in two of my classes. She made snide remarks under her breath, but Josefina just kept telling me to ignore her.

"Pretend you aren't upset. She'll leave you alone," Josefina whispered in my ear.

Lunch was about the same as breakfast. When Betty Ann arrived in the dining hall, Josefina and Miguel tried to distract me as much as possible. Juan and Lena even sat closer to us. When lunch was over, Lena offered to walk Josefina and me back to our room to get our books for the second half of the day.

As we began to leave the dining hall, Thomas stood up and strolled over.

"Do you have a royal guard now?" He laughed, thinking he was being funny.

"Go away, Thomas. You've hurt Jane enough," Juan said coming to my rescue again.

"What's your family's obsession with the human? Maybe you should mind your own business," Thomas retorted.

"Maybe you should mind yours because Jane is none of your business," Juan replied.

"You are human lovers all around. Why don't you go and marry a human? Then you can have half breeds whose magic ability will be below standard," Thomas gloated.

"That's not true," Josefina burst out. "Jane's ability is better than all of your awful friends combined."

"Careful, Miss Martinez. Your brother has already interfered where he didn't belong, and I promised him that was a mistake. I don't think you should involve yourself either."

Josefina mumbled something under her breath and then, very unladylike, she lunged at Thomas. Juan grabbed her before she could get close, but Thomas just laughed in her face. A teacher, Mr. Withermyer by the looks of it, was strolling our way.

"What's going on over here?" he asked looking straight at me. "This better not be the beginning of a fight."

"I was just standing here, trying to talk to Miss Fitzgerald, when Miss Martinez got hostile," Thomas said.

Mr. Withermyer's cold green eyes looked at me again. Juan stepped between Mr. Withermyer and me. "It won't happen again, sir," Juan said.

"Let's see to that. I would teach your younger siblings how to behave, Mr. Martinez. It would be highly improper if they can't act like a young lady and a gentleman. Miss Fitzgerald, I wouldn't start any trouble if you value your education here. I'm sure the pixie government wouldn't be thrilled to know you are starting fights. You three…" he said pointing to Josefina, Miguel, and me. "Don't be late for my class."

Mr. Withermyer stalked back into the dining hall. "You should've let her go," Thomas whispered. "That would've been fun." He left the dining hall snickering to himself.

Juan glanced after him before he turned to us. "You better get your school supplies and hurry off to Charms. You don't need any more trouble with Mr. Withermyer. Josefina, please don't act like that ever again. We all have started at the Jelf Academy and should no longer act like children. It is highly improper for a lady to act as such."

Josefina mumbled an apology to Juan before we ran to our room to collect our books. We actually made it to the room before Mr. Withermyer. Feeling as if I had accomplished something, I rested against the wall outside his classroom and waited for Mr. Withermyer to return from lunch duty. It didn't take long for him to come around the corner, his black jacket billowing out behind him.

"What are you two doing down here?" he asked his lip rising in a sneer.

"We are waiting for class, sir. You told us to get here on time," Josefina replied.

"You shouldn't be loitering in the hallways. This is the second time I catch you up to no good. Don't let there be a third time today, Miss Fitzgerald." He wasn't joking. "Don't get smart with me either, Miss Martinez."

Mr. Withermyer opened the door and entered the classroom while Josefina and I just looked at each other. Why did Mr. Withermyer always assume we were doing something wrong? Josefina and I went to our seats and prepared our table for class. Mr. Withermyer didn't look at us again, but we could feel the tension in the room. I pulled my rock case from my bag and set it on my desk, ready for anything Mr. Withermyer was going to throw at us.

Every student who entered the classroom immediately fell silent. Mr. Withermyer hated conversation in his classroom and a violation of this rule led to severe punishment. He wrote on the board what we would be doing today. The agenda was taking notes on the magical theory of the next charm we would be learning. I didn't even mind the notes today because I wouldn't have been able to concentrate on making a complex charm. I began to settle in when all of a sudden, something slapped me in the back. I cried out in pain and glanced over my shoulder to find Betty Ann smirking.

"Is there a problem, Miss Fitzgerald?" Mr. Withermyer asked as he gave me a dark look.

"No," I said, but I knew Betty Ann had thrown something at me and levitated it back to herself.

"Well, please be quiet. I don't need interruptions in my classroom," Mr. Withermyer shot back at me.

I shook off my anger and focused on the notes. About fifteen minutes later, I felt a sharp pain on my back again. I gripped the table to stop myself from letting out a wail of agony. Josefina looked over with a questioning glance, but of course, I couldn't tell her. Was Betty Ann just going to keep torturing me? Just a few minutes after the thought crossed my mind, I felt the pain again. Unfortunately, a sound escaped my lips.

"What is the problem, Miss Fitzgerald? This is the second time you've interrupted my class. Would you like to enlighten us on what is going on?"

Tired of Betty Ann's abuse, I stood up feeling braver. I would tell the truth, and I wouldn't let Betty Ann walk all over me anymore.

"Yes, I would like to enlighten you!" I said glaring at him. "Since the beginning of class, Miss Barber has been throwing something at me."

"Prove it!" Betty Ann chimed in.

"You are sitting directly behind me, and I can prove it with the red marks that are probably on my back," I retorted.

"That is enough, Miss Fitzgerald," Mr. Withermyer yelled. "This is the third time you have caused a distraction today in my presence. Get out of my classroom and go to Dr. Tweedle's office. I'll send him a memo about your behavior."

I picked up my books and glanced at Josefina. She looked so angry, and I gave her a warning with my eyes. Then, I stalked out of Mr. Withermyer's room. I was madder than I have ever been in my entire life. No other teacher would have dismissed me from their classroom for something like that. Why did Mr. Withermyer hate me so much?

I headed toward Dr. Tweedle's office and knocked on the door.

"You may enter, Jane," his voice called from within. Not waiting for an invitation, I sat down on the pillowed sofa across from Dr. Tweedle's desk. I was so aggravated I forgot common courtesy.

"Hello, Jane. You know, if your stepmother Marie could see how you walked in here, she would frown upon your etiquette lessons," Dr. Tweedle said, but he smiled at me. "To what pleasure do I owe this visit?"

Dr. Tweedle stopped talking as a folded piece of paper flew onto his desk and landed. It was probably the note that Mr. Withermyer had promised to write.

Dr. Tweedle unfolded the letter. His eyes scanned over the page, and he smiled a little as he got to the bottom, but when he looked up at me, he instantly looked serious. "Mr. Withermyer just sent me a notice about some behavior of yours. He said you had a conflict at lunch with Mr. Thomas Whitmore, disturbed the peace, and interrupted his lecture, and he found you loitering outside his classroom. As you know, I'm supposed to be keeping an eye on you, and I'm hoping I won't have to add anything concerning to your report. I don't know how accurate the severities of these accusations are, but I am hoping you can explain." Dr. Tweedle laid down the memo and gazed intently at me.

Where did I begin? For me to be able to thoroughly explain the confrontation at lunch, I would have to give the details of Saturday's dance, and I didn't want to go through that pain again.

"Jane, the only way to sort out this situation is for you to explain yourself. Why don't you start with the lunch incident with Mr. Whitmore?"

I couldn't help myself, but against my better judgment, I broke out in tears. Fresh pain racked my body as I thought of what had been done to me and Thomas's continuing threats. In addition, I didn't want any of this to affect my attendance at the Jelf Academy. It would break me to be expelled.

"Jane, what's wrong? Whatever it is, you can tell me," Dr. Tweedle said.

"Thomas Whitmore was the boy who asked me to the Harvest Festival on Saturday. We were having a wonderful time until Miss Barber levitated the punch bowl and sent it crashing down on me. My dress is ruined, and nothing can be done to fix it. Miss Barber does not like me, and Mr. Whitmore only invited me to the dance to make fun of me. After the physical assault, they continued to verbally harass me until Mr. Martinez stopped them and helped me leave the dining hall.

"The conflict at lunch today started when Mr. Whitmore approached me to continue the verbal insults. Mr. Withermyer happened to notice an argument so he came over to prevent it, but believe me, Dr. Tweedle, there would not have been a fight," I told him as I wiped my tear-stained face.

"How did this happen? Not one staff member reported this incident to me. I'm not saying it didn't happen, but I'm wondering when it happened," Dr. Tweedle replied.

"I don't know, but I overheard Miss Barber's friends speaking about some kind of diversion. I have my dress as evidence, and I have witnesses. Please, I don't want to be expelled from the Jelf Academy. I will do anything," I sobbed.

"I believe you, Jane. Why don't we clear up these other matters before I take care of Saturday night's actions," Dr. Tweedle suggested.

"After Mr. Withermyer approached me at lunch, he instructed Miss Martinez and me to make it to his classroom on time. We collected our materials and were early, to which he said we were loitering and causing trouble. I can assure you, sir that Miss Martinez and I were calmly standing in the hall. I don't see how we can be punished for arriving at the classroom early," I continued.

"Yes, I certainly agree. What happened next?"

"During the Charms lesson, I felt something hit me from behind. It felt like someone was cracking a whip against my flesh," I explained. "It was so painful that I uttered a cry, and when I turned around to see what was causing me such pain, I found Miss Barber sitting directly behind me. She smiled at me, Dr. Tweedle, like she knew exactly what was hurting me. When Mr. Withermyer asked me to explain, I told him the truth and he sent me here."

I leaned back into the sofa upon finishing my story and waited for Dr. Tweedle's response. He looked at the letter from Mr. Withermyer and then back to me as if contemplating what to say. I was terrified as I waited for him to speak. Would this trouble be enough to dismiss me from the Jelf Academy forever? Finally, he took a deep breath and began.

"About Saturday evening, I will have Miss Barber and Mr. Whitmore come to my office for questioning. I would like to hear their account of the evening as well. Also, I would like to see your dress. I'll try my best to repair it if it's possible. I choose to disregard the fact that you arrived early for Mr. Withermyer's lesson. Nothing appears to be wrong with that. I'll speak with Mr. Withermyer. Now head off to your next class and I will get this all sorted out. Bring your dress to me before dinner."

Dr. Tweedle wrote me a pass to Earth Catastrophes, and I left his office feeling much better than I had all day. I hoped he would fix the situation. Once he saw proof that I wasn't lying, everything would be okay.

When I arrived at Earth Catastrophes, Josefina gave me a look that meant she wanted to know what had happened. I gave her a subtle smile, but I knew it wouldn't be reassuring enough. As soon as class was over, I knew she would jump on me for details. Mr. Laruse lectured on the weather again, but I couldn't completely focus on the lesson. Mr. Laruse wasn't the best teacher. Some students couldn't even predict a day-to-day forecast, but at least I had accomplished that and was now working on a monthly forecast. He knew his subject, but his explanations didn't quite reach us.

Sure enough, when the class had ended, Josefina bombarded me with questions about what had happened in Dr. Tweedle's office.

"Are you in trouble? Did you explain that Mr. Withermyer is just being mean? Did you tell him about the dance? You're not being expelled, are you?"

"Calm down! I'll tell you everything," I replied, and while we walked to Zodiac Signs, I explained as much as I could before class started. Then an hour later, I continued my story all the way up to our room.

"Dr. Tweedle is going to call Betty Ann to his office to question her, and he wants me to bring my dress before dinner. I better go down to his office now."

I took my ruined dress from the closet and headed down to Dr. Tweedle's office. I hoped that when he saw my dress, he would know Betty Ann was causing trouble for me. Lena had said nothing could be done to fix it, but Dr. Tweedle was a very powerful pixie. Maybe he had something up his sleeve to repair the damage.

I hugged the dress to me as tears filled my eyes again. Betty Ann had been right when she said this dress was the nicest thing I owned. The hall outside Dr. Tweedle's office was empty, and I took a moment to stop crying. I didn't want to cry in front of anyone again. Raising my head and straightening my shoulders, I took a step toward the door but stopped short when I heard loud voices. I paused startled as I realized they were coming from the office.

I was about to turn around and go back to my room when I recognized the two voices speaking. Mr. Withermyer and Dr. Tweedle sounded as if they were arguing. I froze in the hall and couldn't help but listen.

"The girl is bad news, Oliver. You should just expel her and be done with it," Mr. Withermyer shouted.

"What makes you think that? She has done nothing wrong. I believe she is telling me the truth!"

I inched a little closer, so I could hear better. They seemed to be arguing about me.

"She is deceitful and only wants to get others in trouble. How could you believe her? I can see right through her innocent acts!"

"I still believe Miss Fitzgerald is not lying. She has no reason to. I've seen the people she is living with. She wouldn't want to ruin her education here."

I gulped at the sound of my name. What had I done to make Mr. Withermyer think this? I knew Mr. Withermyer hated me. Sure, he treated everyone with distaste, but it was the way he looked and acted toward me. What had I done to deserve such hatred?

"Oliver, she is just looking for attention. Why can't you see that? She is playing a part for sympathy so we will all forget that she is a half-human. I will not be fooled, Oliver! She should never have been allowed to attend in the first place!"

"Phillip, I do not like discrimination in my school. Though marrying a human is against the law, what's done is done. We cannot change that. Miss Fitzgerald was born. She has been accepted at this school until she proves otherwise. Ever since she was an infant, she has had an uncanny ability. Even you cannot deny that. Surely you have seen her participation in class and if not, you had to have heard your colleagues speaking about her work. That is why I fought with the pixie government to allow her to attend," Dr. Tweedle said defending me.

"She is not her mother!" Mr. Withermyer burst out, and I jumped.

Dr. Tweedle was silent for a long second. At first, I didn't think he was going to reply, but his next words were surprisingly calm and low. I had to strain my ears to make out what he was saying.

"So, this is what it all comes down to; Rachel McCalski. I should've known. In fact, I should've known all along when Miss Fitzgerald first came to my office. I should've expected, if not anticipated, this conversation with you. It's in the past, Phillip, let it go. Rachel chose her life, now get on with yours."

It got surprisingly quiet in the office, but I could tell they were still talking. It was so low that I couldn't hear, and I didn't want to chance moving closer. What did Mr. Withermyer have to do with my mother? I was so confused and disturbed by their commentary. Did Mr. Withermyer know my mother?

I stood still in the empty hallway clutching my dress, pondering on what I had heard. I was so lost in thought that I didn't even hear the office door open. Before I knew it, I was face to face with Mr. Withermyer. I was so startled I almost dropped my dress. Mr. Withermyer cast his green eyes on me and for a second, he seemed just as startled, almost as if he had seen a ghost, but he gained his composure faster than I had.

"Loitering in the halls again, Miss Fitzgerald?" he asked nastily.

"Dr. Tweedle requested an audience with me before dinner."

"Don't let me catch you sneaking through these halls again or I'll deal out my own form of punishment." Mr. Withermyer swept past me. He mumbled something under his breath, but I couldn't make out what he was saying before he disappeared around the corner. Even though Mr. Withermyer was not my favorite teacher, I still longed for acceptance. I couldn't understand why I was disliked and what my mother had to do with Mr. Withermyer. Despite my new forming hatred of Mr. Withermyer, I couldn't help feeling hurt by his comments. Would I ever be fully accepted anywhere?

12

PALM READING
AND PUNISHMENT

D R. TWEEDLE EXAMINED my dress and confirmed that a permanent charm had been used. I was afraid to walk into his office after Mr. Withermyer had come out, knowing that I had been right outside the door eavesdropping. He didn't say anything, but I had my suspicions that he knew. Dr. Tweedle had called Thomas, Betty Ann, and Adam, into his office to question them about what had happened. Thomas and Betty Ann received detention, but Adam was considered a third party, not involved, so he went unpunished.

Betty Ann harassed me more than ever, but I kept my mouth shut during her insults. It was better to be the smarter person and ignore her. My only concerns were on my schoolwork and chores for Marie.

Winter had come at last, and a thick layer of snow coated the grounds of the Jelf Academy. Christmas break was on the horizon along with the midterms. I had much to study, and I was very nervous about the tests. As if that wasn't stressful enough, Marie had big plans for Christmas, including a winter ball. So much preparation needed to be done, and I dreaded going to the manor as much as I dreaded taking the tests.

"I wish you could come to our house for Christmas break. Mother always throws delightful parties this time of year," Josefina exclaimed.

"You know that's impossible," I said. "Marie would never allow it." I looked glumly down at the dining table.

"I know, but it's nice to dream sometimes," Josefina replied as we cleaned up the remnants of our breakfast and headed off to Gemstones 101.

"Sometimes it's worse when you dream about things you know you can't have," Miguel pointed out.

Josefina shrugged him off and took her seat in Mrs. Rowley's classroom.

Today, Mrs. Rowley was going over the happy charm again to be sure we could perfect it before midterms. Everyone took out their pixie dust cases and extracted one cup of diamonds. This was one of the easier charms in terms of ingredients, but difficult because the diamonds had to be crushed into a fine powder. We had learned that diamonds were the hardest mineral. I found it ironic that the happy charm took so much energy to make. Thankfully, we got to use our happy charms after they were made.

"I just can't believe you have to work over Christmas break," Josefina frowned.

"Don't worry about me. I'll have happy charms and quick complete charms on hand at all times." I flashed Josefina a smile, trying to hide my agony from her. I knew she would worry about me and wouldn't enjoy Christmas if she saw what I was hiding.

It was going to be another boring, stressful day with more talk of midterms and studying. In addition, seeing Betty Ann was never a plus and just added to my already stressful life.

"Look who it is!" Betty Ann exclaimed as Josefina, Miguel, and

I walked into Predicting the Future. "A dirty half-breed and her half-breed loving entourage."

I ignored her comment and sat down, waiting for class to start.

Ms. Crescent glided into the room with her big earrings jingled in her ears, and a bright orange bandana on her head. She took her place on the stool in the middle of the room.

"Today, class, I'll be reading each of your palms in my office as a final review of how it should be done. For midterms, you will be reading my palm and the tarots. Depending on how close you are to what I see in my future will determine your grade. I'll call you one by one into my office. Henry Adams, I'll start with you."

A scared-looking boy, whom I never interacted with, walked toward Ms. Crescent. His brown hair stood up at different angles like it hadn't seen a brush in days. His knees visibly knocked together, and I thought he would fall on his way into the office. As soon as he disappeared with Ms. Crescent, Betty Ann began her banter.

"Poor Henry Adams. I hope he doesn't wet himself when he learns of his future. What if she tells him that his precious new puppy is going to die? I hope Ms. Crescent's prepared if he loses the contents of his stomach while in her office," she snickered nastily.

After a few minutes, Henry came out looking whiter than when he went in.

"Betty Ann Barber," Ms. Crescent called. Betty Ann jumped up from her seat and headed toward the office with a smile. She didn't look nervous like everyone else.

"I know what my future holds," she murmured as she disappeared into the depths of the office.

The rest of us sat waiting in anticipation for our names to be called. What exactly did my near future hold? I didn't think I could handle more bad news in my life. Josefina and I continued to exchange glances, each of us with nothing to say. After Betty Ann's exit, the room had fallen completely silent. I was left to my thoughts, which were suddenly interrupted by the calling of my name.

"Jane Fitzgerald", broke the harsh silence, and I stood from my chair. Josefina gave me a reassuring smile as I made my way across the room toward Ms. Crescent's office. Incense stung my nose as soon as I walked in, a strong spicy scent that made me want to cough. I held my breath as I moved through the beaded curtains. Unlike the usual office, Ms. Crescent didn't have a desk. She sat cross-legged on a satin pillow in the middle of the room with another pillow positioned in front of her.

"Come, Miss Fitzgerald. Take a seat and get comfortable. Let the calming scents wash over you and relax all your muscles. Do not fear the future. Embrace it," she said in her soft whispery voice.

I sat on the pillow across from her and crossed my legs in imitation of hers. Relaxing my shoulders, I placed my palms face up in my lap in anticipation of her analysis.

"Relax child and give me your hands."

I held out my hands to Ms. Crescent almost like a sacrifice, hoping they wouldn't shake too much.

"Hmm, a strong lifeline. Your past has made you this way. I can tell right here from your hand. This strength will help you in the future. Now let's see what else we have here. A proposal is at hand!" Ms. Crescent exclaimed excitedly.

"A proposal?" I asked questioningly. What was she talking about?

"Do whatever you can to stop this union from joining. Your future will be very dark if the two unite."

"I'm sorry. I don't know what you're talking about. What proposal? What union? What two are you talking about?" I asked.

Ms. Crescent refused to answer my questions as she continued gazing at my opened palm.

"Hush, child. Only you have the key to your future. Use this information wisely."

She continued looking at my palm, and I had a faint urge to snatch it away from her.

"This dreadful event will occur in the near future in a place far from this school. Stop it or it will become a danger to your life."

Now I was even more confused. A union between two people was supposed to occur, at an unknown location, and I had to stop it because my future depended on it? It sounded quite ridiculous to me. Either this information was false, or I needed to spend some more time studying.

"You will become close with someone who in the past you did not speak to often. When you are warned about this person, you must heed the giver's advice. Do not ignore this information!" Ms. Crescent said as she dropped my palm. "That was a fairly good reading, Miss Fitzgerald. Have a good day."

I slowly got up from the pillow, perplexed by the information I had heard. What exactly had she meant?

I left the perfume-scented room through the beaded curtains. Josefina gave me a questioning look as I left the room, and I just shook my head. Ms. Crescent's prediction didn't make any sense to me, so I decided to forget about it and concentrate on studying.

After packing my bag for History of Pixies, I left my room early and headed toward the classroom. When I entered, the room was empty, and I took a seat pulling out my notebook to study. It wasn't long before I was interrupted. Surprisingly, Betty Ann strolled into the room. I was shocked because she was usually late. Betty Ann gave a jolt when she saw me, but it lasted a second as she replaced it with her smug smile.

"Well, I should've known you were here. The hallway reeked of your dirty human blood."

"I wish Ms. Crescent would have predicted this," I commented not even looking up at her.

"I'd watch that smart mouth if I were you. Don't you remember what happened the last time? Maybe Ms. Crescent should have reminded you of your past. I dare say that punch made your dress rather spectacular," Betty Ann sneered.

I wanted to leap from my seat and wipe that disgusting look off her face, but I contained myself. I decided to ignore her in the hope she would tire of her insults.

"That was one of the finest things in your closet, wasn't it? It was probably the nicest thing you ever owned. Wonder what your mother would have said about it? Then again, she didn't have any taste. She ran off with your father, after all?" Betty Ann spat.

"You didn't know either of them. How dare you speak of them!" I said losing my temper and standing up.

"My father told me all about your parents. Rachel McCalski was the golden student. No one could've predicted she would sink so low. Apparently, she didn't mind tainted blood because she went and had you before she was killed for her stupidity!"

"You have no right to judge my family or verbally insult me!" I shouted losing control.

I felt a strange pressure building up in the back of my head. It felt like a headache was about to come on. The pain was so intense that I wanted to double over, but I would never give Betty Ann that kind of satisfaction. If I could only relax, maybe the pain would go away. The moment I tried to relax the tension, I felt a gust of wind blow by me going straight for Betty Ann. Her eyes widened as she was knocked to the ground. How had I done that? I stood in shock, unsure of what to do.

"Betty Ann, are you alright?" I asked from where I stood too afraid to move closer. "I didn't mean to."

Betty Ann rose from the floor; her brown hair had fallen in her face. Her eyes narrowed, and she gave me the cruelest look as she reached into her pocket pulling out a handful of pixie dust. She threw it at me laughing. The red dust exploded and everything it touched burst into flame. She had cast a fire charm that surrounded me, blocking my exit from the room. A malicious grin spread across her face as she gazed at me through the ring of fire.

"Hope it doesn't get too hot in there. I'll see you later... or maybe not," Betty Ann said as she left the room, leaving me trapped.

What could I do? I hadn't learned a fountain charm to put out the fire. That was a second-year charm. Don't panic, I told myself, but it seemed that the fire was inching closer with each second. Tongues of flame licked at my ankles, and I grabbed my bag and climbed atop a desk. Maybe I could jump over the ring, but that seemed impossible when I realized the height of the flame. Panic set in as a startling truth settled in my head. I could die here. Why hadn't Ms. Crescent predicted this? This was more dangerous than some proposal!

The fire had reached the base of the desk. I screamed for help at the top of my lungs. Please let someone hear me, I silently prayed. Smoke began to cloud the room, and I coughed while I continued to yell. Desperation made me consider walking through the fire and chancing third-degree burns. My cries became weaker after I saw no hope of getting out. Then, my heart fluttered with relief when Mr. Collyworth breezed into the room. In my panic, I had forgotten about History of Pixies class. He looked startled to find me on a desk surrounded by a ring of fire.

"What is going on in here, Miss Fitzgerald?" he asked.

I noticed students piling up near the door. I picked Josefina's face out of the crowd. She looked terrified, and she was trying to push through to get into the room. Mr. Collyworth was frantically searching through his desk, looking completely frazzled. I hoped he would hurry up. The flames were slowly inching closer.

"Please, help me! Hurry!" I wheezed as I coughed over the smoke.

Finally, he found his pixie dust case and opened it to find the charm he needed. Mr. Collyworth threw large amounts of blue pixie dust on the fire that turned into water instantly before my eyes. Sweat poured down his face as he tried to quickly subdue the flames. When he had finished using the fountain charm to put out the blaze, I almost collapsed off the charred desk, my entire body shaking.

Mr. Collyworth rounded on me, his gray hair sticking up.

"What were you doing? You could have been killed. Fire charms should not be messed with. You should know that, Miss Fitzgerald. I am disappointed with you," he accused.

"I didn't cast the fire charm!" I exclaimed as the class pushed into the room.

Mr. Collyworth ignored my statement as he went around the room sprinkling another charm on the brunt objects, repairing the damage instantly. After he was finished, the class filed in, and Mr. Collyworth motioned me to his desk.

"I didn't do it!" I reinstated as I tried to stop my voice from shaking.

"You were the only one in the room! Who else could have done it?"

"It was Miss Barber!" I exclaimed. "She was the one who threw the fire charm at me!"

"That's impossible. Miss Barber got sick after her last class, and she has been confined to her room. I received a memo stating that she was ill, so I knew she wouldn't be in class. I don't know what you're playing at, Miss Fitzgerald, but I'm going to have to send you to Dr. Tweedle."

He bent over his desk and filled out a note, which he folded and then charmed to fly to Dr. Tweedle's office. I looked down at his desk in frustration. I was telling the truth, but I guess no one would believe someone like me.

I left the room as instructed and headed for Dr. Tweedle's office. What would he say about this? Would he believe me? How could I prove that it wasn't my fault?

When I arrived at the office, I knocked and was told to enter. "Hello, Jane. I want to say it's good to see you, but somehow, I just don't think that would fit in this situation. I just received a note from Mr. Collyworth stating that you cast a fire charm in the classroom, which nearly burned everything. Care to explain?" Dr. Tweedle asked as he leaned back in his chair.

I took a seat on the blue sofa and took a deep breath. "Would you believe me if I told you that it wasn't me? I was nearly killed by the charm. You know that I wouldn't cast something like that in a classroom without supervision," I stated.

"Well, who is responsible for this?" Dr. Tweedle said seriously.

"It was Miss Barber. She came into the classroom and started insulting my parents. I became angry with her, and I couldn't control my emotions. I've never felt anything like it before, but somehow, I sent a burst of energy in her direction. It just happened. I tried to explain that it was an accident, but she threw a fire charm at me," I explained.

"Were you aware that Miss Barber fell ill after one of her classes and has been in her room since? This incident is too severe for me to brush under the rug. Are you aware how close you are to being expelled?" he asked.

"Mr. Collyworth implied something like that, but I swear to you, sir, I didn't do it. This school is so important to me. I would never do something like this. I know how much the government would like to see me gone." I looked into Dr. Tweedle's eyes, hoping more than anything that he would believe me.

"Maybe I'm just an old fool and you are manipulating me, but I believe you didn't cast that charm. However, I don't have any evidence that Miss Barber did other than your word. She already has an alibi and no matter what you tell me, others will believe her roommate. I cannot let this act go unpunished, so I hope you will forgive me. If I do nothing, Mr. Collyworth and other teachers will question me. Many already believe I've shown you too much favoritism. I'm very fond of you, Jane, but I cannot treat you any different from the other students, especially with your situation. My hands are tied, so I'm asking you to understand."

"Yes, Dr. Tweedle. I understand," I said hanging my head. "Just please don't expel me from the Jelf Academy forever. This school is all I have."

"I know it is not fair to you, Jane. You've already been through so much. I really hate to do this to you, but I've decided that you will take your midterms at the end of this week. Then, you will be sent home early for Christmas break," he announced.

I looked up with horror. I swallowed the lump in my throat and shook my head back and forth. "Please, Dr. Tweedle, I'll do a hundred detentions. Please don't send me back early!" I pleaded. My stomach lurched at the thought of an extra week with Marie.

"The casting of a fire charm is serious business. The only choices I have is to either send you home early or expel you," Dr. Tweedle explained.

My heart raced wildly at the possibility of the other option. "Alright sir, I see the predicament you're in. I will prepare for my midterms at the end of this week. Then, I will pack my things to start my holiday early," I replied.

"The other teachers will understand my decision since I have explained your home situation. Keep your chin up. You should continue to class since you'll have less time to study for the exams. I feel so awful for putting you through this, but I have no other option. As always, I will escort you away from the school after your midterms are completed. I will still have to report something to the government officials, but I will do my best at pleading your case"

"Yes, sir," I replied as I stood to exit his office. "Thank you for believing me," I said, as I closed the door behind me.

⁓

By the end of the week, I was packed and ready to start my punishment. Josefina was upset that I hadn't been treated fairly. On my last day, I was shown into an empty classroom where I took all my midterms. After I had completed all the tests, I went back up to my room to collect my belongings. Josefina was sitting on her bed when I walked in.

"How were the midterms?" she asked, leaning on her pillows. Her brown eyes stared intently at me.

"Difficult to handle all at once," I replied. While I spoke, I picked up my small bag. I needed to meet Dr. Tweedle before dinner, so I had to be ready to leave.

"Do you think you did well?" she asked as she sat up.

"Hopefully," I said.

"Jane, I'm sorry that you have to leave early," Josefina started.

"Such is my life," I responded. "Don't worry about me."

Josefina got up from her bed and threw her shoes on. "Are you ready to go?" she asked.

All I could manage was a nod.

We exited our room and headed down to the great hall. Miguel was waiting for us in the entrance hall.

Before I knew it, Dr. Tweedle had appeared at the top of the stairs and began descending toward us. I hugged Josefina and Miguel while I tried not to cry. I hoped I would see my friends and the Jelf Academy again.

Dr. Tweedle stared at me with a somber face before he opened the grand front doors. We made our way across the snow-covered garden to the edge of the clouds, a starry night above us. A cold sensation came over my feet as I bounced to the descending cloud in the distance.

"I'm really sorry to do this to you, Jane," Dr. Tweedle said breaking the silence. "This is the only alternative I had."

"I know," I mumbled while I looked at the ground.

We boarded the moving cloud, and I prepared myself for the drop to the bottom. Dr. Tweedle glanced at me with sad eyes, but I didn't trust myself to look at him fully. I didn't want to burst into tears. It would be embarrassing if I were to cry in front of him again. Waiting at the bottom was Dr. Tweedle's carriage. I placed my small bag in the back and Dr. Tweedle helped me to climb aboard. Once Dr. Tweedle was sitting next to me, he held out his hand which I grasped along with the side of the carriage.

I thought about the manor house as Dr. Tweedle cast the pixie dust. I shuddered as I thought of what I was headed towards. The next few weeks would not be pleasant. Marie would do everything in her power to make sure I suffered.

When the dust cleared, I looked out on the dark gate at the end of the drive. Gray clouds hung in the sky, and I took them as an omen. The gate swung open, and Dr. Tweedle steered the horses up the lane. Snow began to fall as we came up the drive. The snow was thick and wet, more to the consistency of sleet. It pelted the windows of the carriage and I shivered.

Dr. Tweedle cleared his throat and I turned to look at him. "Jane, I wasn't going to mention the trouble you are in and explain to Marie that this is the start of your Christmas break," Dr. Tweedle said.

"Thank you for not mentioning it to her," I replied as I lowered my head.

"Instead, I'll tell her that you're one of the brightest students, and I decided to reward you by exempting you from exams allowing you to return home early," Dr. Tweedle explained. "Hopefully after Marie hears of your wonderful progress, she won't be so hard on you."

"I doubt Marie would ever be that nice to me," I answered truthfully. "At least she won't treat me any worse since she won't know the real reason."

Dr. Tweedle stopped the carriage at the manor's front steps. He hopped out and held out his hand to help me down. We ran through the snow to the front door. The house towered over me, and I felt small and cornered between the imposing house and the torrent of sleet. Dr. Tweedle knocked with the brass knocker. I shuddered from the cold snow on my back and the anticipation of

Marie opening the door. Faster than I had time to prepare myself, the door swung opened, and Marie stood in the doorway. Her gray eyes pierced right through me, and I was tempted to run out into the storm. She coldly glared at Dr. Tweedle before her eyes shifted back to me.

"What a pleasant surprise, Jane," she said in a sickeningly sweet voice. "I wasn't expecting you tonight," she said turning to Dr. Tweedle. I could tell from the look in her eye that she was uncomfortable. Dr. Tweedle entered before me and while his back was turned Marie grabbed my arm and forcefully pulled me into the house with an evil glare. I almost tripped over the doorframe and struggled to regain my balance.

"We should discuss why you are here so early in my office," Marie said pronouncing the sentence with authority. She let go of me and walked toward my father's office, her back stiff.

The room was barely lit by the one lamp on the desk and the red curtains were drawn against the stormy night. Marie walked around the desk and sat in my father's red velvet chair.

"Have a seat," she said motioning to Dr. Tweedle, but I stood in the corner.

"I'd like to discuss the matters of why Jane was dismissed early," Dr. Tweedle started.

"Jane had better not have misbehaved. I don't want to be told her attendance at your school is a waste of time. It was out of the goodness of my heart that I let her attend. I won't hesitate to take it away," Marie sneered.

"No, nothing like that," Dr. Tweedle started. "Jane has excelled wonderfully at the Jelf Academy, and my staff is proud of her accomplishments. I decided to reward her by allowing her to go home early for her holiday break. You should be very proud to have Jane as a stepdaughter," Dr. Tweedle smiled. I knew he had said it just to spite her.

Marie looked unsure of what to say, and she looked even more uncomfortable. "Well, this is a wonderful surprise. I'll need as much help as I can get for my upcoming Christmas party. I'm glad she was returned early," Marie said as if I were only a helpful piece of property.

Dr. Tweedle flinched as if he still didn't believe or understand a person could be so cruel. Was he still searching for some good in Marie? I was sure none existed.

"Now if you could excuse us. We have much to discuss. I'm sure you're intelligent enough to find your way to the front door," Marie said rudely dismissing Dr. Tweedle. Instead of commenting on her rudeness, Dr. Tweedle rose from his seat and turned to the door.

"I shall return for you on New Year's Eve if everything is well. Goodbye Jane, I'm sorry I…"

"Goodbye, sir," Marie said cutting him off. Dr. Tweedle looked at me sadly and shook his head as he left. When the door to the office was closed, Marie turned to face me.

"I can't complain that you've arrived home early. There's so much to be done to prepare for my Christmas ball. Since you haven't been around much because of that school, I know exactly what I'll have you do. I think you'll be taking on the balk of the cleaning. It's been so long since you worked for a whole week here. I have been extremely nice letting you go to the school, haven't I, Jane?" Marie asked while she glared at me from across the desk.

I didn't know if she wanted an answer or if it was a rhetorical question. I hung my head to avoid her death stare. "Haven't I, Jane?" she asked in a loud voice.

"Yes, ma'am," I replied softly.

"What did you say, Jane?" she asked oddly calm after she had been shouting.

"I said, yes, ma'am," I spoke up.

"Yes, what?" she asked. I didn't know what she was getting at, but she always played these mind games with me.

"Yes, you are extremely nice for letting me attend the Jelf Academy," I recited.

"That's right, and you will keep to your promise. You have a lot of work to make up for because we need this place perfect for the ball. I suggest you get started," she sneered.

"But ma'am, it's getting late," I replied.

"So? How is that stopping you? I don't care about your opinion on the matter. I asked you to get started. Did I stutter, Jane? Did you not understand? Surely you are not that stupid."

"Yes, I understand," I said nodding my head while I tried to control my anger. I did not need to do the same thing to Marie that had accidentally happened to Betty Ann.

"Good, I suggest you get to work. Surely you didn't forget the rules. What I say goes, and if you do have a brain, I suggest that you do what I have requested," she yelled.

"Yes, ma'am," I said again and then bowed to her for added effect. I couldn't believe she wanted me to clean at this hour.

I went into the kitchen and filled a bucket with soapy water. I began with scrubbing down the kitchen and dining room floors. When I had finished, it was after midnight. I dumped the bucket down the sink and decided to go to bed. I was exhausted, and I slowly climbed the stairs anticipating sleep. Everyone else must be asleep by now, I thought. I could continue with the rest of the cleaning in the morning. When I reached the top, I was surprised to find Marie with her hands on her hips. She laughed when she saw me.

"You didn't seriously think you were done, did you?" she asked.

I looked up at her, my eyes feeling heavy.

"I don't think you are quite done yet. It's not time to relax. Get back to work!" she said, giving me a nasty stare.

Slowly, I turned around and headed back down the steps. I scrubbed the kitchen counters and then dusted the dining room furniture. I also dusted and polished the furniture in the parlor as well. I was so exhausted and didn't try heading up to the attic until it was after three o'clock in the morning. I crashed onto the dirty mattress, too tired to notice how uncomfortable it was.

13

THE FOREVER SLAVE

L OUD NOISES WOKE me from my sleep and my head throbbed.
My eyes didn't want to open.

"Get up! Get up!" said a voice that sounded like Marie's.
I rolled over and buried my head in the pillow.

"Get up now, you insolent girl. There is much to be done and
I will not tolerate your laziness," Marie shouted.

This time I lifted my head in surprise since Marie never entered
the attic. She towered over my little mattress and her figure blocked
out the door. I felt closed in with no escape. Her steel gray eyes
stared down at me making my heart jolt in my chest.

"You have much to do. Get up!" Marie stated.

Quickly, I jumped up from my bed, afraid of Marie and what
she would do. I tried to rub the sleep from my eyes as I stood in
front of her, but every part of my body felt heavy.

"Follow me, I have a list of things for you to do," Marie said,
as she sharply turned from the room.

It would've been foolish not to follow so, in a daze, I went
out after her.

"You'll start in the kitchen and make sure everything's spotless.

I will not have my guests' food prepared in disgusting conditions. Then you'll move into the dining room, followed by the parlor, great hall, and ballroom. Everything must be spotless and look perfect. This party is very important. By no means will you mess up this event for me or Emily," Marie said.

I didn't ask why the party was just as important to Emily. I assumed Marie was throwing the party so Emily would be introduced to the richest men in the area. If I would've asked, she'd have commented on my lack of intelligence. It was better to just listen when Marie talked than to ask questions.

"Now once you're finished with these five rooms, I want you to clean the carpets upstairs in case anyone should wander up there. The bathrooms must be cleaned, of course, taking priority of the one downstairs since it's most likely the one guests will use. When you've finished with the indoor chores, you'll help Robert in the stables for the rest of the afternoon. If these chores aren't complete by dinner, then you'll have to skip it. I'll be finding things for you to do as they come to mind," she said turning to glare at me.

As if in a daydream, I followed her to the kitchen. She handed me a rag and a pail and then left the room. I'd never been so tired as I stared around the kitchen. Marie had woken me at five o'clock in the morning and I had only been asleep two hours. Looking around my eyes closed as I thought about the long list laid before me. Thankfully, I always carried garnet powder for a quick complete charm, so I cast the charm over me and got started. Within twenty minutes, the kitchen was sparkling. The work I completed would have taken hours without the charm.

A half-hour after Marie left me, she was back to examine the kitchen. I froze as she scrutinized everything. I was pretending to polish the sink again, so I wouldn't have to look at her. She seemed completely surprised by the state of the kitchen.

"I see you have been busy," she commented, and I wondered if she would actually praise me for what I had accomplished. Instead,

I was punished. "It seems like you cleaned too quickly. Do this room over. I'm not completely sure that it's clean."

Could she not see how the counters shined? Did she miss the spotless tile floor? Could she be that evil to make me stay in the kitchen when I could be completing other things and saving time? Yes, of course, she could do so without batting an eyelash. She swished her gray skirts as she retreated from the kitchen to leave me staring speechless. I sagged—defeated—at the sink and slowly started running the rag over everything again. All I could think of was the time being wasted and the longer I would have to suffer.

Another half-hour passed, the sun not yet breaking the horizon line, and she was back to inspect for a second time. Holding my breath, I hoped she was satisfied this time. She slowly nodded her head and then ushered me into the dining room. She disappeared again while I cleaned, but I used small amounts of the quick complete charm in case Marie would become suspicious of my fast-paced work.

Thankfully after an hour, when she inspected the dining room, I was allowed to move into the great hall. Here, I couldn't even chance using the charm. Too many people passed through this area. On my hands and knees, I scrubbed the floor until it shone. I'd almost completed the floor when Emily and Preston came stomping in from their Saturday morning walk. It looked like Preston had made it his purpose to trample in every mud puddle, for when he came in, his boots were covered. Emily also had mud on the lining of her cloak.

"Don't..." I cried out as they mercilessly started across the clean floor.

"I'm sorry, Jane. Did you say something?" Emily asked condescendingly as she strode toward me.

"Didn't hear you! Didn't hear you!" Preston shouted as he purposefully ran in circles. He knew exactly what he was doing. He would be fourteen soon and not five.

"Could you please stop?" I asked slowly and quietly.

"Stop what? This?" Emily asked as she started to pace the floor in front of me.

"Please, I just spent two hours cleaning it," I weakly stated.

"Are we getting mud on the floor?" Preston asked with a twinkle in his green eyes. His fire-red hair glinted in the rising sun through the windows.

"What does it matter?" Emily asked. "You have all day. You have no life, so why should you be worried? Sometimes I forget you exist since mother let you attend that school. Why she has allowed you, I don't understand. If it would've been my choice, I wouldn't have let you go. Why should you be educated when all you need to know is how to clean? Which you obviously don't know how, since this floor looks awful," she said laughing. "Come along, Preston. Let's get something to eat since it will be a while for Jane to bring it up to us." She stomped off toward the kitchen with Preston following in unnecessary circles.

I hung my head as I stared at the dirt-covered floor. Why hadn't I anticipated something like this? Just like their mother, they intended to punish me. It was no use fighting for justice around here, I thought as I dipped the rag back in the water and started again. Maybe I would have my revenge someday.

It was almost ten o'clock when I finished the great hall floor. I went into the parlor next and quickly dusted it since I'd done it the night before. Then, I dragged the mop and broom into the ballroom. Back and forth, I went across the wooden dance floor until it looked perfect. I just hoped Emily and Preston wouldn't visit this area with their muddy boots. The rugs upstairs needed a beating, which took longer since I hung them up in the side yard. Finally, with my arms aching, I moved on to the bathrooms, using the charm now that I was away from prying eyes.

I was very relieved when Marie accepted my work in the bathrooms, but the next assignment was physically worse. I walked across the grounds toward the barn to help Robert. He looked up when I entered, and his eyes lit up when he smiled. His auburn hair had grown longer since the last time I'd seen him.

"Hello," I said, walking into a stall to pick up a shovel.

"I see Marie has sent you to assist me," Robert said shaking his head. "A woman shouldn't be assigned a man's job."

"Don't worry about me. I'm used to it," I commented as I began working next to him.

Unfortunately, Robert didn't leave the barn, so I had to work without the charm. My arms burned every time I lifted the shovel, but I wasn't going to stop, no matter how much pain I was in. I was very determined to complete my tasks and show Marie that I wouldn't be easily defeated. I caught Robert staring at me from the corner of my eye. He seemed to work harder when he noticed my determination. I was thankful that the barn was warm for it had started snowing when I glanced outside.

Robert finally broke the silence after a few hours. "How've you been?"

"Do you want me to tell you the truth or a lie?" I asked. As of this week, my life had been pretty rough.

"Why don't you tell me the truth," Robert said as he bent down to continue shoveling.

"I've had the worst week of my life," I started. "I was sent home early from the academy, I had to take all my exams in one day, and Marie has been making me work since I arrived. I haven't had a rest," I said.

Robert stopped shoveling and gave me a strange look. "What are exams like in a school that teaches etiquette?"

I looked at him, confused by his question, and then I remembered the lie I had told. Of course, Robert would think that. Quickly I tried to think of a good answer.

"Oh, you know, the proper way to serve tea, how to bow to a superior, how to politely address guests, things like that…" I replied.

"It's really funny that you would have to take a test on those things," Robert asked.

"I had to serve tea and bow to the headmaster," I quickly said. I wished he would stop asking about my schooling. I didn't think I could continue to lie.

"What kind of classes do you have at the academy?"

I cringed inside as I tried to think of an answer. "I'm taught how to present myself in public, how to serve the wealthy, how to set a table for a meal, and how to behave like a perfect maid," I said, imagining what it would be like to really attend a school for etiquette.

Robert's face fell, and his brow knotted when he heard my answer. "She's sending you off, so you can be a maid the rest of your life. You are so much smarter than that. Marie's suffocating you," his voice had risen quite a bit.

"No, it's not like that!" I replied. "I enjoy going to school. I asked her to go. It's a wonderful opportunity for me."

"How can it be a good opportunity for you? You will be a maid for the rest of your life! Do you want to be Marie's slave forever?" Robert asked angrily.

"What will you do, Robert? Are you going to be Marie's horse boy for the rest of your life? How will you better yourself? Besides, Marie is my stepmother. Where else would I go?" I grabbed my shovel and stalked off to the other side of the barn to continue my work.

He knew nothing about the Jelf Academy. He wouldn't understand that the academy could release me from Marie's oppression.

Robert didn't come after me and stopped talking. I felt bad for walking away and arguing with him, but I couldn't stand him criticizing my choice. Once I was finished on my side of the barn, I hung my shovel against the wall. As I was about to leave, Robert called my name.

"Jane, please don't leave yet. I'd like to talk to you," he said.

I turned toward him and looked into his deep brown eyes. A

shaft of light fell on his auburn hair creating a nice shade. Sweat glistened on his chest where his shirt peeked open. Around his neck was a tarnished silver chain on which hung a ring that I'd never noticed before. I recalled Robert wearing the chain, but I had never seen the ring hanging from it.

"Jane, I would like to apologize. I just don't want Marie taking advantage of you," he said.

"Don't worry, she isn't," I replied. "I choose to attend the Jelf Academy."

"Just as long as it's your choice. You are too smart a girl to be controlled by someone. I wouldn't want you to be unhappy later on. Honestly, you're the only person I can talk to," Robert explained.

I was stunned by his words.

"It's ok, Robert. Thank you for your concern," I replied.

Robert smiled at me. "I assume I'll see you at the Christmas party. Marie wants me to help serve her guests, so I'll see more of the house." He rolled his eyes at his new assignment.

"I'm sure she'll work me to death more than you," I replied. I walked toward the door of the barn.

"Good night, Jane," Robert said, and I could have sworn that he winked at me, but the lighting was too dim to tell.

"Good night, Robert," I replied, slipping out of the barn.

The sun was beginning to fade as I trudged back across the field toward the manor. The snow made it so much harder to climb the hill. Would it be foolish to hope that Marie would let me rest? Sure enough, Marie was waiting for me in the kitchen.

"You look very tired. Would you like to take a rest?" she asked with a sneer.

I stood motionless, just staring at her. I knew she was teasing me. Marie would never offer me a break. I didn't know what to say to her. Would she be nicer if I didn't answer, or would she press me to answer? Uncertain of what to do, I remained silent. I wasn't going to beg for a break.

"No, I don't think you deserve a break. You're away at school, so you deserve to make up all the work you miss on a weekly basis," Marie laughed as she said this.

I hung my head knowing that this was the expected verdict, but I still didn't want to accept it. Marie slowly walked toward me. I could tell she was holding something, but it was close to her side in the folds of her dress. I froze not knowing if she planned to hurt me. When she was finally standing in front of me, she stretched out her hand with the object and I flinched. In her hand was a rag which she dropped at my feet.

"Get to work, and I might let you go to bed this time," Marie snickered.

I knelt down to pick up the dirty rag at her feet. As I glanced up at her, Marie had a strange smile on her face. "At my feet is where you belong. I knew that from the minute I saw you. Your father was foolish to think you were special. I know that he was wrong," Marie stated.

I tried to ignore her because I knew if I listened, I might not be able to control my anger. My father was a wonderful man and Marie was just jealous that he loved me more. I picked up the rag and turned away from her to enter the kitchen.

Unfortunately, Marie followed me. "Your father was never right about anything. You, first of all, are not special, and your abnormality only makes you grotesque. My Emily is smarter and prettier than you," Marie ranted on.

I threw all my energy into scrubbing the sink for the hundredth time that day. I scrubbed until the sink was pristine, but Marie continued with her monologue.

"Your appearance isn't even special. Sure, your eyes are violet in color, but I think it signals you out as an abomination," Marie laughed as she watched me clean the sink. "Ha, Richard believed your mother was special too. In fact, I'm sure she was just like you: an unintelligent abomination."

My hands clenched around the wet rag. Marie sounded just like Betty Ann. "My mother was a good woman!" I said turning to face her now. Please, I prayed, don't let my magic get the better of me.

"Oh? How would you know?" Marie said.

"I know she was special or else my father wouldn't have said so. He knew exactly what he was talking about. My mother accomplished great things in her life, and she gave it all up for him!" I said, my voice rising.

"You are so funny, Jane. You actually believe your mother accomplished something great. Explain what that could possibly be? What would she have done, and what did she give up for your father?"

I clamped my mouth shut so I couldn't shout out the truth. I couldn't tell Marie about the pixie world and the real teachings of the Jelf Academy. Sure, Marie thought I was a freak because she knew about my special talents, but she didn't need to know there were others like me.

Marie leaned back on the counter and smirked at my silence. "Nothing to say now, Jane? I wouldn't make up lies because I certainly don't believe them."

I wanted to call her a liar, but I didn't feel like dealing with the punishment. She had lied to my father when she said she would take care of me Thankfully, Marie had nothing else to say because she swept out of the room.

I stayed downstairs cleaning until the early hours of the morning before I decided to go up to the attic. Just before I fell asleep, I wished with all my heart that my Christmas break would go quickly and that I would be allowed back at the Jelf Academy.

14

THE CHRISTMAS PARTY

OLD AIR RUSHED in the slotted window, rousing me from my sleep. I turned over trying to keep some warmth against the chill. My body ached not only from the cold but from the strenuous labor I was put through in the last week. Today was the day of the Christmas party, and I didn't want to get up. I knew Marie would make me work very hard and any error would be fatal.

I rubbed my arms to shake off the chill and then sat up. Marie expected me to do another cleaning of the house this morning, help Ellen with dinner, take a quick bath, and then dress in my best rags. I was supposed to serve food and keep the trays full. Robert was supposed to help with the food and the serving of drinks.

Standing from the mattress, I had a glimpse out the window at the light snow covering the ground. At least there was a beautiful scene of pure white snow on Christmas. I stretched to wake myself up and then headed down to do my morning chores.

This morning I was lucky to be alone which allowed me to use the quick complete charm. I needed to save as much energy as I could for the party tonight. I couldn't afford to mess up anything. When I entered the kitchen to help, Ellen was already hard at work. Marie had made up an elaborate menu that would have Ellen working all day. A pig was to be roasted for dinner, and Marie wanted small dishes for people to enjoy as they socialized. Marie also requested side dishes to go along with the pig. There was going to be a feast, and I would probably only get a crumb of it.

"Hurry up, girl! Help me husk this corn!" Ellen yelled at me the moment she noticed I was in the kitchen.

I hastily crossed the room to the table piled with corn. As I husked the corn, I watched Ellen prepare the huge pig. She injected the pig with juices to flavor it before putting it into the oven. Ellen then began preparing the other food for the feast. Her face was puffy and red, and her hair was coming undone from her bonnet.

When I had finished husking the corn, I put it into a pot to boil. Unexpectedly, Marie showed up in the kitchen a few hours later. At first, I thought it was to oversee the work, but then she came toward me.

"Jane, why are you still down here?" she asked.

"You told me to help Ellen prepare the food," I replied.

"I didn't tell you to be down here this long," Marie said as if I should know what time she wanted me to finish. I couldn't read minds, yet. I wasn't even sure if it was possible. "Get upstairs and help Emily get ready!" she commanded.

I quickly left the kitchen and headed for Emily's room. When I entered Emily's room, I found her lounging in the tub surrounded by bubbles.

"It's about time you showed up! I feel like my water is getting colder by the second. Don't just stand there like an idiot. Get over here and wash my hair." Emily said to me.

Strolling over to the tub, I grabbed a bottle of her soap and put a drop of the liquid in my hand. Personally, I thought Emily was more than capable of washing her own hair, but maybe she wasn't as smart as her mother thought. I began lathering her long dark hair as she just sat there with her eyes closed. Emily's water was by no means cold. It was nothing compared to the quick cold bath I would have to take later.

"I bet you don't even know how important this party is to me. You don't know a thing about parties or social events. Lots of rich people will be here tonight and of course, I'm going to be the center of attention."

I didn't know if Emily was trying to make me jealous as she often did. I didn't put much stalk in a person's money. A person's status shouldn't be measured by money or riches, but by who they were and how they acted. It was better if I just kept quiet and listened.

"Don't pull my hair while you're scrubbing. I need it to look beautiful tonight, so don't put knots in it," Emily snapped.

Once I was finished washing and rinsing Emily's hair, I helped her out of the tub.

"I'd like to wear the red dress tonight, so my pale skin and black hair will stand out. It's also the perfect color for a Christmas ball. Don't mess anything up tonight, or else I'll see to it that you are severely punished. One small error and I'll make sure you never see that little school of yours again," Emily threatened.

I found the red dress she had requested while she toweled herself dry. Kneeling, I held the dress opened and Emily stepped into it. As I pulled the dress up and buttoned it, Emily made a face.

"Ouch! Watch what you're doing. You're pinching my skin. Do you seriously not know how to do anything? I wonder every day how you got into any kind of school at all," she sneered.

"If you spend your life wondering how I got into school, I think you need a new hobby, Emily." This comment slipped out of my mouth before I could stop it.

Before I could react, Emily whirled around and slapped me across the face.

"How dare you talk to me that way. I will not tolerate your

ignorance. If you ever talk back to me again, I'll make sure the insides of this house will be all you'll ever see again."

My face stung, but I was more shocked than physically hurt. Emily never used physical violence with me before. She normally lashed out with hurtful words instead.

"Now, you'll keep your mouth shut while you finish doing my hair and you'll be on your best behavior tonight," Emily said harshly.

I clasped my lips together, curling her jet-black hair. It amazed me how much she sounded like Marie, but of course, they were exactly alike. When Emily was finished getting ready, I turned to leave. I had to get myself ready before anyone arrived. Marie would be livid if she thought I looked unclean in front of the guests.

"Jane," Emily said calling me back. I leaned back in the doorway to see her face. "I'll make your life a living hell if something goes wrong tonight. That's a promise, not a threat," Emily stated, her gray eyes glowing wickedly in the fading sunlight. She looked so evil standing there, that a chill went down my spine, and I didn't doubt her statement.

Quickly I rushed toward the attic. When I entered my room, I found that Ellen had left a tub of water for me to bathe. I stuck a finger in the water to find it cold. If I had to guess, Marie probably told her to leave it here earlier to make sure the water was frigid. What she didn't know was that I could heat the water with just my mind.

I took off my dirty clothes and slipped into the newly heated bath. I rested my head against the tub, continuing to heat the water so that it would never cool off. I was tempted to press my luck and take longer getting ready, but then I remembered Emily's threats. I climbed out of the still warm water and chose one of my clean servant-like dresses. It was grayish blue and had a white apron that tied in the back. My violet eyes reflected in the tub, and I noticed the red mark on my cheek. Emily's slap was clear and present. I didn't think she had hit me hard enough to leave a mark. My fingers gently stroked my cheek as I continued to gaze at my reflection. Instead of dwelling on it, I found my mother's comb and ran it through my now shinning blonde hair. I held the comb against my chest and looked heavenward.

"Please," I silently prayed. "Protect me from Marie and her family and let everything go smoothly tonight." I took one last look at my reflection, a face supposedly like my mother's, and then I headed down to the party.

The kitchen was buzzing with activity when I entered, and Ellen was busy setting food on trays. "Thank goodness you finally got down here," Ellen barked at me. "Help me with these appetizer trays."

I took the trays out of Ellen's hands and began arranging them nicely on the tables in the great hall. The other servants had done a wonderful job of decorating while I had been busy with the food. A large pine wreath hung on the door decorated with pinecones and poinsettias. Along the banister, a pine garland covered with silver and gold tinsel draped from the top to the bottom. In the right corner stood a very large and perfectly shaped Christmas tree that almost reached the high ceiling. It was decked out with shining red, gold, silver, and blue balls, small candles, and candy canes that flowed from top to bottom. On the very top stood an angel with widespread wings and very dark hair. She looked exactly like Emily which I found incredibly ironic.

Each window held a glowing candle, which from the outside, probably made the house look cozy, warm, and loving. It was amazing how deceiving some things could be. In the hearths, raged warm fires that gave the same cozy effect. Marie had truly outdone herself for this party.

I headed back into the kitchen to retrieve more trays of food and to be given further instruction. I was put to work assembling hors d'oeuvres, which I was instructed to arrange in a certain way.

I was so caught up in remembering what should be placed on each tray, that I was startled when a deep voice spoke close to my ear.

Looking up surprised, my eyes came in contact with Robert. His soft auburn hair was pulled back and his brown eyes sparkled in the candlelight. His radiating smile brought out the dimples in his cheeks and the freckles along his nose. He was well dressed, and I had never seen him so clean. His appearance was a shock. It seemed like my heart had stopped beating. Why did I still feel like I couldn't breathe?

"What's our assignment for tonight?" he asked in a voice deeper than I remembered.

It took me a moment to clear my head before answering. "We're supposed to be carrying trays with drinks around for the guests. It's going to be tedious work, so we have to be careful. Marie will punish us greatly if we spill any of the drinks or break any of the glasses."

Soon, it was time for the party to begin, and guests began arriving. Robert and I were sent out into the great hall with glasses filled to the brim on small rickety trays. I was very nervous, so I used a tiny bit of magic to keep the tray steady. I was very grateful that pixies didn't need charms for everything. I think someone would notice if I kept throwing dust everywhere.

Marie stood at the door in her flowing green dress, with a lace collar that extended up her neck, greeting guests as they arrived. Her hair was pulled severely into a bun making her look, in my opinion, like an evil witch. Emily was nowhere to be seen, but Preston was over at the food tables, probably on the verge of causing trouble. I continued to circle the room, occasionally passing Robert, and returning to the kitchen for refills. The rooms were beginning to fill up, which made it harder to maneuver with a tray full of drinks.

Glancing around, I noticed Marie's disgusted smirk as she greeted the next guest. I was shocked to see Mr. Wicker. Judging by Marie's expression, I couldn't tell if he had been invited or not. I observed their exchange from across the room and was surprised when Marie stepped back, and Mr. Wicker advanced into the room. He must've been invited because I couldn't see Marie allowing him to enter if he didn't have an invitation. Why had she invited him? After their dispute, I didn't think Marie would ever allow him in her house again.

I glanced around the room for Robert, hoping he wouldn't be as startled as I was to see his former master. I noticed him across the room heading for the kitchen. Even though my tray was still full, I headed after him. Weaving through the crowd, I made it to the kitchen in time to catch Robert.

"Robert," I said urgently. "I have to warn you that Mr. Wicker is here. You might run into him among the guests."

All the color drained from Robert's face upon hearing this news. I wondered how Mr. Wicker could have been worse than Marie.

"Robert, are you okay?" I asked as I gripped his arm.

"Yes, Jane, I'm fine," he said shaking his head. "I just never thought I'd see that man again. I thought I'd be free of him for the rest of my life."

"You're free of him, Robert. I am warning you so that you can avoid him the best you can," I replied.

Robert slowly nodded as he lifted his tray full of drinks and followed me out of the kitchen.

The party had increased in size during our absence. People dressed in beautiful Christmas attire mingled around the great hall and were sampling appetizers in the ballroom. It had become harder to navigate the room. I found this task to be easier with magic and every so often I glanced around to see how Robert was faring.

All of a sudden, the noise level in the room dropped drastically. The guests focused their attention to the top of the grand staircase. I turned to see what had caused the interruption.

What I saw looked like an angel, but I knew it was the devil in disguise. At the top of the stairs, Emily stood in her beautiful red dress. Her black hair looked so shiny underneath the light and the sequins on her dress sparkled. She paused dramatically on the landing of the steps and looked out over the crowd. The audience sighed as if they were in the presence of greatness. Slowly, she descended the steps, appearing as if she were floating.

I turned away and continued through the crowd as Emily disappeared at the bottom of the steps. The guests seemed to have gravitated toward her. I wondered what was so special about this Christmas and why this party was so special to Emily. I saw Marie ascend the steps and turn to face her guests on the landing. She clinked her glass to get the room's attention.

"Good evening, fine ladies and gentlemen. If you all head into the dining room, dinner will be served momentarily."

At once, I reported to the kitchen to help Ellen. Marie wanted everything to be perfect, so I was nervous to be serving these many guests. The roasted pig was ready to be whisked onto the table when I arrived in the kitchen.

"Where have you been?" Ellen barked. "Did you forget that you have to serve dinner?"

"I didn't know the time Marie planned on serving dinner," I replied, placing the empty glasses down by the sink.

"Stop your complaining and take this pig into the dining room. Come right back to help me put out the other dishes."

The pig was on a large silver tray laid out perfectly with an apple stuffed into its mouth. I slid the tray toward the end of the table, but soon realized it was extremely heavy. This was nothing a little magic couldn't fix. I risked lifting the tray with my mind while Ellen's back was turned. I was able to get the tray to arm level and make it appear as if I were holding it with my hands. Cautiously, I headed into the dining room.

The guests hadn't entered the room yet, so I had a few spare moments to place the pig on the table as the centerpiece. I was startled when the door was opened, and I almost lost my concentration. It would be earth-shattering if I were to drop the main entrée. Thankfully, it was just Robert coming in to help. He saw me holding the pig and paused for a moment.

"Jane," he said breathlessly. "You're amazing. That pig must weigh a ton, yet you're holding it as if it were nothing. How do you manage?"

"This isn't so heavy, Robert," I lied. "What do you mean by that?"

"You cleaned up most of the barn in less than a half-hour and you somehow managed to lift that broken saddle into the loft without any help," he replied.

I blushed at his compliments and the things he had noticed but acted as if it didn't matter. "Those things weren't that hard. Anyone could have completed them."

"I don't know, Jane, but one of these days I'm going to figure out your secret," Robert said winking at me.

I swallowed the lump in my throat as he passed by. What if Robert found out what I could do? I had to be careful. Swiftly I set the pig down on the table, and I went back to the kitchen to bring out the rest.

Robert and I went back and forth bringing out the food while the guests filed into their seats. Emily sat at the head of the table like a queen, which was unusual; Marie always sat at the head of the table. Once the side dishes were on the table, it was time to bring out the salads and place them in front of each guest. Butterflies churned in my stomach because I had to serve Emily first. I hoped she wouldn't say something about me in front of her guests. Thankfully, Emily was in a deep conversation with the handsome man seated to her right. His dark hooded eyes never moved from her deceitfully angelic face. I could almost feel the heat radiating from his gaze.

When all the salads were served, Robert and I retreated to the kitchen until we were summoned again. My stomach growled at the sight of all the delicious food laid out on the table. I wouldn't be allowed to have dinner until the party was over.

"Why do you think Marie threw this big party?" Robert leaned close to whisper.

"I don't know, but what I do know is that Emily's the center of attention," I replied.

"That can't mean anything good," Robert said.

When the guests were finished with their salads, Robert and I collected the plates and brought them to the kitchen to be washed. It was amazing that Emily hadn't thrown a negative comment in my direction. Ellen came out of the kitchen to carve and serve the roasted pig, which delighted the guests.

When the dinner was over, everyone went back to the great hall and the ballroom to dance and socialize. Robert and I had much to clean up, and I was grateful that he was beside me. We had to carry all the plates and trays to the kitchen and make sure the dining room was spotless. Not only did we have to complete the clean-up, but we also had to get back to serving drinks to all the thirsty guests. It was very nerve-racking because I knew if the slightest thing went wrong Marie would punish me.

Even without the use of magic, the dining room dishes were finished in record time. Robert and I had refilled glasses and left the kitchen. I circled the room and Robert went in the other direction. Every so often we could cross paths and Robert would wink at me. I blushed deeply hoping that he didn't notice. Why did my heart race every time I saw him in the crowded room?

As I continued to circle the room, Mr. Wicker spotted me in the crowd. I tried to distance myself from him, but he came toward me to get a drink.

"I remember you, little maid. You were too curious for your own good. If you were mine, I would've been able to put you in your place," he said looking at me and licking his lips.

I tried to move away from him, but he continued speaking.

"I've thought about you for quite some time. You look familiar. I can't help but wonder if I put you in your place before," he grinned wickedly. Mr. Wicker reached out and caressed my arm with his ugly claw-like hand. I recoiled from his touch.

"What's going on here?" a deep voice said.

I turned around to see Robert standing there. It must have taken a lot of courage for him to stand up for me.

"My old mute horse boy seems to have found his tongue. I knew I should've cut that out of you when I had the chance," Mr. Wicker said nastily.

I could see Robert's face pale, but he kept his ground.

"Come along, Jane. We have guests to serve, not animals," Robert replied. I was equally shocked and proud of his statement.

Mr. Wicker started to open his mouth, but whatever he was about to say was cut off by the clinking of glass. Marie was back on the stair landing with an announcement. Next to her, Emily stood with the handsome young man from earlier.

"I'm sure you all know my beautiful daughter, Emily, who I'd say is as lovely as a rose," Marie began.

The only way Emily was like a rose was the sharpness of her thorns, not her beauty, I thought.

"Tonight is a special night because there's an announcement to be made. I'll let Mr. Drake Doyle do the honors," Marie continued.

The mysterious man nodded at Marie and stepped forward taking Emily's hand.

"What a beautiful woman you've become, Miss Emily. You are truly like a rose, but ten times as lovely. It is my honor that I should have the privilege to be in the presence of such radiance. Without further ado, it seems only appropriate to ask for your hand in marriage," and with that said, he dropped to his knees and produced a ring from his suit jacket.

I stood shocked as I watched the scene unfold. I never expected anything like this to happen. Emily didn't look shocked at all. I realized that this party had been planned for this specific reason.

"Yes, I will accept your hand in marriage," Emily replied, as the ring was slipped onto her finger.

There was a commotion in the vicinity where I was standing. Mr. Wicker had pushed past Robert to get to where Emily was standing. Robert's tray tottered, and it was starting to fall from his hands. I couldn't let Robert get in trouble for this. I had to stop the glasses from falling. Concentrating on Robert's tray, I was able to place the falling glasses on the floor without spilling a drop. Most of the attention in the room was on Mr. Wicker as he began to talk loudly about a promise that was made.

Robert seemed confused as to what was going on and Mr. Wicker paused his rant to turn around and stare at the glasses on the floor. He shook his head and continued speaking.

"Marie, you promised Emily to me. We had an agreement."

"That was months ago, and that agreement is now null. If you cannot conduct yourself in a civilized manner, I will have to ask you to leave. I have invited you here as a truce to settle our indifference. I ask that you remain civil," Marie said in the commanding tone of voice I recognized.

Mr. Wicker quieted down and moved off in the direction of the coat closet. I couldn't tell if he was planning to leave or not. Robert bent down and picked up his tray, still looking confused.

"Jane, did you see that?" he whispered. "How did my glasses fall right side up? None of them have tipped over."

"I don't know, Robert. It happened so fast," I lied again. I felt so ashamed lying to him.

He gave me an odd look before turning toward Emily on the stairs. She seemed to have forgotten the commotion. She was now staring intently at Mr. Doyle as if he was the only one in the room. The expression on her face clearly looked like she had just won a very expensive prize. The audience, who had been stunned to silence, broke out in loud applause for the blissful couple.

"I never thought she would decide on a man," Robert said under his breath. "So many suitors have come through that door."

"I knew it was only a matter of time before she found the wealthiest man she could, especially with looks like his," I replied.

Robert nodded at my statement, both of us sure Drake Doyle had some wealth behind his name. For what other reason would Emily be interested, besides his dark good looks? They stood hands clasped in front of the guests. Then they slowly descended to mingle and be offered congratulations. I watched with disdain, shrugged my shoulders at Robert, and then continued to circle the room.

The party didn't last much longer after Drake Doyle's wonderful announcement. Guests began to leave one by one all wishing their best and asking when the wedding was. It was sure to be a grander event than this Christmas party, and all the guests wanted an invitation. A headache was all I had to look forward to.

When the last guest had left the party, it was time to clean up. I was prepared for a long night, and I knew I would get stuck with most of the cleaning. Sure enough, Marie began to approach me from across the room.

"You're not allowed to go to bed until this place is clean. When I wake up tomorrow, I want it to look as if a party hadn't even taken place. Do you understand me, Jane? I don't care if you ask that stupid horse boy to help you, I just want it done," Marie demanded.

"Yes, ma'am," I replied with my eyes downcast. I didn't want to suffer her wrath tonight.

"Good, then get to it," she said as she climbed the stairs.

I watched her back disappear into the darkness, and then I slowly walked into the kitchen to do the work she had assigned. I should've suspected that I wouldn't get any sleep tonight.

Robert was still in the kitchen when I entered. He smiled at me. I understood it was reflected his relief that the evening was over.

"I'm glad it's over," I said, voicing his expression.

"Yes, and it's back to the barn for me. I just stayed to say good night," Robert replied.

"Okay, Robert, good night." I did want him to go so he wouldn't be stuck helping me clean. Without Robert around, I could clean the house faster, but that didn't mean I really wanted him to go. I wished I could share my secret with him.

Robert turned to leave through the back door, but then paused and turned around. "Marie wants you to clean up the house before going to bed, doesn't she?"

I looked down at the ground and sighed a quiet yes. Robert walked toward me and grabbed my hand. "Let me stay to help you."

"No, Robert. That's not fair. Go and get a good night's sleep. Marie asked me, not you," I protested.

"Let me help you. I'm making it my problem now. Plus, with the two of us working, we can get things done faster." If only he knew things would get done faster without him. Robert continued to look at me intently, and I knew he wouldn't give up.

"Fine. You can help me if you insist on it," I replied, and I felt Robert squeeze my hand.

"Good. I'm glad you didn't fight me."

Robert and I began in the dining room since Ellen had taken care of the kitchen. We changed the tablecloth and put away the Christmas one. I made sure the beautiful china dishes were stacked neatly in the cabinet and that everything was in its proper place. Robert was a big help with cleaning the floor. By using two mops we did finish in good time. I dumped the dirty water and added clean water to the bucket so we could mop the great hall and ballroom.

The great hall and ballroom area were a bigger mess since that was where the majority of guests socialized. Crumbs and fallen decorations littered the floor, and I heaved a sigh when I took it all in.

"Aren't you glad I'm here?" Robert asked as we stood side by side surveying what needed to be done.

I nodded and then began picking up fallen decorations. For being rich and sophisticated, the mess that the guests left was inexcusable. You would think that people who had money and an education would know better than to make a mess. Alas, cleaning and serving were the only things people like Robert and me were good for.

It was getting later and later, and I could feel my body slowing down. Robert looked like he was about to fall over but kept up the work at my side. We spoke very little to save energy. After we mopped and swept the floor, I insisted on polishing it, because I knew it was what Marie expected. Robert looked close to protesting, but he didn't say anything and just went along with my instructions.

When we were finally finished, it had to be close to sunrise. Robert and I collapsed onto the floor for just a moment of rest. "Thank you for helping me. You didn't have to," I said breaking the silence.

"I helped you because I wanted to," Robert replied. "Will you walk me to the back door?"

"Yes, give me just a moment," I answered. I wanted to sit a second longer.

Robert stood before me and held out his hand to pull me up. I placed my hand in his, and he pulled me to my feet. I was surprised by his strength because he hadn't used much effort. "Look," he said pointing toward the ceiling. "Mistletoe." We were standing under the door frame.

I blushed as I joined his gaze skyward. Mistletoe hung above our heads on the doorframe. I knew my face was bright red, and I looked down at my hands. Robert hesitated, and I didn't know what he was going to do. Was he going to kiss me? It seemed like five minutes had passed when finally, Robert just lifted my hand to his lips and kissed it.

"Good night, Jane. I'll see you tomorrow," he said smoothly.

He slipped across the great hall and down the hallway toward the kitchen before I could even mumble goodbye. It had happened so fast that I couldn't wrap my brain around it. I lightly touched the spot on my hand where his lips had been. Confused as to how Robert felt about me, I slowly climbed the steps, dreading the remainder of my Christmas holiday.

15

ROBERT'S STORY

MY HOLIDAY BREAK preceded as it had begun. Each day, I was up early doing chores, some of which consisted of helping Robert in the barn. I didn't mention the Christmas party. Robert was my only friend at the manor, and I didn't want our friendship to end over a misunderstanding. All I knew is that I loved the days that I was sent to the barn. I enjoyed Robert's company and conversation. He made my awful days better.

Today, I was the most hopeful I had been during the Christmas break. Dr. Tweedle would show up at midnight this New Year's Eve and take me back to the Jelf Academy if he'd been able to convince the government officials that I should stay. If Dr. Tweedle came for me, it was going to be the best New Year's Eve I had ever experienced.

Marie had assigned me to the barn, and I tried not to show her how happy I was.

Robert was busy brushing the horses when I entered. I picked up a curry comb and joined him.

"Hello, Jane. You look happier today," Robert commented.

"Yes, I am," I replied. "Dr. Tweedle is supposed to come at midnight to take me back to the Jelf Academy."

"Dr. Tweedle?" Robert's eyebrows rose.

"Yes, he's the headmaster of the Jelf Academy," I replied.

"Wow, you must be very special, Jane, if the headmaster of your school coming to pick you up," Robert said, and he sounded doubtful.

"I know it seems a bit odd, but he knows that I'm an orphan and that Marie wouldn't want to be bothered with taking me. Plus, my mother went to the Jelf Academy, and he knew her very well. Dr. Tweedle believes that I was destined to attend," I explained.

"I never knew your mother attended the school," Robert said. "I thought it was something Marie was making you do. It mustn't be so bad if your mother would've wanted you to go."

"I should've explained it better. I wasn't lying when I said it was my choice to attend. I really enjoy it there, Robert. So far, it has been the best experience of my life. So many people knew my mother, and I've found out more about her."

"When did your mother pass away?" Robert asked. "You've never talked about her before."

"She passed away when I was about a year old. I don't remember much about her, but my father said she was wonderful. He used to tell me I looked just like her. My mother gave up a lot of things because she loved him so much," I said sadly.

"How did she pass away?" he asked.

I paused. How could I tell him about the W.A.S.P. and why they had murdered her? If I did that, then I would have to explain the magical world.

"Look, I understand if you don't want to talk about it. I shouldn't have asked," Robert started. We continued cleaning in silence for a while when Robert spoke again. "I'm really sorry, Jane. I didn't mean to pry. I don't remember my parents much either."

"Did they pass away when you were young too?"

"No, I hope they are still alive. When I was six years old, my mother and I were traveling on a crowded street. I don't remember, but I think my parents were visiting some friends of theirs, so we were in a different town. I was holding her hand as she pulled me through the crowd towards our destination. We had been shopping that day and as a young boy, I was very tired. I remember she was dragging me, and I was shuffling my feet with each step.

"People were all around me. My mother's hand was like my life preserver the sea of people. From every angle, we were shoved and jostled by the crowd. It was very hard to keep up. Before I knew it, my hand slipped from hers, and I was pushed in a different direction. The last thing I heard my mother say was my name as we drifted away from each other. I saw her auburn hair drift away into the crowd. That's the last image I have of her," Robert said.

"I'm so sorry, Robert," I replied, my head hung in sadness.

"I spent my first night sleeping in the gutter on the street, crying for her to come back to me. Mr. Wicker found me the next day and brought me back to his house. I should have been grateful; I would have died in the street. He fed and clothed me, but then the beatings began. If I didn't work hard enough, I was beaten. If I talked, I was beaten. I lived my life in silence, desperate to be back with my parents again. I was only six years old, and I had no way to find them. Mr. Wicker kept a constant watch on me and made me work until I almost passed out.

I endured this for eleven years. For the most part, I'm glad Mr. Wicker sold me to Marie. She rarely comes to the barn and doesn't beat me. The only time she talks to me is when I have to saddle her horse or prepare a carriage. Living in this barn is an improvement compared to my old life," Robert said.

"Do you ever think about finding them? Now that you're away from Mr. Wicker, don't you want to leave?" I asked hesitantly. I didn't want him to leave, but I wanted him to be happy. Even if I had to lose my only friend in this awful place, I would be happy to know he was with his family again.

"I don't have any money, Jane. Marie only gives me food. Plus, I don't even know where to start. All I have from my family is my father's ring. I remember wanting to wear it that day and since it didn't fit my finger, my mother put it on this chain." Robert pulled the ring out from underneath his shirt. It was big and gold, and on the front of the ring was a symbol with lions on it. I assumed it was a family crest.

"I know that my last name is Lyons. The name is engraved here on the family crest. From what I can recall, I believe my father's name was Gabriel. I wouldn't even know how to start looking for him," Robert replied.

"At least you have something. Your family might still be alive, and you can rejoin them!" I said excitedly.

"Yes, but as I said, I need money, which seems impossible to obtain. It'll be another holiday alone. Another year that I can mark off as being an orphan," Robert said sadly.

"Don't be sad, Robert," I said touching his shoulder. "You're not alone. I'm your friend, and I understand what it's like to be alone. I was alone until you came here."

"Yes, and I'm alone when you're gone," he replied.

Now I knew why he looked so sad. I might be returning to the Jelf Academy, and he wouldn't see me as often.

"It'll be ok, Robert. I'm only gone for a week at a time. Then I'll be back shoveling manure beside you." I tried to smile.

He brightened a little and then nodded his head. "I don't know, Jane, but when you are here, the work seems to go faster."

I blushed, hoping he didn't notice. "One day, Robert, I know you will find your family."

He shrugged his shoulders picking up the shovel. "Maybe someday in the future, I will."

We continued our work side by side. I told Robert what I

remembered about my father. I didn't mention my mother again. Even though the work was dirty, I was happy to be in the barn with Robert for most of the day. It was heartbreaking when I had to return to the manor house. Robert surprised me by hugging me goodbye and saying he couldn't wait for my return next week.

As I trudged up the hill to the manor house, I wrapped my arms around myself to combat the chill. It had grown cold in the last week and more snow had fallen. I didn't really have heavy clothes for the winter. The barn had been warm with all the horses inside, but after the physical labor, the wind cut through me. My teeth were chattering, and it was a relief to finally get inside the manor house.

A warm fire was burning in the kitchen as Ellen was bustling around making dinner. Her hair was neatly under her bonnet, and she didn't look as frazzled today. I even thought I heard her humming.

"There you are," she said in a politer tone than she normally used with me. "You should head upstairs because Marie will be looking for you," she warned.

What was going on? Ellen rarely ever warned me about Marie. I gave her a questioning look.

"Only servants for dinner tonight," she said cheerily. "Marie and her brood are going out for the evening to Mr. Doyle's house for a New Year's celebration. Emily's new fiancé is perfect for her. They're two devious snakes," Ellen mumbled.

I almost laughed at her terminology. Ellen would probably be fired if Marie heard her say such things. I left the kitchen in a hurry because if Marie and her family were going out, they'd probably need me to help them get ready.

I entered Emily's room first, figuring she would want and need most of my attention. Emily was deep in her closet throwing dress after dress over her shoulder.

"Where's my green winter dress?" she screamed. "Jane!" Emily flew out of her closet in a rage. She seemed taken aback to see me in her room. "It's about time! Get in my closet and find my green dress. Mr. Doyle likes when I wear green."

Without saying a word, I calmly walked past her and into the walk-in closet. I began my search for the dress and after three minutes, I found it. Stepping over the mess on the floor, I presented it to her and helped her into it. After they left, it would be my job to clean up her closet. What would she do if I just left her room like this? I'd be in serious trouble when they returned, but a smile crept across my face as I imagined Emily finding her room just the way she had left it.

"I need my hair fixed. I need to look better than my best. I must be flawless for Mr. Doyle. Mrs. Emily Doyle, sounds lovely, doesn't it?" she went on in her annoying voice. "I know your jealous, Jane. Then again, you've always wanted to be like me, haven't you? I'm beautiful, smart, and engaged to one of the richest men in the world."

I wanted to choke her for her arrogance, but I stayed quiet as I braided her hair. Why did she always brag and insist on me being jealous?

"I almost feel sorry for you. Not this year, but the spring after I will be married. I'll have my own set of servants to take care of me, and I won't have to constantly wait on you. You'll be left here to rot with my mother while I become the queen of the Doyle mansion. I doubt you'll ever get married. Who would want you? When mother dies, maybe I'll take pity on you and put a roof over your head. I wouldn't count on schooling from me if I were you," Emily rattled on.

Emily lived in her own fantasy world. She was desperate to live like a queen and have power over her servants. Perhaps it would happen, but I knew that running a household was difficult. Even though Marie was constantly in control, she didn't seem to have much leisure time.

"Jane, are you listening to me? I know your head is empty, but can you please try? I want my new rouge on my cheeks. If I have to repeat myself, I think I'll go crazy." Emily said nastily.

I snapped out of my thoughts and pulled the powder out of Emily's vanity. She sat on the stool, face tilted backward, waiting on me to do as she asked. Slowly, I undid the lid and grabbed the tiny brush.

Emily sighed and chuckled a little. "This is exactly how I pictured my life: you at my beck and call and me with a big diamond on my finger." She indicated the sparkling ring on her left hand. The ring was definitely hard to miss; the diamond covered most of her finger. Drake Doyle was, without a doubt, a rich man. The diamond was cut in a princess style which had to be a few carats, and the band was bright gold. I wondered how extravagant the wedding ring was going to be.

I didn't make eye contact with her as I dipped the brush into the jar. Rage was building in me, and I had to keep control. I was tempted to spill some of the powder on her dress and ruin it. My magic was so hard to control, but I couldn't let it escape me. I took a deep breath as I leaned over Emily to apply the blush. When Emily's cheeks looked rosy, I put down the brush. As I tried to screw the lid on the blush, I accidentally dropped it. My mind was so clouded with anger that I wasn't fast enough to catch it with my magic. The powder hit the hardwood floor with a bang as glass and powder flew everywhere.

Emily turned around so fast, her eyes blazing with anger. I dropped to my knees and began picking up the shattered pieces. I put the pieces in a wastebasket that was located under her vanity. I hurried into her private bath to get some damp towels to clean up the mess. While I was cleaning up my mistake, Emily was yelling at me.

"Fool! How could you be so stupid? That was my new jar. Why do you have to ruin everything? Just because your hideous cheekbones will never have rouge doesn't mean you can ruin my things."

I tried to tune her out as I went about scrubbing the floor, but her voice raised a few octaves as if she knew I wasn't listening.

"You are the stupidest thing I've ever seen in my entire life. You don't know how to do anything right, and you make a mess out of everything. Why your father ever loved you is unknown to me. I've heard you are like your mother, two aberrations with strange violet eyes," Emily shouted at the top of her lungs.

Even though Emily had insulted my mother and me, my pride rose as I was compared to her. I hoped I was like my mother even if it meant being unnatural in Emily's eyes. I hoped everything about me was like her because she had been an amazing pixie. I was interrupted from my thoughts by a sharp voice.

"What is going on in here?" Marie stood in the doorway of Emily's room, her eyes on me.

"Jane dropped my new jar of rouge, and it broke on the floor," Emily wailed giving her mother tearful eyes as if she had just lost a very close friend.

"Jane, come to my room as soon as you clean up the mess you created." Marie demanded. "Don't even think about wasting time."

She acted like I always did things slowly, but most of the time she was the reason it took me so long to do anything. She always asked me to do things a second or third time when they were perfect the first time. I rushed to clean the floor, hoping that I would be able to handle anything Marie punished me with. Emily stood gazing down at me with a satisfied smirk on her face. She always had that look on her face when I got yelled at. I scrubbed as hard as I could, and when I finished, I dragged myself to my feet. With a determined glare, I headed towards Marie's room.

Marie was sitting straight in her vanity chair staring coldly into the mirror. She saw me enter from the reflection, but she didn't turn around. I paused in the doorway unsure of what to do.

"Come here and put my necklace on," she demanded.

I crossed the room nervously. She always had a way of acting calmly before she punished me. My fingers shook as I took the necklace from her. It was a string of beautiful pearls, some of which were pink in color. They were so lovely, and I knew they were very expensive. When I had fastened it around her neck, I stepped back, waiting for her to scold me. Marie rose from her vanity, her regal figure stood out in her long black dress that had a white sash around the waistline. Her spine was like steel as she turned to face me.

"Why does it seem like every time I turn around, you are in the middle of doing something wrong?"

I hung my head unsure of what to say. It didn't matter what she found me doing. To her, it would always be wrong.

"Now you listen. I don't want any more nonsense from you. Your father stuck me in this predicament. Unfortunately, you're my responsibility. As of this moment, I don't want to see any more mistakes. You will bow your head and do as you're told or so help me god, I'll throw you out into the cold. One more step over the line and that school of yours will be a thing of the past.

"Emily is now engaged and has come into womanhood. Snide comments from you will not be tolerated, and she has every right to punish you as she sees fit. You are our servant, Jane, because I had no choice. If anything, you should be grateful for my kindness. Just remember that I don't have to keep you here or send you to any school. You are a burden to us, Jane."

I kept my head down and didn't want to look at her. I hated her and her offspring. I kept breathing deeply to control my emotions. I was tired of being told I was worthless.

"I don't want to have this lecture again. Go into Preston's room and make sure he is ready to leave soon. Remember, no more problems," Marie smirked as she wagged her finger.

My shoulders sagged as I left her room. Since I did everything wrong, it might be five minutes before I was thrown from this house if Marie was true to her word. I shuffled down the hall to Preston's room, wondering what kind of chaos I would find. I gave two sharp knocks on the door before I entered. Preston was on the floor in his best suit playing with something in the corner. His clothes were covered with dust and lint, and I knew I would have to tackle that situation before he left the house.

"Preston," I preceded slowly, not knowing how he would react. "Could you please get off the floor? Soon, you'll be on your way to a New Year's Eve party."

At first, Preston didn't look at me or attempt to get up from the floor. If Preston didn't get ready, his actions would be my fault. I began mentally packing what few items I owned. Suddenly, to my relief, Preston stood up and turned to face me. He was holding something in his hand, but I couldn't tell what it was.

"Come on, Preston," I almost whispered. "Let's clean you up and get ready for Mr. Doyle's party."

It was odd how Preston kept staring at me with a smirk on his face. Deciding to ignore him for the moment, I searched the top drawer of his armoire for another pair of pants. My hand clasped around a matching pair, and I pulled them from the drawer. Preston watched me as I unfolded them and held them out.

"You'll have to change out of those pants," I narrated just because he was staring at me.

When I stepped closer to him, Preston finally said something. "I have a present for you, Jane."

This startled me, and I knew he was up to something.

"Oh really, Preston? Well, that's lovely, but you really need to get ready because your mother will be prepared to go soon," I replied.

I stepped closer to him, and his smile widened. He shifted what he was holding in his hand and quickly unveiled my *present*.

"Here, Jane. It reminded me of you."

I had to control myself, so I wouldn't scream. Dangling between his thumb and forefinger was a dead rat which he was holding by the tail.

"My God! Where did you get that?" I had been so shocked I had almost dropped the pants.

"I killed it," he replied nonchalantly with that wicked grin on his face. He tossed it toward me, and I had to jump back to keep it from hitting me. He laughed maliciously.

"Preston, I think it is time to get ready," I said trying to control my voice.

The main thing on my mind was getting Preston ready and having the family sent off to the party so I could dispose of the thing before Marie saw it. Thankfully, Preston didn't give me any trouble and in five minutes he changed his pants. I quickly ushered him down to the front hall where Marie and Emily were already waiting.

"Make sure you clean this place up while we're gone," Marie demanded.

"Yes, ma'am," I replied. "I won't be returning to school until midnight." I figured I should remind her in case she had forgotten.

Her nose turned upward at this statement, seeming disgusted. "Oh, I forgot about your stupid school. We won't be home to escort you back to school, so you'll have to return tomorrow," she said matter-of-factly.

"Someone's coming to get me as usual," I said slowly. It was ridiculous of Marie to claim she couldn't take me back to school. She had never taken me to the Jelf Academy, and I wasn't even sure she could.

"Midnight is such an odd hour and especially on New Year's Eve," Marie said suspiciously, as her face scrunched up again.

"The arrangements have been made, none of which were my decision. I'll be sure to leave the house in absolutely perfect condition."

Marie looked defeated as if she were being cheated out of another day of my servitude. Graciously, Marie turned her head to leave. It was obvious she was done discussing the matter.

"Very well, Jane. Try to have a nice week at that ridiculous school, but just be prepared for strenuous work when you get back. I'm sure we'll need to keep the house orderly since Emily is newly engaged. Without a doubt, many visitors will be stopping by to pay their congratulations," Marie smirked.

Emily had a scow on her face as she observed our exchange. Preston was fidgeting where he stood, the devious wheels in his brain probably turning. I nodded toward Marie to show I understood I would be working twice as hard.

"Come along, children, or else we'll be late for our wonderful party," Marie said stressing the word wonderful.

Preston scampered out the door first with Emily behind him, her arms crossed in irritation. As Marie closed the door, I could have sworn I heard Emily say, "Honestly, mother, I don't even know why you send her to school." I smiled at the closed door and then decided it was best to start working upstairs.

My first task would be disposing of the dead rat. The whole incident had disturbed me. How had Preston killed the rat? I didn't even want to know where he had found it in the first place. My stomach churned at the thought of it lying on the carpet in his room. I retrieved a bag from the kitchen and slowly ascended the stairs. I don't know why, but I crept toward Preston's room as if I would find the thing alive. I knew it was impossible because as Preston changed, the rat had lain motionless.

When I peered around the corner into his room, I could make out the gray lump of fur lying where Preston had thrown it. I felt nauseous as I entered the room, but I forced myself to approach it. It looked so pitiful lying there twisted on the rug. After inspection, it became clear that Preston had snapped its neck, but as I continued to stare, I saw other marks too. A sickness welled up inside me as I realized Preston had tortured the poor creature before sentencing it to a final end. How could he do such a thing?

I didn't want to touch the rat with my bare hands, so I opened the bag and focused on levitating it. The lifeless body lifted off the rug and plunked into the bag. I had to fight off a sick stomach as I wrapped up the bag and prepared to take it outside. Holding the bag out from my body, I exited Preston's room and climbed down the stairs. I decided to dispose of the animal by throwing it with the other garbage kept on the side of the barn. It was already dark outside when I crossed the property, and I couldn't cross my arms against the cold because of the bag. I made my way to the barn and deposited the dead rat with a shudder.

I shivered from the cold, and when I opened the front door, I welcomed the heat. The next task I had to tackle was reorganizing Emily's closet. Slowly I climbed the steps then sighed when I got to Emily's room. It was messier than I thought. With Marie gone, I decided to use the quick complete charm. Within twenty to thirty minutes, I had Emily's room back to perfection. Very satisfied with my work, I went around the rest of the house making sure everything was in top shape.

After I had finished with my chores, I climbed the steep attic steps. It was chilly here since the harsh wind worked its way through the cracks in the roof. My teeth chattered as I gathered my school supplies. I hoped that soon I would see Josefina and Miguel. I couldn't wait to tell them about Emily's engagement and how awful Marie was. I prayed that Dr. Tweedle would be knocking at my door, and I would be taken away to the world I belonged. The thought of expulsion made my stomach hurt.

Once I had my belongings packed, I moved around the attic and explored old things I had snuck up here many years ago. Several articles of clothing felt like pixie material, and when I searched even deeper, I found a wallet in one of the coat pockets. I had never thought to search my mother's belongings. Inside the wallet, I was startled to find several hundred dollars in pixie money plus several human bills as well. I was surprised that my mother had stowed it in a coat pocket. It was lucky of me to have snuck this particular coat into the attic. If I would've found this wallet earlier, I might have thrown the money away, having no idea what it meant.

Since the coat seemed to be made out of pixie material, I slipped it on. It fit me perfectly and was nice and warm. This coat would be perfect for when I had to cross the grounds of the Jelf Academy. I decided to store the wallet with the money in a secret compartment of my pixie dust case where it would be safe.

With every last hope, I trudged down all the stairs and sat on the steps in the great hall. My eyes stayed focused on the grandfather clock, anticipating the stroke of midnight.

16

NEW YEAR'S EVE

THE CLOCK BONGED its deep chime twelve times, and I jumped at the noise. A loud knock at the door soon followed. My stomach leapt in excitement. I threw open the door to find Dr. Tweedle clad in a wool trench coat that came down to his mid-calves.

"Happy New Year, Jane. Are you ready to go?" he asked.

"Yes, more than ever!" I exclaimed picking up my suitcase. I closed the door behind me and stepped outside into the chilly air.

"After reviewing the details of the incident with the fire charm, the government officials have decided to give you a second chance. They based this decision on the progress you have made so far in your classes. Unfortunately, they're not entirely convinced that you should be enrolled at the academy. If you can finish the rest of the year with good academic progress and no other incidents, they could change their minds."

"Thank you, Dr. Tweedle. I was so nervous that you wouldn't come."

"I know you didn't receive that coat as a Christmas present," Dr. Tweedle said, looking at my mother's coat.

"Marie had a change of heart over Christmas break," I said sarcastically.

"Where would Marie get a coat made out of pixie material?" Dr. Tweedle chuckled.

"I found it in the attic with a few of my mother's old things Marie didn't throw away," I told him as we both settled in the carriage.

"I hope that your Christmas was good. How were the past few weeks?" Dr. Tweedle asked.

I looked down at the floor of the carriage instead of answering. Dr. Tweedle must have sensed that I didn't want to talk about it, so he didn't say anything else as he dug the teleporting charm out of his coat pocket. I didn't want Dr. Tweedle to know the whole truth about my life here. I clung to the carriage and before I knew it, we were in the meadow awaiting the cloud to drop from the sky.

"You haven't answered my question, Jane" Dr. Tweedle pressed after a few moments

"Marie threw a huge Christmas party with many guests. It was a lovely grand event," I stated.

"Oh, well I'm sure that was wonderful. How nice that you got to attend," Dr. Tweedle replied.

"I got to serve drinks and clean up afterward. I also worked hard for days before the party," I said dully, forcing the words from my mouth. Why would he think I would attend the party as a guest?

"I'm sorry, Jane. I've never known anyone to be treated so cruelly by their family. I'm sorry I assumed. Knowing your mother as well as I did, it's hard to believe that her daughter wasn't brought up by someone as kind as she was," Dr. Tweedle replied sympathetically. "I wish there was something I could do."

"Don't worry, Dr. Tweedle. I'm okay," I lied. "I don't consider Marie or her children, family anyway." I tried smiling at him.

Dr. Tweedle gave me a worried look, almost as if he could

see right through my lie. Before he could reply, the cloud had descended. I boarded it quickly. Dr. Tweedle climbed on after me but remained silent. Despite the depressing conversation, I couldn't help but be excited to see Josefina and Miguel. They would understand my situation with Marie.

When the cloud came to a stop, we stepped off and walked toward the school. I could see fireworks in the sky above the Jelf Academy. I instantly began to feel better. As soon as the huge front doors creaked open, I heard loud laughter. I turned to face Dr. Tweedle in the entrance hall.

"Thank you so much, Dr. Tweedle. I really appreciate that you came to get me."

"It was my pleasure, Jane. The students are having a New Year's Eve party in the dining hall if you'd like to join them," Dr. Tweedle replied.

"Thank you again. This will be the most special New Year of my life," I exclaimed.

What greeted me when I entered was the pleasant shouts of laughter and music. Everywhere I turned, students were dancing and talking. The dining hall was packed. Some of the tables were pushed against the walls, leaving just enough room to sit at them. I looked for a familiar face, but it was overwhelmingly crowded. Suddenly, I heard my name. I turned toward the voice, as Josefina rushed toward me, throwing her arms around me.

"Jane, I've missed you! I'm so glad you're back! I couldn't wait to see you. How was your Christmas? Was Marie awful to you?" She was so enthusiastic that I couldn't help but forget about Marie's cruelness earlier in the evening.

"I've missed you too. I was so worried that I wasn't coming back," I replied.

"I prayed you wouldn't be expelled. How was Christmas? You haven't said."

"There's so much to tell you. I don't know where to begin," I said breathlessly. It was just like Josefina to ask me a million questions and expect an answer for them all at once.

"Come sit down. Miguel's already at a table. I know he'll want to hear about you too," she said tugging on my hand.

I followed her across the crowded room until we finally reached the table where Miguel was sitting. He smiled when I approached, and I sat down between the two of them.

"Hi, Jane. How are you?" Miguel asked.

"I'm just glad to be back," I replied.

"Jane was going to tell us about her Christmas break," Josefina told Miguel.

"Yes, where do I begin? It was so awful. From the minute I arrived, I was put straight to work. I barely got any sleep."

"That's awful! I wish you could stand up for yourself," Josefina commented.

"Marie's been threatening to throw me out. This time, I don't think it's an empty threat. Just before I left, she threatened me again," I said.

"That's terrible. Is there any way to get away from her?" Miguel asked concerned.

"No, I wouldn't have anywhere to go, and I am too proud to become a burden to anyone," I answered.

"Why did she have you constantly cleaning? Was that her way of punishing you for being dismissed?" Josefina asked rapid-fire.

"No, Marie wasn't told. Dr. Tweedle didn't think it would be wise. We just told her I was home early because it was a reward for my academic excellence. If Marie would've known it was because of trouble, I would never have been allowed to return," I responded.

As soon as I paused for breath, Josefina was back to her questions. "So, why did you have to clean so much?"

"Josefina, I was getting to that," I laughed. "I can't even pause to breathe because you're so impatient. Marie was throwing a huge Christmas party, and she wanted the house to be perfect before the guests arrived. Of course, Emily and Preston made my tasks more difficult. On top of that, I had to help Robert in the stables shoveling horse manure."

"Who's Robert?" Josefina asked. "You've never mentioned him before."

"I didn't? Robert is my only friend at home. He's the stable boy Marie was given by one of Emily's suitors. He hasn't been working for her very long. Anyway, sometimes I'm sent out to work with him, and since he is about my age, we've become friends. He was separated from his family when he was very young, and he has been forced into a life of hard work. I feel very sorry for him."

"That's so sad. At least you have a friend at home," Miguel replied. "It's a shame that Marie makes you do a man's work."

"I can't believe she makes you do that!" Josefina exclaimed. "It's not proper for her to make you work outside."

"It really doesn't matter. When no one is around, I use the quick complete charm to save my energy."

"Oh Jane, you have to be careful not to get caught. Humans can't find out about what we are. You haven't told Robert, have you?" Josefina asked worriedly.

"No, I haven't told Robert. I know the rules. I only use it when I'm sure no one will see me. If Marie ever saw me using any magic, she would certainly throw me out. I've been very careful," I replied.

"I'm just worried about you. The W.A.S.P. could be anywhere. You can never tell which humans are members. I just wouldn't want any of Marie's servants to belong to that organization!" Josefina wailed.

"Don't worry. I am always cautious. Besides, you didn't let me tell you about the Christmas party!"

Josefina and Miguel leaned closer becoming even more attentive.

"Robert and I had to serve drinks and food to the guests. I have to admit everything was decorated beautifully and all the guests were elegantly dressed. Emily made her grand entrance before dinner and all the guests gravitated toward her. I didn't understand why this party was so important to Emily. She even took special preparations when getting ready.

"I was so nervous. I thought I was going to do something wrong or that Emily would embarrass me in front of all the guests. Thankfully, Marie and Emily were too distracted and didn't pay much attention to me. After dinner, there was dancing and socializing. That was when Marie decided to make the big announcement. I was startled when Emily and a young man were called to the front of the room and even more so when he got down on one knee and purposed to her."

Josefina gasped and looked just as startled. "Your stepsister is going to be married?" she exclaimed.

"Yes, the Christmas party was Emily's engagement party as well. A year from now, in the spring, she will be married to Drake Doyle, one of the richest men Marie could find."

"Didn't you say she was mean and awful? Who would want to marry her?" Miguel said.

"According to what I've heard, he's just like the rest of them. This wedding is going to be a nightmare, and if anything goes wrong, I'm going to be blamed for it. I can't even be happy that Emily will be moving out of the house. Somehow, I think that she will still visit and be there to punish me. Before I left, they were headed to Drake Doyle's mansion for a New Year's Eve party. Preston even went along, despite his childish nature.

"The strangest thing happened before they left. When I entered Preston's room to make sure he was dressed, he was playing with something on the floor. Then, he told me that he had a present for me. He proceeded to drop a dead rat at my feet, which after examination, it was obviously tortured to death."

Disgust was mirrored in both the twin's eyes. Finally, Josefina spoke, "How horrible! Why would he do such a thing? I'm almost ashamed to tell you about our Christmas and how wonderful it was. I wish that you never had to return to that awful woman and her two demented children."

"Enough about me. After all, it's the New Year, and I am back. Marie and her children are in the past, and I won't have to deal with them until next weekend. I would be happy to know how your holiday was," I suggested.

"We had a very good Christmas," Josefina replied. "My parents bought both of us a small pet to keep here at the academy. I got a Cactus Cat and she's so pretty. I named her Cocoa after the Peruvian cat god, which some of my Peruvian ancestors worshipped. At least, that's what my mom told me,"

"What's a Cactus Cat?" I asked.

"A Cactus Cat feeds off the juice of the cactus plant and their fur can become pointy like a cactus when they're angry. They originated in the north and south American deserts. Cactus Cats become extremely loyal and protective of their owners. They make good pets for pixies," Josefina explained.

"I can't wait to see her. It's so nice that they allow us to keep pets here. What kind of pet did you get, Miguel?" I asked.

"It's called a Gwilingi. It looks just like a small black dog," Miguel said. "I just named him Blackie."

"That's wonderful. I'm so glad that you both had a splendid Christmas," I said sincerely.

"Other than that, we didn't do much over the holiday. We've missed you," Josefina said.

"Have you been practicing your predicting the future over the break?" Miguel joked.

"No, I haven't had the time for that. I have a feeling that Mr. Withermyer will give us some kind of surprise quiz since he likes to torment students."

"Jane's probably right. I'm horrible at his tests, but you've been able to complete everything he assigns, Jane," Josefina replied.

"I don't know how I manage to do it. It must be beginners' luck."

"I swear it must be from your mother. You're more like Rachel McCalski than you think. Maybe even greater than..." Josefina was interrupted.

"Greater than Rachel McCalski? Well, that wouldn't be very hard. I will say that I'm very surprised to see you here, Jane."

I spun around to see Betty Ann. She had on a party dress decked out in pink lace with her brown hair down below her shoulders. The dress had a deep V neck which made her bosom stand out. She looked very cheap for being so rich.

I felt my rage building within me, but I had to stay calm or else I'd be trouble again. Betty Ann was probably trying to goad me into an argument so that would happen.

"Betty Ann, I really don't see how we were talking to you," Miguel said in my defense.

"Well, I was just coming by to congratulate Jane for fooling Dr. Tweedle and some of the government chairs. My father isn't duped by you, though. He knows exactly what you are."

"Betty Ann, I don't know what your obsession with Jane is, but every time I turn around, you're talking about her. It's a pity your life is so boring and unsubstantial that you have to talk about Jane just to have something to say," Josefina said.

Betty Ann glared at Josefina, and I thought for a second that she was going to slap her. "It upsets me that the Jelf Academy would allow such pixies into this establishment. Dr. Tweedle needs to take out the trash," Betty Ann replied nastily.

Miguel was on his feet after Betty Ann stopped speaking, but I quickly reached out and grabbed his arm. "Sit back down, Miguel. Let's be smart and not associate ourselves with the trash at this academy," I said.

I could tell from Betty Ann's silence that she was dumbfounded. Soon after, I heard her stalking off to bother someone else.

"How can you be so calm when she insulted your mother again?" Miguel asked. "I wanted to shout at her for demeaning you."

"I'm not calm. I'm very angry, but I don't want to get in trouble because of her again. I've been working so hard, and I've just been given a second chance. I'm not going to get expelled because of Betty Ann. She doesn't know what she's talking about. I'm not going to stoop to her level with unladylike behavior. Someday, when she no longer has friends, she'll wonder why," I replied.

"You're right, Jane," Josefina replied. "Did you see the dress she had on?"

We laughed at Betty Ann's ridiculous outfit and then helped ourselves to the buffet that had been set up on one side of the dining hall. We spent the rest of the morning listening to music and dancing. It was right before daybreak on January first that we headed to our rooms.

When Josefina and I reached our room, she smiled. "You're going to meet Cocoa. I hope she likes you." She placed her hand on the panel and the door swung open. Josefina entered slowly, and I followed her. Curled up on a big pillow was the most beautiful cat I'd ever seen. I wouldn't have been able to tell that she wasn't a normal cat if I hadn't already known. It wasn't until I got closer and saw that her dark fur seemed to shimmer green on the tips of her hair. When she heard us enter, she rose from the bed and ran to Josefina.

Josefina bent down and petted her sleek fur. "Hello, Cocoa," Josefina giggled as she stood up.

As I drew closer, Cocoa seemed to tense. All of a sudden, her hair stood up, becoming bright green and pointy like a cactus. I was sure it was just as sharp.

"It's ok, Cocoa, this is Jane, my best friend, and roommate. She isn't going to hurt me," Josefina soothed the cat.

Cocoa seemed to have understood what Josefina said, and she calmed down. Cocoa's fur turned back to the gray color and the spikes disappeared. She came towards me, and I bent down to let her smell my hand. She rubbed against me, and her fur was surprisingly soft, despite being sharp only a moment ago.

"She's really beautiful," I told Josefina.

I crossed to my side of the room and sat down on my bed. I didn't realize how much I had missed sleeping here until now. Cocoa climbed back into her cat bed and Josefina scratched behind her ears. She purred in satisfaction.

"It feels so good to be back here. It feels normal. Like I belong in this world and not in the other one. Sometimes, I feel like my life with Marie is a horror story and the world of pixie magic is the real world," I said as I reclined on the bed.

"This is your world, Jane, and you do belong here," Josefina replied.

"Some people don't seem to think so, and humans would think I'm an abomination," I said solemnly.

"Don't listen to what anyone else thinks, especially Betty Ann. You definitely belong here. Who cares if you're half-human? You're one of the best pixies I've ever met." Josefina said smiling.

"Thanks, Josefina. You're the best friend I've ever had. I was very lucky to have met you."

"I'm very lucky to have met you, too," she replied.

I crawled under the covers, feeling exhausted but happy. I did want to belong in the pixie world. I hoped I would be able to prove it.

17

Day of Freedom

I AWOKE TO JOSEFINA shaking me and the feel of fur against my face. Cocoa was curled around my head, and Josefina was sitting on the side of my bed.

"Good morning, Jane. It's eleven-thirty. If you get up now, we might make it in time for lunch," Josefina said.

"It's eleven-thirty?" I asked sleepily. "I've never slept so late in my life!"

"I'm sorry to wake you, but I'm hungry," she laughed.

I crawled out of bed and quickly put on an informal dress to wear to lunch. It felt strange to be at the Jelf Academy and not attend classes.

"Are you ready to go now?" Josefina asked.

"I still need to fix my hair and brush my teeth," I said, shuffling to the bathroom.

In a few minutes, I was ready. Josefina and I headed down to the dining hall and saw that the tables were back in order. There was no sign that a party had taken place the night before.

"What do you want to do today?" Josefina asked as we waited to select our meal.

214

"I don't care what we do," I replied. "I'm just happy to have a day of relaxation."

"Josefina told me that you were here," Miguel said as he approached us. "I thought I would join you. My roommate still hasn't returned from Christmas break. I thought it was strange, but we don't have class today so, maybe he'll come back tonight or even tomorrow morning. He isn't very social. Perhaps that's why he didn't come back for the party last night."

"Who's your roommate?" I asked.

"Do you remember Henry Adams in our Predicting the Future class?" Miguel said.

Josefina and I nodded. I remembered he was a small anxious boy.

"We were placed together since we both didn't know anyone to room with. He's very nice but extremely quiet. He never says much."

"I'm sure he'll be back soon. Maybe his family went on vacation over Christmas.," Josefina suggested.

"If he had any holiday plans, he didn't mention it to me, but then again, he never told me anything," Miguel pondered.

We finished our lunch and then debated on what to do. Finally, we decided to have a snowball fight on the lawn outside. I was thankful for my mother's coat because it kept me warm, and I didn't even feel like I was outside. Pixie snowball fighting was very different from what I witnessed between Emily and Preston. Instead of picking up snow and forming it into a ball with our hands, we were able to use our minds. I had better aim by using my mind than if I would've thrown it with my hand. I could visually direct the snowball to land exactly where I wanted. Also, by not having to form the snowballs with my hands, I could make them as enormous as I wanted. I couldn't remember laughing so much.

We came in from the cold to get ready for dinner. My coat and the bottom of my dress were drenched. Josefina and I sloshed up to our room, our noses and ears red. Josefina began changing out of her wet clothes, but I stood by the door thinking.

I wanted to experiment with my abilities to see what I could do without charms. I knew I could heat other objects using my hands, but would I be able to heat my entire body? I closed my eyes and concentrated. Soon after, I felt a warm tingling sensation.

"Jane! What are you doing?" Josefina exclaimed after a few minutes. "You're smoking!"

My eyes snapped open, and I glanced down. Steam was rising from my clothes. Soon, the warm sensation intensified, and I figured it was because my clothes were drying. Sure enough, when I touched my coat, it was no longer damp.

"Don't worry, Josefina. I'm only drying my clothes. Look," I said showing her my sleeve.

"Wow, Jane. I can't believe you have the ability to mentally dry your clothes. That kind of mental concentration takes a lot of practice," she said touching my coat.

"I wanted to see what I could do by only using my mind. I thought if I could warm my hands, maybe I could emit heat from everywhere."

"How'd you do that?" Josefina asked still awed.

"I just concentrated on what I wanted to happen," I replied.

"See, I've been telling you that you're talented," Josefina giggled.

Josefina stopped changing and attempted to dry her damp dress. I stood watching her, and after a moment, steam rose from her dress.

"Josefina, you're doing it! I told you it was easy," I said with delight.

"I'm sure it is for you. After a few minutes of trying by myself, I had to ask Miguel to help me and finally, they began drying," Josefina sighed.

"Wait, you and Miguel can combine thoughts to do magic without charms?" I asked startled.

"Yes, that's what makes twins special. We can talk to each other and combine our magic," Josefina shrugged her shoulders as if it was nothing special.

"Dr. Tweedle told me the more we practice, the better developed our minds will be. Can you imagine how powerful you and Miguel will be by the time we graduate from here?" I stated.

"I know, but it seems like your mind is already developed."

I laughed at her confidence in me. I didn't know why Miguel and Josefina thought so highly of me.

Josefina and I headed down to dinner in our newly dried clothes, meeting Miguel at the entrance to the dining hall. He looked worried.

Josefina grabbed Miguel's arm with concern on her face now. "He hasn't come back yet?"

I gazed at them, trying to understand what they were talking about. It didn't seem fair that they could read each other's minds, especially when they didn't explain.

"No, he hasn't returned," Miguel replied looking solemn.

"I'm sure there's a perfect explanation," Josefina said reassuringly.

"Excuse me," I interrupted. "I can't read either of your minds, so I have no clue what you're talking about."

"Sorry Jane," Josefina apologized. "Miguel's roommate Henry still hasn't returned."

Miguel looked anxious, so I said, "Maybe Henry will be back later tonight or tomorrow."

Miguel smiled at me and shrugged his shoulders. I followed the twins into a line and waited to get dinner. "Where do pixies go on vacation?" I asked. Were there special places only pixies could go?

"Pixies go to similar places that humans travel to. Humans just don't understand the significance of certain places. The Mayan temples in Mexico were built by pixies. So were the Egyptian pyramids. Humans wouldn't be strong enough to build those structures with primitive tools. That's why back in ancient times, pixies were rulers and healers, and humans were our subjects. Pixies have their own forms of government now because humans became aware of what we truly are. We no longer look like gods to them anymore.

"When humans realized that pixies could become ill or die, they knew we weren't gods. Some humans, like the W.A.S.P., think they can kill us and take our powers. That's why pixies have to hide. It's too much of a risk," Miguel explained.

"Miguel, I'm impressed! I didn't know you knew all this history!" I exclaimed. "No wonder you and Josefina are getting top marks on all of Mr. Collyworth's tests."

"Our Uncle Fernando is a historian," Josefina explained. "What he knows is fascinating, but I just can't listen when he talks about how the Mayans sacrificed humans to their gods. He goes into detail about that stuff," she made a disgusted face.

"Josefina, that stuff's interesting," Miguel replied. "Uncle Fernando told us that Stonehenge was built by Anglo-Saxon pixies. Who else would've been able to build a huge astrological calendar or move those stones? Uncle Fernando gets to travel to different places around the world to research ancient cultures. He's a pixie archeologist. I've considered going into his field, and then we could travel together. My dad isn't too enthusiastic about me following in his brother's footsteps. He thinks that I should help Juan with the family gem business or go into government law."

"We have plenty of time to choose a career. It's only our first year. We don't have to have an idea until the fifth year," Josefina said.

I was fascinated to learn that pixies could be tracked through ancient history. I was having a hard time remembering things about the current pixie world, it was hard to imagine learning about the past. For a brief moment, I wondered if I did belong here, but I pushed the thought from my mind as I looked at Josefina and Miguel's smiling faces.

18

A CHARM OF CONFUSION

CLASSES BEGAN TOO early the next morning. I was surprisingly tired even after having a day of rest. Gemstones 101 went smoothly and soon we entered Predicting the Future. Ms. Crescent was sitting in the middle of the room holding sticks of incense. She cast what I guessed to be a mild fire charm and they sparked to life. Then she dramatically blew out the flame, causing the incense to smoke. Ms. Crescent looked at me as I took a seat, and I could have sworn she had a frown on her face.

When the whole class arrived, Ms. Crescent stood up and paced the room.

"Today, class, I was going to begin lecturing on mystical auras and how you can see someone's energy, but I've changed my mind. Instead, we'll be discussing the importance of future predictions and why we should pay attention to them. When we receive future insights, they come to us for a reason. They're warnings of events that could come to pass if we do not act on them. When they are ignored, all sorts of trouble could occur.

"For example, if you are warned about a certain place, you shouldn't venture to that location. If we don't listen and open our minds to the signs we're receiving, then disaster could strike," Ms. Crescent said very dramatically.

Some students shifted uncomfortably in their seats.

"It is also very important when a person with significant practice in the art of seeing the future shares their insights of the visions they received. You should listen to me during our meetings. I have had significant training and would deem myself highly qualified when it comes to interpreting the future. You should heed my predictions for they are of the utmost importance. Class is dismissed since my inner eye can't focus today. Tomorrow, we'll start auras," Ms. Crescent sighed. We looked at each other in confusion before we filed out of the classroom.

"Full of herself, isn't she?" Miguel asked once we were far enough down the hall. "All she told me when we had our private session was to study or else, I would fail midterms. As if that wasn't obvious."

"Maybe she had nothing life-threatening to tell you," Josefina said.

"Come on, Josefina. Why are you defending her? She just acted like her insights into the future were the most important things in our lives," Miguel complained.

"Maybe you're right, but I do feel like I've learned a lot in her class. What do you think, Jane?" Josefina asked.

"When I had my private session, Ms. Crescent told me things that didn't make sense. You think she would've foreseen that I was going to be sent home a week early. I would've liked to avoid that," I agreed with Miguel.

"Something just tells me that we should listen to what she has to say and not blow it off entirely," Josefina commented.

Miguel just shook his head at her as we sat down in History of Pixies.

"Did you notice that Henry Adams wasn't in Predicting the Future today?" Miguel pointed out looking very troubled.

"I didn't notice, but I also wasn't looking for him," I said.

"It's odd because he doesn't strike me as the kind of person to miss class. He was always too nervous about it," Miguel replied. "He wasn't in our room this morning either."

Before we could continue our conversation, Mr. Collyworth entered the room and began another boring lecture about the Civil War telling us pixies fought for both sides.

"The Southern pixies believed that if they could keep slaves, they would still be in control of humans. The Northern pixies disagreed because they decided a long time ago to let humans have their own society. The Civil War was the official end to pixies 'ruling' humans, at least in America. Pixies in the past fought in human wars because they believe in the cause, or they want to be inconspicuous. This still happens today," Mr. Collyworth droned on.

After what seemed like hours, we were finally dismissed from class and made our way down to lunch.

"I'm so glad to be out of there. I felt like it lasted five hours," Josefina complained.

"I thought it was fascinating. If you would just listen for once! I'm going to start blocking my mind during tests if you don't start soon," Miguel countered.

I kept my mouth closed and my amusement to myself. I could understand both of their points. Mr. Collyworth was boring, but the information had the potential to be interesting. Maybe it was only that way for me because I found everything about the pixie world interesting.

Of course, lunch went quickly because my least favorite class was right after. Whatever Mr. Withermyer had planned would seem like punishment for having a holiday break. Josefina, Miguel, and I cautiously entered the classroom and took our seats. Mr. Withermyer wasn't seated at the front of the room, but we knew better than to talk. Even without his presence, his eyes still seemed to be on us.

I pulled my pixie dust case from my bag, along with the mortar and pestle. The classroom filled up and still, Mr. Withermyer hadn't entered. We all sat in silence, no one daring to even murmur. Finally, five minutes after the start of class, Mr. Withermyer strode into the classroom. He acted like he was on time and looked as if he was daring someone to comment on his lateness.

"Open your books to page 102. Today you will craft a confusion charm, and then test your charm on one of your classmates. Depending on how confused they become will inform me of who was successful. Don't worry, I may use an undoing charm to reverse the effects afterward, but I'll judge that by the performance of the class," he grinned wickedly. "You have until ten minutes are remaining in the class to perfect your charm. As a side note, I will know if you're faking the effects of the charm. So do not attempt to save your friend's grade."

I swallowed the lump in my throat and opened my book. I measured out one and a fourth cups of peridots and began heating them in my cupped hands. When they were slightly warm, I began crushing them into powder with the mortar and pestle. As I crushed, I looked to my left and noticed Josefina was sweating. I took a deep breath and read the third step. I had to measure the same number of peridots, but I had to chill them instead. How was I supposed to do that? If I could heat my body, did that mean could I cool myself down too? I closed my eyes, trying to concentrate with all the noise in the room. Dr. Tweedle said pixies could do anything with firm concentration and discipline of the mind. I held the second cup of peridots in my hands and imagined my hands were freezing.

Suddenly, I began to feel a numbness in my hands, almost as if I had gone out on a cold day without gloves. I kept concentrating like this for a few minutes, and then I touched the stones. I could feel a temperature change, but not drastic enough to chill them.

I knew my time was limited, so I tried to think faster. Compelled by an idea, I brought the stones up to my mouth and blew on them. I imagined that both my breath and hands were icy cold. This odd idea seemed to be working, and soon my peridots were chilled. I quickly crushed them, the whole time praying that Betty Ann hadn't seen what I had done. She had passed other charms by copying off me, so I hoped she was too distracted to notice.

Now, I had to measure half a cup of the cold pixie dust and mix it into the warm bowl. The directions stated that the pixie dust needed mixed in three complete rotations clockwise and then five rotations counterclockwise. I counted slowly. Once the rotations were completed, I had to add the remaining dust half a cup at a time repeating the instructions. I was just making my last rotation when Mr. Withermyer asked us to put down our equipment.

"I will be choosing the classmate on whom you will test your charm. Let's begin with Mr. Brian Nickels testing his charm on Miss Lacey Stevenson."

A brown-haired boy with a small number of freckles on his face slowly walked to the front of the class along with a pretty blonde-haired girl who looked nervous.

"Do you have a glass of water to put my charm in? The book says it could be added to a beverage," Brian stuttered.

"I hoped you read how to make the charm better than you read the description of how to use it," Mr. Withermyer sneered. "The charm can be added to food or drink, but that's only to be inconspicuous. Miss Stevenson knows what you are doing. I hardly see the point in wasting the time to conceal it. Move along, Mr. Nickels, and cast the charm."

Lacey looked like she was bracing herself as Brian stepped closer. He cast the light green dust into the air above her. Then, he stepped back, waiting on her reaction. Lacey opened her eyes and blinked rapidly. "Why am I in Charms class?" she blurted. "I thought I was on Christmas break."

"What is your name?" Mr. Withermyer asked.

"Lacey Stevenson of course," she replied as if it was the dumbest question in the world.

"Only semi-satisfactory, Mr. Nickels. Miss Stevenson only managed to forget what day it was. A powerful confusion charm wouldn't have allowed her to remember her name or where she was. Please take your seats."

Mr. Withermyer then proceeded to call up other students. Everyone was able to remember at least something after they'd been charmed.

"Miss Betty Ann Barber will test her charm on Miss Jane Fitzgerald," Mr. Withermyer said. His smile seemed malicious.

Betty Ann skipped to the front of the room as if she had been awarded the best prize of her life. I glared at both of them, a wave of anger bubbling in my chest. I should've seen this coming. If she had copied me like before, then I might be in trouble. I was sure Mr. Withermyer wouldn't undo the effects of the charm on me. Slowly, I rose from my seat and made my way to the front of the room. Betty Ann's smile grew larger as I stood in front of her. I braced myself for what was about to happen and imagined my mind surrounded by a wall. This was my feeble attempt at protection other than fleeing the room completely.

Betty Ann began casting her charm over me and instantly I felt my mind begin to cloud. I could almost visualize it happening, and I knew I had to fight it. I mentally pushed against the thick fog that was entering my mind. I clung to my identity and what I knew was happening around me. The fog hung in my mind, and I thought I was going to be sick. I knew that if I succumbed to the fog, the sickness would go away, but I also understood if I did, Betty Ann's charm would take over. I fought the fog as hard as I could and slowly, it started to recede. My mind became stronger until eventually, the fog lifted, and I felt normal again.

"What is your name?" Mr. Withermyer asked, pulling my attention to him.

"My name's Jane Fitzgerald. I feel perfectly fine," I said firmly.

"She's lying," Betty Ann shouted. "I saw her eyes glaze over. It has to have affected her!"

Mr. Withermyer glared at me. "Ask me any questions you want to," I replied.

Mr. Withermyer began asking me a series of questions about my life, and with each correct answer, his frown grew deeper. Finally, he ceased his interrogation. I was sure it bothered him that I had answered all the questions correctly.

"Return to your seat, Miss Barber," Mr. Withermyer growled. "Stay at the front of the room, Miss Fitzgerald. It is time to test your charm. You will test it on Miss Taylor Miller."

Taylor rose from her seat, looking very scared and vulnerable. My heart rose in my throat. Why did I have to test my charm on her? Taylor had a childlike quality about her and casting my charm felt wrong. Hopefully, since she was so smart, she would be able to fight it as I did. Taylor stood in front of me with her eyes cast down, managing to look smaller than usual. Slowly, I cast my charm over her and prayed for the best. Instantly, her eyes glazed over, and her body shuddered.

"Where am I?" she wailed before Mr. Withermyer had a chance to question her. Obviously, she wasn't fighting it. Taylor crossed her arms over her chest and slightly bent over.

"What is your name?" Mr. Withermyer asked her.

"Am I Tammy?" she asked. "Please don't hurt me," she screamed.

Her shrill scream shook me to my core, and I just wanted to help her. I wished I knew how to cast an undoing charm.

Taylor crouched down and placed her hands over her eyes. She started rocking back and forth as she screamed. "Help me! Help me! Don't let them kill me!"

The whole class looked shocked. No one else had reacted like this. Mr. Withermyer looked taken aback, but he quickly composed himself. "Class is dismissed." he snarled as he walked toward Taylor and cast his undoing charm on her. I stood rooted to the floor, terrified by what my charm had done to her. I watched Taylor relax and then collapse into a faint. Mr. Withermyer bent down and gently lifted her head off the ground.

"I'm… I'm sorry," I stammered as the rest of the class fled the room. What had I done?

Mr. Withermyer turned on me. "I said the class was dismissed, Miss Fitzgerald. You may now leave," he demanded.

I collected my materials and quickly made my way to Earth Catastrophes. I felt horrible about what my charm had done to Taylor. Who did she think was going to hurt her? Did I complete my charm correctly? My stomach fluttered about the possibility of being called to Dr. Tweedle's office. This would be it. The pixie government would definitely vote to expel me now.

Josefina and Miguel were already in the classroom when I arrived. They both looked as shaken as I was.

"I don't know what I did! I completed the charm exactly as the book said," I said frantically.

"Calm down, Jane. I'm sure it'll all be okay. Mr. Withermyer did the undoing charm. Once Taylor has a minute to recuperate, she'll probably be okay. I don't think it was your fault, Jane," Josefina said trying to comfort me.

"No one else acted like that. I feel terrible. The way Taylor screamed frightened me," I choked back my tears. "I'm afraid I did something wrong and any minute I'll be sent to Dr. Tweedle's office. I'll be packing my bag and leaving the Jelf Academy forever."

"Jane, I know of students who have done worse at this Academy. Juan has told me that students have been expelled for intentionally causing harm to others. You didn't set out to hurt Taylor. Mr. Withermyer had us cast the charms on each other. It's not your fault," Miguel said.

Even though they both assured me that everything would be okay, I couldn't help feeling disturbed. With the arrival of Mr.

Laruse, we had to end our conversation. I couldn't concentrate on the lesson. When Taylor didn't come to class, I really began to worry. Any minute I would be called to Dr. Tweedle's office to explain myself. I also feared for Taylor's wellbeing.

I followed Miguel and Josefina to Zodiac Signs, not feeling very talkative. I knew they thought it wasn't my fault, but they weren't the ones who cast the charm on Taylor. I knew that I wasn't going to be able to concentrate on Zodiac Signs. As the other students filed in, I noticed that Taylor wasn't coming to this class too. I felt even sicker. What had my charm done for her to be absent from two classes? Through Zodiac Signs, I sat on pins and needles. I planned to go straight to Dr. Tweedle's office after class unless I was called sooner than that.

My anxiety made it hard to breathe, but I wasn't requested to leave the room. As soon as we were dismissed, I sprinted from the room.

When I got to Dr. Tweedle's office, I knocked as calmly as I could. Slowly, the door swung opened, and I could see Dr. Tweedle sitting at his desk.

"Come in, Jane. I figured I would be seeing you."

"How's Miss Miller? She didn't come to our other classes. Is she okay?" I fired off quickly.

"Miss Miller will be fine. Right now, she's resting in the hospital wing until she feels better," Dr. Tweedle replied.

"Is it my fault? Did I do the charm wrong?" I asked alarmed.

"No Jane, it isn't your fault. Mr. Withermyer brought me your confusion charm and after testing it, I determined that it was completed correctly. Very well done on the first try if I can say that, but do you understand the effects of a confusion charm?" Dr. Tweedle asked.

"I know they confuse the person who gets placed under one," I replied.

"Yes, but a person may entirely forget who they are. Past events may influence how someone reacts. A person may have suffered a traumatic event in the past, so when they become confused, they may believe the event is still happening. Feelings caused by the past event may arise," Dr. Tweedle said.

"Is that what happened to her?"

"I can guess that something of that nature must've happened, but I wouldn't be at liberty to discuss it."

"So, I'm not going to be expelled?" I asked terrified.

"No, as I said, I have analyzed your charm and it was executed correctly. I don't feel the need to mention this in your report," Dr. Tweedle said reassuringly.

"Dr. Tweedle, is it possible to mentally fight off the effects of different charms?" I asked. I was curious about what I had felt when Betty Ann had cast her charm on me.

"Yes, it's possible to fight off the effects, but it takes a much-trained pixie to do it. Some of the most advanced pixies can't even fight off the total effects of a charm. It all depends on the charm's strength. Not even I can fight off every charm."

"I'm only asking because when Miss Barber cast her charm on me, my mind clouded at first, but then I was able to push away the fog and think clearly again."

Dr. Tweedle stared at me for a moment with a surprised expression, but then he quickly tried to hide it. "It's unheard of for first-year pixies to mentally combat charms and completely disarm them. Miss Barber's charm must've been weak or not concocted properly. Surely you must have been a tad confused."

"I wasn't confused at all after the charm," I insisted. "I felt like I was fighting back the fog in my head."

"Miss Barber's charm must've been very weak then. As long as I've been headmaster of this school, I've never seen a young student accomplish that. Don't worry, Jane. Disarming charms will come with time. Most students develop this skill in their fifth year if they are lucky."

I bowed my head in acceptance. After all, Dr. Tweedle was the headmaster, and I should take his word for it. I just couldn't ignore the nagging feeling that I had fought Betty Ann's charm.

"Would it be possible for me to visit Miss Miller to see how she's doing? I'm devastated by what happened."

"Yes, you may," Dr. Tweedle said brightening. "I'll give you directions to the hospital wing."

I thanked him as I exited his office. I took the stairs to the third floor. Rounding the balustrade at the top of the stairs, I then turned to my left. The first door I came to, had a plaque that read 'Hospital Wing'. I took a deep breath and pushed the door open.

When I entered, I glanced around the reception room. Several students sat on the chairs waiting their turn. The walls were bleached white and so was the outfit of the woman behind the counter. Her badge said Nurse Adelina, and she had a kind, round face.

"How can I help you, dear?" she asked when I walked up to the counter.

"I'm here to see Taylor Miller. Dr. Tweedle told me I could come by."

"All right, dear. Let me show you to Miss Miller's bedside." Nurse Adelina rose from the desk and took me through the door on the far left. We entered the true hospital wing, each bed sectioned off by a curtain. When we got to Taylor's bed, I found her propped up on a pillow looking very sad.

"Hi, Taylor. How are you feeling?" I asked.

Taylor looked down at her fingers and shrugged her shoulders.

"I'll leave you girls alone for a while," Nurse Adelina said, making her way back to the office.

"I'm really sorry about the effect my charm had on you. I didn't expect that to happen. I wanted to let you know that I had no intention of causing you or anyone else harm."

"I know it wasn't your fault. What happened to me was my fault. I was the one confused," Taylor said in her small voice.

"No, Taylor, we shouldn't have tested our charms on each other. It wasn't right. Mr. Withermyer should've known someone could be harmed," I replied.

"The confusion charm isn't supposed to hurt people, just confuse them. People forget who they are, or what they were doing, or where they're at. I read about almost all of the charms in our book."

"Then why did the charm harm you?" I asked her.

"I was confused, and I just can't seem to forget," Taylor mumbled. Her eyes looked glassy, with a faraway gaze.

"I don't understand."

Taylor finally looked at me. "I don't want to talk about it!" she said loudly, startling me. "I'll be fine!"

I stood speechless. Suddenly, nurse Adelina was at my elbow. "Is everything okay in here?" she asked. Taylor didn't speak again and had gone back to looking at her hands. "Maybe you should let her get some rest," Nurse Adelina said touching my arm to steer me out of the room.

"I'm sorry, Taylor. I didn't mean to upset you. I just wanted to stop by to tell you that I was sorry and to see how you were feeling. Get some rest. I hope you're feeling better soon," I said.

"Thank you for visiting me, Jane. I appreciate it," Taylor whispered in her usual quiet voice.

Nurse Adelina led me back to the front office. "I'm sure it'll take a while longer for the undoing charm to take full effect. She should be fine soon. Nothing to worry about."

"Thank you for allowing me to see her," I replied as I exited the hospital wing.

On the way back to my room, I stopped at the closest restroom. When I finished, I was just about to exit the stall when I heard Betty Ann and her friends enter. It sounded like they were on their way to dinner, so I hesitated in the stall and decided to wait.

"I don't know what happened in Charms today," Betty Ann

was complaining. "Jane must've cheated somehow. There's no way she felt nothing from my charm. She was lying."

"Why do you say that?" one of the girls asked. "Did you see what Jane's charm did to that ugly, weird girl? Maybe Jane's more powerful than you think."

"Be quiet, Marsha. There is no way a stupid half-human like Jane is more powerful than me. My family's bloodline dates back farther than anyone can remember. I come from a long line of powerful pixies. I know Jane must be cheating because I copied how she did her charm," Betty Ann said.

I couldn't believe my ears. So, Betty Ann was copying off me.

"Are you sure you copied Jane's charm exactly? Maybe you missed something," another girl said.

"No, I didn't miss anything. I did exactly what she did. Jane should be the one in the hospital wing. If her charm put 'Miss Know It All' there, my charm should've had the same effect. I wonder how she managed to cheat," Betty Ann fumed.

"Betty Ann," the one named Marsha spoke. "If Jane's terrible at everything and isn't a true pixie, then why were you copying her charm?"

"Marsha, just be quiet. Let's just go to dinner," Betty Ann commanded.

I heard them leave the restroom, but I was too stunned to move. If Betty Ann had copied my charm, then why didn't it have the same effect on me that it had on Taylor? Dr. Tweedle told me that I had completed the charm correctly. If Betty Ann had copied my charm, then wouldn't it be the same? I was so sure I had fought off the effects of the charm. Was Dr. Tweedle correct about charm disarming, or had he lied to me about it?

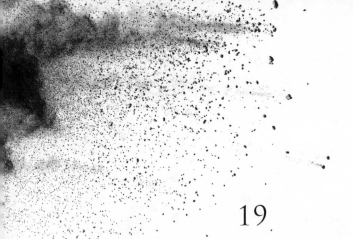

19

AURAS AND FALSE ACCUSATIONS

"SHE'S THE CHEATER!" Josefina exclaimed. I'd just finished telling her about visiting Taylor and what I had overheard in the bathroom. "I've seen her looking at you in Charms, especially for the harder assignments. It's no surprise to me that she would copy you!"

It was after dinner, and Josefina and I were back in our room. I hadn't mentioned my unintentional eavesdropping at dinner for fear of being overheard. I knew Josefina would be able to tell Miguel, so I waited until we could be in the privacy of our room.

"She has a lot of nerve with all this talk about how you're a human and that you have tainted blood. Well, I'd like to ask her why she's copying you when she's supposedly better than you!" Josefina said excitedly.

"Promise me you won't," I said. "Betty Ann's not worth the time."

"Okay, I won't say anything. I'm glad you found out that Taylor's all right, though," Josefina said brightly, but I couldn't look at the incident as something to be relieved about. Taylor had been so distressed. It was hard getting the image of her screaming out of my head.

⁓

Taylor was in class the next day, quiet and withdrawn as ever. Miguel's roommate, however, hadn't returned to the school. Miguel hadn't received any word from him, and we could only surmise his whereabouts.

"Oh, Miss Miller! I'm so glad to see you in class," Betty Ann said, her voice dripping with sarcasm. "I thought Miss Fitzgerald had permanently damaged you. The way you screamed sounded like you were dying. I thought she'd made you go mentally insane."

Taylor just kept her head down and continued staring at her books. I could see she was biting on the inside of her lip, doing her best to ignore Betty Ann.

"Hello!" Betty Ann yelled when Taylor didn't answer. "I'm talking to you. Maybe Miss Fitzgerald did mess with your brain," Betty Ann said nastily.

Just when I was about to stand up and defend Taylor, Ms. Crescent breezed into the room.

"Take a seat, Miss Barber. Why are you still standing?"

"Sorry, I was asking Miss Miller if she was okay. She was hurt by Miss Fitzgerald's charm yesterday, and I was just concerned. I don't know how she mixes a confusion charm, but obviously, it's lethal."

"That's enough, Miss Barber. Please take your seat so that I can begin my lesson. I know this class will have a wonderful time learning about auras and how to detect them. Can anyone tell me what an aura is?"

No one in the class raised their hand.

"No one?" Ms. Crescent asked. "Not even you, Miss Miller? I'm surprised."

I heard Betty Ann's snicker.

"An aura is the energy field that surrounds everything in the universe: pixies, humans, animals, etcetera. Without knowing it, we project our emotions as colors. Knowing how to detect and read auras will give you a deeper insight into the world around you. You have to be able to open your mind and fully concentrate. This will be one of your first lessons of using your mind and eyes as one."

I heard Miguel sigh.

"Please open your books to page 226 and we'll briefly discuss the colors. Then, you'll practice opening your minds to detect one of your classmate's auras."

"Great, more practicing on classmates since that turned out so well yesterday. I don't want Miss Fitzgerald as my partner," Betty Ann said loud enough for me to hear, but Ms. Crescent didn't respond.

"As you can see, there are many different shades of each color, so you must be specific. An aura cannot just be red or yellow. You must describe precisely: deep red, muddied red, bright red, or maybe even light or dark pink. If you're not specific with the color, you'll get the aura reading wrong. I want you to read over each aura color meaning, and then we'll get started on reading them for each other."

I began reading. There were so many colors and each color had four or five meanings attached to it depending on the specific color description. How could anyone be accurate with all the different meanings?

"When you have finished reading, pick a partner, and then I'll explain how to open your mind and see what is normally unseen," Ms. Crescent announced

I partnered with Josefina, and we waited for further instruction.

"Gaze at your partner and imagine that you see a fuzzy outline around their body. Clear your mind and project your energy toward them. Focus and connect with their energy. A color should start to form around their body. This color will reveal their emotional state," Ms. Crescent explained once everyone had a partner.

Josefina and I began staring at each other. I pushed my mind out to her hoping to get some kind of reaction. I focused on the area surrounding Josefina just like Ms. Crescent told us to do.

"Oh wow!" Josefina suddenly exclaimed breaking my concentration. "It's so beautiful!"

"What do you see? I don't see anything around you yet," I said.

"I see this beautiful light blue around you. It's amazing!" Josefina replied.

"How did you see it?" I asked. "Nothing has changed around you since I began."

"Just keep concentrating. I not only tried to look at your outer features, but I imagined that I was trying to look into your soul too."

My eyes returned to Josefina. Suddenly, I felt like I was looking at her for the first time. A bright gold light surrounded her, shinier than anything I had ever seen. "Oh, I can see it!" I exclaimed.

"I knew you would. If I could do it, I was sure you could."

Other students around the room were also gasping with excitement as they discovered their partners' auras.

Ms. Crescent's voice interrupted the class. "Once you have discovered the aura, look up what the color means, but remember to be specific."

"Your color was a light blue. We'll see if it describes what you're feeling right now." Josefina's hand went down the page searching the blues, while I searched for gold. "A light blue means that you are feeling peaceful and calm."

"I guess I feel calm right now," I replied. "Maybe you should look at my aura during Charms class."

I found gold under the section headed 'Yellows'. "Your color says that you're feeling awakened and inspired. Is that true?" I asked.

"I do feel that way. To be honest, I'm kind of excited to have seen your aura before you saw mine. You're so good with mental focus. I just figured that you'd master this. I guess that's why I feel inspired because I realized that I might actually be good at something," Josefina gushed.

"Josefina, you're good at a lot of things. You know so much about the pixie world and you're doing well in our other classes. Do you want to know what you're the best at? Being a great friend," I replied.

Josefina smiled. "It means so much to hear you say that."

Ms. Crescent came over to us since she had seen us talking. "Were you both successful at identifying each other's auras?"

"Yes, and they were very descriptive," Josefina replied.

"Yes, of course, they are! That's wonderful!" Ms. Crescent then turned to the class. "Once you've seen an aura, you may leave. You have until the bell for your first attempt. Tomorrow, we'll pick new partners and practice more aura detection."

Josefina and I collected our bags and waited for Miguel in the hallway. He came out of the classroom at the sound of the bell, with a scow on his face. He was mumbling under his breath.

"That was a pointless lesson, which isn't a surprise since every lesson of hers is like that," Miguel grumbled.

"That lesson wasn't pointless. I saw Jane's aura almost straightaway. I really enjoyed that class," Josefina said.

"I saw nothing, not even the outline she was talking about. Anyway, even if I had seen the color, what description would I choose? I mean what's the difference between deep red and muddied red anyway? It's too confusing, and you have to guess at everything. Why do we even have to take this class? Half the students have no idea what she's talking about most of the time. I don't think any of us are going to become seer pixies," Miguel ranted.

I didn't speak up because I had thought auras were very interesting, and I had eventually seen Josefina's. If I hadn't, I might be a little skeptical.

"Miguel, you can't be good at everything!" Josefina was insisting. "You need to practice opening your mind to someone other than me."

Miguel shrugged her off, and he didn't look happy until we got to History of Pixies.

"Now this is a real class with facts," Miguel said ecstatically as we entered.

Mr. Collyworth continued his lesson on the American Civil War. He talked about the important battles that pixies had fought in and how a higher percentage of pixies supported the Union over the Confederates.

"It was a very bloody war," Mr. Collyworth droned on. "There is only so much pixie magic can do. A pixie would be lucky if he could protect himself let alone his comrades. Not many pixies were severely wounded, but many humans were lost."

"Why would pixies fight with humans for a human cause? I would never fight alongside a human especially for human affairs," Betty Ann mumbled from the back of the room.

Mr. Collyworth continued with his lecture, choosing to ignore her.

When class was over, it was Josefina's turned to complain. "Now, what was so important about that class?"

"When learning about history, we can learn peoples' past mistakes so that we can try not to repeat them," Miguel answered smugly.

"Not all of us are going to be historian pixies," Josefina returned sarcastically, and their small argument was over.

I was grateful for lunch and the much-needed break. As we entered the dining hall, I noticed several students handing around flyers.

"I wonder what they're passing out," Josefina said between mouthfuls.

When they got to our table, Josefina's eyes lit up but then darkened with disappointment.

"The Valentine's Day dance is coming up, but only third years and up can go," Josefina sighed when she looked at the pink flyer.

"I've had my share of dances this year," I replied sadly. Just remembering the last one made me sick. "Maybe Juan can take you to this one?"

"Juan will be taking Lena. I bet she's very excited. When's he going to wake up and see how madly in love she is with him?" Josefina lamented. "I can't wait until I can go to a dance."

I shuddered as I recalled Thomas's smile when he had come by my room, a sinister smile of anticipation, not adoration. How stupid I had been to have been swept away by that handsome smile when all along it was Betty Ann's forever. Unconsciously, I looked across the cafeteria at Thomas and Betty Ann. He had an arm around her, whispering in her ear. She was clutching one of the pink fliers. Were they going as a couple or plotting the destruction of some other poor soul's evening? Before I could look away, Thomas caught my eye. His lips curved upward maliciously and from behind Betty Ann's back, he waved at me. Quickly, I looked away disgusted.

"Jane? Are you finished with lunch?" Miguel asked shaking my arm.

"Yes," I replied slowly.

"We asked you that question twice. Are you okay?" Josefina asked looking concerned.

"Yes, I'm fine. Let's get ready for Charms," I said halfheartedly.

We disposed of our dirty dishes and exited the dining hall. Leaning against the wall with his hands in his pockets stood Thomas. I didn't even see him exit the room.

"Jane, can I escort you to the Valentine's Day dance? I saw you watching me across the hall." Thomas raised his eyebrow suggestively.

"I wouldn't accompany you to the dance even if you were the last man on earth," I said as I walked by him.

"Jane, I just saw you daydreaming about me asking you. I know you're jealous of Betty Ann. Since you think I'm so handsome, I'll invite you again. You don't have to beg me like you did last time."

"Me? Jealous of Betty Ann? I would never be jealous of her. How can I be jealous of someone who cheats off me in class? It sounds like it's the other way around," I called over my shoulder.

Suddenly, he was at my side, following me down the hallway.

"Jane, I'm just letting you know that you don't have to beg me this time. I'm willing to sacrifice so you can go to the dance."

"Are you delusional? I would never beg you, and I didn't beg you to go last time. You're a snake, and I'll never have you escort me to another dance. Leave me alone, Thomas. By the way, you need to check your collar. Betty Ann seems to have you on a tight leash. You wouldn't want to choke," I said loudly.

Other students who had overheard me were stifling their giggles and pointing at Thomas. His mouth dropped open, and he stopped following me down the hallway.

I was shaken by my encounter with Thomas, but Josefina touched my hand. "I'm so proud of you. Thomas is an idiot and Betty Ann's puppet. They must think you're really that stupid."

We abruptly stopped talking when we entered the Charms classroom. Mr. Withermyer was early today and was sitting at his desk with his dark overcoat still on. His piercing green eyes followed me across the room with a glare that made me shutter. Why were his eyes always following me? Why did he hate me so much?

At this point in my life, I was used to people hating me. I could understand the reasons of others, but what was Mr. Withermyer's reason? I was torn between looking away or defiantly looking back at him. I wanted to look into his eyes to show him I was not intimidated by him, but then again, I didn't want any more trouble.

Mr. Withermyer's lecture focused on the importance of carefully reading the textbook and adding the right ingredients for our assignments. He mentioned the harm we could cause our fellow students if we didn't read the directions carefully. Occasionally, he glanced at me, as if my charm had been wrong. I was angry that he was insinuating it was the reason Taylor had been sent to the hospital wing. I noticed out of the corner of my eye that Taylor was looking at Mr. Withermyer with an angry expression. It was the first time I had ever seen her look so hostile, especially toward a teacher.

I was relieved when class was finally over, and I could escape into the hallway. It was hard trying to mask my anger when it was obvious what Mr. Withermyer was implying. As we got further down the hall, Miguel finally spoke.

"I don't know why we had to listen to a lecture like that. Why did he make it sound like you had done something wrong when he knows very well that your charm was completed correctly?"

"I don't know," I said.

I was about to continue down the hallway when I felt a slight tug on my sleeve. I turned around to face Taylor. She looked better than when I had seen her in the hospital wing, and she seemed fueled by anger.

"No matter what he says, Jane, what happened to me isn't your fault. He was trying to make everyone believe you had done something wrong. I'm so mad he's making you the class scapegoat when you just happened to be the one to cast the charm. After all, Dr. Tweedle analyzed your charm and said you had done it correctly. It's only because of my memories," Taylor sighed, and then she seemed to realize what she'd said.

"Why do you think your memories caused your reaction to the charm?" I asked slowly. I didn't want it to seem like I was prying. The last thing I wanted was to make Taylor uncomfortable.

"My memories haunt me. I don't want to talk about them," she said matter-of-factly as she breezed past me on the way to Earth Catastrophes, leaving me standing puzzled in the hallway.

20

COLD WORK AND
WARM HEARTS

THE NEXT FEW weeks flew by since I was very busy with classes. At the Academy, preparations were being made for the Valentine's Day dance, while at home, Marie was making me sew embellishments on the new dress Emily was going to wear to a party at the Doyle mansion. As I pricked my fingers over and over again, Emily sat watching, laughing, and instructing me on how she wanted the dress to look. Several times she had me redo the same seam of black lace on the purple fabric because she had suddenly changed her mind. My fingers hurt so much, but Emily seemed to revel in my small torture, bragging about being invited to such an extravagant party and how wonderful Drake Doyle's mansion was. She couldn't wait to be married to him, so she could live in such opulence. I tried not to roll my eyes.

"The place is absolutely beautiful. Drake and I will be married there in a little over a year now," she gushed.

I paused in my stitching. I was unaware that the wedding

would take place at the Doyle mansion. I had always thought that it would take place here.

"Unfortunately, you are invited, but only because I need help with preparations for the ceremony. After that, you will serve the guests as you did for Christmas. I don't doubt that we will also need the help of that silly horse boy again. There is so much that needs to be done, but I'm not worried about it. It's a shame mother sent you off to that school. You're going to be making all the decorations and favors so I guess you'll just have to work extra hard when you come home. I don't understand why mother is wasting time on educating you."

I already couldn't wait until this wedding was over. Marie and Emily were going to work me until I died just to get everything done. I imagined myself repeating the same tasks over and over until they were up to their standards.

After several hours, Emily was finally satisfied with the dress, and I was dismissed. Marie sent me out in the snowy cold to clean off the long drive and paths around the house, so no one would slip on the ice. I put on my mother's coat, once again grateful for its warmth, and headed out into the cold with the shovel. The icy air hit me in the face, causing me to shudder. Though the coat kept my body warm, my hands and face were unprotected. At least my hair hung over my ears. I started at the top of the driveway, my breath creating warm puffs of vapor as I worked quickly to escape the cold. Being out in the open, I knew it would be impossible to use the quick complete charm.

Within minutes, my hands felt frozen, and I was nowhere near being done. Maybe I would freeze to death, and Marie would finally be rid of me. I thought about being warm and how good it felt to sit in front of a fire. Suddenly, my hands started to tingle, causing me to drop the shovel in surprise. I held my hands out in front of me but didn't notice a difference. After the tingling feeling had passed, my hands felt warm, as if I weren't even outside. It took me only a moment to figure out what had happened. I chuckled for not thinking of it sooner.

Ever since I started attending the Jelf Academy, I noticed I had an easier time focusing my mind on certain things. It barely took any effort to do minor magic, like levitation.

Feeling warmer allowed me to be content with the chore. At least Marie and Emily were not breathing down my neck. If only they knew I wasn't being tortured right now, they would probably give me a different chore.

I was about halfway down the drive when a hand gripped my shoulder. I dropped the shovel and spun around to come face to face with Robert.

"I'm sorry if I scared you," he said grabbing my hands to steady me. "I thought you heard me approaching." Suddenly, Robert dropped my hands and stepped away. He gave me the strangest look and then stared at my hands. "Your hands are surprisingly warm," he said questioningly. "You've been out here for quite a while. How is it that your hands are not frozen?"

I wrung my hands as I tried to think of an answer. Oh, why did he have to grab my hands? "I guess I've been working so hard that I'm sweating," I replied.

Robert gave me a sideways glance and then he smiled at me. "Anyway, I'm glad to see you. It has been a while since I've seen your smiling face."

I shook my head as I picked up the shovel. "Yes, Marie and Emily have been keeping me busy with Emily's chores. Today, I was sewing lace on Emily's party dress," I replied.

"I guess you're getting some extra training to be Emily's personal maid," Robert said with a smirk.

"I don't need to train. I've been doing this my whole life," I stated with a small smile on my face, trying to make light of the situation. When Robert realized that, he chuckled.

"Oh, I forgot I was speaking to a veteran."

"Yes, I was stripped of my childhood at five years old and thrown into a life of servitude."

Robert frowned and glanced down the driveway. "Which pathways have they asked you to clear?" he asked, changing the subject.

"I have the rest of this driveway, and paths around the house in case we receive guests," I explained.

"Let me get a shovel from the barn, and then I'll help. I can't allow you to be out in this weather for much longer," he said turning toward the barn before I could protest. He had so many other chores to do pertaining to the horses, and this was my job. I wasn't sure if Marie would be mad if he helped. I didn't want to get Robert in trouble.

He came back with the shovel, bounding across the snow with a smile on his face. I couldn't help but smile back at him. Robert had a way of erasing the gloom. He dove right into the task, and I had to hurry to keep up with him. Within half the time, we had completed the driveway and were heading toward the garden paths. I noticed Robert's hands were red and my heart hurt at the sight. I wished there was a way to warm his hands without him knowing.

"Why does she want you to clean off the backyard garden paths anyway? Who comes back here?" Robert asked.

"Sometimes Emily and Preston walk these to get fresh air. Occasionally it's part of their morning routine," I replied with a roll of my eyes. "I swear Marie sits in her room and comes up with the most painful chores for me to do."

"Wouldn't it be nice if we could just leave?" Robert asked. His face was red, and I couldn't tell if it was because of the cold.

"I couldn't leave. I have nowhere to go. At least you have the potential to find your family," I replied.

"If I ever have the nerve or the resources to leave, I'm taking you with me," Robert stated so passionately that I had to look up from my shoveling. He looked down and wouldn't meet my eyes.

"You're the closest thing I have to a friend. I just wouldn't leave you if I found a way out," he finally said after a while.

"Thanks, Robert. I really appreciate it."

We continued to shovel sections of the garden path. I was grateful to have Robert's help, but I felt bad about him being out in the cold. As we got to the farthest part of the garden, closest to the woods, I noticed something strange on the path ahead. When I drew near, I saw bright red blotches in the snow.

"What's that?" Robert asked.

"I don't know, but it looks like blood."

"Look," Robert pointed. "There's a trail heading toward the woods." He walked toward it and I followed.

There was a larger amount of blood splatter as we came closer to the woods. If an animal was wounded, it was probably close to death considering the amount of blood. We entered the woods, and I stopped short as soon as I saw the deer carcass. It had been so mutilated that I almost retched. The body was chopped and thrown about savagely, but it didn't look like another animal had done this. Then, I saw the boot prints in the snow. Obviously, the deer hadn't been hunted for food.

"What the hell?" Robert exclaimed as he covered his mouth. "Why would someone do this?"

I shook my head in horror. Robert crouched down to examine the animal. I watched as he took his shovel and moved the deer's body around to get a better look. The body had been sliced from throat to stomach and all the internal organs had been thrown about. I looked away disgusted, very disturbed as to why someone would dismember an animal this way. Why wasn't killing it enough? Why kill the animal if it wasn't going to be used for meat?

"The only organ that's missing is the heart," Robert said as he stood up.

I shivered, but not because of the cold. "Let's continue shoveling the walkway. I can't bear to be here anymore."

I dragged my shovel back out of the woods and continued to clear off the pathway. Whoever had mutilated the deer was a sick person. Who would've done that so close to the manor? I shuddered at the thought.

Robert joined me to finish the work, but he didn't say anything. I just wanted to finish so I could get inside to distance myself from what I had seen in the woods. Once we finished with the garden paths, I followed Robert back to the barn to put the shovels away. He kept glancing over at me as if he were worried. Outside the barn, Robert took my shovel.

"I'll hang them both up inside," he paused for a minute. "I'm sorry that you had to see that. No lady should have to see something so gruesome."

"It's not your fault Robert. I'm fine, really," I said even as he raised his eyebrows. "I'm really am. Just disturbed."

"Would you like to come inside?" he asked stepping back from the doorway.

"I would like to, but I should get back to the main house. I know Marie will have something for me to do," I replied.

Robert nodded his head in understanding, and I turned to head back up to the house. I hadn't realized how late it had gotten. As I entered the house, I was instantly rushed to the kitchen to help prepare dinner.

Ellen was busy seasoning a whole chicken when she commanded me to chop potatoes, boil them, and finally mash them. I got to work immediately, and it took my mind off of the horror I had seen. When the food was ready, I took it out to the table for Marie, Emily, and Preston. Preston gave me a devilish grin which probably meant he planned on breaking something or causing some kind of disturbance. I sighed to myself as I laid out the meal, and then I retreated to the kitchen to eat my own.

I became surprised when I was not interrupted immediately, and I started to think that maybe Preston had been trying to trick me into thinking that he was up to something. This thought occurred too soon because all of a sudden, I heard a loud crash coming from the dining room. I put down my fork and headed for the mop and broom. When I entered the dining room, Preston's chicken bones had been casually thrown on the floor beside his chair, but I couldn't tell what had made the crashing sound. Then, I saw the wet wall across the room. Preston had thrown his glass, and it had smashed on the wall.

"My water was too warm. Why didn't you put enough ice in it? It wasn't cold enough," Preston yelled at me.

I chose to ignore him and swept up the broken glass on the other side of the table. I looked up at Marie, wondering why she didn't scold him. After all, it was her glassware he was breaking. Trying not to shake my head, I cleaned the broken glass off the floor and wiped the wall clean.

After disposing of the broken glass, I came back out to sweep up Preston's chicken bones. It was hard to fathom why he had thrown them on the floor as if he were a wild animal. This was definitely not how a thirteen-year-old boy should behave. Not only that, throwing chicken bones on the floor was not good etiquette at all. Ironically, Marie was always yelling at me about being proper. She was always worried about me being an embarrassment, but her son was doing the most inappropriate things I had ever seen.

"Mom, Jane should be punished for not putting enough ice in my water. She's so stupid," Preston whined. At this statement, a smile broke out on Emily's face.

"Jane, Preston likes a lot of ice in his water. Do you understand?" Marie turned toward me as I scrapped the last of the chicken bones into the dustpan. I knew she wasn't going to see the immaturity of her son.

"Yes, ma'am. I understand," I replied. I was used to humoring them by now. Robert was right, I was a veteran.

"Good, now don't forget it, Jane, even though I know how

often you forget the most obvious things," Marie commented. This comment was rewarded by Emily and Preston's snickers.

I tore into the kitchen feeling angry. Preston never complained about his water before and had never stressed how much ice he wanted. He was only being difficult to get on my nerves and make Marie punish me. Marie always leapt on an opportunity to punish, scold, or tell me how stupid I was. For me, it was a lose-lose situation.

I didn't hear any other smashing sounds coming from the dining room, so I assumed nothing was amiss. The next time I entered the dining room, everyone was gone. Preston had thrown more chicken bones on the floor, which he must have found amusing. As I washed the dishes, I daydreamed. What would my life be like if I never had to come back here? Maybe if Robert ever got the nerve to leave, I would go with him. I didn't know what we would do without money, but it had to be better than here.

I knew I could never give up attending the Jelf Academy though. My life in the pixie world was too important. If I did get expelled from the Jelf Academy, perhaps it would be easier to leave. I sighed deeply at the thought of freedom, but then I pushed it from my mind. I wasn't free at the moment and there was still much I had to do before I could go to bed.

Taking a bucket, I filled it with water and began mopping the dining room floor. I knew the chicken bones would leave the floor sticky, and I didn't want Marie to complain about it. Since it was late, I chanced a pinch of the quick complete charm. I was so relieved that some of my chores could be completed with a charm, but it didn't stop me from being exhausted by the end of the night. My small mattress in the attic never looked so good.

I climbed the stairs, trying to be as quiet as possible. When I had reached the door of the attic without anyone stopping me or yelling at me, I let out a sigh of relief. It would be typical of Marie to walk out of the darkness and demand that I return downstairs.

It was cold in the attic, but I imagined warmth, to make it manageable. I wished I would have known I could warm myself a long time ago. I wondered what it was like for my mother to have grown up in the pixie world. Would it have seemed wonderful to her, or did she take it for granted? What had my grandparents been like? They must have disagreed with her marriage or else she wouldn't have left the pixie world completely. There were so many things I wanted to know about my mother. I wished I could ask her everything about her life. Most importantly, how did she end up meeting my father and falling in love with him?

I crawled onto the mattress imagining how my parents met for the first time, and I wondered if it was love at first sight for both of them. Did love at first sight even exist? My father must have meant so much to her. She left the pixie world behind because she simply could not live without him.

Reaching for the small blanket, I pulled it over my body. I froze when my hand collided with something cold and slimy beneath the blanket. Leaping from the bed, I ripped the blanket away from me. A shrill scream of terror rose in my throat as I stared at the bed. Lying in the middle of my bed was the heart of the deer.

21

A HORRIBLE PREDICTION

THE PINK DRESS sparkled and reflected light as Lena twirled around in a circle. I was grateful to be back at the Jelf Academy and in Lena's bedroom. She had put on her Valentine's Day dress, to show Josefina and me what it looked like. She looked absolutely beautiful.

"What do you think?" Lena asked as she spun around again.

"You look very beautiful," Rosie, Lena's roommate, replied. She flipped her chestnut red hair to the other side of her neck as she lounged on her bed. I had liked Rosie immediately. She had a heart-shaped face with pale skin and freckles on her nose. She had a slight Irish accent because she moved to America from Ireland five years ago. Rosie was also in her third year and had met Lena when she began at the academy. She had a great sense of humor and that was what kept me from focusing entirely on last weekend.

I was still terrified from finding the deer's heart in my bed, and I shivered as I remembered touching it. As I watched Lena spin in a circle, I tried not to think about who had placed the heart in my bed. I had a sneaking suspicion that Preston was guilty since he had given me the tortured rat for Christmas. It bothered me greatly that anyone would do that to a harmless animal.

"Juan's going to love it!" Josefina gushed, breaking my thoughts. I was grateful to be pulled back to the present. I needed to forget what I'd experienced.

"Do you truly think so?" Lena asked excitedly. "I'm embarrassed to admit, but I think I'm in love with Juan," Lena stammered, turning very red.

Josefina started jumping up and down as she embraced Lena. "I knew it!" she said exuberantly.

"I hope it's not obvious," Lena said covering her face with her hand.

"Not to him," Josefina replied trying to make Lena feel better. "Juan hasn't a clue of your true feelings."

"Maybe you should tell him," Rosie suggested. "He takes you to every dance and spends so much time with you. He must feel something for you."

Lena paced the floor. "I would be too nervous to tell him," she wailed. "Besides, if he has any feelings for me, he should be the one to show them. It would be improper of me to pursue him."

"Don't worry, Lena. You look so beautiful in that dress. My brother would be a fool not to have feelings for you," Josefina said with a small wink. I got the impression that she knew something we didn't.

Lena smiled. "I'm glad everyone but me is so confident. Thank you for the compliments on my dress. I hope it looks okay on me."

"You look wonderful. We would never lie to you," Rosie replied.

Lena excused herself to the bathroom to change.

"That dress is so pretty on her. She's so lucky to be going to the dance. I'm glad she fancies Juan. I know they're perfect for each other," Josefina gushed.

Rosie chuckled. "You act like they will be engaged soon."

Josefina gave a small knowing smile, but before she could say anything, Lena came out of the bathroom. "It's the Valentine's Day dance, so maybe I will hint at my feelings," Lena said determinedly.

"Promise to tell me all about the dance," Josefina said.

Lena promised and since it was getting late, Josefina and I left Lena's room and headed to our own.

"You were unnaturally quiet tonight," Josefina remarked as we walked down the hallway. I mentally cringed that she was so observant. I hadn't told her what was bothering me.

"I didn't have much to say," I shrugged.

"Jane, something is wrong. I can always tell when you're upset. Something's on your mind. I'm very intuitive. You can always tell me your problems. You're my best friend. I'll always be here for you," Josefina said gently.

I proceeded to tell Josefina what had happened on the weekend and the horrific details about the deer. She was very sympathetic, but I knew she was worried. I explained why I thought Preston had done it by reminding her about the rat he had killed on New Year's Eve. Josefina gagged and rubbed her arms to shake off the chill my story had given her.

"That's not normal, Jane. It's very disturbing that a thirteen-year-old boy would do such things."

"I know, and Preston's never acted normal. I try not to pay attention to him since I can't stand his behavior," I replied.

"I can't even imagine what it would be like to live with Marie, Emily, and Preston. I wish you didn't have to live with those nightmares."

"Let's not talk about it anymore. When I come to the Jelf Academy, I like to forget about my stepfamily as much as I can. Anyway, it's great that Lena and Juan are going to the dance. I hope they have a better time than they did at the Harvest Festival," I said.

"I think they're the perfect couple," Josefina replied.

"Josefina, they aren't even courting."

"Oh, I think they will be soon," she replied cryptically.

"How can you be so sure?" I questioned her.

"I've been practicing predicting the future techniques and have been trying them out on my family. Last week, I predicted that Miguel would choose the chicken salad for lunch, and he did!"

"Since you and Miguel have a mental connection, are you sure it's a true prediction?" I asked giggling.

"Well, maybe not, but that's why I started making bigger predictions on other members of my family. I'll be so excited if my predictions come true. Maybe I'll be gifted at predicting the future. That sometimes happens when a pixie gets a certain affinity for different subjects. Ms. Crescent has it for divination," Josefina said.

"Good, then you can tell me when Preston is going to defile my bed," I said in a joking way.

The days went by quickly at the Jelf Academy, and I was nervous to return to the manor house. Josefina and I had lots of homework, and I thought the teachers seemed on edge about something. Ms. Crescent acted even more dramatically and constantly complained of headaches. Even Dr. Tweedle looked distracted when I saw him in the hallway. I didn't have time to ponder on it because every night Josefina and I were busy with assignments. Despite all the extra work, nothing could squash the excitement Josefina had for the Valentine's Day dance. She was so certain that Juan would realize his feelings for Lena.

On Friday, the whole school seemed to buzz with electricity. It was very hard to pay attention in class. While I wasn't going to the dance, I still felt somewhat uplifted by the charged atmosphere. This didn't stop the teachers from giving out assignments, however. Mrs. Rowley gave us a surprise quiz on the properties of astrological gemstones. Afterward, I felt I had done well with the number of assignments we had concerning the properties.

Ms. Crescent was very frazzled when we got to her classroom.

She was pacing while she waited for us to take our seats. Josefina and I looked at each other with worry. We had yet to see her this nervous.

"Good morning, class. Although you should always keep your mind open when divining the future, it's possible your mind can become overrun by all the insights you are receiving. This may cause confusion, hence why I've been experiencing headaches. Something very important is going to occur in the near future. Though don't worry. There are ways to concentrate and let your mind focus on the important events. Meditation is the best way to center your inner eye.

"The purpose of this exercise is to clear your mind and decipher the events or information shown to you. You must be willing to dive deeper into your mind to discover the future. I'll need the room to stay completely quiet during this demonstration, so I don't lose my focus."

Ms. Crescent took deep even breaths as she sat with her eyes closed. Everyone watched her with rapt attention waiting for something to happen. Several minutes passed, but Ms. Crescent stayed on the pillows, her breath calm and even. Miguel looked down the row at Josefina and me rolling his eyes. Soon, other students began fidgeting in their seats, but no one dared to speak. Ms. Crescent began rocking back and forth on her pillow when suddenly, her eyes snapped open. She looked frightened.

"The terrible news will be announced on the twenty-fourth of February," she gasped with a sharp intake of breath. Then, she began shaking and fell backward, her eyes rolling backward. Everyone in the room looked shocked prior to Josefina jumping up and running to Ms. Crescent's side. She shook Ms. Crescent several times before she cried out, "Find Dr. Tweedle!"

Suddenly the room became noisy as students ran to get Dr. Tweedle while others crowded around Ms. Crescent. I remained in shock, frozen in my seat. My birthday was the twenty-fourth of February.

I regained my senses when Dr. Tweedle swiftly entered the room and began clearing students away from Ms. Crescent. He checked her vitals and then levitated her up onto the gurney Nurse Adelina pushed into the room a few minutes later.

Dr. Tweedle then turned to the class. "What happened?" he questioned.

"Ms. Crescent was showing us how to meditate. She said that her mind was so full of events she couldn't concentrate," Josefina stepped up to explain.

"Did she have a vision? What did she say?" Dr. Tweedle asked calmly, but I could tell he was anxious to hear of it.

"She didn't say much, Dr. Tweedle," Taylor said in her small voice. "The only thing she said was we would hear some terrible news on February twenty-fourth."

"Did she give details about the news?" Dr. Tweedle asked frantically.

"She didn't get a chance to say. She passed out right after declaring the date," Josefina said.

"I must go to the hospital wing to check on Ms. Crescent's condition. Class is dismissed. Use this time as a study period," Dr. Tweedle replied looking stunned as he headed out of the classroom.

Some of the students began to collect their books while others stood motionless. A loud cackle broke the silence in the room, and I turned around to see Betty Ann laughing.

"Is this an act? I can't believe she just fainted in the middle of class. This is completely ridiculous," Betty Ann said as she mimicked Ms. Crescent fainting. "Wait until I tell my parents about this! I can't fathom why Dr. Tweedle even believes half of the predictions she makes. Ms. Crescent doesn't know the future! She's a fraud!"

No one responded to Betty Ann, but Josefina gave her a nasty look as she left the classroom. We gathered our books and exited into the hallway.

"I hate to admit this," Miguel whispered as we walked down the hall. "But for the first and only time, I actually have to agree with Betty Ann. Ms. Crescent seems like a fraud, and I believe her class is a waste of time."

Josefina gave Miguel the same look she gave Betty Ann. "Ms. Crescent isn't a fraud. Sure, she is a little eccentric, but there's truth to her predictions. Why would she fake what just happened? You just don't understand the art of telling the future. Dr. Tweedle must have faith in her since he hired her."

Miguel stifled a laugh but didn't say anything else.

"You can laugh all you want, Miguel," Josefina scoffed. "I've been practicing the techniques we've been learning in class, and maybe my predictions will come true. Don't be surprised if something terrible does happen on the twenty-fourth of February."

"When Ms. Crescent mentioned that date, you lost all color in your face," Miguel said turning to me. "Are you okay?"

"The twenty-fourth of February is my birthday. I hope the terrible event has nothing to do with me."

"Oh Jane, there is nothing terrible about your birthday. Why haven't you told us? You'll turn seventeen in a few weeks!" Josefina responded.

"My birthday has never been an exciting event. Marie and her children made me feel punished for it," I sighed.

"Not anymore!" Josefina declared. "From now on, Miguel and I will make sure your birthday is a special event."

"You don't have to do that!" I protested.

"Nonsense!" Miguel shouted. "Your birthday is important to us, and you deserve to feel special. Ignore everything Marie has ever told you."

I couldn't stop the smile that spread across my face, and at that moment, I managed to forget the impending disaster.

22

NEVER CLEAN ENOUGH

"JANE, COME HERE right away!" The shouts of Marie echoed throughout the house. What did she want now? I was trying to do everything as perfectly as I could. I should know by now that pleasing Marie was not possible.

"Yes, ma'am?" I said softly as I entered Marie's bedroom.

Marie was standing in front of her vanity looking at herself in the mirror. She pulled at the skin around her eyes. I could see crow's feet where her skin used to be smooth. She glanced at me through the mirror with a look of disgust.

"Have you cleaned my bathroom yet?" she asked with a raised eyebrow.

"Yes, ma'am. I was in there this morning," I said.

"It doesn't look like it. There's dirt in between the tiles and the tub still has a ring. If you can't complete your chores correctly, I'll never let you return to that school. I don't know how I'm benefiting from it yet, but at least you're someone else's problem for a while. You've been a useless burden around my neck for all these years."

Marie looked back at her reflection and dabbed some powder around her eyes. I headed for the bathroom since she was obviously done with me and would rather pretend that I wasn't there. Switching on the light, I surveyed the room. The tiles looked clean to me. Either Marie claimed there was dirt because she wanted to make me clean again, or she was crazy and honestly believed that dirt never left her floors. From under the sink, I pulled out a bucket and rag and proceeded to fill the bucket up with soapy water.

I could still hear Marie in her bedroom. I assumed she would stay there until I finished. That meant I had to clean the old-fashioned way. I got on my hands and knees, making sure I paid special attention to the grooves in the tile.

After an hour of scrubbing, the joints in my fingers started to hurt and the palms of my hands were all red. My knees had the pattern of the tile imprinted on them. Slowly I got to my feet. It felt good to stretch my back after being hunched over for so long. Now, it was time to tackle the spotless tub.

I bent over again and took my time scouring the invisible ring. For good measure, I also touched up the faucet. Muscle spasms coursed down my back, and I thought about the Valentine's Day dance taking place this evening. How I wished I could have been invited by a gentleman who cared about me just so I could escape this. As I fantasied, I heard the tap of a shoe on the tile floor. Turning around, I saw Marie glaring at me.

"When you're done, don't even think about dumping that dirty water into my tub. Take it outside. Tonight, Emily and I are going to Mr. Doyle's house to meet his mother and discuss wedding plans. I expect you to complete all your chores by the time we get back. I don't want a thing out of place." Then, she turned on her heel and left me to finish.

Good riddance, I thought as I rinsed the soapy water down the drain. Now I wouldn't have someone breathing down my neck. I carried the bucket of water down the stairs and left it by the door while I did a quick cleaning of the rest of the house. When

I thought my work might please Marie, I slipped on my coat to take the water outside.

The cold February air froze my face as soon as I opened the door. I shivered as I made my way down the walk and dumped the dirty water into the snow at the edge of the path. The sky was full of stars, but the moon was only a small crescent. Looking across the grounds, I noticed a light in the barn. Robert must still be awake. I glanced back at the house, and with a shrug, I began walking down the slope. Marie and Emily might not be back for a while, and I hadn't seen Robert this weekend. My feet made crunching sounds as I tramped across the hard-packed snow. I pulled my coat firmly around me and stayed huddled that way until I reached the barn.

After a few knocks, Robert finally answered the door. He looked surprised to see me.

"Jane, what are you doing here? Come in quickly, it's freezing out there."

"I just came for a visit. Marie and Emily have gone out this evening, and I'm finished with my chores," I replied with a smile.

Robert's smile filled up his face. "Here, let me take your coat. The horses keep this place nice and warm." He took my coat and hung it on a nail by the door. Then, I followed him up the ladder and into the loft.

"How've you been?" I asked as we sat down in the hay.

"Lonely when you're not around. I have no one to talk to. I tend to the horses all day so sometimes I talk to them. I rarely see anyone except Marie occasionally, and she's only out here long enough to recite what needs to be done. At least with you around, I know what a human voice sounds like."

"I'm sorry, Robert," I said sadly.

"It's okay, Jane. I'm sorry to sound depressed. Don't frown. I'd rather see you smile. I love your smile," he said.

I giggled and blushed at his admission. "Sometimes it's so hard to smile in this place."

He nodded in agreement. "No wonder you like that school so much. The classes must be boring though. How fun could it be to learn about etiquette and manners?"

"It isn't so bad. Some of the classes are interesting, and I made a few friends," I slowly replied. I hoped he didn't ask many questions. I hated lying to Robert.

"That's great! Tell me about your friends," he said eagerly.

I had to be careful. I couldn't tell him about Miguel and Juan because boys wouldn't attend a school to learn manners and table setting.

"I share a room with Josefina. She was my first friend. She has a bubbly personality and always knows how to make me laugh. She's also very determined and doesn't take no for an answer. Just last week, Josefina said that she was going to make my birthday special even though I told her it wasn't important."

"Did your birthday pass already or is it soon?"

"I'll turn seventeen on February twenty-fourth," I replied. "Honestly, my birthday has never been special," I added.

"Maybe Josefina's right. Maybe it's past time that you have a special birthday," Robert said smiling at me. "If you would be here on that day, I'd make it special for you."

I blushed again. "Thanks, Robert. That's so nice of you. My birthday is not that special, and neither I am," I protested.

"That's not true, Jane, and I hope that deep down you know that. It pains me to hear you speak that way. Continue to tell me about your friends instead," Robert said with a smile.

"Alright," I said with a sigh. "Josefina is my closest friend, and I was so lucky to have met her the first day. We have all our classes together. I've also connected with a girl named Lena. She's in her third year at the school, and she knows Josefina's older brother. Lena's extremely nice. Josefina compares Lena to a big sister since she has two brothers," I told Robert.

"It's good to hear that you have people who you've grown close to. At least you can get away from the people who make your life miserable," Robert replied.

"Unfortunately, that isn't true. Even at the Jelf Academy, I'm not liked by everyone. A girl named Betty Ann has been nasty to me since the first day. Do you remember me telling you that my mother had attended the school? My mother was a very good student and every teacher praised her. They all expect me to be the same, and I think Betty Ann is upset by that. She's constantly insulting me and disrespecting my mother's memory."

"Ignore her. It seems like jealousy. She's just mad that all the teachers like you."

"That's not true either. Most of the teachers do like me, but there's one who doesn't at all. I've never done anything to make him dislike me, but he always finds faults with everything I do. I shouldn't be so bothered because he's mean to everyone and almost every student is afraid of him. I wonder what happened to make him that way," I said as I pondered Mr. Withermyer's behavior.

"I don't know why a teacher would hate you," Robert said looking thoughtful. "but I wouldn't worry, especially if he treats other students negatively."

I described the other teachers that I liked, and I told Robert how wonderful Dr. Tweedle was. It was hard to explain everything without giving too much away, so I tried to be as vague as possible. I wished I could tell Robert about my magic and that there were other people just like me. He probably would think I was abnormal or insane and stop talking to me. I wanted Robert to continue to be my friend since I needed someone to shine a glimmer of happiness in this terrible house. I had to do what I was told ironically by both Marie and Dr. Tweedle. In both situations, I would be expelled, whether it was from this house or the pixie world.

Soon, I realized how late it was. I needed to get back to the house before I got in trouble. I bade Robert goodbye and climbed down the ladder.

"Thanks for visiting me, Jane," Robert called down to me as I was putting on my coat. "I do miss you when you're away," he said softly as he shyly ducked his head so I couldn't see his face.

"It's always a pleasure to visit you. I miss your company as well. I do wish you could escape this place for a while," I replied.

Swinging open the barn door, I walked out into the cold night. A chilly breeze was now blowing. Looking up, I noticed that dark clouds covered the stars and the moon, plunging everything into darkness. A chill went down my spine, making the hair on my neck and arms stand up. I rubbed my arms, trying to shake it off. Halfway to the house, I had a weird feeling pass over me as if I was being watched. It was the same feeling I had gotten before I had met Dr. Tweedle. I glanced around me with unease.

"Hello? Is anyone there?" I called into the darkness.

I received no answer and I stood very still. My unease grew stronger. Fear rose in my throat, making me feel like I was choking. Something had to be out there in the darkness. I sprinted to the house as fast as my legs would carry me, hoping whatever I had sensed wouldn't catch me. I prayed that I wouldn't stumble and fall. Finally, I made it to the house. Flinging the front door opened, I charged inside, slamming the door behind me. I locked it as quickly as my fumbling fingers would allow.

My heart was pounding out of my chest, and I rushed up all the stairs to the attic. Adrenaline, from fear, was coursing through my veins, and I tried to calm down. I didn't know why I felt so scared. Maybe it was the pixie part of me that could sense danger, or perhaps I had some type of sixth sense that was not related to the pixie blood at all. It was possible that I had imagined the feeling of being watched, but the more I thought about it, the less I could shake the chill that had run down my spine. Something was out there, and I was glad that I had not stuck around to see who or what it was.

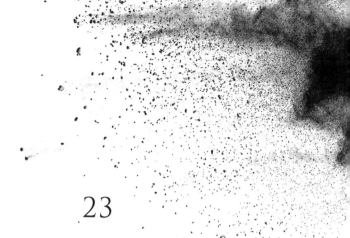

23

FEBRUARY THE
TWENTY-FOURTH

MY EYES SNAPPED open, and I gasped for breath. Where was I? Slowly, the dream receded, and I recognized the ceiling above my bed at the Jelf Academy. It was the third time this week I had the dream and woken up in a cold sweat. Something was chasing me. Something sinister was hiding in the dark waiting to harm me. I took deep breaths trying to calm myself. All of a sudden, Josefina's face hovered into my line of view.

"Good morning and happy birthday!" she shouted.

I blinked and then rubbed my eyes, trying to orient myself. Yes, today was my seventeenth birthday. I sat up in bed and threw off the covers. Josefina was standing next to my bed with a big smile on her face.

"Good morning and thank you for the birthday wish. This is the first acknowledgement I got since I turned five," I replied.

Josefina walked over to her desk and riffled through the drawers. She quickly spun around and held something behind her back. Slowly, she approached me, the enormous smile still on her face.

"I wanted to get you a little birthday present." Josefina held out a small, gift-wrapped box with a large purple bow on it.

"Josefina, you didn't have to do this!" I said taking the box from her.

"I know I didn't have to, but I wanted to. Jane, you are my closest friend. You deserve something nice," she replied.

I smiled. "Thank you. This means the world to me."

"You don't even know what it is. You might hate it," Josefina giggled.

I raised my eyebrows at her and then looked down at the gift in my hand. This was one of the nicest things anyone had ever done for me. Tears started to form in the corners of my eyes. Slowly, I slid the ribbon off and opened the wrapping paper. Inside was a box, and I slowly opened that too, savoring the only present I had received in a long time. Lying on a soft cushion inside the box was a silver crescent moon-shaped pendant with a small stone on the inside of the moon. It hung on a thin silver chain that glittered in the light.

"Thank you so much!" I cried. "It's beautiful. I love it."

"The stone is garnet. When you wear it, you'll be able to do your chores a little faster. Other charms and enchantments were placed on it so that humans won't detect your quick movements. It doesn't work as well as the quick complete charm of course, but it will help. Also, the chain is made of elf silver, so it's unbreakable," Josefina explained.

"Oh, Josefina, I love it. It must have been so expensive!" I exclaimed.

"My dad owns a gem mine, remember? We have several pixie jewelers that my dad sells the uncut gems. The jeweler that uses my father's jewelry designs is the one I asked to make this gift for you. Since he's such good friends with my father, he was happy to make it."

"It's wonderful and means a lot to me," I said taking it out of the box and clasping it around my neck. I looked at myself in the mirror and watched the gem sparkle around my neck. Maybe today would be the first good birthday I would remember.

Josefina and I got ready to go to class, and I remembered, that yet again, we wouldn't be having Predicting the Future. We would be given another free period. So much had happened in the last week. Ms. Crescent still hadn't returned from the hospital wing, so Dr. Tweedle had declared all of her classes cancelled until her return. Dr. Tweedle wouldn't tell us what was wrong with Ms. Crescent, but we assumed her visions were making her ill. Betty Ann made nasty comments throughout our study periods, but no one responded to her. Realizing her effort was fruitless, she eventually stopped.

Also, the Valentine's Day dance had taken place without a hitch. Lena described it for Josefina and me when we came back to school after that weekend. She said the great hall was decorated beautifully with pink, red, and white glitter hearts hanging from the ceiling and off the staircase. The lights had been low, setting an ambient and romantic scene. The tabletops had been set with white tablecloths and in the centers were vases full of big red roses. Strings of diamond-like stones hung off the vases and confetti hearts were scattered on the tables. The small red candles had flickered, adding a soft glow to the room. Josefina and I had listened in awe of Lena's description and sighed wishing we could have seen it. It all sounded so romantic.

Lena then told us that she had gotten too nervous and hadn't attempted to hint at her feelings for Juan. She was afraid and didn't want to jeopardize their friendship. Josefina was disappointed that the prediction she made didn't come true, but she claimed that maybe the vision had occurred somewhere other than the dance.

Josefina and I got through our morning classes and my birthday went along like a normal day at the Jelf Academy. The only difference was that it was the best birthday I had ever had. Mrs.

Rowley somehow knew it was my birthday and said something in Gemstones 101. I was feeling so buoyant when I got to lunch because, for the first time, my birthday wasn't an awful reminder or a disgrace. I couldn't help but feel happy.

"Hello, Jane. Happy birthday!" Juan called as he and Lena sat down at our table. "How does it feel to be seventeen?"

"It feels better than being sixteen so far," I replied, making everyone laugh.

"So, are you having a wonderful day?" Lena asked.

"Yes, I am. The only bad thing is I have Charms next. I'm sure Mr. Withermyer will find some way to ruin it," I replied.

"I wish that wouldn't happen," Josefina moaned.

"If I only have one bad hour today, I guess it's not so bad compared to birthdays of the past," I said.

Soon lunch was over, and it was time to go to Charms. Slowly, Miguel, Josefina, and I entered the classroom. Mr. Withermyer was sitting at his desk as usual and grimaced when he saw me. His eyes locked on me, and I shuddered. What if he knew today was my birthday and was planning on making it miserable for me?

When the class was full, Mr. Withermyer rose from his seat. "Today, we are going to attempt another charm from your book. We'll see how many of you are competent enough to complete this charm correctly. Open your books to page…"

Mr. Withermyer was cut off by a knock on the door. His eyes scanned the classroom looking for empty seats. When he found none, he turned to the door with a confused look on his face. As soon as Mr. Withermyer opened the door, Dr. Tweedle breezed into the classroom looking distraught.

"I'm sorry, but I'm afraid that I need to cancel this class for today. Could you please escort all the students to the dining hall? There's a terrible announcement that must be made," Dr. Tweedle exclaimed before he quickly turned on his heel and left the room.

"Apparently, I will not be teaching Charms today. Obviously, there is something more important," Mr. Withermyer said dryly.

Everyone stirred nervously in their seats. All of us were wondering what Dr. Tweedle had to tell us.

"Stand up in an orderly fashion so we can make our way down to the dining hall. I expect no pushing or shoving. If anyone speaks a word, you'll have detention with me," Mr. Withermyer commanded.

I stood in line behind Josefina as we marched down the hall like army cadets. I almost expected Mr. Withermyer to tell us to solute each other too. When we got to the dining hall, we all filed in and claimed a seat quietly. Most of the students were already waiting in anticipation for Dr. Tweedle's terrible announcement. Panic fluttered in my chest. Today was my birthday, the day Ms. Crescent predicted something bad would be announced. I hadn't remembered until just now. I felt frozen in my seat as dread washed over me. I wanted to alert Josefina, but Mr. Withermyer would punish anyone who spoke. The only thing I could think to do was reach over and squeeze her hand. Her brown eyes mirrored mine, and it was obvious she had also remembered Ms. Crescent's warning.

Dr. Tweedle ascended onto the dais and stood behind the lectern. He looked very somber, and I couldn't fathom what he had to say. The entire room became so silent and still, you would think someone had stopped time. Every person had their eyes focused on Dr. Tweedle and their faces held anxious looks. I had never seen anyone take command of a room like Dr. Tweedle. Not even Marie with all her poise and power was capable of doing it. Dr. Tweedle straightened his glasses as he looked down into the faces of all the students.

"The news I have to tell you is very terrible and very sad, but I feel that you must be aware. I'm not telling you this to make you panic or be afraid, but what I'm about to tell you affects the entire pixie world. Others have told me that it was someone else's responsibility to discuss these events with you. I believe it's only fair and reasonable that I do. Yesterday evening, pixie officials discovered four pixie bodies, two adults and two children. The family appears to have been murdered by the W.A.S.P."

Several gasps were heard throughout the crowd.

"Unfortunately, I must also report that some of you knew a member of this family. He just started his first year last fall. Since he is a student, I felt obligated to tell you this news. I'm sorry to inform you about Henry Adams and his family," Dr. Tweedle said sadly, and I watched a tear glisten on his cheek.

"What a tragedy for such a young individual to perish. The rest of today's classes will be cancelled so we can all pay our respects to the Adams family. Although this is painful news, I would like you to take it as a warning. Despite what you may think, humans can be dangerous. I'd advise that you don't communicate with them, but if you must, use the utmost caution. Never reveal what you can do. The W.A.S.P. is becoming more knowledgeable about the pixie world, and we need to do whatever we can to protect ourselves," Dr. Tweedle said concluding his speech. Everyone was still motionless as we watched him walk away from the lectern and off the stage.

I glanced around at the faces of the other students in the crowd. Everyone appeared somber. Some were crying while others looked angry. There was only one group of students that didn't look sad or upset: Betty Ann and her friends. They stood in the back corner laughing and talking as if Dr. Tweedle didn't just deliver the terrible news about the death of one of our classmates. I watched them in disbelief, wondering how they could react so casually to Henry's death.

Even though most of the people didn't know Henry, we all felt the sadness of an innocent pixie life lost to the horrors of the W.A.S.P. These same people had killed my mother all those years ago, murdered Mrs. Dimple's husband, and were responsible for countless others. Josefina, Miguel, and I glared at them for their disrespect.

Betty Ann must've seen us because she approached with her friends in tow. I stood my ground keeping my eyes on her. She gave me a malicious grin.

"Jane, why do you look so sad? I didn't know that Henry was a beau of yours," Betty Ann said laughing. "Josefina looks pretty sad too. I didn't know that you were competing for his affections."

"A pixie was murdered, Betty Ann. That should make everyone sad," I replied dryly.

"Henry Adams was hardly a pixie. He could barely concoct a charm. He obviously couldn't foresee a single thing, and the only class that he could do anything right in was History. History isn't even really a pixie class; a human could do it," she looked me up and down.

"Henry Adams was a pixie regardless of how talented he was," Josefina said angrily.

"It's the law of natural selection. It doesn't matter if both his parents were pixies. Henry didn't act like a pixie. His family must not have been smart or talented because they were all caught by the W.A.S.P." Betty Ann replied.

"It's a wonder you haven't been caught yet," I quickly replied. Then, I turned on my heel and walked away.

I exited the dining hall and angrily stomped in the direction of my room. Josefina and Miguel were following quickly behind me.

"You should've seen her face," Miguel said once we got to the top of the stairs.

"Her jaw was hanging so low I thought it was about to drop off!" Josefina added.

"Good, that proves she's more of a dunce than I thought. Let her think about it for a while. Maybe she deserves to be caught by the W.A.S.P." I muttered out of anger.

Josefina and Miguel shuddered. "I know Betty Ann's awful, but the W.A.S.P. is the worst thing that can happen to a pixie," Josefina replied.

I stopped abruptly and looked at the twins. "What do you mean?" I said, struggling to keep my voice steady.

"It would be awful to tell you," Miguel protested. "Your mother…"

I gave them both a stern look. "I need to know," I said determinedly. "Despite what happened to my mother, I need to know about the W.A.S.P. They're murdering pixies, and I need to be aware for my own safety."

"What we know is only speculation because everyone caught by the W.A.S.P. hasn't come back alive," Josefina started grimly. "We can only guess from the evidence found. Pixie officials hypothesize that the W.A.S.P. tortures pixies in an attempt to steal our magic powers. No one knows whether this is even possible and as far as we can tell, the W.A.S.P. hasn't succeeded. Pixies don't even know where the root of our power comes from. Is our power in our soul where it's intangible or is it in our brain or heart? The W.A.S.P. isn't stupid, and they know we can move things with our minds, so they perform tests and operations," Josefina said as she shuddered again.

"The W.A.S.P. also tortures pixies for information about the pixie world and where they can find others. I can't even think about the secrets they already know. Did they figure out twins' powers? A chill runs down my spine every time I think of the W.A.S.P." Miguel said.

I swallowed the lump in my throat. Who knew what the W.A.S.P. had done to my mother? I felt tears well up in my eyes, and I struggled not to let them fall.

"Thank you for telling me. I needed to know, but if you two don't mind, I would like a moment alone. I'll be in the library. I just want to sit in silence," I said with a sigh.

Josefina and Miguel nodded sympathetically, and I headed back downstairs. After Dr. Tweedle's horrible announcement, I needed to be alone with my thoughts and I assumed the library would probably be empty. With the rest of the day free, I doubted anyone would be studying.

I pushed open one of the double doors, entering the library. The lights weren't overly bright, and Miss Pierce sat behind the front desk with her head tilted down reading a book. Slowly, I walked around, not sure what I was looking for. Eventually, I came to a section that caught my attention. The books in this section had titles like *The Gods of the Pixies* and *Pixie Religions*. I didn't even know that pixies practiced any kind of worship. I plucked one of the books from the shelves and sat down in the aisle to look through it. I needed a distraction from the recent news and Josefina and Miguel's speculations.

Pixie religion was based on the worship of multiple gods and goddesses. The pages were adorned with colorful works of art depicting the gods and the function of life they controlled. The gods created the pixie race and gave them the ability to do magic. It was a gift that the human race didn't receive. There was Adharin, the god of the sky, controller of the weather. He supposedly lived on clouds much higher than the Jelf Academy. The book depicted him with stormy gray hair and piercing blue eyes that matched the sky on a clear day.

I flipped through the other pages in the book and read about Kyla, the goddess of water; Aden, the god of fire; Lana, the goddess of the earth; Cillian, the god of war; and Karenza, the goddess of love. There were so many gods and goddesses that I was amazed and intrigued. It was nice to think of some godly power watching over and controlling different aspects of your life. I wondered if my mother worshipped the gods. Was this something all pixies believed? No one had mentioned religion before.

I flipped to the next page of the book and my eyes fell upon a cloaked figure with a hood drawn up over his dark hair. The caption beneath the picture read Cian, god of death, which caused me to shudder. Death wasn't exactly what I wanted to think about, but I couldn't help but be curious about what happened to pixies after they died.

The book described two different kingdoms Cian ruled over. One kingdom was called Speura, and it was described as beautiful and bright. If a pixie was good during their lifetime and believed in the gods, then Cian would reward them with eternal life in this beautiful kingdom. The other kingdom, Ifrinn, was described as dark and painful. If a pixie committed evil acts, then Cian punished them in Ifrinn by making them his eternal slaves. I looked at the artistic drawings, and I felt goosebumps on my skin as I glanced at the depictions of Ifrinn.

I was so absorbed in the book that a sobbing sound from somewhere close startled me. I nearly jumped out of my skin, making the book slam shut in my lap. I sat quietly for several minutes, my ears straining to hear anything in the now quiet library. I didn't move a muscle and my breathing had become shallow. Hadn't I heard someone crying?

Just as I was beginning to believe that I had imagined it, another small sob echoed. I quietly got to my feet and gently slipped the book back into its slot on the shelf. Slowly, I picked up my bag while continuing to listen. Suddenly, the sobbing slightly increased, and I was positive someone was crying. I was unsure of what to do. Should I stealthily slink away, or should I find the source of the sound?

Slinging my bag over my shoulder, I walked down the aisle of bookshelves. I rounded the corner and was surprised to see Taylor huddled on the floor with her arms wrapped around her knees. Tears were streaming down her face, and when she saw me, she tried to hastily wipe them away. It wasn't my intention to intrude, and I had been trying to slip away, but now that I knew it was Taylor, I couldn't leave.

"Taylor, are you alright?" I asked.

She looked away from me and continued to dry her eyes with

the back of her hands. I felt terrible about finding her like this. I had come to the library for the same reason: to be alone. I wondered why she was crying so hard.

"Taylor," I repeated when she didn't answer me. "Is everything okay?"

Finally, she looked at me with her bloodshot eyes. "Nothing will ever be okay," she muttered.

"I'm sorry about Henry," I offered. I didn't even know they had been close. "I believe everyone is struck with grief for his passing."

Taylor looked away from me, and then she put her head down on her knees. "It's not just Henry." She was barely audible, and I had to strain to hear her.

"What is it then?" I whispered back, remembering that I was still in the library.

Taylor shook her head as it still rested on top of her knees. I knelt next to her very confused. What else was Taylor so upset about besides Henry? My heart went out to Taylor, and I knew something was bothering her even before Dr. Tweedle's announcement. I wanted to help her, but I didn't know how. Taylor always seemed so depressed. I couldn't remember if I had ever seen her smile since we had started at the Jelf Academy.

"Taylor, you can tell me. I promise I won't tell anyone else," I tried again. "I want to be your friend. I've had great losses in my life too, so I understand," I said sadly.

Taylor looked up at me through her blurry eyes. "You're genuinely a nice person Jane, and I appreciate that you care. I know you would have some understanding, but I can't talk about it. You have no idea what I've been through, and it hurts too much to discuss it. If you don't mind, I'd like to be alone."

She slowly rose from her crouched position and softly touched my arm. Her lips lifted a tiny bit into what I assumed was a grateful expression, and then I watched her walk away into deeper parts of the library.

24

A DEEP HATRED

"I'M SORRY THAT your birthday didn't turn out as you would have liked," Lena said at lunch the next day.

I just shrugged my shoulders, swallowing a bite of the sandwich. "Birthdays have never held much of an importance to me."

"Yes, but yesterday was supposed to be your first special birthday," Josefina sighed as she picked at her macaroni.

"It started out special," I said as I fingered the necklace Josefina had given me. "I found a book that was all about pixie gods, and I forgot to ask you about it. Do all pixies believe in the gods?"

"I don't think all pixies believe anymore, but we do," Miguel replied. "Our father always prays to Lana, goddess of the earth, since our business is in mining."

"So, Lena, have you prayed to Karenza lately?" Josefina asked jokingly with a small smile on her face since Karenza was the goddess of love.

Lena blushed a bright red and gave Josefina a death stare. Juan was sitting right next to her at the table. "I'm sure everyone's prayed to Karenza at least once in their life," she replied coolly.

"I just thank Heulfryn every day for making the sun rise," Miguel said sensing the tension.

"I found the book so interesting. I'd like to believe that there are godly beings watching over us. I want to believe that when my mother passed away, she went to live with Cian in Speura. Why didn't anyone mention pixie religion before?" I asked.

"Religion isn't as popular as it used to be. Years ago, every pixie believed and worshipped the gods. Now, more and more pixies are falling away from religion. Some pixies, like Betty Ann's family, believe since they are rich and powerful officials, they're like the gods. Maybe one day the gods won't like their arrogance and strike them down," Juan said.

"If only that would happen," Josefina sighed glancing over at Betty Ann's table. "However, I don't think Cian wants to deal with her soul yet."

Everyone chuckled softly. No one seemed in the mood to laugh loudly after yesterday's announcement.

At the end of lunch, Josefina and I dropped off our trays while Miguel went back to his room to grab something he'd forgotten.

"Why did you ask Lena if she was praying to Karenza? Juan was beside her, and she hasn't hinted at any affections." I asked.

"Okay, I'll admit what I did was a bit cruel, but I know that Juan has to be just as enamored with her. He doesn't stop talking about her on the weekend. That has to mean something, right?" Josefina asked me.

"Don't look at me. I know absolutely nothing about love. Maybe you should ask Karenza," I replied. "How's Miguel doing since Henry Adams was his roommate?"

"He's upset about it, but even though they shared a room, I don't think they were close. At least that's what I can tell from Miguel's mind. He seems just as upset as we are."

It was on the tip of my tongue to tell her that Taylor was very upset about Henry's death, but I managed to stop the words before they came out. Even though Taylor hadn't told me anything, I had promised not to tell anyone. It would also be awkward explaining the situation to Josefina, and I didn't feel like getting into it. I fell silent because we were approaching Mr. Withermyer's classroom.

When we entered, Mr. Withermyer was already up at the board, mentally writing instructions for what we were going to do today. I tried to swallow the lump in my throat when I realized we had another charm to attempt. The instructions on the board looked complicated, and I could tell it wouldn't be easy. My stomach felt like it was going to drop out of my body, and I could feel an anxiety attack coming on. I was determined to do my best, but I knew Mr. Withermyer would find something wrong with the charm I turned in.

When the whole class had filed in, Mr. Withermyer told us that we had forty-five minutes to complete and perfect the charm he had written on the board. As usual, he wouldn't accept any late charms. I wiped the already forming sweat from my brow and began when Mr. Withermyer started the timer. I was in the middle of crushing my first mineral when Mr. Withermyer was suddenly at my desk. He signaled for me to stop what I was doing. What had I done wrong?

"You continue to surprise me with how bold you can be. You really must have some nerve," Mr. Withermyer said looking at me with those intimidating green eyes.

I looked up at him, confusion evident on my face. What was I doing other than what he had instructed? I gave him a blank stare.

"Of course, you would pretend not to know what I'm talking about, but I won't stand for cheating in my classroom," he spat at me.

"How am I cheating by doing step one? My eyes have stayed on my own work. I haven't copied anyone." I made a point to flash my eyes at Betty Ann.

"You don't have to copy off someone to be cheating in class,

Miss Fitzgerald," he said very condescendingly as if he was talking to a very stupid person and needed to slowly pronounce every word slowly. "My assignment is a timed assignment of forty-five minutes. That necklace you are wearing is proof enough that you are cheating."

I looked down at the necklace Josefina had given me.

"Didn't you learn in Gemstones 101 that wearing certain gem-stones enhances your ability?" he said looking down his straight Grecian nose at me. "Since I know that a garnet is hanging around your neck, I hope that you have studied enough to know what that kind of gemstone does."

An icy feeling moved down my spine as I realized that Josefina's gift was supposed to help me work faster when I went back to the manor. I felt the blood drain from my face.

"I'm sorry, Mr. Withermyer. I received this necklace as a birth-day present yesterday. I forgot I was wearing it," I replied.

At first, he looked taken aback, but then he chuckled dryly in a very rude manner. "I keep hearing from other faculty that you are gifted. Don't try to put on an act with me now."

"I honestly didn't remember that I had it on," I cried.

"Maybe cheating is how you get by in your other classes, but it's not going to happen in this one. Get up!" he demanded nastily.

I stood up from my seat and determinedly faced Mr. Wither-myer. "I'm telling you the truth. I've never cheated a day in my life!"

"I am not accepting any of your excuses. I caught you today, and I'm going to have to send you to Dr. Tweedle. Come up to my desk," Mr. Withermyer said.

I followed him to his desk with my head held high as all the students in the class watched me. I hadn't intentionally worn the necklace to cheat. I knew I was telling the truth. I wasn't going to walk with my head down ashamed. Mr. Withermyer sat at his desk and began writing a letter to Dr. Tweedle while I stood in front of him. I could tell that everyone's eyes were on me. I just knew that

Betty Ann had that smug smile on her face, so I just stood with my back straighter.

When Mr. Withermyer had finished his note, he folded it up so that I couldn't see what he had written. He then levitated it off the desk and pushed it with a hand motion out the door and down the hallway in the direction of Dr. Tweedle's office.

"Dr. Tweedle has been notified of your arrival. You are dismissed," he said with a malicious smile. "Oh, and by the way, you will receive an F on today's assignment since cheating isn't tolerated in my classroom, or at the Jelf Academy."

I spun around from his desk, rolling back my shoulders, and walked out of the classroom. I was fuming that Mr. Withermyer had accused me of cheating. He wouldn't even let me try to explain. Not only that, but he also made it look like I cheated all the time. I bet Betty Ann was having a field day. When I got to Dr. Tweedle's office, I felt like smoke was coming out of my ears. I knocked on the office door and patiently waited with my arms crossed over my chest.

"Please come in, Jane," Dr. Tweedle said in a voice that sounded disappointed. I knew he had already read Mr. Withermyer's letter.

I pushed opened the door and stepped out of the hallway. Crossing the room, I took a seat on the couch in front of Dr. Tweedle's desk.

"Hello, Jane. According to the letter I just received from Mr. Withermyer, it appears that you were cheating in his class by wearing an object of enhancement," Dr. Tweedle stated and then looked up at me pointedly as if asking me to explain.

"I won't deny that I'm wearing one," I said reaching for the pendant around my neck. "I didn't wear it so I could cheat. I forgot I was wearing it. I received it yesterday as a birthday present," I replied calmly.

"You do know that wearing a charm like that is a form of cheating?" Dr. Tweedle asked.

"Yes, sir. That's why I am telling you I wore it unintentionally. With the news we received about Henry, I had completely forgotten that it was around my neck," I explained. "I have never cheated in my life, nor at this school."

"I never thought you would be one to cheat, Jane. Maybe I'm an old fool, but I still believe that. I know that you're still new to this world and that it's easy to forget things when everything's a new experience. I'm going to forget about this and let you go without punishment. I'm going to trust that you simply forgot. Everyone deserves a warning. You're such a good student, and you're doing so well in your classes. I'll ignore this misstep. I know how important this school is for you. I don't believe you would intentionally do anything to jeopardize your attendance here. Please do not break my trust, Jane, and please try to work harder in Mr. Withermyer's class," Dr. Tweedle replied.

"Yes, sir. The worst thing I could do is break your trust. I will try to work harder in Charms, but no matter what I do, Mr. Withermyer finds fault in it. He never recognizes when I do well. I don't think he likes me much," I said.

Dr. Tweedle looked down at his hands. The expression on his face made me think that he knew something I didn't, but the second passed and he looked up at me with a bright smile. "I don't think Mr. Withermyer hates you. I know he's harder on his students because he wants them to succeed. Plus, Charms is one of the most important classes for life after the Jelf Academy. If a student cannot create a basic charm, they have no hope in a pixie career. A pixie can get by without knowing every detail of the future, but charms are a way of life. Don't take it to heart. I'm sure he's just looking out for the best in each student," Dr. Tweedle explained.

I nodded my head, but I didn't agree. Mr. Withermyer had some personal vendetta against me. Sure, he was hard on the other students, but I was the only student that his eyes followed about the classroom, waiting to point out my failings. I was the only student he dismissed from his classroom. Other students who performed worse hadn't been treated this way. His behavior was a mystery to me. Why did he hate me so much?

"Jane, you're allowed to return to your classes now. By the way, happy belated birthday," Dr. Tweedle said with a smile.

I thanked him and stood up from the sofa. When I checked the clock on his desk, I saw that it was almost time for Earth Catastrophes. I decided to just head in that direction. As I walked to class, I couldn't stop thinking about Mr. Withermyer and his disdain for me. My gut feeling told me that Dr. Tweedle knew something about why Mr. Withermyer treated me so badly. I couldn't explain why I felt that way. Of course, Dr. Tweedle would say Mr. Withermyer was just hard on his students. I thought about it all through Earth Catastrophes.

Mr. Laruse couldn't even hold my attention when he mentioned we would be learning tornado detecting techniques until the end of the year. As interesting as it sounded, I couldn't muster enough enthusiasm. Josefina and Miguel both looked very excited since it would probably be the most thrilling lesson we would have in this class. Even Taylor looked like she had perked up. I tried my best to concentrate as Mr. Laruse described the warning signs that would indicate a tornado was likely to happen.

"After some practice, you should be able to feel it in the air. The visual indicators are very dark clouds and sometimes you'll be able to sense hail," Mr. Laruse explained. He wrote down these examples on the outdoor chalkboard. I absentmindedly scribbled them down into my notebook.

As we left the class, Josefina and Miguel began talking excitedly about the lesson Mr. Laruse had planned for this week. He had mentioned simulating a magical tornado for us to practice.

"Finally, we will be predicting earth catastrophes. I've had enough of predicting rain and snow!" Miguel said.

Josefina agreed. They both looked at me, waiting for me to

answer. "Yes, I'm excited to be doing something else," I replied trying to sound upbeat about it.

Thankfully, the twins didn't say anything about the mood I was in, and I managed to pay attention to Zodiac Signs. I was glad when that class ended. Slowly, I picked up my books and slung my bag over my shoulder. Josefina was waiting for me in the hallway outside the classroom.

"You can go on ahead," I told her. "I'm thinking about going to the library before dinner."

"Is everything okay?" Josefina asked. "You seem to be going to the library a lot lately."

"Everything's fine," I replied. "I just want a quiet place to study the charm I failed today."

"I'm sorry about that. I should've told you not to wear it to class. I should've reminded you to take it off," Josefina said.

"It's not your fault. Please don't blame yourself," I said giving her a friendly squeeze on the shoulder. "I know better now. I didn't even get into much trouble for it. Dr. Tweedle understands. What does it matter if I failed my first assignment? I'll show him by acing the charm he gives us for our finals," I replied determinedly.

"If you don't mind some company, I might come later. I still haven't started that paper Mr. Collyworth assigned us," Josefina laughed.

"Okay, I'll see you later," I stated as we both headed in opposite directions.

The halls were mostly empty as I headed down to the first floor. It seemed very quiet since most students went to their rooms to start on homework or relax before dinner. When I made it to the second floor, I thought I heard angry voices. It sounded like they were coming from Dr. Tweedle's office. I slowed my gait and almost came to a complete stop when I heard Mr. Withermyer's voice. What was he doing in Dr. Tweedle's office?

"Phillip, we've been over this before," I heard Dr. Tweedle say calmly.

"I can't believe you didn't punish her! She was cheating in my class! You should write to those government officials and have her expelled!" Mr. Withermyer's harsh voice yelled back.

Unless Mr. Withermyer had sent another student to see Dr. Tweedle, I could safely assume they were talking about me. This was the second time I had accidentally stumbled upon a discussion about me. Maybe it was fate or that sixth sense I was starting to believe I had.

"Don't you think the girl has been punished enough? First, she lost her mother and then her father at such a young age. You should see the people she has to live with! They're absolutely horrible to her. I really can't see punishing her over something so small when I know she's telling me the truth about it," Dr. Tweedle replied.

"Are you telling me that just because the girl has had a hard life, she can't be punished for any rules she breaks now? Is that what you're saying?" Mr. Withermyer demanded.

"No, that's not exactly what I'm saying, Phillip. Miss Fitzgerald's a good student, and she's been working very hard at this school. I believe that she wore the necklace by accident. She told me it was a birthday present from her friend, Miss Martinez, and I'm sure she was probably excited to have received it. It might be the only birthday present she has ever received, knowing that awful stepfamily of hers. Have some compassion for the poor girl."

"I can't," came Mr. Withermyer's sharp reply.

"Phillip, it's been seventeen years," Dr. Tweedle sighed. "The past is the past. You can't change it. That's one thing pixies can't do: go back in time. You need to move on and forget about it. As much as you would like to think so, Miss Fitzgerald isn't stupid. She has sensed the hostility that you have for her. She has brought it to my attention today, and I'm telling you that you need to stop.

Regardless of the situation, every student must be treated fairly. She has nothing to do with her mother's past," Dr. Tweedle said.

"If she is so smart, then why do you keep accepting it when she pretends that she doesn't know things because she wasn't born in the pixie world?" Mr. Withermyer sneered.

"I believe her because I can sense that she's telling the truth. Besides, Miss Fitzgerald doesn't have much to look forward to when she goes home. Why would she spoil her chances here? She's a very good student. I think it's time for you to start acknowledging that. You have to agree that she does belong here, despite the government's hesitations."

"Do you even know how painful it is for me to look at her?" Mr. Withermyer asked in anguish. I was taken aback by this statement. What did he mean by it, and if that was the case, why did his eyes seem to follow me around the classroom?

"I understand, Phillip, but for the sake of your professional career as a teacher you need to put your past behind you," Dr. Tweedle said.

"Are you saying that you would let me go?" Mr. Withermyer asked in a voice I had never heard before. A voice that sounded both scared and sad.

"No, that's not what I'm saying. I'm just asking you to bury any bad feelings you have and start treating Miss Fitzgerald like any other student. I know it will be hard for you, but you need to stop targeting her for being Rachel's daughter," Dr. Tweedle commanded.

The doorknob to the office began to jiggle. I quickly hurried down the stairs and into the library, hoping I had made it in time and wasn't seen. Mr. Withermyer didn't like me, and it had something to do with my mother. At least I knew I hadn't imagined Mr. Withermyer treated me worse than everyone else. I couldn't fathom what had happened in the past to make Mr. Withermyer hate my mother and me.

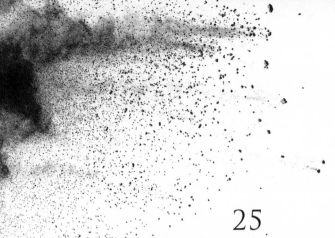

25

SO MANY TESTS AND
SOME STARLING NEWS

THE WEEKS FLEW by and before I knew it spring had come, melting away all the snow. In the gardens on the grounds, flowers were starting to bloom, and trees were gaining their leaves. Finals swiftly approached, so I didn't have time to think about what I had heard outside Dr. Tweedle's office. I didn't want my first year at the Jelf Academy to be over. I was dreading going back to the manor house for the summer. It seemed like only yesterday I had found out I was a pixie and that I would be given the opportunity to go to the Jelf Academy. Now, I felt like I had learned so much, and found the one place I belonged. What if I never saw the academy again? I didn't even want to think about what would happen if I failed to impress the government officials.

I was also fearful to leave the academy and the pixie world. Every week, Josefina and Miguel returned to school with the news of other pixies who were missing or dead. The attacks had become more frequent than ever before, and pixie authorities were becoming increasingly nervous. Josefina, Miguel, and I speculated the reason for the rise in W.A.S.P. attacks, but no one knew what had triggered their aggressive behavior. Dr. Tweedle told us any human could belong to the W.A.S.P., and we had to be extremely careful.

I tried to push these new horrors from my mind as I concentrated on studying. Mrs. Rowley told us the written portion of the exam would consist of gemstone properties, and in the practical portion, she would randomly select the charm we needed to create. I hoped she would choose the quick complete charm since it was the one I had mastered.

Ms. Crescent had returned to the classroom and seemed to have recovered from the stress of her visions. She still received flashes of information about the W.A.S.P., but none of her visions were ever detailed enough to stop the attacks. Even though she had resumed teaching the class, she looked pale and withdrawn. Josefina and I felt sorry for her, but Miguel just sighed when it came to her sporadic visions. Upon her return a few months ago, she had quizzed us on tarot cards and palm reading since these would be on our exam along with aura detection.

Mr. Collyworth droned on about American pixie history, determined to cover as much information as possible. His exam would consist of a multiple-choice test and two essay questions. Though it seemed easy enough, I was still worried about the history test. We had covered so much information. What if I couldn't remember specific dates, places, or names?

Mr. Withermyer's final exam was sure to be the hardest of them all. The practical exam would consist of several charms and the written exam would test our knowledge of ingredients. Mr. Withermyer had stated that we wouldn't be allowed to use our books at any time during the exam. The only positive change about his class was that he hadn't tried to make a fool out of me over the last few months. It seemed as if he had decided to listen to Dr. Tweedle, but he still gave me nasty looks.

In Mr. Laruse's class, we were still practicing the prediction of tornadoes, reviewing predicting rain and snow. I doubted his exam would be hard. I felt the same way about Mrs. Harris's class. From what she had told us about the exam, it seemed straightforward. Also, we had been reviewing the material for weeks now. With the pressure of the exams, I hoped that I could balance the amount of work. Despite believing that two of the six exams would be easy, I was beginning to feel as if I lived in the library.

The day of our first final exam was scheduled on Monday, with the rest of the tests continuing on Tuesday and Wednesday. The regular class schedule wouldn't be followed during this week and students would be taking two exams per day. The tests lasted longer than the fifty-five-minute class periods, and any remaining free time during the day was used for studying. Josefina explained that the teachers would have time to calculate our grades so we would receive them before we left for the summer.

Thursday and Friday would be for gathering our belongings and preparing to leave the academy. I was grateful for the freedom of the last two days before I had to return to the manor house. I prayed with all my heart that it wouldn't be the last time I would see the Jelf Academy.

On the morning of the first exams, I forced myself to rise before the sun. I gently woke Josefina as she had asked. I couldn't believe this day had come, and I was extremely nervous. How I performed on these exams would be a determining factor of whether I could return to the academy. Josefina and I planned to go down to the library to practice for our Charms test and to quiz each other on charm ingredients. My stomach felt sick, and I hoped that I would remember everything during the exam.

After a little over an hour in the library, Josefina and I went to breakfast. I was feeling slightly more confident about the tests since we had gone over the material again. Juan and Miguel were already at a table, so we joined them.

"Have either of you seen Lena today?" Juan asked when we sat down.

"No, we've been studying in the library all morning," I replied.

"I didn't see her last night either, but Jane and I were studying in our room," Josefina added.

"I was just wondering because it isn't like Lena to miss breakfast," Juan said.

"Lena and Rosie were probably studying late into the night. She could've accidentally overslept. We've all been under pressure because of final exams. Don't worry about it. Lena isn't the type of pixie to miss her tests," Miguel stated.

"No, she isn't," Juan replied with a concerned expression.

In the blink of an eye, breakfast was over, and we were walking into our first test. I hadn't been able to eat much, and my heart pounded uncontrollably. Mrs. Rowley greeted us with a smile on her face. When we were all seated, she passed out the tests. I gained some confidence as I worked through the first part of the exam. I had memorized all the properties for the twelve astrological gemstones, and it wasn't long before I moved on to the second part.

Mrs. Rowley had a jar full of paper slips on her desk. Written on each slip, was the name of a charm. Whatever charm you picked was the charm you had to complete. With a deep breath, I reached into the jar and my hand closed around my fated charm. Slowly, I unfolded the paper and released a sigh of relief. I couldn't believe my luck at choosing the quick complete charm. Mrs. Rowley gave me a knowing smile, and I performed the charm with ease.

Thankful to have one test completed, I moved out into the hallway to wait for Josefina and Miguel. As soon as they had finished, we returned to the library to focus on our next exam: Predicting the Future which was scheduled after lunch.

"The Gemstones 101 test was easy, but I'm not so sure about

Predicting the Future. I might have to make something up," Miguel said.

"I told you to pay attention in that class!" Josefina scolded him. "I'm guessing you want my help now."

Miguel gave her a sheepish smile. "If you help me out a little on this one, I'll help you out on the History exam," he offered.

We spent an hour in the library studying. At lunch, no one was very talkative, and I could understand why. All I could think about was my remaining exams, but Predicting the Future was the one now looming over my head. The tarot cards, auras, and palm readings swirled around my brain, and I silently visualized the pages of *Divination for Beginners*. I couldn't worry about the future exams. I had to focus on conquering one test at a time.

The Predicting the Future final began with matching each tarot card and aura color with their meanings. The last part of the test consisted of reading Ms. Crescent's palm in the back room. I was fairly confident that I had remembered the tarot cards and the aura colors, but the palm reading made me nervous. When it was my turn, I walked through the beaded curtains into Ms. Crescent's office. She had the cushions on the floor, and I sat down in front of her.

"Whenever you're ready to begin," Ms. Crescent said to acknowledge me, and she held out her right palm. I took a deep breath and began examining her hand.

"You'll have many horrible upcoming predictions," I said. I shuddered as I saw flashes of them in her future. I concentrated harder. I touched on the meaning of her lifeline, and then I moved on to the other lines of Ms. Crescent's palm. Throughout the reading, a face continued to flash in my mind. A face that was very handsome with dark brooding eyes and jet-black hair. He looked so familiar to me, but I couldn't place him at first. When I was almost finished with the reading, I finally realized to whom the face belonged. "How do you know Mr. Doyle?" I asked.

"Who's Mr. Doyle?" Ms. Crescent replied. "I've never met anyone with that name."

"Oh," I flushed with embarrassment. "I must've mistaken him for the young man I saw in my vision of your future. Mr. Doyle is my stepsister's fiancé and a human. I'm sorry. I should've realized that you couldn't possibly know him."

"I don't know any humans, but I have been getting visions of a dark-haired man myself. No matter, your allotted time for this part of the test is up. You're dismissed," Ms. Crescent said abruptly.

I got up from the floor cushions and exited through the hanging beads. I was confused. Did I do a good job at palm reading because she had seen a dark-haired man in her future as well? I could've sworn he looked like Mr. Doyle, but it must have been my imagination.

I was relieved when the first day of tests finally ended. How I had done on the Predicting the Future exam was out of my hands, and I needed to focus on the exams for tomorrow. Josefina and I studied for the upcoming tests before dinner and we both agreed to go to the library to continue studying that evening.

When we sat down at our usual table for dinner, Juan was still concerned. No one had seen Lena today. Apprehension crept into my mind, but Josefina refused to think the worst. She suggested that Lena might have fallen ill, but Juan didn't appear to agree with Josefina's explanation.

The next morning, Josefina and I rose early again and pulled out our History and Charms books. Keeping the same schedule as the day before, we spent time in the library before breakfast. Miguel joined us later and tried to help us with historical facts. He knew good memorization techniques, and I hoped they would help me. I kept reciting the major dates and figures in my head as I left the dining hall.

I hoped the History of Pixies exam wasn't too long or difficult. I wanted as much time as possible to look over my Charms notes again. As I waited to enter the History classroom, I pulled out my class notes in an attempt to study one last time. Miguel amazed me again with his knowledge of the topics we covered. I knew he was going to ace this test. Sooner than I expected, Mr. Collyworth was calling us into the classroom, and it was time to begin.

As I stared down at my exam, dates swam through my head. For some of the multiple-choice questions, I second-guessed myself and started overthinking the available answers. My eyes kept straying to the clock. I wanted to make sure I had enough time to finish the entire exam. The two essay questions were easier because we had just gone over the topics in class during our review. I was satisfied with my short essays on the American Revolution and the American Civil War.

A small weight lifted from my chest as I placed the exam on Mr. Collyworth's desk. My stomach rumbled for lunch, and I hoped I would be able to eat something with the Charms exam looming. Miguel had finished the History exam faster than Josefina and me, so he was already in the dining hall. I picked a small meal just in case I would start feeling sick. It wasn't long before a very worried-looking Juan joined us.

"Lena wasn't in any of the classes today to take the finals. I'm really worried about her," Juan said distressed. "Have you heard anything?"

We all shook our heads as he sat down with his lunch.

"This isn't like her. There has to be something wrong," Juan said. He picked at his lunch. His face looked sallow, and he had dark circles beneath his eyes.

Our unease about Lena grew when Rosie approached our table. "Has anyone seen or heard from Lena? She didn't come back to the academy last night or the night before."

Juan's face became even more drawn. "No, I haven't seen her. I'm really worried about her."

"Perhaps Lena has fallen ill and stayed home to recover," Josefina suggested again to Rosie.

Now that another day had gone by without Lena, Juan wasn't satisfied with Josefina's explanation.

"If Lena's sick, perhaps Dr. Tweedle would know," Rosie commented. "I'll ask him if he's heard anything."

We all looked at each other, our appetites lost with our concern for Lena. I didn't have time to contemplate explanations, however, because it was time for Charms.

I knew I was shaking as I entered the Charms classroom, but I tried to breathe deeply to calm myself. I hoped I was prepared for whatever Mr. Withermyer had in mind for this test.

"Please sit down quickly so we can begin. You have ninety minutes to complete the exam. The first part of the test is a true or false section about what ingredients are used in certain charms. This should take you ten minutes at most. Then, you will create the two charms I have written on the board. Since we will not have time to test them, I expect you to bottle them in the tubes on my desk. Make sure your name is on both tubes and put the name of the charm on the label as well. I expect to know which one is which. Failure to do this will result in an automatic point deduction. I will be testing them later. As soon as all exams are passed out, you may begin," Mr. Withermyer said with a sneer.

Then he projected the two charm names on the board: the See All charm and the confusion charm. I took a deep breath as the test was passed out. Once given the signal to begin, I quickly flipped the paper over, sensing that I would need the entire ninety minutes to complete everything.

The true and false section wasn't as bad as I thought, but I did notice some trick questions. I slowed my reading and double-checked my answers, so I wouldn't fall victim to the nuances.

When I had finished the written part, I pulled out my pixie dust case. I started with the confusion charm since it was the more recent of the two. As I chilled my cup and a half of peridots, I remembered Taylor's scream after my charm had been cast. I wondered who Mr. Withermyer was testing these charms on. I prayed to the gods that mine wouldn't have the same effect on them as it did on Taylor.

When I had completed the confusion charm, I went to Mr. Withermyer's desk to collect a test tube. He gave me a strange look as I approached. As I glanced around the class, I noticed I was the first one to have completed a charm. Some of the students were in the middle of the first charm, and I cringed for the ones who were still working on the true and false section. I gave Mr. Withermyer my first charm, labeled with the charm and my name. Then I gave him what I thought was a polite smile. I walked back to my desk with my head held high, and I was startled to hear a short, amused chuckle. Never mind him, I thought, it was time to begin charm number two.

I had studied the concepts of the See All charm, but it had been a while since I created one. I recalled that it was easier than the confusion charm. I pulled out the tiger eye I needed and began. Halfway through my making the charm, I got the feeling I was being watched. Sure enough, when I glanced over my shoulder, Betty Ann was eyeing me intently.

Thinking quickly, I pulled out another type of rock from my pixie dust case and displayed it so she could clearly see the name of it. Thankfully, I had chosen talc, so it crushed easily, and it didn't take me any extra time. I pretended to dump the dust in with my ingredients, but instead, I dumped it into an empty dish. I then stirred the talc several times making it look like I was finishing up the charm. When I noticed Betty Ann's head down and quickly working, I turned my attention back to the real ingredients and finished the charm. Quickly, I put the talc powder back into my case and then took my second finished charm to the front of the room to be bottled and labeled.

I was the first one to finish the Charms exam, and I breathed a sigh of relief as I exited into the hallway. Now, I only had two more tests tomorrow, and then it would be over. I became saddened when I realized that by the end of the week I would be returning to Marie. I scolded myself for thinking about it and pulled out my Earth Catastrophes notes from my bag.

Continuing with our routine from the previous two days, Josefina, Miguel, and I studied after dinner in the library. With only two more exams to complete, we were feeling better about the remaining tests. The Charms test was now in the past, so we could relax a little. Though the next tests seemed easier, we stayed late at the library studying for Earth Catastrophes and Zodiac Signs.

The next morning Josefina and I rose later than the previous two days and only had time to make it to breakfast. Miguel and Juan were already at the table, and I could sense that the atmosphere was tense. It soon became apparent that Lena had not returned last night, nor this morning. Rosie didn't approach our table, and Josefina couldn't think of another reason why Lena had not come back to the school. I couldn't eat and left the table so Josefina and Miguel could try and bolster their brother.

The sun was very bright, casting shafts of light through the tree branches of the large willow tree. A nice spring breeze blew through the air, and it was hard to believe we would soon be tested on predicting rain, snow, or even a tornado. The weather was so perfect. When Mr. Laruse arrived at the classroom, he looked as frazzled as always. He handed out the test sheet which had the numbers one through five down the left side. The top of the paper explained that Mr. Laruse was going to simulate five weather events which we had to predict before they happened. He also mentioned that events could be duplicated. Mr. Laruse stated he would give us five to ten minutes to predict the events and, then we had to put our pencils down in between.

The test was so simple, we knew our results as soon as it was over. Mr. Laruse simulated two rain events, one snow event, one small tornado, and as a trick he summoned hail. I was so glad I had not been stumped by the predictions and got a five out of five. I joyfully handed in my test.

"I can't believe he fooled us with hail. It wasn't something we went over in the review," Miguel complained. "I could sense something cold was going to happen, so I wrote snow even though I knew it didn't feel right."

"I had that feeling too, but I remembered one of his lectures about hail, so I rethought my answer," I replied.

"I knew it was going to be hail, too," Josefina added. "I just had a feeling."

"Why didn't you tell me?" Miguel teased. "Some twin you are!"

We enjoyed another quick lunch, coupled with studying for Zodiac Signs. The pressure I had felt earlier in the week seemed to subside since there was only one exam left. Zodiac Signs seemed like it would be the least difficult test. Mrs. Harris had been very helpful during our reviews the week before, and I doubted she had any surprise questions in store for us.

We arrived at the Zodiac Signs classroom early. All I had to remember was a few facts about each zodiac sign. After all the students had arrived, Mrs. Harris passed out the test papers and told us we could begin. Like the history test, it was also a multiple-choice and essay test. At least we didn't have to make any charms or predict any events.

We were only fifteen minutes into our test when a knock sounded on the door. Dr. Tweedle entered the room looking solemn, and he spoke with Mrs. Harris quietly. Most of the students looked up from the test curious about their exchange. A few minutes later, Dr. Tweedle left the classroom and Mrs. Harris stood in front of the class.

"Excuse me," she said with a sad look on her face. "We'll have to resume this test sometime tomorrow. Dr. Tweedle has asked me to escort you to the dining hall for an announcement," she said with sadness in her voice, and we all looked at each other with a terrified expression. Obviously, Dr. Tweedle didn't have good news.

Mrs. Harris collected our tests, and we all left the classroom in an orderly fashion. Mrs. Harris hadn't said anything about remaining silent, so Josefina rushed to my side.

"What do you think Dr. Tweedle has to tell us? I know it doesn't sound like good news, but I don't know if I can bear the bad news. What if something happened to another student, like Henry Adams?" Josefina cried.

"I know. That's why I'm terrified by this announcement," Miguel said grimly.

As we filed into the dining hall, the scene was eerily familiar. My stomach felt sick. I wanted to run away and cover my ears to block out what Dr. Tweedle was going to say. The room grew quiet instantly when Dr. Tweedle ascended to the podium. I was having horrible flashbacks, and I swallowed the lump in my throat.

"My dear students, it is unfortunate that I have to come before you again with another terrible announcement. I wish it weren't so, especially during your most important exams. This morning, the parents of Helena Rodriguez were found in their home. Miss Rodriguez was nowhere to be found, and she has been declared missing. We have reason to believe that something terrible may have happened to her. The pixie authorities are certain the W.A.S.P. are involved and the outcome doesn't look good," Dr. Tweedle said as he bent his head.

I felt paralyzed I processed the information. The world around me had gone hazy as my vision shifted in and out of focus. Lena was missing and believed to be dead. I felt like I was going to fall over, but I snapped back to my body when a loud cry echoed through the hall. Juan was wailing like a strangled animal. The people around him were trying to keep him from falling to the floor. He tore at his hair and large tears rolled down his face.

Josefina was also crying. She ran over to hug her brother followed by Miguel, who had not come to tears yet but looked just as grief-stricken. My cheeks felt wet, and I wiped at my face. I headed toward them, still not completely believing anything this terrible could have happened to Lena. Beautiful, kind, fun-loving Lena couldn't be dead. Juan took a long time to calm down. When he finally did, Dr. Tweedle continued speaking.

"My deepest sympathies go out to the Rodriguez family and any friends of theirs. Please keep them in your mind and hearts. Remember to remain cautious and constantly alert when you return home for the summer. Again, Nurse Adeline is available for those who need grief counseling during this very difficult time." Dr. Tweedle half-heartedly stepped down from the dais. Even though he always seemed strong, I could tell he was on the verge of breaking down.

"I loved her, and I never got to tell her," Juan sobbed pulling my attention away from Dr. Tweedle.

"She loved you too," Josefina cried. "She admitted her feelings to me before the Valentine's Day dance."

Juan sobbed harder and tears glistened in everyone's eyes. I didn't know what to say, so I put my arms around both Josefina's and Miguel's shoulders. My brain couldn't comprehend what had happened. Lena was the nicest person I had ever met besides the Martinez siblings. She was the one who had defended me from Betty Ann and Thomas, and she comforted me afterwards. My heart ached, and I supported both Josefina and Miguel. They leaned on me, and we mourned for our friend.

I was interrupted by a hand tapping me on the shoulder. I turned to face Mrs. Rowley. Her eyes glistened with tears.

"Miss Fitzgerald, Dr. Tweedle has asked me to send you to his office. He has something important to tell you." I heard what she said, but my mind felt clouded. I nodded my head as I let go of Josefina and Miguel and followed Mrs. Rowley away from the anguish in the hall.

Mrs. Rowley must have known I was confused because she made sure I arrived at Dr. Tweedle's office. Why did Dr. Tweedle want to see me? Did they decide to expel me already? Why would Dr. Tweedle tell me this immediately after the devastating news of Lena's disappearance?

I entered the plush blue office in a daze and saw Dr. Tweedle seated at his desk, wiping his eyes with a handkerchief. When he saw me, he quickly put the handkerchief down and straightened his glasses. Like a ghost, I had floated to the sofa and took a seat. I almost felt like I was looking down at myself from a distance as if I were no longer in my body.

"Jane, I know you were close to Miss Rodriquez, so I'm sorry for your grief at this time, but there's something important I must tell you. When the Rodriguez's were discovered, a note written by the W.A.S.P. was also left at their residence."

Dr. Tweedle reached into his desk drawer and pulled out a dirty crumpled piece of paper, which he unfolded. He laid it between us on the desk. I shuddered as I looked at the letter because the smudges looked like dried blood. Stamped at the bottom, was a picture of a wasp. I could make out the striped body, the wings, legs, and the dark black stinger. The wasp was inside of a hexagon shape that reminded me of a honeycomb. The symbol was the only form of a signature.

"This letter was written as a threat, and the only reason I am bringing it to your attention is that it concerns you."

I leaned forward and tried to concentrate on what he was saying.

"When the W.A.S.P. attacked your mother all those years ago, they celebrated a great victory because your mother was a very powerful pixie. They had discovered her powers through the torture of other pixies and became determined to capture her. They hadn't discovered that your mother bore a child. If they would've known about you, I fear they would've killed you too. Maybe that was the only good thing about your mother leaving the pixie world.

"This relates to the note because it seems the W.A.S.P. has finally discovered your existence. They don't seem to know anything about you other than your mother's bloodline continued. The W.A.S.P. isn't privy to your name or gender, but in this note, they have threatened to find you," Dr. Tweedle said as I blinked in confusion.

"The W.A.S.P. knew nothing of your mother's marriage, so they believe you have the last name of McCalski. They've assumed someone in the pixie world has raised you for all these years. We're fairly certain they have no idea you live in the area where your mother died. This gives us an advantage in protecting you. I believe you will still be safe with your stepmother, and I will take it upon myself to set up special defenses when I take you back for the summer," Dr. Tweedle stated.

I felt like a large cube of ice had fallen into my stomach. The W.A.S.P. had murdered my mother and now they were coming for me. Why? "Dr. Tweedle, the W.A.S.P. harms any pixie they come across. Why are they so determined to find me?" I asked with a shaky voice.

"The W.A.S.P. is under the impression that someone from your mother's bloodline will be more powerful than she ever was. It's rumored that they received some kind of foretelling from a pixie they captured. They firmly believe the progeny of Rachel McCalski will have the ability to destroy them. Since you're your mother's only child, they assume it will be you."

26
RETURN TO THE MANOR

I WENT THROUGH THE next few days in a daze. The W.A.S.P. had a goal to find and kill me because they thought I was powerful enough to stop them. That wasn't possible. I couldn't be more powerful than my mother. Dr. Tweedle assured me that no matter what happened, he would keep me safe while I was at the manor. I trusted that he would, but nothing he could tell me would ever shake the dreadful fact that people were trying to murder me.

My Zodiac class met on Friday morning to finish our exam, so we had Thursday to mourn the Rodriguez family. Juan was so depressed, he never came out of his room, and Josefina had to beg him to eat. She also suggested that Juan visit the hospital wing. Josefina wasn't handling Lena's disappearance any better than her brother, though. Every night she cried herself to sleep. Josefina had known Lena for most of her life, so I was sure it felt like she had lost an older sister.

On Thursday, Josefina asked me why Dr. Tweedle had pulled me into his office for a private word. I wished Josefina wasn't so observant and didn't have such a good memory.

"You're going to want to sit down for this," I told her. Her legs shook as she sat on her bed.

How would I tell Josefina that the W.A.S.P.'s main goal involved my capture and death? I paced in front of her and then stopped when I saw the anxious look on her face.

"Dr. Tweedle called me to his office because a letter was found with the Rodriguez's," I started.

"A letter?" Josefina asked. "What kind of letter? Why did he tell you about it?" Josefina asked.

"The letter was written by the W.A.S.P...."

Josefina interrupted me. "I've never heard of the W.A.S.P. leaving letters before. What was it about?" Her eyebrows creased as she looked at me.

"The letter contained a threat. They mentioned my mother and how it was a great victory when they eliminated her," I said irritated. "What the W.A.S.P. didn't know at the time of my mother's death was that she had given birth to me. Recently, they've discovered my mother's bloodline hadn't ended with her. Dr. Tweedle speculates that they gained this information from the pixies they tortured. The W.A.S.P. seems to think my last name is McCalski like her."

"What does the W.A.S.P. want with you? Don't they want any pixie they can find?" Josefina asked, a frightened look in her eyes.

"The reason they are looking for me is they learned of a prediction that states I will be more powerful than my mother. Only I will have the ability to defeat their society. So, their main goal is to find and kill me," I replied gravely.

Josefina gasped and laid her hand on her throat. Her eyes were wide with fright and the color had drained from her face. "Oh, Jane. We have to keep you safe. How could you possibly return to Marie for the summer? You'll be surrounded by humans!" Josefina cried.

"Dr. Tweedle says it's one of the safest places I can go. The

W.A.S.P. expects me to be living with a pixie family. They won't be looking for me as a servant to a human and her family. Plus, Marie's so appalled by my magical abilities, she would deny them. Dr. Tweedle said he would place defenses around the house which will alert him if I'm in any danger. I have no idea why the W.A.S.P. believes I'll be more powerful than my mother. I guess they want to get rid of me just in case."

"You must be terrified! I'm terrified! The W.A.S.P. is bad enough, but to be personally hunted," she gasped. Her reaction was normal, but I was trying so hard not to panic. This predicament seemed like it was happening to someone else, and I felt like an outsider looking in. How did someone deal with knowing other people wanted to kill them? I wouldn't be able to function if I thought about it too much.

"I will be okay, Josefina. You won't have to worry about me. I'll have some protection and the W.A.S.P. won't think to look for me if I live among humans," I said.

Josefina looked at me skeptically. Slowly, she rose from her bed and approached me. Suddenly, she threw her arms around me, wrapping me in a humongous hug. "Please be careful this summer. You're like my sister. I don't know what I would do without you, especially since I already lost my other sister," Josefina cried as tears streamed down her face. I kept hugging her tightly, afraid that I would start crying too.

"I'll be fine, Josefina. I'm supposed to be a powerful pixie, right?" I joked as emotion overwhelmed my voice. "The W.A.S.P. will have to watch out for me."

"I'm going to miss you so much, Jane," Josefina said as she pulled away from me. "I hope the pixie government allows you to return to the Jelf Academy. I don't know what I'll do without you. You deserve to be here. You are a pixie, Jane."

"My life would feel like it was ending if they decide to expel me. I would be trapped with Marie and she might be worse than the W.A.S.P.," I joked boldly. I smiled even though my eyes were brimming with tears.

❧

The unfortunate day came when it was time to leave the Jelf Academy for the summer. Some students looked joyous about this, but of course, I couldn't be anything but sad. We had gotten our grades for the year, and I was very pleased with the marks I had received. I had achieved an outstanding level, the highest mark, in Gemstones 101, Predicting the Future, Earth Catastrophes, Zodiac Signs, and surprisingly Charms. I was sure Mr. Withermyer hated that he had to be fair and give me the grade I deserved. I hoped my scores would prove that I belonged in the pixie world.

Rumor had it that Betty Ann failed half of the Charms exams which gave her a mark of satisfactory. I wondered if it was because she had used talc in the See All charm. The only class I received an average level was in History of Pixies. Perhaps I was following in my mother's footsteps. I shuddered about what that would mean for my future.

Everyone at the school was busy packing up their belongings and preparing to leave. My heart clenched at the sight of so many packed suitcases. The day of departure had arrived and there would be no avoiding it. Josefina and I carried our luggage into the great hall with the other students and waited our turn to ride the cloud down to the meadow below. We both had somber faces. I bent down to pet Coco goodbye and a small tear escaped my eye. I would miss her too. After my goodbye, Josefina knelt to put Coco in her cage for traveling.

We were soon joined by Miguel and Juan, both of them looked dismal. We all boarded the cloud together and began the descent down to the meadow. I watched the school until it disappeared from my line of view. Would this be the last time I would see it? Why did it feel like I was leaving home instead of heading towards it? I wiped the stray tears from my eyes and tried to be strong. I prayed I would be allowed back in the fall.

That's if I survived the summer, the nasty thought snuck into my head. It was a fact that was hard to ignore.

In the clearing, Juan, Josefina, and Miguel moved toward an empty carriage, and I followed them to say my goodbyes. My heart was aching because their family had become my family. They were the three people who cared about me and hoped that I would be okay. What would I do without them? I helped them load their bags into the back of the carriage and then we all stood facing each other. I hugged Juan first and whispered how sorry I was about Lena. She was still missing, and no one had heard anything else concerning her disappearance. Then, I hugged Miguel.

"Be careful this summer, Jane," he said to me. "I hope Dr. Tweedle is right about sending you back to live among humans."

"I'm going to miss you all so much. I hope this is not the last time I ever see you," I said, tears blurring my vision.

Josefina hugged me the longest and hardest. "Please, Jane. Be cautious this summer. I don't want anything to happen to you. Don't let Marie crush your spirit and stay positive. I know this isn't the last time I'm going to see you."

"You three better be careful, too. No one's safe from the W.A.S.P. I don't know if I'd want to come back to the Jelf Academy without you."

They all smiled, though their eyes glistened with tears, and then they all converged on me for a group hug before they climbed into the carriage. The winged horses pawed the ground and flapped their enormous wings. I watched the Martinez's fly into the sky, the whole time Josefina waved out the window until the carriage disappeared from view. My eyes felt swollen, and my cheeks were wet, but I quickly wiped my tears away with my sleeve.

"I know saying goodbye to your friends is hard, but it's time for us to leave now, Jane," Dr. Tweedle said gently as he came up behind me. "I know you're feeling sad and scared, but I do have something to tell you. The government officials were most impressed when I gave them the report of your academic achievements. It's hard to deny that you've done extraordinarily well in your classes. That alone should have convinced them that you're indeed qualified to attend the Jelf Academy of Magic," Dr. Tweedle said.

I hung my head and tried not to cry. "So, I wasn't able to convince them? I won't be returning to the Jelf Academy?" I said sadly.

"It took a lot of persuading, but finally, the pixie government agreed that you belong in the pixie world. Since the W.A.S.P. declared they are hunting for you, it was agreed that it was highly unlikely for you to reveal the pixie world since you are also in danger. Your education at the Jelf Academy has been approved, and you no longer need to worry about your status. You've done it, Jane. You've been accepted."

I couldn't believe the relief that washed over me at the news. I had been able to prove to the pixie government that I belonged at the Jelf Academy. I had been terrified of losing my connection to my mother's world, but now I wouldn't have to give it up.

"Thank you, Dr. Tweedle. I'm so glad you believed in me. How can I ever return the gratitude I feel?" I said with emotion.

"No need to thank me, Jane. You've proven you're talented enough to attend the Jelf Academy. Somehow, I knew you would," Dr. Tweedle replied with a wink.

I couldn't contain my smile as I followed him to his carriage. When I climbed inside, I gripped his hand as he teleported us to the manor. Teleportation still took my breath away, and it took me a moment to orient myself. When we arrived at the end of the driveway to the manor house, Dr. Tweedle leapt out of the carriage, and I watched as he sprinkled pixie dust around the entrance. I knew that he was casting the charms that would hopefully protect me over the summer. When he finished, he climbed back up beside me.

"I've placed several charms to protect you. I'll be alerted if you're in any danger and no matter where I'm at, I'll teleport back here to come to your aid. Nothing will happen to you, I promise. Behave yourself, Jane, and keep your abilities secret. I'll be back for you on August twenty-first. We will return you to Jewel Caverns to collect everything you will need for your second year at the Jelf Academy."

The carriage pulled up outside the front door, and I looked at Dr. Tweedle. "I'm going to miss you, Miss Fitzgerald. Please be on guard this summer."

I hugged Dr. Tweedle on impulse, not knowing if it was the proper thing to do. He accepted my hug and I mumbled, "I'll really miss you, too."

Then, I quickly turned away, so he wouldn't see me cry. I grabbed my small bag of belongings and climbed out of the carriage. This parting was bittersweet for me. I would miss the pixie world during the summer, but at least I would be able to return to the Jelf Academy in the fall. Bravely, I climbed the manor's front steps and prepared myself for all the things that would be waiting inside. With a deep breath, I pushed the door open, already calculating the number of days until I would return to my true home: the Jelf Academy of Magic.

THE END

ACKNOWLEDGEMENTS

This book wouldn't have been possible without the help of so many people, and I am so grateful to have you all in my life. To my parents who have always stood behind me and encouraged me to follow my dreams. You saw potential in *Pixie Dust* when I began the manuscript at seventeen and have helped me through every step of the process. Without your love and support, I would never have had the confidence to publish.

I am thankful for my loving husband, Christopher, who took the time to read the manuscript even though *Pixie Dust* was not "your kind of book". Thank you for your continued support of my lifelong dream.

For my son, Clayton, you are the light of my life. Thank you for the few moments of quiet time, so I could work on all my edits, preparing this book for publication. I hope you know that anything is possible, and when you choose to follow your dreams, I'll be behind you every step of the way.

Thank you to my brother, Regis, for reading this novel despite the fact that you're not a book person. Your perspective and ideas helped enhanced the story and allowed me to expand on a few details.

Thank you to all my beta readers, family, and friends who assured me that this story had potential. I will be forever grateful for your suggestions, guidance, and encouragement. Your reviews boosted my confidence and convinced me that *Pixie Dust* could be in a book store someday.

Many, many thanks to my wonderful editor and friend, Alexandria Groves. From the beginning, you have bolstered my spirit and been a tremendous help. Thank you for reassuring me when I had my doubts. Your positive energy and fantastic edits have been greatly appreciated. *Pixie Dust* wouldn't be as polished without you.

Thanks to the team at Damonza, for designing my amazing cover. It was so exciting to see my vision turn into a reality. I felt like my book was really coming to fruition when the cover was complete.

I am extremely lucky to know so many amazing people who believe in me and this novel. Thank you for everything you do and continue to do. I value each and every one of you.

EXCERPT FROM DRAGON SCALES

Please enjoy the following excerpt from
Dragon Scales, the second novel in the
Jelf Academy Series.

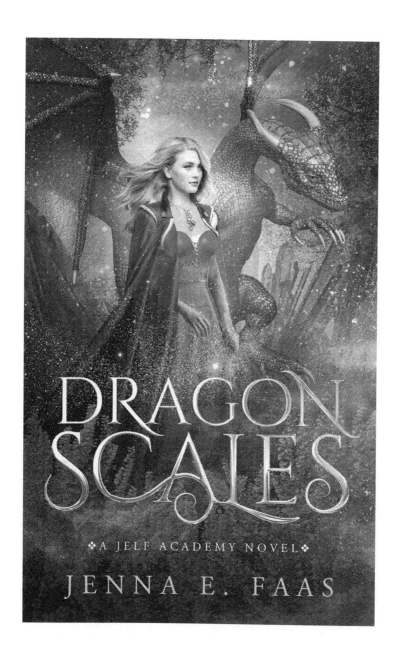

DRAGON
SCALES

❖ A JELF ACADEMY NOVEL ❖

JENNA E. FAAS

1

LONG DAYS OF SUMMER

THE SWELTERING SUN radiated down on my back as I worked. It was so hot outside that I could see the heat waves in the air across the field. I wiped the sweat from my brow and continued to dig the shovel into the hard ground. Ever since I had returned for the summer, Marie assigned me more outdoor chores. Marie was my stepmother and ever since my father passed away, she treated me like a slave. She even moved my bedroom into the attic. Marie hated me because she knew I looked like my mother who passed away when I was only one year old. She had always been jealous that my father loved my mother more.

However, that wasn't the only reason Marie couldn't stand me. Not only did I look like my mother, but I was also "special" like her as well; I could move things with my mind. Marie thought I was a freak and told me she would throw me out if anyone found out about the things I could do. What she didn't know was there were other people just like me. I was a pixie. Pixies could move things with our minds and create charms from rocks and minerals. Marie was also unaware that I was attending a school called the Jelf Academy, a school that taught pixies how to manage their magic.

Marie believed she was sending me to a school to learn etiquette, so I could become the perfect respectable servant. If she ever found out the real purpose of the Jelf Academy, she would stop me from attending and follow through on her threat.

The Jelf Academy was such a special place for so many reasons. First of all, it was the school my mother had attended. I instantly felt connected to her once I had started attending. The academy also made me feel as if I finally belonged. It had become my home. However, there was a third and most important reason as to why I had to finish my five years at the Jelf Academy. My mother hadn't passed away because she had been sick. She had been murdered by an evil group of people know as the World Association for the Slaying of Pixies, abbreviated W.A.S.P. These people hated all pixies and had the intention of eliminating them one by one. My mother had been a very powerful pixie, so the W.A.S.P. had rejoiced when they had defeated her. They didn't know about me when they ended her life.

Just recently, the W.A.S.P. gained information from the pixies they tortured that I would be responsible for dismantling their organization. Since I was my mother's only child, it made sense for the prophecy to be about me, which currently made me their primary target.

I was not in immediate danger since the W.A.S.P. knew nothing about me. They believed I went by my mother's last name, McCalski, instead of Fitzgerald and that I was being raised by pixies. For once in my life, I was thankful I lived with Marie. Unfortunately, my safety was temporary because it would only be a matter of time until the W.A.S.P. discovered my true whereabouts. That was why it was essential for me to attend the Jelf Academy. I needed to know everything about being a pixie in order to defend myself if I was ever found. I tried not to think about being hunted by the W.A.S.P., but I couldn't help but to always look over my shoulder.

I couldn't wait to be back at the Jelf Academy to start my

second year. Since Marie knew nothing about the magic school, Dr. Tweedle, the headmaster, always transported me to the academy. A year ago, he had appeared in my life and explained who I was and what my abilities were. He was the one who changed my world around, and I'll be forever grateful for that.

I was accepted at the Jelf Academy of Magic, but not everyone in the pixie community had accepted me. Last year, I had to prove I was worthy to remain in the pixie world. Since it's illegal for pixies to have relations with humans, there had never been a student who was half-human before. Fortunately, I had been able to convince the pixie government of my abilities, and the fact that the W.A.S.P. was hunting me also helped my case. I would be less likely to expose the pixie world now that my life was in danger.

I continued to work in the field and tried not to think of the potential peril that could befall me. Soon, I was interrupted by Robert, the only friend I had at the manor. Robert was the auburn-haired boy Marie had hired to work in the barn and help with the horses. Unfortunately, he was paid in room and board and had to live in the loft above the horses. He used to live with a man named Mr. Wicker who was actually worse than Marie. When he first began living at the manor, he never spoke to me. I thought it was because he didn't like me, but that wasn't the case. Since then, Robert and I have grown closer and became friends. He eventually told me that Mr. Wicker didn't allow him to speak, and if he did, he would be punished.

"Good afternoon, Jane," he said to me as he approached. "I see Marie has you doing outdoor chores again." He shook his head as he inspected them. "A lady shouldn't be out in the sun doing a man's job."

"Haven't you heard? I'm not a lady," I replied with a chuckle. Robert looked at the ground, ignoring my comment.

"When you're finished cleaning up dinner, do you want to come down to the lake again?" Robert asked referring to the small lake in the woods on the manor's property. Sometimes, if Marie and her children were preoccupied, I would sneak down to the lake. It was the only relaxing thing I could do at the manor. It was refreshing after a long day of working under the sun.

"We'll have to see, Robert. It depends on Marie. Sometimes she has me working well into the night," I replied.

Robert looked sympathetic. "You start school again soon, don't you?" he asked with an upset look on his face. Robert told me before that he missed me when I was gone. I wished he was also a pixie, so he could attend too.

"Yes, in a week I will be picked up from here, so I can begin my second year!" I said excitedly.

"How much do you have left to learn about etiquette? I can't believe you go to that school for five years," he replied.

"Oh, I couldn't believe how much there is to learn either," I lied and instantly felt guilty.

I always hated lying to Robert. I wished I could tell him the truth, but since humans were not allowed to know of the pixie world, I would be jeopardizing my position when I had just worked so hard to prove myself. Any human could belong to the W.A.S.P. so you couldn't trust anyone. My mother took that risk and broke the rule for love.

"You'll have to tell me all about it then," Robert chuckled, breaking my thoughts.

"Yes, sure," I replied noncommittally. I hoped he wouldn't ask me.

I finished up the tilling with the shovel and followed Robert to the barn. It was the hottest part of the day, and I was using most of my energy to keep myself cool. Pixies had the ability to change their body temperatures. We just had to stay focused on the task, which was sometimes hard to do. Your mind had to be able to multitask.

My body ached all over, and it was such a relief to enter the cool barn. I hung my shovel on the wall next to the others and took a deep breath. I knew I would have to get back up to the house to help with dinner, but I found myself sitting down on a bale of hay. I hadn't realized how tired I was.

"Would you like some water?" Robert asked me.

"Sure," I sighed. It felt so good to sit, and my throat was so parched.

He handed me a bucket full of water. I cupped some in my hands and brought it to my lips. Robert stood watching me intently. I tried not to spill water down my dress because sometimes his firm gaze made me nervous and, for no reason, I felt self-conscious. I didn't know why he made me feel that way. He was just my friend.

"Thank you," I said, handing the bucket of water back to him.

He smiled at me as he took the bucket from my hands and, again, his brown eyes met my violet ones. I quickly looked down at my hands because I could feel my cheeks reddening. Sometimes that look of his made me react funny. I looked back up at him and smiled.

"I should head back up to the house. I know Marie will want me to help with dinner. She's probably already mad that I'm not up there already slaving away," I sighed as I got up from the hay.

"Hopefully, I'll see you tonight at the lake," Robert said.

"I'll have to see what Marie is doing and if I can sneak away or not," I replied.

He smiled again as I left the barn. My legs burned as I walked up the slightly inclined terrain that led up to the side of the house. I had worked very hard today and had exhausted myself. I walked around the back of the house and entered through the kitchen door.

"Where the hell have you been?" This was the greeting I got from Ellen the cook. Her mousey brown hair was concealed beneath a blue bonnet and her apron was ruffled over her round stomach.

"I just finished my work in the field," I replied used to her tone with me.

"Wash your hands immediately and get over here!" she yipped.

I inwardly sighed as I washed my hands in the sink and joined her in the preparation of dinner. Ellen told me to begin boiling the corn on the cob and then instructed me to cut all the kernels off the cobs. Apparently, Marie didn't want to bite it off the cob today. The hot corn burned my fingers as I held it upright with one hand and cut off the kernels. Marie would think of this as a punishment for me. I was almost certain she sat around all day and thought of things I could do that would make my life miserable.

After I finished, I added butter to the bowl and stirred it in until it was well mixed. Then, I helped Ellen finish up the preparations by taking the rolls out of the oven and placing them on a nice dish. Marie always wanted to have dinner served on the best china, no matter what day it was. When the chicken was done roasting, we carried the food out to the table. Marie, Emily, and Preston were usually seated at the table when Ellen and I served dinner. We never had to call them down to the dining room. I always wondered how long they sat there.

Marie sat straight in her chair as if a metal rod had been inserted in her spine. Her midnight hair, streaked through with gray, was always in a severe bun and she always wore a stern look on her face. I had never seen her smile or laugh. When she did smile it always seemed cold and malicious, not genuine. Marie probably had been pretty when she was young, but her cold demeanor overshadowed any features that I would consider beautiful. Even her gray eyes matched the stoniness of her heart.

Emily was like a carbon copy of Marie. She had the same black hair and her eyes were also gray. Emily wasn't distasteful to look at, but like her mother, she lacked inner beauty. Emily delighted at anyone's misfortune and that was the only time she laughed. Making my life miserable was one of Emily's favorite activities. Another favorite of hers was verbally insulting me to make me feel insignificant and beneath her. Of course, I didn't listen or believe anything she said, but what she said was hurtful. Soon, I wouldn't have to worry about Emily's verbal insults because she would be married next spring. After that, she would move in with her new husband Drake Doyle.

I couldn't say I would be upset to see her go, but as the wedding drew nearer I would have more chores to do. Marie and Emily already told me I would be slaving away at the favors and other decorations needed for the wedding. On the wedding day, I would act as a server to the guests at Drake Doyle's house where the wedding would be held. I couldn't wait for the whole thing to be over.

As I laid out dinner, I glanced at Preston. His appearance was so unlike his mother and sister that it would've been easy to think he was adopted. That was until you got to know him. His personality was the same if not more malicious. Preston was fourteen years old, but he acted like he was still a child. He would throw temper tantrums when he didn't get his way. His green eyes always had a mischievous glint in them and his bright orange hair was always messy. Preston was never able to sit still for long, and compared to Marie and Emily's posture, his was quite the opposite. For as ridged as Marie was, it was hard to believe she let Preston act the way he did. I always assumed these traits came from his father, Marie's first husband who was missing and believed to be dead.

Ellen placed the roasted chicken in the middle of the table, and I put out the bowls of corn and potatoes. I returned to the kitchen to bring out the rolls and butter. When I returned to the table, Preston was already digging into his chicken, like an animal. I tried not to laugh because Marie complained about my manners but didn't say anything about Preston's. As soon as I placed the rolls on the table, he snatched one and stuffed the whole thing into his mouth. I turned away disgusted. Back in the kitchen, I waited in case I was summoned for anything. I wouldn't be able to eat my dinner until they were done. I got whatever was left.

I waited patiently and when they were finished I started clearing off the plates. Preston had made a mess, so I needed to get the mop. How he had gotten food all over the floor was beyond me. I swear it amused him that I would have to scrub the floors after dinner. What other fourteen-year-old would act like that? I put the dishes in the sink and then filled up a bucket so I could mop the dining room floor. I had the bucket halfway full when I heard my name being called.

"Jane! Where are you? Why do you disappear every time I need to talk to you?" Marie's harsh voice echoed outside the kitchen. I stopped what I was doing and went back into the dining room. Marie sneered when she saw me. "There you are."

Where else would I be besides cleaning up after dinner? I looked at her, waiting for the commands she was sure to give me.

"Emily and I will not be home this evening. We were invited to Drake Doyle's mansion to discuss plans for the wedding. His mother will also be there to help us with the planning," she stated with a roll of her eyes. "I expect you to clean up this mess. The floor is so sticky. I expect it to be mopped." She looked at me as if the floor was my fault.

"I was just getting the mop, ma'am," I replied.

"Good. Make sure this floor shines. Perhaps a wax would also do," she said with a nasty smile. I nodded at her in understanding. "It better be perfect when we return home. I don't know how late we'll be, but you better get to work," she commanded me and then turned on her heel to leave.

She thought she was making my job harder by commanding me to wax the floor. Unbeknownst to her, she was actually making it easier on me by leaving the house. Since she wasn't going to be home, I could use a pixie charm called the quick complete charm. This charm allowed me to move faster than a human and complete the chores quicker than I normally would. I had learned to master this charm last year. Ever since then, I have kept small amounts of the charm in tiny bottles that I always carried with me.

I listened to make sure everyone was gone. All the hired help should've retired to the servant's quarters by now, so I would be able to use the charm. I went into the kitchen to finish up the dishes the human way just to make sure. Finally, I reached into my pocket and pulled out a bottle full of maroon-colored dust. The charm was made completely from garnet. I tapped some of the dust onto my hand and then sprinkled it over my body. The familiar sensation tingled in my limbs. I could feel my muscles tighten with energy straining to be used.

I rushed around the dining room, rolling up rugs and moving furniture, to clear the floor. My muscles felt good now that I was moving quickly. Using the charm gave me a boost of energy without exhaustion afterward.

Within five minutes, I had the floor mopped. My hand moved in wide fast circles as I waxed, and I managed to complete the task within a half hour. The quick complete charm was just starting to wear off as I rolled out the rugs in their usual positions. My muscles twitched, and I finally relaxed. I sat down on the floor with my back against that wall and glanced at the grandfather clock. It was only eight o'clock. Marie and Emily were gone for the evening, and I deserved some fun.

2

THE LAKE

T HE NIGHT AIR felt hot and humid against my skin. I
trudged down the small hill toward the back gardens.
Beyond them lay the woods. The small lake was not very
far. I could hear the sound of insects making their night noises as
I walked through the gardens. On the horizon, the sun was just
beginning to set, shinning an array of colors across the sky. The
flowers in the garden were beautiful in the soft light.

The woods stood before me, a mass of dark greens and black
shadows. When I entered beneath the leafy green branches, it felt
slightly cooler, but it was still humid. I picked my way over sharp
sticks and stones, heading in the direction of the lake. The forest
at dusk was incredibly breathtaking and peaceful as dim shafts of
light shown through the trees from the setting sun. I felt my body
start to relax despite the heat.

When I got to the lake, my clothes were sticking to me, and I
knew how wonderful it would feel to swim in the cool blue water.
There was no sign of Robert yet, and I paused to appreciate the
beauty of the scene in front of me. The water looked crystal clear,
and I could see all the rocks at the bottom. Tall pines surrounded

the lake, making the area seem secluded which was exactly why I liked coming down here. I pulled off my sweat-soaked dress, kicked off my shoes, and slid out of my stockings. I laid them on one of the rocks and entered the lake in my underclothes.

At first, the water felt cold, but as my body got used to it, the water felt great. I swam out to the middle of the lake and floated on my back. I gazed at the sky and watched the clouds and the tops of the pine trees towering over me. A flock of birds flew into my line of vision, and I watched them soar over the treetops and disappear. How wonderful it would be to be a bird, I thought. You could fly away from your problems and land in a better place than the one you left. This summer, I had felt like a caged bird waiting to be set free.

I closed my eyes and put my hands underneath my head as I continued to float on the water. I only had to survive the week, and then I'd only see my step-family on the weekends. I was happy summer was almost over. This thought was a calming one. I relaxed in the water and felt the tension in my muscles disappear. I thought about all the new things I would be learning in the upcoming year. I couldn't remember if I would be getting a new class or not. I was excited to find out. However, I knew this next week would drag by since I was so eager to get it over with.

The crunch of a stick snapped me out of my daydreams. I sat up in the water and glanced at the woods around me. My stomach dropped when I didn't see anyone. The noise could have been made by an animal, but it would be foolish of me not to be cautious. Thoughts of the W.A.S.P. remained at the forefront of my mind. I sank in the water so only the top of my head was visible. Treading water slowly, I tried not to make a sound as I scanned the forest around me. My heart raced in my chest, and I breathed deeply to calm myself.

Relief flooded my body when Robert walked out of the woods. I moved and Robert spotted me.

"I didn't think you were here," Robert called out to me. "I didn't see you out there."

I swam toward him. "I was just floating. The water feels great after a day of hard work," I replied.

I couldn't help glancing down as Robert removed his shirt. I felt my cheeks redden, and I didn't know why. I had met Robert at the lake for a swim over the summer, but I still blushed at his undressing. I glanced at him from beneath my eyelashes and saw his broad chest muscles. Around his neck was a tarnished silver chain. Dangling from the chain was a silver ring. Robert had confided to me that he had been separated from his family when he was young. He had roamed the streets until he was picked up by Mr. Wicker. Since he was so young and scared, he didn't have a choice. The only object he had to remind him of his family was his father's ring, which he wore around his neck. As far as I knew, he never took it off. Robert told me that he intended on finding his family if he ever had the resources. I felt sorry for him and wished I could help him somehow. At least his family might still be alive.

I looked down again as Robert unbuckled his belt. To prevent my eyes from looking, I laid on my back and continued to float again. The sky was growing darker with each minute. Robert and I always swam in the lake at night, so the darkness didn't bother me. Before Robert came to the manor, I used to swim in the lake alone. I was very familiar with the surrounding woods and could probably make it back to the manor blindfolded.

I heard a splash and looked to see Robert in the water, swimming toward me.

"When did you get down here?" he asked me.

"Only about five minutes before you did," I replied.

"I'm glad you decided to come. I only have a few days left with you before you return to school. I guess Marie had something important to do," Robert said.

I smiled at his first statement. I guess he did miss me when I was away. "Yes. Marie and Emily went over to Drake Doyle's house to meet with his mother. They were going to discuss some plans for the wedding," I grimaced.

"I bet you can't wait until that wedding's over," Robert replied.

"Yes. I'll have one less nuisance to look after. I'm counting the days until Emily's gone. I'll no longer be her personal slave. May the gods have pity on Mr. Doyle's servants when they have to deal with her," I sighed.

"Gods?" Robert asked questioningly.

I bit my tongue. Just last year I had found out that pixies believed in gods and goddesses. I had decided to worship the pixie religion because I had wanted something to believe in. I hoped there were superior beings who controlled our universe. If we had lived a kind-hearted life, we would be able to live with Cian, the god of the dead, in his beautiful kingdom when we died. I hoped this was true because when I died I wanted to see my mother.

"It's just an expression," I shrugged thinking quickly.

"Well, yes. Emily's extremely hard to handle," he laughed accepting my explanation.

"Tell me about it," I grinned.

"Marie told me I'll be coming along to help serve the guests. Apparently, this joyous event will be taking place at the Doyle mansion," Robert replied.

Marie and Emily had already informed me about the location of the wedding. I had been surprised to hear that it wasn't taking place at the manor. Supposedly, Mr. Doyle's house was much grander and that's why it had been the chosen location.

"I'm so excited to see the house Emily incessantly brags about," I said sarcastically.

Robert smiled and playfully splashed at me. "At least you will be rid of her and that's all that matters," he stated.

I splashed him back and he dove beneath the water to avoid it. Before I knew it, he was tugging at my ankles and pulling me under.

I was able to take one deep breath right before he dragged me down. I opened my eyes under the water and saw a murky outline of him swimming to the surface. I kicked my legs to swim toward him. Robert broke the surface of the water and I playfully jumped on his shoulders to send him back under. We both resurfaced laughing.

"I love the sound of your laugh," Robert said. "I wish you would laugh more often."

"I wish I would too," I said blushing again. "But there's never much to laugh about."

Robert gazed at my face intently. "No more depressing conversations tonight. I'd like to have a good week with you. How about a race around the lake?" Robert asked.

I nodded my head and with that, we took off. I had taught myself to swim and had become what I considered a strong swimmer. I was able to keep up with Robert, but soon it became clear that Robert had more stamina than me. He made it back to the starting point, and I got there a few minutes later. I turned on my back and began to float trying to catch my breath.

"I beat you, Jane," Robert gasped as he turned on his back and floated beside me.

"I let you win," I said jokingly.

"No, I saw you trying your hardest," he laughed.

"Okay. You beat me," I replied.

We fell into a comfortable silence as we just drifted, looking at the stars as they popped out brightly against the black sky. I was able to pick out some constellations I had learned in Zodiac Signs. The moon was almost full, and it cast a nice glow over the forest. It felt like we were in a world of our own and no one else existed. I pondered on whether I would mind that so much.

"Do you think I'll ever be able to find my family?" Robert asked breaking the silence.

"I don't know, Robert. Maybe you will someday," I replied.

"Sometimes, I stare at the night sky and wonder if they're

looking at the same sky thinking about me. I know that sounds silly, but I hope they haven't forgotten me," he sighed.

"I'd want to believe that my son was alive," I replied.

Robert sat up in the water and so did I. "Come on. Let's dry off. It's getting late and you don't know how long Marie and Emily are going to be gone," he said sadly.

I swam behind him to the shore, and we crawled up on a boulder. My skin felt chilled as the beads of water dried. It felt good because even though the temperature had dropped, it was still humid.

"Sometimes I look up at the stars, hoping there is a better place we go to when we die. I hope my mom's watching over me from that other place," I stated.

"There has to be someplace better than this. If not, life's the biggest joke," Robert replied darkly.

I glanced over at him and noticed how beads of water fell across his sun-tanned chest, how his muscles stood out beneath his skin, and how he had a slight line of freckles across his nose. His brown eyes captured my violet ones, and I felt like Robert had a way of looking into my soul. He looked at me as if I was the only person on earth. This thought made my cheeks redden again, and I was grateful for the pale light of the moon.

"We should be heading back," I said as I leapt off the rock, reaching for my clothes.

"Yeah, I wouldn't want you to get in trouble. I'll walk you back," Robert said as he also slid off the rock.

I dressed quickly, now self-conscience of his gaze. I turned my back to him as he gathered his clothes and stared at the moon wondering what time it was. Hopefully, it wasn't too late and Marie and Emily were still out. Normally when I was with Robert, I always managed to lose track of time. I heard Robert clear his throat and when I turned around, he was dressed.

I turned to the woods, ready to head back when Robert

extended his hand to me. We had never held hands before. "It's dark. I figured we could lead each other back," was his explanation. I reached out my hand and clasped his warm damp one. His fingers were shriveled from being in the water so long and somehow, they slid perfectly into the spaces between mine. He grasped my hand tightly and I followed him into the woods.

Even though I was familiar with the pathway back, I felt comfort in the warm feel of his hand against mine. The trees, which were formerly green, were now black. If I wasn't so familiar with the woods, I would've been scared. My eyes were beginning to adjust to the darkness, and I continually glanced down to make sure I didn't trip. I didn't want to embarrass myself in front of Robert.

When we were halfway through the woods, a chill went down my spine. I got the odd feeling that I was being watched. This wasn't the first time I'd felt this way. I clutched Robert's hand tighter and walked closer to him.

"Jane, what's wrong?" he asked me.

"I just got this very strange feeling, Robert, like we're being watched," I replied.

"I'm sure it's just because of the dark. It's probably nothing," he said as he squeezed my hand.

"No, I feel like something sinister is out there. I just got a chill down my spine," I said anxiously.

Robert chuckled. "Don't worry. Nothing too bad could be in these woods."

I froze. Of course, Robert wouldn't be aware of the possible dangers, not necessarily for him but for me. I couldn't ignore the nagging feeling in my stomach. I knew I might have to choose between flight and fight. I'd rather get out of the woods than expose what I really was to Robert or whoever was watching us.

"Are you okay?" Robert asked, looking into my eyes.

"Could we please get back to the house quickly?" I asked nervously.

Robert must've seen the fear in my eyes because he nodded, and we picked up our pace. My fear grew stronger, and it felt like any moment something was going to jump out and grab us. I pumped my legs harder and was almost pulling Robert along. When we broke the tree line, my fear abated a little bit, but I didn't slow down. I didn't stop until I reached the barn. Robert let go of my hand, and I took deep breaths trying to slow my racing heart.

"What was that all about?" Robert asked between gasps.

"I can't explain it," I replied. "I felt like we were in danger." I continued to breathe heavily.

"What could possibly be in those woods?" Robert gasped.

I shook my head. "I don't know, but I never felt that way about the woods when I was younger. Maybe I was imagining things," I lied to make Robert feel better.

"I think the darkness of the woods just got to you," Robert said gently touching my arm.

I nodded, though I knew what I had felt in the woods was real. Robert smiled at me.

"I better head back to the house before Marie returns," I said, sadly glancing at him. His eyes found mine, and once again, I felt flush with color. I prayed he would mistake it for exertion.

"Good night, Jane," he said, reaching for my hand and squeezing it. "If Marie keeps us apart this week, enjoy returning to school."

"Good night, Robert," I replied as I squeezed his hand back. I couldn't believe how much I would miss him. I still held onto his hand as I turned to go. Slowly, his hand slipped out of my grasp. Robert's eyes looked at me sadly and I turned away and walked toward the house, feeling guilty for leaving because of who I was.

ABOUT THE AUTHOR

Jenna E. Faas is the author of *Pixie Dust*, the first book in the *Jelf Academy Series*. She lives in Pittsburgh, Pennsylvania, with her husband, son, and two Australian shepherds. From the very first time Jenna turned the pages of a book, she was obsessed. As a young girl, she always made up stories, which she jotted down in school notebooks. An avid reader, she would get lost in fantasy and wished magic existed. Jenna began the concept of Pixie Dust when she was seventeen and expanded her creation of the world through her college years. Her bachelor's degree in Geology helped inspire pixie magic since gemstones and minerals are the ingredients to create pixie charms.

When Jenna isn't writing or reading, she enjoys spending time with her family, working on arts and crafts, and singing her favorite songs. She is currently working on the next installment of the *Jelf Academy series*: *Dragon Scales*.

Find Jenna on the web at
https://jennaf14.wixsite.com/jennaefaas-author